THE MAN FROM BURNT ISLAND
A Novel

Wendy Sura Thomson

Copyright © 2021 Quitt and Quinn, Publishers
All rights reserved.
ISBN: 978-1-7372600-4-2
Published by Quitt and Quinn, Publishers
Michigan

ACKNOWLEDGMENTS

I want to thank Carol Hunter for her unwavering support and for being a wonderful sounding board for this work.

Jefferson from First Editing has now saved me twice. His keen eye and deep knowledge of all things grammar are truly amazing.

Andrew Lark, whose invaluable insight and knowledge added depth and polish to this work.

I am deeply indebted to Ron Clark of the United Kingdom who researched the 42nd Blackwatch on my behalf. His findings were beyond anything I could have ever imagined.

I also wish to thank my Beta reader, Carol Aiken, for her time and energy.

PREFACE

The protagonist in this story is a hardscrabble Scot who grew up speaking Broad Scots. While I have softened some of the dialect, which would be perfectly unintelligible to an average American, it's important to the storyline because this man's language mirrors his ambition-driven transformation.

I am offering a guide here to help those of you unfamiliar with broad Scots. Stick with me here: his heavy Scots accent disappears fairly early on.

(1) "Ken" is Scottish for "know." "Ah dinnae ken" means "I don't know."

(2) "Dreich" is one of the most popular Scottish slang words. It means dreary, misty, rainy, generally miserable weather. Very prevalent in Scotland.

(3) "Hawd yer wheesht" is another very popular Scottish slang term. It means "be quiet."

(4) Vowels, in particular, change.

    a. A short "i" often becomes more of a soft "u" ("will" becomes "wull").

    b. An "o" at the end of a word often becomes more of an "ae" ("to" becomes "tae").

    c. The diphthong "ow" becomes "oo" ("out" is "oot"; "now" is "noo").

d. A soft "o" becomes a soft "a" ("off" becomes "aff"), as do words ending in "y" ("my" becomes "mah").

e. A soft "a" becomes more of a soft "i" ("what" becomes "whit").

f. "Good" becomes "guid"; "you're" becomes "yuir."

(5) Wee = small. Gang = going. Dee = day. Sair = sore. Bairns = children. Weans = young children ("wee ones"). Neeps = turnips; neeps 'n tatties are very traditional: mashed potatoes and turnips. Braw = big, strong, healthy. Fàilte = welcome. Blether = gossip.

(6) A bannock is a fried oatcake.

(7) Ending letters get dropped left and right.

First Day Down the Mine

Three years on the pithead, it was time
For me to down the mine.
I was nervous on the day
As Jock Sharp showed me the way.

Hard hat and carbine lamp,
Through the air-doors, everything smelt damp.
Jock climbed on the trolleys and sat down.
Sit by me, he said, and hang on.

-   David Johnston

CHAPTER ONE

Robert Funkie Thomson Sharp stood in the back row, center, for the annual class picture one last time. The tallest in his class, he was always positioned there.

The schoolmaster called up the students one by one.

"Frank Sharp."

Frank walked up to the schoolmaster.

"Frank Sharp, you have completed primary, with distinction, as of the twelfth of June, nineteen twelve." He handed Frank his certificate. "I recommend you continue your studies, young man. You are clever in mathematics and the sciences."

Frank took his certificate, shook the schoolmaster's hand, and searched for Jamie Campbell, his best friend. The two didn't wait for the end of the ceremony; they started walking down High Street towards Wellsgreen, where they both lived.

"So, Jamie, whit wull ye dae noo?"

"Mah da says ah wull join him carting. An' ye?"

Frank hung his head. "Mah da has me aff tae th' Rosie colliery tae join mah brothers, Jock and Jimmy."

"'N' whit wull ye dae thare?"

"Da says ah wull likely be a drawer."

Jamie stayed silent for several seconds. "I'm sorry fer ye, Frank. That's sair wark." He suddenly stopped and faced his friend.

"But yer sae braw – mibbie they wull put ye elsewhere! Drawers needs be wee, an' yuir nae wee!"

Frank stayed silent as they walked. The lads usually ran home, but today they were in no rush – in no rush to leave their youth behind. Frank was always home doing chores when Jock and Jimmy came in from the colliery, black with coal dust and bone-weary. Frank would soon be one of them.

Jamie picked up a stone from the road and threw it over the low stone fence towards some grazing sheep. One looked up, still munching, as the stone fell three feet short.

"Missed thaim."

A fresh gust of damp, cool air brushed past the boys. Frank turned to spy the western horizon.

"Storm clouds comin' in, Jamie. We'd best git alang."

They heard a clap of thunder in the distance, glanced at each other, and started to run. By the time they got to Wellsgreen, the rain had started. Frank ducked around back of his rowhouse.

"Bye, Jamie!"

He stopped to remove his shoes – hand-me-downs with pieces of sheep leather inserted to cover the holes in the soles.

"Mammy, ah'm hame."

Bess Sharp came out from the scullery, wiping her hands on her apron.

"Yer late, Frank. Was it th' last dee doins??"

Frank handed her his certificate of completion.

"Aye, Mammy. But ah'm done noo."

Bess put her hands on her son's shoulders. "Aye, yer be a man now, Frank. We kin use anither set o' workin' hands. Noo haste ye tae th' back garden 'n' help th' bairns bring in some neeps fer supper."

Frank glanced over at his older sister Jeannie, who was darning socks by the small front window. He waved in greeting as he picked up his shoes and headed out back, following his mother as she headed back to the scullery.

Maggie and Lill were kneeling in the garden, laughing and chatting. But instead of digging out turnips, they were busy making mud pies in the rain.

"Och, Mammy's gonnae be crabbit fer sure," said Frank as he peered into the nearly empty wicker basket between them. "Luik at ye! All mud 'n' mess, 'n' nae neeps! Git tae it, lassies. I'll help ye."

Frank knelt and started digging out turnips, knocking the mud off them and placing them in the basket. His example settled the young girls down and encouraged them to tend to the small harvest. The rain was starting to come down harder, and by the time the three of them had enough turnips for the nine people who would be sharing supper, they were soaked to the skin and shivering. Even so, they stood in the rain, rubbing the mud off of their knees before they came in, taking off their muddy shoes and rinsing them in the rain before they set them by the back door.

The three quickly stripped down and placed their wet clothes on the wooden drying rack by the cast-iron stove that heated the row house, then they ran upstairs to get into some dry clothes. By the time they came back down, Jimmy, Jock, and Da – John Paton Sharp, as he was formally known – had returned from the mines. The rain turned the coal dust they always brought home with them into black streaks on their faces and work clothes. The three stood outside, scrubbing their hands, hair and faces in the rain before they, too, stripped down. They took their filthy clothing off and dumped them in the washtub by the back door, like they did every night, before heading upstairs for some clean clothes.

Bess, meanwhile, had commandeered her small army of children into getting supper on the table: fresh haddock, bannocks, crowdie cheese, potatoes, and turnips. She looked at the washtub and the drying rack and sighed. She would be up late tonight with the washboard. Laundry was hard to do when it rained: she had to wash the clothes at night and dry them on the rack overnight instead of washing them in the morning and hanging them outside. The children's wet clothes would have to wait; work clothes came first.

"Ah hope it doesn'a puir doon rain fer days," she commented to her husband when he and the two older sons came down for supper. "Come sit."

The family headed to the table.

"Up, then," said Jeannie as she tapped her knees. Andrew clambered up into her lap while Maggie, Lill, and Frank waited for a place at the table. The parents and the eldest children – Jimmy, Rob, Jock, and Jeannie – ate first.

When Rob was finished, Frank quickly sat down and hungrily addressed a big splat of potatoes and turnips, a smallish piece of fish, a spoonful of cheese, and a bannock.

It was like this both morning and night in this small row house with a table for six, two rooms, scullery, privy, and one window – just like the homes of most of the other miners. The scene played out throughout Wellsgreen. Many people – a few hundred in total. Not an extra pound of fat anywhere to be seen - work was too hard; food was always a challenge. A sea of vastly predominant blue-eyed men, women, and children, all fair and lean and muscled. The Sharps were no different. Oh, some were taller than others; some blonder, some with redder hair; some even brunette. But to a one – lean and muscled. The legacy of a lifetime of hard, physical labor. Frank was the tallest by a good six inches already, although no one knew why that was. He was a physical anomaly – perhaps a throwback to some long-forgotten Viking ancestor.

"Frank, Monday you'll be comin' wi' us tae th' mines. Th' overseer wull be waitin' on ye." Da spoke between bites, not looking up. "Half o' yer wages are yers – half ye gie tae yer mither fer yer upkeep. Yer a man noo, laddie." Da's face was splotched red, the result of too many Friday nights at the pub. His hair had already gone pure white, prematurely like so many other Scots. He was square-jawed, well wrinkled, and rugged looking. His shoulders and biceps were broad and strong from decades of swinging a coal pick.

"Ye ken whit job I'll hae? Mibbie pit head worker?"

Jock laughed at that. "Frank, are ye daft? Lads start as drawers. Ye ken?"

Frank stared at his plate. He dared not mention the schoolmaster's comments about continuing his education. The family could not afford it, he knew. He would become a drawer – spending all day, every day, pushing and pulling carts loaded with coal to the windlass, which would lift them to the surface, and walking down empty ones through narrow shafts that were so small that children frequently could not stand up. Hour upon hour underground. Knowing he was going to have money for the first time in his life did not overcome the dread he felt. Jamie was right – it was sore work.

After supper, Jeannie helped her mother with clean-up. Jock picked up his fiddle, took a place near the stove, and began playing a lilting melody. Lill and Maggie began to dance. Frank couldn't help but smile. Jimmy came over and started to sing, and Jock picked up the melody.

"*I love a lassie, a bonnie, bonnie lassie. She's as pure as the lily in the dell.*"

Da Sharp looked up. "Yer no Harry Lauder, lad. Nae, nae at aw." He lit a pipe and peered out the small front window. "I'll nae be goin' tae th' pub in this waither." He dropped his eyes back to the newspaper he had been reading. "Sure 'n' you laddies won't be gang tae Kirkcaldy to th' dance tonight, either."

Jock and Jimmy had to agree. Jock picked up his fiddle again and played, and Lill and Maggie danced the Gay Gordons together. Bess and Jeannie came in from the scullery -- Jimmy grabbed Jeannie and joined in the dance, which made her laugh.

"Come, Frank, dance wi' me," said Bess, taking Frank's hand.

"Just one afore ah'm needin' tae wash th' clothes." She was smiling. She had always been a pretty one: eyes that sparkled when she smiled; a clear, rose-blushed complexion; and wavy strawberry-blond hair. She didn't smile broadly anymore; she only smiled with her lips closed. It wasn't because most of the joy had walked out of her life; it was because, like everybody else, several of her teeth were missing, and most others rotting.

"Mammy, I'm nae a dancer."

"Follow me, then. Four steps forward, turn aroond, 'n' four steps back... Thare ye hae it! Noo again... You'll need this when yer aff wi' Jock 'n' Jimmy tae dances."

Frank blushed. "I'm still a bairn, Mammy. They'll be callin' me a wee laddie. I dinnae want tha."

Da put down his pipe and folded the newspaper.

"The mines'll make a man oot a' ye soon enough."

He turned to his wife.

"Bess, is there a wee dram left afore ah go tae bed?"

"Nae, Jock. Tae close tae payday."

Da sighed, picked up his pipe, lit it, and moved his chair closer to the stove. He sat in silence, staring blankly at nothing at all as he puffed away.

* * *

Frank came down early the next morning, joining Da, Jimmy, Rob, and Jock at the table for porridge, oatcakes, and tea. Bess had packed lunches for the lot and now was turning over the clothes she had placed on the rack the prior night to better dry the backsides. Mornings were silent; they were almost always silent. Bess had been up a good hour before for breakfast and laundry, and the long list of chores ahead for the day made her less than cheerful. Rob left first; he had the longest commute to the merchant in Kirkcaldy where he was a clerk. He had been ill as a small child and was too frail for mine work. The rest ate quietly, grabbed their sack lunches, and left...but Frank stopped and ran back in. He gave his mother a hug.

"Bye, Mammy." He turned and ran back out.

It was another dreary day, with low gray clouds hanging over the heavy mist that had settled near the ground.

"Dreich. Damn dreich." Jimmy pulled his cap down over his eyes and shoved his hands deep into his pockets.

As they headed towards the mine, they were joined by others, men and women, headed to work.

"Aye, Sharp, who's that ye git wi' ya? Is that wee Frank? He's aw' groon up, tha' one."

"Aye, Robertson. That's me wee Frank. He's thro' wi' primary. He'll be startin' at th' mines th' day. Ah spoke tae Low aboot him last week."

"He's a braw one, tha'. Guid tae hae anither wage in th' hoose, eh?"

"Yer nae only sayin' it, man. Couldn'a even ha' a dram last night. None left."

Robertson laughed. "Times bein' tough, wi' nae a dram in th' hoose!"

Conversation drifted off as the gaggle of miners reached the main gate of the Rosie Mine and broke off to head to their various stations.

"Come wi' me, lad. Yull need tae catch up wi` Low, th' Overseer."

Da and Frank headed over towards the low, grime-covered building that held the offices. Charles Low was speaking to a couple of engineers. Da and Frank stood to the side, waiting for the conversation to finish.

"Mr. Low, this is mah son Frank. He's thro' wi' primary noo, an' he's reportin' fer work."

Frank grabbed the cap off his head and shook Low's hand.

"Glad tae meet ya, sir."

"Yer a braw one, noo. Howfer auld are ye?"

"Twelve, sir. But ah turn thairteen next month."

Low threw a sideways glance at Da Sharp.

"Thairteen's th' age fer mine work, Sharp."

Da Sharp fidgeted a bit as Low turned his attention back to Frank.

"Bit yer close tae th' age, an' yer sae tall that none wuid mistake ye. Ye kin start, laddie. Gae over tae th' bursar an' git enrolled. Come back when yer done." Low pointed to the door next to the pay window, halfway down the wall. Frank ducked his head in acknowledgment.

"Thank ye, sir." He hurried off.

"Ye dinnae tell me he was sae tall, Sharp. He cannae be a drawer – he cannae fit in th' cart shaft. But he's nae auld enough tae work th' coal face or th' pithead."

Low stopped and thought.

"Ah wull shift Campbell fra' messenger an' hae him apprentice as a reddsman. Yer Frank kin be a messenger."

"Thank ye, Mr. Low." Now Da Sharp had his hat in hand as he gave a little nod of thanks. "He's a guid worker an' a clever lad. Ye willn'a be disappointed."

As Da headed to the coal face, Charles Low headed over to the office.

"Are ye done wi' yer paperwork, laddie?"

Frank looked at the clerk and raised an eyebrow.

"Aye, Mr. Low, we only need his wage," said the clerk.

"Laddie, we'll be payin' six shillings a week. An' yer tae tall tae be a drawer. Ye kin be a messenger."

Frank lit up. "Thank ye, Mr. Low!"

"You'll need tae ken names 'n' positions right quick, laddie. Yer da said ye were clever. That's tae see. Come wi' me – I'll show ye aroond."

Frank followed the overseer around, marveling at the industry

8

of it all and furiously memorizing the locations as he and Low toured.

When they met other workers, they stopped to make introductions.

"Yer th' new message boy? What's yer name?"

"Sharp, sir. Frank."

"When I call ye, Sharp, step lively."

"Aye, sir."

"No dawdlin', laddie."

"Nae – no dawdlin'."

"Low, a braw one, aye? Ye sure he's nae fifteen?"

"Juist oot o' primary – nae, he's aye a laddie, Paterson."

"Haste ye when Ah call, Sharp." Paterson turned back to his work.

It seemed Frank had just gotten started when the lunch whistle blew. The miners came up from the pit, and Frank sought out his da.

"Da, they've pat me as message boy!"

"Aye, Frank. Low said it was."

Frank's eyes gleamed with excitement, and he could barely stand still.

Da couldn't help a weary grin. "Ye soon will lose tha' excitement, Frank. You'll be runnin' hither and yon aw day. Save some of tha' energy fer ya' work. You'll need it." He sat down to eat.

"Here – sit here. We only ha' thairty minutes tae eat." He patted the bench next to him.

Frank swung his legs over the bench and sat, opening his sack lunch and pulling out the food his mother had packed.

"Mr. Low says I need tae ken buildings 'n' names, da. Ye ken tonight you an' I kin practice?"

"Dinnae bother me when ah'm eaten' lad. It kin wait."

Frank and his da finished lunch in silence. When the whistle blew, Da Sharp swung his legs over the bench and headed back to the pit, leaving Frank alone to retrace the path Low had taken him on.

"That's th' office – Mr. Low's office. The clark's name is Barrowman."

He walked a few steps further.

"That's th' bursar's window. Th' bursar is…is…Reid!"

Proud of himself, he headed toward the pit head.

"There's th' pithead, and there's Paterson o'er thare. And there's Broon, by th' craw pickers."

"HEY, SHARP!"

Frank turned towards the call – it was Paterson. He ran over.

"Aye, Mr. Paterson?"

"Gae tell Purdie tha' he kin send half th' drivers aff. We've awfy much water in th' main shaft, an' we hae tae stop an' dry it afore we kin bring more coal up."

Frank hesitated, trying to place Purdie.

"O'er thare, lad!" Paterson swung his arm over to the horses and coal carriages that took the coal to the railway loading dock. "Purdie! Him – wi' th' broon jacket!"

Frank took off running.

* * *

Before Frank knew it, the whistle blew for quitting time. He waited for Da, Jock, and Jimmy by the main gate. The three were midstream in the river of grimy men and women wearily heading home. Frank jostled his way to them, and once they got through the gate, they walked four abreast for the mile or so it took to get to their rowhouse. Weary, the four trudged along in silence. The rain had long since stopped, but it was still gray, with low clouds darkening the day. The unpaved road was rutted and muddy until reaching the tenement, where it had been cobbled.

The four ducked around back and began their daily ritual of stripping off their work clothes into the laundry basket and washing their hands and faces in the bucket of fresh water that Bess left out every non-rainy day for them, and then they went upstairs for clean, dry clothes.

Supper was called just as Frank was coming back down the stairs. He went into the scullery to help his mum, but she shooed him out.

"Yer a workin' man now, Frank – nae mair a bairn. Take yer place wi' th' men, as ye are now. Jeannie, can ye let Frank eat afore ye? He's a miner noo. Take wee Andrew, wait, an' eat wi' the weans."

Frank hadn't thought about that. He smiled to himself as he headed towards the table.

"Mammy, I'm too tall fer drawin', so Mr. Low made me a message boy. I'm learnin' th' places and names fast. There's Paterson, Reid, Barrowman...Mr. Low, of course..."

"Hawd yer wheesht, laddie! Let me eat in peace!" Jock loaded his plate. "Yer be dead tired by week's end."

The wind out of his sails, Frank silenced himself.

After supper was over, he stood and let Jeannie have his seat.

"Think I'll fin' Jamie Campbell." Frank stood up.

"Haste ye back, Frank. Work comes early," Bess called from the scullery.

Frank went out the back, slipped on his shoes, and ran three doors down. He went around back and knocked at the door. Mrs. Campbell opened it, smiled, and beckoned Frank to come in. He removed his shoes and walked in. Supper was over, and Jamie was sitting at the table, reveling in his first day of not helping clean up.

"Hey, Jamie! Want tae gae doon tae th' streetlight? There's a group doon thare talkin' – some just oot of primary like us."

"Mammy?"

"Off ye go, lad. Jus' be back early – ye ken? Ye hae work th'morra."

Jamie and Frank slipped into their shoes, tore out the back door, and headed down to the streetlight in front of the local pub. A group of teenagers had gathered there and were chatting, laughing, and passing around a cigarette.

"Hey thare, Campbell! Sharp! Fresh fra' work, are ye?"

Frank and Jamie approached the group.

"Broon! Saw yer da at th' works th' day. Ah had tae gie him a message."

"Yer a message laddie, then. Mah da said sae. He git hame early fer th' rain in th' pit. Nae a guid message, Sharp. Dinnae like losing a wage, he. Came home in a foul mood."

"Nae me fault, Broon. Jus' doin' me job."

"Yer lucky tae be sae braw, Sharp."

"Yer th' one? Th' one tae git th' job ah was tae git?" A short teen walked around the group and stood in front of Frank. "I'm still drawin' after a year. An' yer th' one that's keepin' me in th' pit?"

"I dinnae ha' a thing tae dae wi' it, Kilgour. 'Twas Mr. Low tha' said ah was too tall fer th' tunnel."

Kilgour shoved Frank. "'Twas me job ye took, laddie."

"Back aff, Kilgour," a voice from the crowd said.

"Nae, ah willn'a. Ye gae tae Mr. Low th'morra, Sharp, an' tell him ye dinnae wan' tae be a message lad."

"Nae, I cannae do tha', Kilgour. I'm too tall fer th' tunnel. Mr. Low said sae."

Kilgour shoved Frank again, this time harder.

"Ah wouldn'a dae tha' again, Kilgour. Ah dinnae hae a thing tae dae wi' it."

Kilgour shoved Frank one more time. All it took was one haymaker for Frank to lay him out flat. There was a collective gasp from the crowd.

"Is he oot? Oot cold?" A lad bent over Kilgour and peered into his face.

"Aye, that he is. Fetch some cold water, wull ye?"

Another lad ran over to the horse trough, scooped up some water in his cap, ran back and splashed it over Kilgour's face. Kilgour coughed, raised his head slightly, moaned, cupped his jaw, then dropped back down onto the pavement.

Jamie turned to Frank. "Frank, let's be gang." Frank looked around at the group questioningly. To a one, they were standing back a bit.

"Awright thare, MacIntosh. Afore ah gae, a fag?"

MacIntosh handed over the cigarette, and Frank took a puff before handing it back.

"Thank ye. We'll be aff noo."

Jamie and Frank walked back to Jamie's house.

"Frank! Ah dinnae ken ye could fight like tha'! Ye laid that laddie oot cold in one blow!" Jamie's voice was low.

"Ah dinnae ken where tha' cam' from, Jamie. I've ne'er bin in a fight afore."

"Yer a puir tough one, Frank. I'll nae be getting' on yer ill side. You'll be gettin' a reputation after tonight, Sharp. Guid or ill, ah'm nae sure."

Jamie ducked around the side of the rowhouse.

"Guid nicht, Frank."

"Nicht, Jamie." Frank headed home.

* * *

"Laddie, ah heard ye were in a fight last nicht?" Da Sharp asked as the four passed the gate and were headed home the next day. "Wi' Kilgour, th' drawer?"

"Aye, Da. He came at me. Thrice 'twas. Pushed me. Ah just punched him once."

"Word spread at th' coal face fair quick, laddie. Ye watch; there'll be they tha' luik tae take' doon th' tough one."

Frank looked down and rubbed his knuckles. They weren't even bruised or red – just a bit tender.

"He came at me, Da. Ah dinnae want tae stairt a fight, but he wouldn'a stop. He was red-faced that ah git th' message lad job. Ah tellt him ah ha' no a lick tae dae wi' it, but he wouldn'a listen."

"Ye watch, lad."

* * *

After supper, Frank went looking for Jamie.

"Jamie – doon tae th' streetlight?"

"I dinnae ken, Frank. Kilgour might be luikin' fer a fight."

"An' if we dinnae gae, might think we're afeard."

Jamie stopped. "What aboot askin' Cunningham tae come wi' us? 'Twould make' better odds."

"Aye, that it wid. We dinnae wan' tae luik like were itchin' fer a fight, though. Ye fetch Cunningham – when ah see ye half way tae th' light, ah'll come after ye."

Jamie ran a few doors down. Minutes later, he and Robbie Cunningham headed over to the streetlight where a half-dozen teens were congregated. Robbie was pulling out a cigarette when Frank joined them.

"Hae a fag, then, Sharp?"

"Think ah wull, Rob, 'n' thank ye." Frank took one puff and gave it back.

"Broon, howfer ye be?"

Tommy Brown looked cautiously at Frank.

"Ah be guid, Sharp." He hesitated. "'Twas some fight lest night. Ah dinnae ken ye could punch like tha'."

"Wasn't luikin' tae fight, Tommy. Tha' Kilgour was pure ragin', he was. He dinnae come tonight?"

"Nae. He's nursin' a bruised jaw, but nae as much as his bruised pride."

There was gentle laughter at that.

"Sharp, yer a braw laddie, ye are. Ye gang tae Kirkcaldy end o' th' week?"

"Nae, nae this week. Mibbie next – need mah wage paid first, ye ken?"

14

"Watch ye. Word o' lest night wull head thare afore ye. But we lads o' Wellsgreen, we stick th'getherrr, aye? Dinna gae wi' oot us, Sharp. We stick th'getherrr."

"Kilgour?"

"Aye. Dinnae matter if we ha' oor oon squabbles. When we gae tae toon, it's Wellsgreen agin' th' lot o' thaim. Mind ye tha'."

* * *

It's hard to tell the time in June in Scotland. It never gets pitch black like in the dead of winter…more like a dark twilight is all it can manage when the days are their longest. It was nearly eleven when Frank got back home, and everyone had already gone to bed. Frank slept on the floor downstairs.

The next morning, Bess said, "Yer back hame late last night, Frank. Git ye up, yer in me way." She had already started breakfast and had hung the laundry out back. "An' yer runnin' wi' tha' crood – it's nae guid. You'll be havin' th' constable after ye."

"Aw, Mammy, they're mah friends, aye? Only ones tae hang wi' – let me be." Frank rubbed his face and shook his head, trying to get the sleep out of him.

"It'll come tae nae guid. Mark mah words, laddie." Bess busied herself with laying out tea, bannocks, porridge, and jam, and then she called upstairs. "Come an' eat now, lads."

She looked outside, scanning the western horizon. "Och, looks tae rain."

She hurried out back and pulled the laundry down, and when she came back inside, she lay the clothes out on the drying rack. By then, Da Sharp, Jock, Jimmy, Rob, and Frank were nearly finished with breakfast. They grabbed their lunches and headed out towards the Rosie.

"Damn. Anither dreich day. Win' an' rain wull be th' death o' me." Jock pulled his cap down and quickened his step against the wind, rain, and chill. "Step lively… Better tae be dry afore we gae doon th' shaft, aye?"

Jock had a point... It was miserable working the coal face with a wet cap and shirt. The damp cold worked right through a man. Frank just looked glum... He had to run back and forth through the rain and mud no matter how hard it came down.

It started to drizzle just after Jock, Da, and Jimmy were down in the pit. Frank hadn't even broken stride when his day started. "Sharp!!!" It was Purdie. Frank took off running.

By nine, the skies opened up. The pumps draining the pit were running full bore. At ten, the whistle blew, and the pit was closed for flooding. Frank was with Purdie, delivering his final message of the day, when he heard a frantic cry from the first coal cart.

"Help!! Git a crew 'ere! Crawford's stuck under th' wheel 'n' canna git free!"

Frank rushed over and saw Robbie Crawford with his leg crushed under a wheel. The wheels on the other side of the cart were stuck in a deep, muddy rut, and the horses couldn't pull the cart free. Crawford was screaming in agony as the three other carters pushed the full coal cart, trying to free it but to no avail.

Frank didn't waste a second. He ran to the side of the cart closest to Crawford, bent his knees deeply, and put his back under the cart. He put his hands up on the cart bottom and heaved with all his might. Several of the miners had been running to help, and when they saw what Frank was doing, they grabbed Crawford and managed to pull him out right before Frank's legs gave out. He dropped the cart heavily back into the mud and fell to his knees.

By now, a full gaggle of miners were behind the cart, pushing as the drover commanded the draw horses to pull with all their might. The cart finally released, and several of the miners fell face first into the mud.

Purdie grabbed Frank under an arm and pulled him up.

"Laddie! Are ye aw richt? Ah ne'er saw a laddie o' twelve ha' th' brawn tae raise a cart!'"

Frank looked around, not realizing fully what he had just done. Several miners were just staring at him – in awe, in disbelief…he wasn't sure. He became very uncomfortable, stuck his hands out in the rain to clean them before wiping them on his trousers, and looked down, red-faced.

"Aye, Mr. Purdie. None th' worse fer th' wear." He glanced at the still-staring men, tipped his cap a bit, and left towards the gate. He didn't even wait for Da, Jock, and Jimmy before heading home.

* * *

"Men were sayin' ye raised a topped-oot coal cart, Frank. That true?" Da asked between bites.

"Aye, ah did. But nae aw th' way. Just enough tae git Crawford free."

Jock and Jimmy were silent, but they looked at Frank with newfound respect.

Bess broke in. "Ye raised a topped-oot coal cart? Howfer many stone wuid tha' be? Laddie, what were ye thinkin'? Yer aye a laddie, nae yet thairteen. Whatever possessed ye tae hae a go tha?"

"Ah wasn'a thinkin', mammy. 'Twas Crawford – his shank was crushed 'n' stuck. Wasn'a much. Ah dinnae lift th' whole cart, just th' corner where Crawford was. Just enough fer him tae be pulled free."

"Ye've gotten a name fer yersel' noo, laddie. You'll be th' blether o' th' mines. Might even git yer name in th' papers." Da finished his last bite and pushed his plate away. "Crawford wull be in yer debt noo. Willn'a be a man nor lass at th' Rosie tha' dinnae ken yer name."

* * *

Frank and Jamie made a habit of heading down to the streetlight in the early evenings to meet up with the lads from Wellsgreen to smoke, joke, brag, and jostle one another.

"Aye, th' streetlight's on. Time tae head hame, lads." Constable Murray made it his duty to clear the street. "If ye wan' tae stay up later, gae tae th' dance hall Friday. Ye cannae hang 'ere when th' light comes on."

The lads started back to the rowhouses.

"Let's gae tae Kirkcaldy end o' th' week! Ever been tae th' dance?"

"Gae t'getherrr? Ah dinnae wan' tae gae by m'sel'.'"

"T'getherr. Cunningham?"

"Aye, ah'll gae."

"Campbell?"

"Aye."

"Kilgour?"

"Aye."

"MacIntosh?"

"Aye."

"What aboot ye, Broon? An' ye, Paton?"

"Aye."

"Aye."

"'Tis settled, then. Meet a' th' streetcar a' six."

Back at home, Frank walked in the back door, looking for Jock or Jimmy.

"Jock, whit's it cost tae gae tae th' dance in Kirkcaldy?"

"Ye gang, Frank? Aren't ye th' groon man noo. Tuppence fer th' bus, sixpence tae git in."

Frank made a face at the slight, tipped his head slightly for the information, and headed upstairs.

*   *   *

After supper on Friday, Frank rushed to clean himself up and put on his Sunday clothes. The amusement on the faces of his parents and older brothers irked him, but he brushed it off and headed to the bus stop. He wasn't the first one from his group there.

"Tuppence fer th' bus, ye ken?" Frank reached into his pocket as he spoke.

"Aye, Frank. Aw set." Kilgour turned to see Cunningham and Jamie approach… Paton, Brown, and MacIntosh were not far behind. Coming from the other direction were several girls accompanied by several lads.

The bus pulled up just as the second group made it to the stop. It was half full, but the next stop – East Wemyss – was sure to fill it. The last stop before the dance hall was near the Michael Mine.

"Aye, luikt tae be th' crood from Michael."

A good dozen or so young people piled on, and the bus was quite packed. The passengers were laughing and smiling. It was a lovely night for the dance, and most of the young folk agreed.

The bus pulled up in front of the dance hall. Frank and his buddies stood to the side for several moments, watching as the crowd bought their tickets, walked past the doormen, and entered the double doors. Once they understood the process, they got in line, bought their tickets, and went in.

The hall was deeper than wide, with a well-worn wooden floor. At the far end was a stage, and along either side were small wooden pub tables, each with seating for four. None had tablecloths or ashtrays – they were bare. Next to the stage was a lemonade stand. Four chandeliers ran the length of the dance floor, and the walls were split with wainscoting: dark, cherry-stained wood on the bottom and dark red wallpaper above. It appeared that the sides of the hall were split by gender: the left side was getting populated by the lads; the right, by the lasses. The lads from Wellsgreen headed to a couple of tables mid-center of the dance floor and sat down to watch. The group from the Michael mine came in shortly, and they sat at tables next to Frank and his friends.

It was not long before the master of ceremonies headed toward the stage. He
stopped in front of a funnel with a cable attached to it that ran down a pole stand.

"Whats tha'? Ye ken? That funnel thing?"

Frank didn't get an answer. The MC spoke into the funnel, and a loud, fuzzy voice suddenly filled the room.

"Fàilte one an' aw! Guid tae see ye 'ere tonight. Th' band is ready, sae ah wuld like tae invite aw tae participate in th' grand march. Th' laddie chosen tae lead th' grand march tonight is a lad fra' East Wemyss just promoted tae clark in th' solicitor's office... Andrew Reid, please invite a lassie an' come up tae th' stage."

"Ye ken what he's sayin'?"

"Nae – it's aw garbled."

The band started playing "Mhaire's Wedding," and Andrew, who had chosen a pretty redheaded girl, marched down the center of the ballroom, followed by other couples. At the far end, the couples peeled off, one right and one left, and both queues circled the perimeter and headed back to the stage, front center. There the couples joined together, making four across, and headed back down the dance floor, where they split off again, two right and two left. Every lap around the perimeter doubled the number of marchers abreast of one another until there were too many to fit across and the ends of the lines wrapped back. At that point, a bit of chaos ensued to great laughter, and the band ended the traditional song and then immediately broke into a popular reel.

"Ah'm aff tae git a lemonade." Frank rose and walked down the side of the tables to the lemonade stand. Several people were ahead of him, so he waited patiently.

When he headed back to his table, he noticed that Kilgour was standing in front of one of the Michael lads. His face was flushed.

Such a hothead. This doesn'a luik guid.

Frank quickly walked over and put his lemonade down. Paton, Cunningham, and Jamie were now standing, as were three of the Michael lads.

"What's gang on?" Frank put himself between the two groups

of lads.

"Blyth 'ere says ah cannae ask th' broon-haired lass fra' Michael's tae dance."

"An' why wuid ye say tha'?"

"She' ma sister, an' I cannae hae her dancin' wi' Rosie trash."

At that, Kilgour took a swing. Frank caught his arm and pulled him back.

"We cannae fight 'ere – we'll no be comin' back. Th' constable wull see tae tha'. Tak' it ootside."

"An' who are ye tae tell us tha'?" Tommy Blyth stopped and stared at Frank. "Ye th' lad a' the Rosie tha' lifted th' topped-out coal cart? Think yer sae braw, dae ye? Wull see aboot tha.'"

The two tables got up and walked back past the bouncers, out to the road and down a few storefronts.

"Wull, ye say Rosie is trash? Ye an' who else?" Kilgour's face was flushed scarlet. He didn't wait for an answer – he head-butted Blyth midsection and punched him right and left in the ribs as hard and fast as he could manage. That was all it took; mayhem ensued. That is, until Frank laid out one of Blyth's companions, Tommy Millar, with one swing.

Three chaps from Michael stopped for a moment, looking down at their fallen buddy. They then turned their attention to Frank. Robbie Bell took the first swing; the others quickly followed suit.

Cunningham, Paton, and MacIntosh tried pulling the three off of Frank, who had punched Bell right in the face, breaking his nose and causing it to bleed profusely. Frank took a punch to the eye, which started to swell up immediately.

Frank swung Bell around, lifted him up, and was about to body-slam him to the ground when the constables appeared and carted everyone off to the hoosegow.

* * *

"Dinnae ah tell ye tha' crood was nae guid? Dinna ah tell ye th' constables wuld be after ye?" Bess scolded Frank as she placed a small piece of raw potato on his eye.

"An' noo ye hae tae pay th' fine. Ah dinnae care, Frank – it comes fra' yer wage – after ye pay fer yuir upkeep. Ah'll nae be takin' less fer ye git in trouble."

Rob spoke up: "Is it true ye picked up that laddie an' were aboot tae slam him tae th' ground?"

Frank smiled. "Aye, tha' ah did."

Rob laughed. "Aye. Ah'll no be gittin' on yer ill side. Yer a tough one, Frank."

"Tough enough tae take mah given name back?"

"Frank, it's nae me fault tha' Da was drunk when he registered yer name an' called ye Robert, too. Cannae hae two Robert's in one hoose."

"Ah wull take mah name back one dee, Rob. One dee."

CHAPTER TWO

"Aff tae th' dance t'nicht wi' us agin, Frank?"

The shillings in Frank's pocket wanted to be set free. He pushed his hand down into his pants pocket and jiggled the coins around a bit.

"Aye, ah might."

"Loads o' bonnie lasses, aye, Rob?" Jimmy grinned and poked Rob in the side with his elbow. "But ye've git yer eye on Jess Ireland an' none ither."

"Och, clam up, Jimmy." Rob's face flushed pink. "Nae a maiter tha' ye hae yer oon eye on Ness Thomson, aye?"

"An' ye, Frank. Yer tae be fifteen th'morra, aye? Mibbie ye kin lead th' grand march tonight."

Going to the dance had become a biweekly habit for the Sharp brothers; it was the only socially acceptable way to socialize with young ladies without parents hovering. Frank went with them once a month or so.

It was as balmy as a July evening could be in Scotland, with an uncharacteristically gentle breeze under clear skies. The bus to Kirkcaldy was on schedule and was packed with adolescents and young adults, high-spirited and laughing as they anticipated a fun evening. It wasn't a long ride into Kirkcaldy, and the bus stopped right in front of the dance hall. The bus quickly emptied as the riders walked past the bouncers on either side of the double doors and entered the ballroom.

The music had yet to start, and people were milling around on the floor or heading to one of the small tables that lined either side of the newly varnished wooden dance floor in the middle of the large room. At the back, the band was setting up.

Frank headed over to the lemonade stand and bought a glass. Spotting his brothers, he headed to the table they had commandeered.

"Aye, Sharp!" Frank nodded towards a group to his left as he made his way. He was similarly hailed several times before he reached Rob, Jock, and Jimmy.

"Ness or Jess 'ere t'nicht?" Frank glanced over at the bevy of girls chatting across the room.

"Aye, Ness is ower thare," said Jimmy. "Soon as th' band starts, ah wull gae ask 'er tae dance." He stood. "Aff tae gie a drink noo."

Frank sat and surveyed the room. His eyes landed on slender, tall lass with long black hair pulled back so ringlets fell over her shoulders. She had luminous porcelain skin and eyes so blue he could see their color from across the room.

"Ye ken tha' lassie thare, Jock? The one wi' th' lang black ringlets?"

"Nae. Ah ne'er saw her afore. Bonnie, though."

Jimmy returned with a lemonade just as the MC walked up to the mike.

"Fàilte one an' aw! Guid tae see ye 'ere tonight. Th' band is ready, sae ah wuld lik' tae invite aw tae participate in th' Grand March. Th' laddie chosen tae lead th' Grand March tonight has a birthday th'morra... Frank Sharp, please invite a lassie 'n' come up tae th' stage."

Frank's face reddened. "Jimmy, is this yer daein'?" Jimmy just grinned, and Jock laughed.

Frank stood up to applause, nodded slightly in acknowledgment, and headed over to the lass with the long black ringlets.

"Ah dinnae ken yur name, but wull ye join me in th' Grand

24

March?"

The lassie blushed. "They ca' me Margaret Ferrie, an' ah wull dance wi' ye, Frank Sharp."

She held out her hand, and they walked up to the front of the stage as couples formed and congregated on both sides of them. Frank and Margaret proceeded down the center, leading the Grand March.

When the march ended and the band broke into a lively reel, Frank said, "Wull ye hae anither dance wi' me, Margaret?"

Margaret looked directly into Frank's eyes. "Aye, Frank, ah wull." Frank smiled, placed his hand on her waist, and the two were off. The two stayed on the dance floor for the next three songs before Frank spoke again.

"Wull ye hae a' lemonade?"

"Aye, thank ye."

Frank shepherded Margaret over to the lemonade stand and bought two glasses. They headed to an empty table and sat.

"Ah dinnae see ye here afore, Margaret. Thank ye fer leadin' the Grand March wi' me... Ye dinnae e'en ken who ah wis."

"Ah ken ye, Frank Sharp. Yer th' lad wha' works a' the Rosie. Th' braw one. Th' one tha' saved Crawford, aye?"

Frank's face reddened, and he quickly changed the subject.

"Wha' aboot ye, Margaret? How come dinnae ye come 'ere mair often? Ah dinnae see ye here afore tonight."

"Ah hae tae help me mum. Ah am th' eldest, an' most times, ah need tae tend tae th' bairns – Fridays me mum an' da gae tae th' pub."

"That's nae fair." Frank took a swig of lemonade. "Ye dinnae work, then?"

"Ah hae a job – ah'm a domestic fer a solicitor."

"Ye dinnae gae tae primary 'ere: Ah wuid hae seen ye."

"Nae. We moved from Newburgh two years ago. Nae more work for a loom weaver thare noo. Da came tae work th' mines."

"Guid fer me." That made Margaret blush.

The band started another reel, and the dancers began dancing the Gay Gordons.

"C'mon! Let's dance this!" Frank grabbed Margaret's hand and pulled her towards the dance floor. He silently thanked his mum for teaching him as the two took up a position and joined in.

* * *

Frank climbed out of the coal shaft as the whistle blew, stretched his arms up far over his head, bent right and left, and then touched his toes. He disliked delivering messages to the coal face – it was dank, dirty, and cramped. It had been a dry and sunny Tuesday, so most worked late to make up for work missed due to rain the prior week. He waited for Da, Jock, and Jimmy, and then they headed towards the gate.

"GREAT BRITAIN DECLARES WAR ON GERMANY!! Get your papers here!"

The newsboy could barely keep up with the demand from the miners as they jostled for their copies. Da finally got his, and he and the brothers stood to the side as he started reading – just like all of the other miners, each in their own little groups. No one headed straight home that August 4.

"Read it aloud, Da!"

Da dismissed the request with one hand as he kept reading. He finally looked up. "Germany invaded Belgium," he said. "Nae guid ye dinnae ken howfer tae drive a motorcar. Th' army wull pay thairty-five shillings a week! Th' army is askin' fer recruits."

"Thairty-five a week? That's mair than th' lot o' us mak' th'getherrr!"

"Nae guid ye dinnae ken howfer tae drive a motorcar, laddie." Da folded the paper and tucked it under his arm, and the four headed towards Wellsgreen.

Once home, one by one, they washed their face and hands with the water in the bucket left by the back door and placed their filthy work clothes in the washtub. They were on their way upstairs for clean clothes when Da noticed Jeannie and Bess in the front room, all smiles and excitement. The three lads headed up, but Da stopped.

"Wha? Did a rich uncle die?"

Jeannie grinned, lowered her chin a bit, glanced at her mum, and held out her left hand.

"Weel, yer gonnae be wed! Ah wis wonderin' whin th' ring wuid come. Rabbie asked me fur yer haun weeks ago. Said he'd bin savin' fer years sae he cuid rent a hoose fer th' two o' ye. You'll mairie 'ere, in th' front room. Ye saved fer a dress?"

"Aye, Da."

"Well then." Da said nothing more. He turned abruptly and headed upstairs for a clean set of clothes. Halfway up the stairs, he paused and called over his shoulder, "Och – we're a' war wi' Germany."

* * *

Saturday couldn't come soon enough. Frank rose early and slipped out the back. He climbed onto his bicycle and rode into Kirkcaldy, straight to the recruiting station on High Street. It wasn't difficult to spot – there were a couple of dozen men outside the door, waiting to enter. Frank parked his bike and got in line.

"Next!"

Frank walked in and approached the table where two British recruiting officers sat.

"You are here to enlist?"

"Aye, that ah am."

The recruiting officer peered at him intently.

"Yer Frank Sharp, are ye?"

"Aye."

"Yer a fine, tall lad, but you need tae be eighteen tae enlist. You, Sharp, are noways eighteen. Come back in a few years. Next!"

Frank fetched his bike and rode east. He passed through Methil; too many there knew him. Past Leven, too, for the same reason. He needed to go where his reputation could not follow him, so he rode all the way to St. Andrews. He was not sure exactly where the recruitment station was, but he thought it must be on Market Street – that was the main drag. It didn't take him long to find a crowd of young men gathered on the side of the street, waiting to enter an open door. He parked his bike and walked up to the crowd.

"Urr ye waiting 'ere tae enlist?"

"Aye, tha' we are."

"Well then, ah think ah will join ye. Bum a smoke?"

Someone handed Frank a cigarette.

"Thank ye."

A man came out the door, and a voice from within called out. "Next!" The man closest to the door entered.

"Are ye in?" Frank asked the exiting man.

"Aye, tha' I am. Forty-Second Blackwatch. Ah'm tae report next week."

"Guid luck, then."

The voice from within again boomed. "Next!"

Frank was not quite finished with his cigarette when he was up. He dropped the remainder of the cigarette onto the ground, rubbed it out with the toe of his shoe, and walked in.

"Name?"

"Frank Sharp."

"Full name?"

"Frank Sharp."

"Address?"

"Three Wellsgreen, Rosie-Near-Buckhaven."

"Occupation?"

"Miner."

"We need miners, lad. You need not fight – the war effort will need coal."

"Ah've a da an' two brothers tha' werk in th' mines, sir. Ah'm just a messenger thair."

"A messenger? How old are you, lad?"

"Eighteen, sir."

"You don't look eighteen, laddie. Go back home."

Frank dropped his head, turned, and walked out the door.

"Laddie!" the recruiter called out. "Come back in here."

Frank turned around and walked back in.

"You look eighteen now. Birthday?"

Frank quickly subtracted three years from his birth year. "July 15, 1896."

"Birthplace?"

"Burnt Island."

"Next of kin?"

"Bess Sharp."

"Same address?"

"Aye."

"Relationship?"

"She's mah mither."

"All right. Sign here, laddie. You're in the Forty-Second Blackwatch. Report back here a week from next Friday."

"Aye, thank ye, sir."

"Don't thank me yet, soldier. Next!!!"

Frank walked out, quickly headed to his bicycle, and rode back to Wellsgreen. He stopped off at Jamie Campbell's house.

"Aye, Jamie. Dae ye ken whaur Margaret Ferrie bides?"

"Somewhaur in Kirkcaldy, ah think. Yur sweet on 'er?"

"Ah'm needin' tae talk tae 'er. Hope she goes tae th' dance next. Thanks, Jamie."

Frank headed home.

"Whaur hae ye bin, laddie? Ye missed dinner!"

"Mammy, ah went tae St. Andrews." He paused and took a deep breath. "Ah joined th' Forty-Second Blackwatch."

Bess dropped the laundry basket she was taking outside to hang.

"Hae ye lost yer mind, lad? Whit wur ye thinkin'? Yer nae auld enough!"

"Tis dane, maw. Ah signed th' papers. Ah report back in a fortnicht."

"How come, lad?"

"Ah kin git up tae thairty-five shillings a week, maw. Ah've bin earning only six shillings since ah wis twelve. Ne'er git a raise. Ah dinnae even lik' it."

Bess didn't say another word – she merely picked up the laundry basket and headed out the back door, shaking her head as she went. She never said another word about it.

* * *

Frank didn't wait for his da or brothers Monday morning. He left early to find Mr. Low before most of the miners were to arrive.

"Mr. Low? I've come tae tell ye tha' ah'm quittin' tae join th' army. Ah've git two weeks here, an' then ah'm gang."

Yer nae auld enough, lad! An' the wa' wull need coal tae run! Ye need not gae tae wa'."

"Ah've signed on, sir. Ah'm tae report end o' week next."

Mr. Low walked around his desk and approached Frank. "We need ye, lad. Ah kin move ye to th' pithead. Or th' coal face. Git ye a raise. To ten shillings."

"Thank ye kindly, sir, but ah cannae dae tha'. Th' army's payin' up tae thirty-five shillings for motorcar drivers. Wi' wages lik' tha', I bet ah kin top tha' offer. Ah'm gang awa'."

Frank extended his hand to shake Low's. The overseer hesitated and then rather half-heartedly reached out to shake.

"Best 'o luck tae ye, lad. We'll miss ye."

Mr. Low spent the next several days in similar conversations with many young men. It didn't take a week before mine management decided to offer raises across the board to all the men and to post job openings in the local paper. The moves had only limited success – the fever and excitement of war met the perceived invincibility of the young men. That being said, the lure of higher wages enticed carters, slaters, and clerks to apply at the mine – including Jamie Campbell and his father.

"Yer leavin', Frank? Ye joined up?"

"Aye, Jamie. Only one dance afore ah leave. Gang tae th' dance end o' week fer sure."

'Yer only fifteen, lad. Howfer did ye sign up?"

Ah fibbed, Jamie. Th' soldier told me tae leave a' first. He called me back, though. Said ah luikt eighteen an' signed me up."

Jamie shook his head. "Yer sair young, Frank. Th' army finds oot an' yull be drummed oot on yer bum."

Frank smiled broadly. "Ah'm sae tall, ye ken? Tall an' braw. Ah kin hold mah oan. An' ye kin tak' me messenger job. Ask Mr. Low right awa', though. It's a fair set better than drawer. Ye come wi' me tae th' dance Friday? Ah'm gang fer sure."

"Ye told me tha' aw' ready, Frank. Yer mind's gang addled." Jamie laughed and jostled Frank's arm.

"Aw, leave me be, Jamie. Ah'm gang nae matter if ye come o' no."

"Don't fash yersel', Frank. Ah'll gae wi' ye."

* * *

Friday was not long in coming. Frank and Jamie caught the bus and headed to the dance hall in Kirkcaldy. Frank scanned the crowd.

"De ye see Margaret, Jamie? Ah need tae tell her ah'm leavin' soon. Ah want her tae hear it from me an' nae ither."

Jamie scanned the crowd with Frank. "Nae, Frank. I dinnae see her." He swirled around.

"Frank – Ah think she just walked in. Thair!" He pointed at the door.

"Thank ye, Jamie," said Frank as he hurried toward Margaret.

Margaret was turned away, speaking to some girlfriends. Frank tapped her shoulder.

"Margaret? Kin ah speak wi' ye?"

"Frank! Guid tae see ye! An' wha's the rush?"

Frank cupped her elbow in his hand and led her over several feet.

"Margaret, ah'm gang a wa'. Ah leave Friday next. Tae th' Forty-Second Blackwatch. An' I was wonderin'…"

Frank dropped his head, and then he held both of her hands in his.

"Ah ken ye an' me are nae far from bein' bairns. But ah was wonderin' if ye wuld wait fer me. We wull be aulder then – grown. Closer to marryin' age. An' ah wuld sair lik' it if ye wuld wait fer me."

Margaret's face reflected her utter astonishment.

"Ah dinnae ken wha' tae say, Frank. Ah'm nae sixteen!"

"Margaret, please. Th' army pays guid wages – up tae thirty-five shillings a week! Gie me a reason tae come home. Gie me a chance. When ah come home. An' kin I write ye? Kin ye gie me yer address? An' wull ye write me back?"

Margaret's impossibly blue eyes gazed intently into Frank's.

"Aye, Frank. Ye kin write me. A' Greenbrae Hoose, Garden Close, Cowdenbeath. An' I promise tae write ye back. But nae mare than tha'. I cannae promise mare than tha'."

Frank lifted Margaret's hands and kissed them gently.

"Tha's enough fer me fer now, lass. Dance wi' me t'nicht. An' then just wish me well."

"I kin dae tha', Frank. An' wish ye Godspeed."

Frank took one step towards the dance floor, holding Margaret's hand in his.

"Then let's dance, lass."

The two danced with no one else that evening.

CHAPTER THREE

"Line up, men, with an arm's length between you and the man next to you. Second row an arm's length behind the first. You tall ones, back row."

Frank headed to the back; he was a good head taller than the men in the first few rows. He took a position near the center, where he stretched his right arm to the front and then to the side.

"Hands down! Atten...TION!"

The sergeant looked at the hapless recruits as they struggled to get into formation.

"No! ATTENTION! Arms to the side! Heels touching! Chin down! Shoulders back! Straight up tall!"

He walked along the rows, correcting postures where needed. Frank took good mental notes, and by the time the sergeant got to him, he was standing properly. The sergeant finished and walked around to the front.

"Now we are going to march. You will start with your left foot. You will keep in formation. Do not veer left; do not veer right. Do not get ahead of your line and do not lag. Now, when I say 'right face,' you are to sharply turn ninety degrees to your right."

He paused and took a deep breath.

"Right face!"

This maneuver was a not executed well – at all.

"NO! Turn towards me."

The recruits turned back as instructed.

"Now, watch. This is how you will turn." The sergeant lifted his left heel and his right toe. He pivoted ninety degrees to the right on heel and toe and brought his feet together.

"Lift your left heel and your right toe. Pivot right sharply. Bring your heels back together." He paused for several seconds before yelling, "Right FACE!"

He watched in dismay as these lads, who had never been exposed to anything faintly close to military discipline, struggled. He walked around to the far side of the three columns.

"Right FACE!"

The men turned to face him.

"You! You! You!" The sergeant pointed at two lads and Frank. "Step forward and show the rest how it's done."

The three looked at each other and positioned themselves abreast of one another. Before the sergeant could issue the command, Frank piped up: "Right, FACE!"

The three executed the turn smartly.

The sergeant walked up to Frank.

"You seem too young to have been in the military before, Private. Have you experience as a drill instructor?"

"Nae, Sergeant. Ah just come oot o' th' mines."

The sergeant smiled a bit and took a couple of steps down the line before coming back.

"You just came out of the mines. So, please, tell me why you decided to issue an order?"

"Ye tellt us tae shaw th' lads howfer it's dane. Ye didn'a ask us tae hauld oor horses."

A wave of laughter swept through the lines.

The sergeant again weakly smiled. "Private, you have a lot to learn. The first thing you need to learn is respect." His conversational tone had turned loud and cold. "You will not speak unless spoken to. You will not issue orders. You will start and end every response with 'sir.' Do you understand?"

"Yes, sir."

The sergeant shouted his correction: "Sir! Yes, sir!"

"Sir. Yes, sir," Frank answered less than enthusiastically.

"SIR! YES, SIR!" the sergeant bellowed.

"Sir! Yes, sir!" Frank replied with more energy...but still, it was fairly apparent that he thought the exercise to be rather pointless.

"Back in formation, men."

The three recruits took their positions in line.

"Right...FACE!"

The turn, while far from perfect, was better.

The sergeant turned with the platoon.

"Forward march!"

A second later: "Halt! Men – start with your left foot! LEFT FOOT!" He waited a moment.

"Forward march!"

The platoon took off down the road and marched for several hours. It was a ragtag bunch. There were no barracks, so soldiers were garrisoned in private homes. There were no uniforms; soldiers trained in whatever clothes they had brought with them, wearing white armbands stamped with "RH" for Royal Highlanders. That was the only indication this was an army regiment.

When Frank got back to his quarters, he removed his shoes and checked the linings he had inserted to cover the holes in the soles. They would not last much longer.

The next morning, Frank went with shoes in hand to his lieutenant. He held up the shoes, soles toward the officer.

"Sir, I dinnae think th' shoes wull last anither march."

The lieutenant looked at the soles. "I agree. Let me see what I can do. Until then, use them."

Frank left to join the formation. When the platoon returned from their march, he was summoned by the Lieutenant.

"I managed to find these boots for you, recruit."

Frank looked at them. They were the finest boots he had ever owned, and they had intact soles.

"Thank ye, lieutenant!" He saluted and left for his quarters. When he got there, he tried on the boots. They fit poorly. He put on both pairs of socks he had – better, but not good.

Frank wore the boots to training the next day, and by the end of the march, he had very blistered feet. When he returned to his quarters, he gingerly removed the boots and socks. Barefoot, he limped out of his room to the mistress of the house.

"Ma'am, ah wis wonderin' if ye had some wrappin's fer me sair feet."

The matron looked down to Frank's feet, shook her head, and returned from the kitchen with clean strips of cloth.

"Thank ye, ma'am." Frank went back to his room and carefully wrapped his feet. He put a pair of socks back on and fell into a deep sleep.

Frank limped into muster the next morning.

"Sharp – are you injured?"

"Na, nae much, Lieutenant. Just a few blisters."

"Get those tended to. You'll be marching again tomorrow."

Sharp put his socks back on and headed towards the door, carrying his boots.

"Ah'd gie a poun' sterling fer mah auld boots, even wi' th' holes 'n th' soles. At least ah cuid walk in thaim wi'oot blisters."

"Oh: and soldier – you'll fare better in the army speaking proper English. This might be the Forty-Second Blackwatch, but we're still a King's Regiment. You learned the King's English in school, no doubt. It's time to use what you learned."

Frank bobbed his head as he headed out.

* * *

Frank's mess plate was piled high with beef, potatoes, bread, carrots, and peas.

"Ah've ne'er eaten so well," he said to the recruit next to him. "Ah must hae gaint a full stone here."

The recruit smiled. "Ah've ne'er been so built." He flexed his arms. "Ma girrl back hame wull be happy." He grinned broadly.

"Ah lik' this part well enough, but I dinnae lik' so much marchin'."

"Ye ken? I dinnae ken wha' we spend aw day marchin' around, ither."

Frank wolfed down his meal and then headed back to his bunk, where he pulled out paper and pen and wrote to Margaret.

October 14, 1914

Dear Margaret:

I hope this finds you well. I am well here, gaining weight and muscle. The lads here are friendly enough, but I'm not the favorite of the drill sergeant. I am quickly learning that questions are not appreciated, nor are smart remarks. I keep finding myself being disciplined, marching all night long by myself, back and forth across the parade field. I finally got a pair of boots that fit. The first boots I was given fit poorly and gave me blisters. I've new knit stockings that are warm and thick – the best I have ever had. And I'm making 10 shillings 6 pence a day – and don't need to give half up for my upkeep! Basic training is almost over. I don't know what's next, but I think they'll be sending us to a real military base. All we have done here is march – and march with broom handles instead of rifles. I don't know why this has been so important. I think we've overstayed our welcome here in St. Andrews, although the mistress of the house where I have been staying has been very kind.

I hope you will wait for me. Write me soon? My lieutenant says they will forward letters no matter where they send me.

    Yours, Frank

He sealed the letter, addressed it, and took it to the post. When he got back to his room, he pulled out the two letters he had from Margaret and re-read them. Once finished, he folded them up very carefully and placed them back in his rucksack. He then fell asleep on his bunk, rousing only to crawl under his covers as night fell.

* * *

"Congratulations, men! You've passed basic training. You are now officially privates of the Forty-Second Blackwatch. You have worked hard and gained both skills and discipline. You will need them in the coming weeks. You are being deployed to Hawick for additional training. Departure is at oh-six-hundred hours tomorrow. For king and country!"

The commander was regaled with a loud and enthusiastic echo: "For king and country!"

"Dismissed!"

The newly graduated soldiers broke rank. Some milled around, others headed back to their quarters, and some broke out cigarettes. Frank headed back to his bunk to write a letter to Margaret.

January 13, 1915

Dear Margaret;

We are heading out soon – going down to the Borders for additional training. We leave tomorrow. We still don't have proper uniforms. But I think we are going to a true military base and not staying with civilians.

I will keep your letters by my side while I am gone. I am not

*sure I will be able to write you often or not. Please don't let that
deter or worry you. I will write as soon as I am able.*

Wish me Godspeed, Margaret.

Yours forever, Frank

After supper, Frank walked out to the end of the ancient
cemetery that ended at the edge of the North Sea, passing the centuries-
old tombstones that crowded this somber space. As he headed towards
the white-capped waves, the constant wind whipped at his face. It was
cold, and the skies had already darkened. Here, above the windswept
coast, the stars hung in a magnificent, dense, magical masterpiece
against the blue-black velvet of that northern sky. Frank lit a cigarette
and sat down, cross-legged. He looked out north across the water and
then up at the sky.

"Ah'll be leavin' ye th'morra, Fife," Frank said to the wind and
the North Sea.

He stopped.

"Ah'm leaving you t'morra, Fife," he repeated, using proper
English – the English he had learned in school.

He snubbed out his cigarette on an old, weathered, lichen-
covered grave marker and gazed across the water at the horizon.

"Ah'm leaving you, an' Margaret. Ah hope ah come back tae –
to – something better than a messenger lad. Ah dinnae – don't – want to
work in th' mines when Ah return."

His musing was interrupted by a glorious green glow dancing
on the northern horizon. It was soon joined by yellow, magenta, and
purple. Mirrie dancers – aka the aurora borealis – had decided to give
Frank a spectacular send-off. He sat spellbound, watching the display.

"Aye, are ye meanin' to tell me tae come back, oor are ye giein'
me a guid-bye?"

Frank stopped again. He repeated the phrase in grammar school
English.

"Are you meaning to tell me to come back, or are you giving me a goodbye?"

He sat until he was thoroughly chilled, and then he rose, brushed off his backside, and started back. A moment later, he paused, turned, and addressed the sea and sky.

"Ah will bring Margaret here when I come back. Wait for me, will ye?"

With that, he headed back into St. Andrews.

* * *

The men mustered early, as always…but today there was more energy: the excitement and anticipation of invincible youth going off on what was sure to be a grand adventure. The men heaved their rucksacks and headed toward the waiting transports, where corporals and PFCs lowered the tailgates and ordered the privates to cram up and in.

April 6, 1915

Dear Margaret:

We've been in Hawick now for several months. I'm not used to being so far inland – I miss seeing the water. This is more of a proper camp, though. They have us in barracks, sleeping in bunk beds. We still don't have proper uniforms, but they have managed to get us utility clothes for training. They are of sturdy fabric. Mum would like them.

We continue our training here. We are finally training with real rifles. We are with a brigade from the Gordon Highlanders. We keep our distance, though. We Fifers stick together. We're not just marching anymore, which is good. We are learning military maneuvers. Some have peeled off to learn how to fire machine guns and mortars. They won't let me do that. I think they know I'm not eighteen, so I am doing other things.

We have been told that one of these days, we will be moving again. I think it will be to a larger base where we can train with other units.

I read your letters every night, Margaret. I enjoy them so.

Ever yours, Frank

July 4, 1915

Dear Margaret:

Sorry I haven't written for a while. They moved us back to Fife – to Kinghorn – but we were only there a couple of days before they moved us again. I wish we had been there longer. You were so close! I would have loved to see you on leave. We are now up in Perth.

This is a proper base, with barracks, a mess hall, a quartermaster, and an infirmary. We are involved in advanced training. I applied to learn to drive a transport but was denied. I think it is due to my age.

I have been able to hold my tongue enough to keep from marching all night long. I would have saved myself many sleepless nights had I figured that out earlier. In any event, I think you might not even recognize me now. I was told I was braw before, but now even more. My mum would even have a hard time, I think.

Some of us have been deployed to replace the 1/7 in France, but we "young ones" have been held back. I'm not the only one that enlisted too young. The officers here have figured that out and are keeping us on base for now. We are not hearing too much about the fighting. Except for me needing to hold my tongue and be very obedient, this is far better than working in a coal mine. The pay and food are way better, that's for sure. I am proud to be in the 42nd, I can tell you that.

I look forward to your next letter.

As ever, Frank

October 30, 1915

Dear Margaret:

I hope this finds you well. We have moved again – we are now in Grangemouth. I do not understand why we move so often.

I have big news: I have been made calisthenics instructor! This is a great honor and is much more enjoyable than anything I have ever done before. It is keeping me from some of the drudge work assigned to privates. I've never been in charge of anything before, but I have been told that I have a talent for it. I hope that if I excel, I can get a promotion. I would not mind doing this for the remainder of the war.

I do think of you often, Margaret, and hope that when I return, we can see each other often. Please wait for me.

Yours, Frank

March 18, 1916

Dear Margaret:

We have moved – again. For the first time in my life, I am not in Scotland. We are in Norwich, down in England. I thought I had seen a proper base – this camp is like nothing I have ever seen. It is quite large, and it is not only for army personnel. There are air forces here, too. Thousands of men, I would think.

I am still a calisthenics instructor, but now I have larger classes. We have equipment and obstacles here, unlike Grangemouth. I am enjoying the challenge. I still have weapons training, but except for that and daily marches, I exercise men all day long.

The discipline here is stricter. We must march to and from mess as a squadron. The lieutenants inspect our barracks every day. Everything must be shipshape. Sometimes the lieutenant tests our bed-making by trying to get a tuppence to bounce off the blanket. I don't much mind. It's not difficult to keep things tidy. Some of the lads, though, are having a rough go of it. More men have been sent to relieve men on the front. Some news has gotten back to us by way of recovering wounded men. The stories are terrible. I will not sorrow you with the details, but I wish more than ever to stay here and train men.

Please write soon.

Forever yours, Frank

August 14, 1917

Dear Margaret:

We have moved again – this time to North Walsham. We are closer to the North Sea now, and when I have leave, I can cycle to the sea. It's good to be nearer the water.

I have big news: I have been promoted to lance corporal! I am still instructing calisthenics, but at a higher rank. And more pay. I am very glad I enlisted. I am doing so much better than I would be doing if I had stayed at the Rosie. When I return, I hope I can find other employment. I do not wish to return to the Rosie.

I have news of my family. Jeannie has a bairn. All of my brothers of working age are still at their same jobs. They tell me that conscription started last year for men nineteen years and older, but coal miners are exempt. Not only exempt, but they are highly discouraged from leaving the mines in the name of the war effort. Rob is exempt due to his frailty – I'm the only one in my family enlisted.

More and more men are replacing the fallen. We hear the 42nd had very heavy losses on the Western Front. They were the first ones out of the trenches and were, nearly to a one, done in by machine-gun fire.

I remain safely on British soil, where I hope to stay. I think of you very often.

Forever yours, Frank

April 3, 1918
Dear Margaret:
This might be my last letter for a while. I am in Dover, England, and am being deployed to the front. The 2/7 42nd has been disbanded, and we are being assigned to the Seaforth Highlanders when we cross the Channel. We have been issued proper kilted uniforms.

We have to carry everything we need with us. They piled us high with equipment and rations. The strangest thing we got is this piece of canvas that goes over our kilts. To tell you the truth, I wish we were in trousers instead. My rucksack must weigh 4 or 5 stone with everything in it. I have your letters right in the middle, all protected. I like to read them, especially at night. I think I've memorized most of them.

We're off for France tomorrow. I need to turn in – we have a big day tomorrow.

Wish me Godspeed, Margaret.
Yours, Frank

*   *   *

Frank sealed this last letter and took it to the camp post. Then he walked back to the tent where all the deploying soldiers were spending their last night in England in row upon row of cots. A small group of men stood outside the tent, smoking. Frank walked up to them, pulled out a cigarette from his pocket, and lit it.

"Mind if I join ye?"

"Naw, not at all, Sir. Can't sleep?"

"Haven't tried yet. Should, though. T'morra's going to be a big day."

"Aye, tha' it is."

The men smoked in silence. Frank took a couple of drags, dropped his cigarette into the dirt, and snuffed it out.

"Godspeed tae ye, lads. Think I'll turn in."

He entered the tent, found his cot, and slipped off his boots, and he lay there a while, hands under his head, staring at the top of the tent. Finally, he drifted off to sleep.

May 15, 1918

Dear Margaret:

I haven't been able to write you for several weeks. I hope you haven't been worried. I am fine and have yet to see battle. That will be coming soon enough.

We are up near the front lines. I don't know where, exactly. We rode some in trucks to get here and marched the rest of the way. We can hear the shells from camp here, behind the lines.

We will spend four days in the trenches and then switch out and come back to camp for a while. The men coming back are filthy – all muddy and wet. There's a problem with lice. Some have bad sores on their feet from being in wet boots for so long.

They don't complain much, though. They take their turns and get on. There's training and calisthenics here in camp in between trench shifts to keep strength and skills up. My very favorite training is marksmanship. They do try to keep our weight up, but that depends on the supply lines. If supplies are late, then food is a bit on the light side. They try to make it up when the trucks finally get here.

I start my first trench shift tomorrow. When I rotate back out, I will write again. I miss you, Margaret. When I come back, you and I will dance the Friday nights away.

Yours forever, Frank.

* * *

Frank marched down into the trenches with his company, weaving his way through the narrow, winding mud held up by planks to keep the trench walls from collapsing. There were sections of trench where wood planks floated in mucky water and to lose one's balance off the plank often resulted in pulling a bootless foot from the sucking muck. Soldiers crouched and snatched bits of sleep in small dug-outs in the walls, and these were mostly a refuge from the muck of the trench floor. The rats apparently thought so too. Artillery shells flew overhead, towards the German line. Most hit in no-man's land – an otherworldly collection of shell holes, barbed wire, and obstacles of various sorts intended to make traversing this stretch of hell next to impossible. German shells were also regularly fired, but they rarely came close to the trenches.

Frank had excelled in marksmanship, so he was assigned as a sniper. He took his place toward the top of a makeshift ladder, firing when he saw a head or helmet. He rarely knew whether he made a kill or not, but the occasional thunk of a bullet piercing a German helmet proved his skill as an expert marksman. There was little to do between shifts but try and get some rest. The first four days seemed to last forever.

July 15, 1918

Dear Margaret:

I got your letter today. It was the very best thing that has happened to me since I came here – the best birthday present I could wish for. I am glad for you that you got a job as a domestic for the Earl of Wemyss! Such an honor. I am sure you will do very well.

I sorely miss trousers. This kilt is so heavy when it's wet, and my legs get terribly scratched by barbed wire when I am on patrol.

New troops are arriving every day... I think they must be getting ready for something different. One of the new lads said they are bringing in tanks. I don't exactly know what those are, but I will find out soon enough.

Sorry that this is short, but I have to go and direct a class. I think of you constantly, Margaret. I can't wait to see those blue eyes of your again.

Yours faithfully, Frank

Frank didn't mention the lines of men who didn't manage to get their gas masks on in time – the men who were blinded, the men with bandages wrapped around their heads. He didn't mention the men who had been shot by German snipers, the ones who were wounded, or the scores who were dead. He didn't mention the foot rot some men had from constantly wet and infected feet.

The camp became crowded with the amassing of hundreds and hundreds of troops. Frank had his hands full conditioning both them and the men switching out of trench duty. It seemed that the encampment couldn't hold one more soldier...and then Frank heard a rumble, a loud, ominous, rather thundering rumble that was coming closer and closer. He was still on the training field when the first tank appeared from the west. Dozens of them were rumbling in. Training stopped as everyone turned and watched the caravan of these fierce war machines roll in on their treads. The extra men, these fortified machines – Frank knew that something big was going to happen, and happen soon.

It was a gray day when the mass of regular foot soldiers was ordered into the trenches – all shifts. Frank watched as his unit, in their kilts, lined up with the others to enter the trenches. He couldn't imagine them all fitting in; they must have been shoulder to shoulder. The tanks were assembled, ready to cross a makeshift bridge across the trench into no-man's land. Frank waited for the artillery barrage to start, but the guns were silent. That was unusual. This felt different. Frank stood back and watched as best he could from his poor vantage.

And then the call came. The Seaforth Highlanders were the first to climb the makeshift ladders and charge across the land that had become hell. There was an eerie silence from the German side until the machine guns opened up, mowing down the Scots as they ran into range. They fell, and the men following them fell – but still, the men behind them charged. They stampeded toward the German line, their numbers compensating for the carnage, and when the first of them reached the German trenches, the tanks crossed. They rolled over piles of fallen Scots, men from other regiments, and rolled inexorably toward the German trenches, immune to the machine guns. They plowed right into the Germans, and between the tanks and the foot soldiers, the German line was taken. What was left of the enemy fell back.

Frank watched in horror as the bodies were deposited on his training field. The mangled were doctored as best as possible and loaded into transports then taken to the field hospital several miles behind the encampment. The next morning, as the remaining men were mustered into formation, he was aghast at how few of the Seaforth Highlanders were left – hardly a one. His regiment had been annihilated.

October 12, 1918

Dear Margaret:

I am sorry if you have been worried about me. We were pulled back and merged with another unit. We have been on the move, and we just got to where they have cots we can sleep on.

I sorely want to come home. I am fine but very weary. I could not have imagined war would be like this. We all left thinking we would be such fierce warriors; that part is true. But war is a horrible thing. I never even want to talk about it. There's nary a one of us that wouldn't give a year's pay to be back in Fife.

I don't know where we will go next. Keep me in your prayers, Margaret. I fall asleep dreaming of you every night.

Yours forever, Frank

* * *

November 11, 1918

Dear Margaret:

The Great War is finally over. It's been years, I know — but I'm coming home! The letters you sent kept me going throughout this terrible time You have always been in my thoughts.

I can't wait to see you again! I hope you feel the same. I should be back in Fife in a fortnight.

Yours faithfully, Frank

CHAPTER FOUR

It was raining when Frank got off the bus from Edinburgh and walked up to the Kirkcaldy ticket station to buy a ticket to Wellsgreen. He kept looking around to see if he recognized anybody in the crowd, but no. These were all strangers. He wondered if anyone would recognize him now that he was nineteen, several stone heavier, and even taller than when he left. He stood waiting, still in his tattered and filthy uniform, awkwardly watching civilian life. As he stood, he mentally ticked off the things he needed to do. First, he needed to buy civilian clothes. Then he needed to get a job. And he needed – desperately needed – to see Margaret.

The bus lurched to a stop as Frank mused over his impending tasks. He waited as a few elderly ladies boarded the bus… *so many ladies, hardly any boys my age*, he thought as he climbed aboard.

"Just back fae' the wa'?" the bus driver asked. Frank hadn't heard such a broad accent in some time.

"Aye, I am," he replied.

"Guid luck tae ye, lad. Failte hame."

Welcome home. That was the first time he had heard that. It felt good.

Frank got off about thirty minutes later. He stopped and looked around. Same shabby old town. The streetlight he and the the boys used to congregate around – there was a new group of young lads under the light. They stopped their conversation to watch Frank walk by. He walked slowly to his parents' house, but instead of walking around back, he walked up to the front door and knocked.

After a few moments, the door opened.

"Hello, Mum."

Bess stared at this near stranger in disbelief. "Is tha' you, Frank? Are ye home fae th' wa' now? Let me luik a' ye! Ye've groon tae be a braw man!"

Frank leaned over and gave him mum a kiss on the cheek.

"Aye, I'm home, Mum. May I come in?"

"Yer speakin' lik' a Brit, lad! Howfer?"

"Folk do better speaking proper English in the army, Mum. It probably saved my life. That and being braw."

Bess stepped aside.

"Come in, then. Are ye hungert? Ah've some bannocks just baked."

"I'll wait for the others. Where are the bairns?"

"Th' weans are nae home fae school. Andrew and Lill. Maggie's a' job a' th' mine wi' yer da. Rob an' Jimmy ur merreet: Rob merreet Jess Ireland, an' Jimmy merreet Ness Thomson."

"They were sweet on those lassies afore I left. Good for them!"

"An' Jeannie ha' a wee bairn wi' anither on th' way."

Frank looked around the room. Nothing had changed. He didn't know why he thought it might be all different. He certainly was.

"Mum, I'm going to go ask for a job at the Rosie for now. Until I find a better job. Do you know whether Mr. Low is still the overseer?"

"Ah dinnae ken, Frank. I dinnae ken whether thair any jobs. Miners weren't subject tae th' draft, sae th' jobs fillt up fast."

"I'll go anyway. And tomorrow I need to go into town to buy some civilian clothes. I'll be back later."

Frank kissed his mother on the cheek and left for the coal mine.

It was mid-afternoon when he walked through the familiar gate.

He headed over to the overseer's office and knocked on the door jamb, even though the door was open.

Mr. Low was standing in front of his desk, his back to the door. He turned around.

"Aye?"

"Mr. Low, it's Frank Sharp. Home from the war, and I was wondering if there was a position here for me."

"Frank Sharp! Luik a' ye! I ken ye were braw afore, but luik at ye noo!"

"Thank you, sir. A job?"

"Nae, laddie, thair's nae jobs open noo. We're full up. I kin put yur name on th' list, though."

"Do you know of anyone that's hiring?"

Low thought for a minute. Then he walked behind his desk and pulled out a pen and paper. He scribbled something, came around, and gave the piece of paper to Frank.

"Ah hae a cousin in Pittenweem tha' makes golf clubs. 'Ere's his address."

Thank you, Mr. Low."

Frank turned and left. In a way, he was relieved. He didn't want to be a coal miner – stay a coal miner – like his father and brothers. He needed a job, but he would look elsewhere. And if anyone asked, he could say he had tried.

Instead of returning to his parents' house, Frank went to the bus stop. He was headed to Kirkcaldy to buy some new clothes – something he had never done before. And then he was going to Cowdenbeath. He needed to see Margaret.

* * *

Cap in hand, Frank knocked on the door of Greenbrae House. A pleasant-looking matron with white hair and wearing a fresh apron opened the door.

"Ma'am, my name is Frank Sharp, and I was wondering if I

could call upon Margaret Ferrie."

"Sae yer Frank, fresh fae th' wa'! Ye writ many letters, lad! She'll be glad tae luik on ye. Come in an' bide a while. I'll fetch 'er."

She stood back to allow him entry and closed the door after him.

With a grin, she said, "If ah'd known ye wair comin', I'da baked ye a cake." She laughed and motioned for him to sit while she climbed the stairs. A few minutes later, Margaret came flying down the stairs.

"Oh, Frank! Ah was wonderin' if ye'd come soon! Luik at ye! Yer sae braw! An' e'en taller than ah remember!" She took both of his hands in hers, beaming.

"Mrs. Ferrie, would you mind if Margaret and I took a stroll?"

"Nae, laddie. Hae a guid time." She waved them off.

Frank reached over to open the door and then stood back and put on his cap. As he and Margaret stepped out, she glanced back at her mother, grinning widely as she left.

"Margaret, you look exactly as I remember you."

"Ah cannae say th' same, Frank. Yer aulder…nae a laddie. Nae mair. An' ye talk different – ye a Brit noo?"

Frank laughed. "No, Margaret. But I was told I would go further speaking the King's English. It was true, I think. The men I instructed assumed I went to school beyond primary. It gave me greater authority in their eyes."

Margaret changed the subject. "Yer wearin' store-bought clothes! Ye luik sharp, Frank." She laughed at the pun.

"Aye. I could do little else but save my wages. I've got a tidy sum, but it has to do me until I find wages. I went to the Rosie, but there were no openings."

"Aye, 'tis rough noo, Frank, wi' all the men returnin' a' once."

"The overseer gave me the name of a cousin that might need help building golf clubs. I'm going to go see him next week."

The High Street trolley pulled up to the corner. Frank grabbed Margaret's hand.

"Let's go!"

"Gae whair?"

"To the edge of town...out to the countryside. I don't know. Somewhere we can be alone."

The two hopped on the trolley and took it to the edge of town. Then they walked away from town, up the road to the rolling farmland. There were still some bales of hay scattered across the harvested fields. Frank hopped a low stone fence and lifted Margaret over, taking her to a hay bale that was not tightly secured. He made a comfortable hay pile for them to sit on and motioned for her to sit with him.

"Margaret, I sore missed ye." Frank leaned over to her and gently moved one of her ringlets from the front of her shoulder to the back with the back of his hand. Margaret blushed but made no move to stop him. He then cupped her cheek in his hand.

"I thought about you every night, Margaret. I'm telling you now: I mean you to be mine."

Frank leaned over and kissed her gently. He moved his right hand to the back of her head, drew her nearer, and kissed her again. His kisses became more and more intense, moving from her lips to her neck and ear. His left hand moved to Margaret's waist, and he leaned down until she was lying under him in the hay.

"Margaret, I cannae help m'sel'. Ah want ye fiercely," he whispered in her ear as his hands moved over her body. Margaret couldn't hide the fact that her body was responding in kind. In no time, her skirts were up around her waist.

* * *

Frank rolled off of Margaret and lay next to her.

"I hope I didn't hurt you, Margaret."

She straightened her frock, placed her coat over her like a blanket, and rolled over to face him. A tear rolled down her face.

"Frank, ah love ye. Ah fell in love wi' ye mair wi' every letter ye sent. Ah expect ye tae intend tae marry me. If ye dinnae intend tha', tell me noo, an' ah'll ne'er see ye agin."

Frank rolled to face Margaret.

"I love ye, lass. I will ask for your hand when I've a proper job so I can well care for you. That I promise." He kissed her.

Margaret smiled and rolled onto her back.

"I mean tae hold ye tae tha', Mr. Sharp."

* * *

Frank rose the next day, put on his new clothes, and headed to the address Low had given him. He found himself standing in front of a nondescript stone storefront in Pittenweem, quietly tucked on an out-of-the-way side street. The faded, painted sign that hung over the door read "Alexander B. White, Proprietor. Golf Clubs." Frank tried the door handle; the shop was open. He walked in as the bell over the door announced him.

A spry, white-haired man came in from the back, wiping his hands on a cloth. The shop smelled of sawdust and varnish, and the wood floor creaked with every step.

"May I help you?"

Frank pulled out the note Low had given him.

"Sir, I am fresh from the war and am looking for work. Charles Low at the Rosie said you might be hiring." He handed the address he had been given to the man. "Are you Mr. White?"

"Aye, that I am, lad. So, you are looking for work? Are ye good wi' yer hands?"

"I believe I am, but honestly, I've never been tried. I worked at the Rosie as a messenger. I joined the Forty-Second when I was but fifteen."

"The Forty-Second, aye? From St. Andrews?"

"Aye, the Two-Seven. I made corporal."

Alexander White studied Frank closely.

"And wha's your name, lad?"

"Frank Sharp, sir."

"Did you see action?"

"Aye, sir. I was stationed on the Western Front."

"Well, ye must ha' been lucky to come back in one piece. I lost two sons to the Western Front."

"I am sorry fer yer loss, sir." Frank hung his head and looked down on the cap he held in two hands.

After an uncomfortable silence, the man said, "Aye, I can use a lad. Where do you bide?"

"Wellsgreen, near the Rosie."

"Ye don't mind coming o'er to Pittenweem?"

"I don't mind going anywhere in Fife for work."

"I cannae pay ye much tae start. I'm thinking that the links will start up again as men come back and spend the money they earned in the service. I promise ye I will gie ye a raise as soon as I can, but I cannae afford more than eight shillings a week. Not now. But if ye show promise and if the business picks up, I would like tae get ye fifteen shillings a week. But for noo, that's just a goal."

"Any work is better than none. I have ambition. I want to marry. I will take the work, and thank ye. I've been told I'm a clever lad. I won't disappoint you."

"Start Monday, then. Nine o'clock."

"Thank you, Mr. White. Thank you very much." Frank shook Alexander White's hand firmly, and then he turned and left.

As he rode his bike back to Wellsgreen, he smiled. He had a job until something better came around.

* * *

It was a ninety-minute bike ride to Pittenweem. Frank rose early on Monday morning and headed out. He decided he would ride as often as he could, only spending bus fare when the weather demanded it. He was fifteen minutes early.

"Hae ye ever worked with wood?"

"Nae, Mr. White."

"Come wi' me, lad."

Mr. White headed to the woodworking shop in back. The back room was crowded with various lathes vises, saws, and other woodworking equipment hanging from hooks on the walls. Mr. White went to a workbench that stood underneath the only window.

"I want ye to sand this smooth." Mr. White picked up a partially finished driver and a piece of sandpaper and demonstrated to Frank what he wanted. "Make this smooth as a baby's bum. And here's an apron fer ye." He handed Frank a sturdy canvas apron. "Any questions?"

"No, sir."

Frank put on the apron and started sanding, mimicking Mr. White's actions. Mr. White watched for several minutes.

"Mind ye to sand equally all aroond. The shape must stay the same."

"Aye, Mr. White."

"There. Ye hae it. Bring it to me when yer done." Mr. White went up front to answer the bell that told him someone had entered the store.

Frank sanded carefully, admiring the beautiful grain of the beech club head as he turned it to maintain shape as he worked the sandpaper. He stopped to examine another club head that was on the table. It was extremely smooth – Frank worked on his clubhead until it was just as smooth, and then he went out to the front room, looking for Mr. White.

"Mr. White, is this good?" Frank handed the sanded clubhead to Mr. White.

Mr. White took the sanded clubhead and examined it closely.

"Well done, lad. Ye have a knack for workin' wi' yer hands."

Mr. White walked to the back room, motioning Frank to follow.

He pointed to a basket on the floor, next to the workbench.

"Thair a half-dozen heads in tha' basket. Sand them aw."

"Yes, sir." Frank got to work.

* * *

Frank found himself smiling as he rode back to Wellsgreen. The money wasn't great, but he found he liked woodworking. He liked the smooth coolness of the sanded beech. He liked admiring the curves of the wood as he sanded, noticing the fine grain and how the curves of the club head revealed it. He certainly liked it more than being a messenger.

Frank turned off, but instead of heading home, he headed to Cowdenbeath, Garden Close. He knocked on Margaret's door.

"Hello, Mrs. Ferrie. I was wondering if Margaret would like to take a stroll?"

"Well, how ye be, Frank. I'll fetch the lass." As she turned, Margaret came down the stairs.

"Hello, Margaret!" Frank's face lit up as he saw her. "Care to take a stroll?"

"A fine idea!" Margaret grabbed a shawl, gave her mum a quick peck on the cheek, and left with Frank.

"I have a job, Margaret! It's in Pittenweem, and I'm not making much money to start, but I like the work. I'm making golf clubs."

"Golf clubs?"

"Yes. I like working with wood. A fair sight better than running messages at the Rosie."

"Tha's no aroond the corner, Frank...Pittenweem."

"Until something better comes up, Margaret. No much work these days, ye ken?"

"Ah ken yer right, Frank. Me brothers cannae find guid work, ither. Ah'm happy fer ye."

"Happy for us, Margaret." Frank reached around and gave her a little hug.

"No in public, Frank! Wha' wull people say?" She wiggled out of Frank's arm, alarmed.

"So, I cannae gie ye a little hug?" Frank teased.

"No in th' street, Frank. It's unseemly."

"All right, then, Miss Ferrie." Frank spun off, turned towards Margaret with great solemnity, and took a deep, deep bow.

"I beg your forgiveness."

At this, Margaret laughed and shook her head.

"Ah dinnae ken wha' tae dae wi' ye, Frank Sharp."

"You're going to marry me one day, Margaret. That's what you'll do with me."

CHAPTER FIVE

Frank climbed out of the bus and headed towards home in the icy drizzle. It was a cold February day, so he turned his collar up and pulled his cap down to keep the weather out of his eyes. He quickly walked around to the back, took off his shoes, and entered the rowhouse. The aroma of a savory vegetable stew – with a scant hint of beef bone broth – filled the room. He was late, and everyone else had finished supper. Frank grabbed a bowl and served himself some stew, and then he sat at the table and finished it off quickly. He washed the bowl and spoon and headed into the front room, where Da was reading the paper.

"Any chance there's an opening at the mine, Da?"

"An' how come de ye ask, Frank? Golf clubs no fer ye?"

"I haven't gotten a raise in salary ever, Da. It's been over a year, and all I hear is business isn't good. Couldn't be so bad, seeing that I need to stay late more than not."

"Wull thair may be, Frank. Yer brothers Jimmy an' Jock hae been talkin' aboot bein' aff tae America."

Frank was stunned. "Really? When? And why?"

"Jobs are waiting wi' guid pay 'n' advancement. Thay heard it from Robbie Hooks, who is in Detroit making cars a' Ford. Wage is five dollars a dee fer eight hours' work, tho' I dinnae ken whither tha's guid o' puir. Hooks says it's guid. Ye kin ask tae replace one o' thaim once they tell Low thair leavin'. Eight hours a dee – ah jus' might tak' a notion tae gie m'sel'."

Frank sat in silence, taking it all in.

"Da, have you read any articles in the paper about work in America?"

"Aye. Talk o' many lads leavin' fer greener pastures. They say ye kin even buy yer oon hoose! Nae rent – buy!"

"I'm going to the pub for a pint, Da. Want to come?"

"Nae – th' weather's tae raw fer these auld bones."

Frank headed out and ducked into the corner pub.

"What do you hear of work in America?" Frank addressed the question to the barkeep, but he intended for the men sidled up to the bar to also hear.

"Ye thinkin' o' gang, Frank?"

"No – just curious. But I hear people are going. Just wondering. Any of you get any letters from kin that are there?"

"Aye, mah sister an' her husband are in Canada. Thay wur given land an' hae built a hoose o' thair oon. Say ''tis wide open, an' thare ur help wanted signs aw ways. Ah'm thinkin' o' gang m'sel'. Ye shuild think on it yersel', Sharp. Here's a pisshole wi' nae guid work an' nae guid wages tae gie wi'."

Frank finished his pint. "See you later, lads." He went home and had a hard time falling asleep. He was thinking of America.

* * *

Frank headed to Margaret's to take her to the dance in Kirkcaldy, as he did every Friday. Mrs. Ferrie opened the door and greeted Frank icily. Margaret, her eyes red and puffy from crying, came up behind her.

"Margaret! What's wrong? Are you all right?"

Mrs. Ferrie stormed into the kitchen as Margaret walked up to Frank. She looked at him and started to cry.

"Frank, ah'm pregnant."

Frank put his arm around her and led her to the loveseat. They sat together, holding hands.

"Ah cannae work whin ah start tae show, Frank. Ah cannae be seen in such a state."

Frank squeezed her hand. "Margaret, I will give your mum three shillings a week during your confinement. I can't afford a place for us – not yet. But I will take care of you until the bairn is born. And when I find a better wage, we will marry. And until then..." Frank's voice trailed off.

"Until then, I will stand by you. Margaret, I won't let you down."

Frank stood up. "Let's go for a walk. It's dark – no one can see you. Come with me, Margaret. Let's get some air."

Frank and Margaret walked away from Cowdenbeath, towards farmland.

"Wull ye meery me noo, Frank? Afore I show?"

Frank fell silent, his head down. Finally, he said, "I can't afford to rent a place, furnish it, and support the three of us on eight shillings a week, Margaret. Even if I took everything I have saved, I can't arrange any of that before you start to show. I don't want to live that poor – I don't want you to live that poor."

Frank took a breath.

"My da says Jock and Jimmy are thinking of leaving for America. He says he thinks I can replace one of them at the Rosie. I can make fifteen shillings a week there – that's nearly twice what I make now. But that can't happen for a while, and our bairn might even be born by then. But I promise you, when I can make fifteen shillings a week, I will make you my wife."

Margaret started to cry.

Frank turned to stand in front of her. "Margaret, please don't cry. I will come every night to be with you. Every night as long as your parents allow it. I will stand by you – on that, you have my word. Please don't cry. I love you, Margaret. I love you with all my heart. I have never loved another – I have never even called on another. I saw you across that dance hall, and I knew you were the one for me the night we led the Grand March. That was over five years ago, and my feelings have not wavered. You are the one."

Margaret wiped her eyes with the backs of her hands and tried to clear her sniffles.

"Ah wuid lik' ye tae come nightly, Frank. Mah parents willn'a mind a' taw, ither. Ah will resign mah post in a month's time, afore th' reason becomes clear." She sighed.

"An' then mah confinement starts." She hung her head resignedly.

Frank took Margaret's hand. "Come, let's walk."

The stars were out – it was unusually clear and crisp, with nary a breeze and a bright full moon. A lovely night for a stroll. Frank and Margaret walked away from town, as they usually did – out past the farms towards Loch Gelly. The moonlight glittered on each small wave as they crested and then lapped against the rocky shore, which was surrounded by trees. Frank laid his overcoat down, and he and Margaret sat on it as they stared at the inky blackness surrounding the reflection of the pale yellow moon extending towards them. Margaret shivered a bit, and Frank drew her close, wrapping his arm around her.

"Have ye a chill, Margaret? Should we go?"

"In a bit, ah think, Frank. Thair's a nip in th' air."

With that, Frank stood up, extended his hand to Margaret's, and pulled her up.

"Cannae have ye cauld, lass."

"Ah'm glad yer so braw, Frank. 'Twill be hard tae dae tha' in a few months."

Frank grinned. "You'll never be too heavy for me, Margaret."

They slowly headed back. Frank left Margaret at her door, preferring not to deal with her parents at the moment. He needed to present a sound plan to them… He just wasn't ready.

"I'll come for you tomorrow night, Margaret. Sleep well." Frank gently kissed her and left.

* * *

Frank took the bus to Pittenweem on Tuesday to avoid riding in the first snow of the season. Not that it ever snowed much in Fife…just enough on that cold and windy Tuesday to make bike riding dicey. He quickly walked the three blocks from the bus stop to White's, where he stomped his feet before entering the store to the familiar ringing bell.

"Aye, Frank. Guid mornin'," called Alexander White as he came from the back room. "A dustin' o' snow, aye? Winter's upon us."

"Mornin', Mr. White." Frank headed to the back room to hang his coat on the coat rack and don his carpenter's apron.

"Mr. White, I was wondering if we could speak about my wage. I've not had a raise."

"Ah've told ye afore, Frank – business is nae tha' guid."

"I need the money, Mr. White. I need to marry my girl."

Mr. White's eyes narrowed as he deciphered Frank's meaning.

"Wull, lad, it cannae be from th' store. But ah've an idea. Ever been tae a whippet race?"

"Nae."

"Ah've a whippet ah race. She's a quick one, tha'. Made some shillings on 'er. Come tae th' race in Kingsbairns once they start up again. Two o'clock. Bet on mah whippet and win a week's wages if th' odds are guid an' the crowd is large."

"Are you saying I should gamble?"

"If ye need th' money, lad. Easy money."

"I'll think about it, Mr. White." Frank turned to get to work.

He finished off the last of the clubs and shafts early and left for Wellsgreen – he had two hours before he needed to be at Margaret's. He hoped the mine closed early with the weather.

Rob and Jimmy had rowhouses in Wellsgreen – next to each other, around the corner from their parents. Frank knocked on Jimmy's door.

"Wull, howfer ye be, Frank?" Ness Sharp opened the door wide to let Frank in. "Yer here fer Jimmy, no doubt. She turned and called upstairs, "Jimmy! Yer brother Frank is here fer ye."

"Hello, Ness. I hope you're well."

"Aye, tha' we be. Care fer a cup o' tea?"

"Lovely. Thank you, Ness."

Jimmy came down, tucking in his shirt. "How ye be, Frank? Still aff tae Pittenweem, makin' golf clubs?"

"Aye, I am, Jimmy. But I've come to ask you about going to America. Are you considering it?"

Jimmy scowled at Frank. "E'er since ye came back from th' war, yer talkin' lik' a Brit. Ah cannae git used tae it. Wha…we're nae guid enough fer ye noo?"

"It served me well in the service, Jimmy, and I believe it will serve me well in the future. I've got ambition, and the King's English helps."

"Ye've got airs is wha' ye hae, Frank."

"So, tell me, are you serious about leaving for America?"

"Luikin' into it. Hooks – ye remember Hooks? He's in Detroit. Makin' motorcars. Says wages ur guid an' thair are help wanted signs aw ways. An' he said th' St. Andrew's Society helps Scots settle in. Lots o' us thair – enough tha' they built their oan hall. Makes it feel lik' home."

"When are you thinking of leaving?"

"Mibbie in a year. It wull tak' a bit o' doing tae save twenty pounds: ten fer steerage an' ten fer once we arrive."

"Are you still working the coal face?"

"Aye, whyfer ye ask?"

"I'd like to replace you when you leave."

"Ye dinnae lik' mine work, Frank. How come ye want tae gae back?"

"I'm not making much, and Mr. White won't give me a raise. I need to make more… I told Margaret we'd marry once I was making fifteen shillings a week. White said if I wanted more money, I should bet on his whippet."

"He races whippets, does he? Ne'er been much o' a gamblin' man m'sel'. Money's tae hard tae come by."

"Yer no even sayin' it, Jimmy. I'd rather swing a pick."

"Afore I leave, ah'll tell ye, an' ah'll mention to Low yer interested."

"Thanks, Jimmy."

Frank finished his tea and took his teacup back to the scullery, where Ness was busy cleaning up after supper.

"Thank you for the cup of tea, Ness. Good to see you." He gave her a peck on the cheek.

"An' tae you, Frank."

Frank headed towards the front door. "I'm off to Cowdenbeath. See you later!"

"Gie oor regards tae Margaret!"

"I will. Thank you!" And with that, Frank was out the door.

* * *

Frank's curiosity got the better of him, so on the first Saturday in May, he caught the bus to Kingsbairns to attend his first whippet race. The course was a flat, rather narrow but long grassy area defined by strung rope on either side, where spectators gathered. Four men were at the start of the course, and four men with white cloths were at the end.

Frank walked up to the ropes halfway down the course and watched as the judge got ready to start four dogs. At his signal, each of the dog handlers – slippers, as he learned later – picked up their dogs by the back of the neck and their tails. When the judge dropped his hand, all the men hurled their dogs down the track towards the men with the white cloths, who were waving them frantically and calling the dogs to them. The race was over in less than a minute. Frank looked around for Mr. White.

There must have been twenty dogs competing, four at a time. Mr. White was down behind the starting line – it appeared that he was not in the next heat. Frank walked over to him.

"Hello, Mr. White."

"Frank! Ah see ye cuildn'a stay away! Did ye bet on my Lady here?"

"No – I thought I would first watch. I've never seen whippet racing before."

"Yer gang tae miss oot, laddie. Th' man o'er thair wi' the black apron is takin' the wagers. Yer gang tae lose oot, nae placin' a wager o' mah Lady here."

"Maybe next time, Mr. White."

"Lady's in th' third heat. Ye watch... She'll win."

Frank tipped his cap and walked back to a spot along the course. The second heat was about to start. Four men with dogs stood at the start, ready to hurl on command; four men with white rags waited at the end, ready to call the dogs home. In less than a minute, three more dogs were eliminated, and a second dog had made it to the semifinals.

Frank watched Mr. White closely as he prepared to race Lady. White patted his dog's head, left her with his slipper, and headed down to the end with his white cloth. At the judge's command, the slipper, who was down on one knee, hurled Lady forcefully. When she landed, her front paws were already out and ready to run. The slipper nearly fell face down on the grass. Lady's long and slender legs gave her sleek body remarkable stretch as she positively flew down the course to a very encouraging Mr. White, a good dog and a half ahead of her closest competitor. She was a remarkable dog.

After the race, Frank sought out Mr. White, who was giving Lady a treat and praising her while she rested during the last two qualifying heats.

"Your Lady is quite fast. You were right," said Frank, patting Lady's head. "The odds on her must be poor – she is obviously quite a contender."

"No sae bad, Frank. Third heat, middle o' th' pack. Slowest in th' first heat – fastest in th' fifth. Nae a big reputation yet. Wait a month, though. Then odds willn'a be sae guid."

Frank looked intently at White and then headed off to find the man in the black apron. He bet sixpence on Lady and walked away that day winning three shillings – more than two day's wages and enough to cover the money he needed to give Margaret for the week. He caught the bus home, smiling.

* * *

"Mr. White, the Saturday race was interesting. Lots of racing whippets... Must be dear to keep them, aye? Is there a winner's purse to help with the cost?" Frank made sure to sound nonchalant as he turned a golf club.

"Aye, Frank, thair is. Whyfer wuild ah keep a dog wi'oot a benefit?"

"You must have a lot of experience with whippets."

"Aye, a bit. Lady's mah third pup. Ah was lucky tae git her. Breeder didn'a think she was th' best o' the litter. Mah guid luck, tha'. She'll mak' me a pretty penny, ah think."

"How often do you race her?"

"No in th' rain, but if th' weather's guid, thair's a race every weekend until winter. She's a wee bit young, sae ah dinnae want tae race her every week. Ah've been restin' her a fortnight between races."

"Have I turned this club enough, Mr. White?" Frank held out a No. 2 wood for Mr. White to inspect.

"Yer becomin' a master turner, Frank. Yu'v a knack fer workin' wi' yer hands."

Frank smiled as he picked up the next club head.

On the way home, Frank grabbed a newspaper and turned to the back. He was looking for ads for whippets. He had a lot to learn – and that's just what he intended to do.

* * *

"Mrs. Ferrie, here's three shillings for Margaret." Frank held out the money to a still-icy Mrs. Ferrie, who took it without comment. Margaret came into the front room from the scullery, took off her apron, and grabbed her coat. She was starting to waddle a bit, and Frank held her coat so she could put it on. The two left for their evening walk.

"Your mum is never going to like me, Margaret."

Margaret laughed. "Praise doesn'a come easily tae her, tha's fer sure. Dinnae fash yersel', Frank. She'll come aroond." She laughed again.

The two strolled towards the fields north of town, up a gentle hill on a pebbled footpath lined with recently blooming wildflowers.

"Margaret, my brother Jimmy says he should have enough money for steerage to America by next year. He said he'd put in a word for me when he tells Mr. Low he's leaving, but I need to ask you: would you ever consider leaving for America with me?"

Margaret stopped in her tracks.

"America? Frank! Leave wha' we ken fer wha'? It's no easy here, tha's true. But gang sae far awa'…" Margaret's voice trailed off.

"It's not for sure, Margaret. I don't have any solid plans – my current plan is to ask for Jimmy's job when he leaves and stay with you. Marry you. Might even be able to take over his rowhouse. Just thought I'd ask. Lots of men are finding good work in America. That's all."

The two walked up the path until they got to the crest of the hill. The path wound down the hill before turning left to cross a small, old stone bridge that traversed a little rivulet. The couple stopped at the crest, turned around, and headed back to Garden Close.

* * *

Frank had just returned from the whippet race, where he'd won five shillings, when a messenger came to the door.

"Frank Sharp?"

"Aye, that's me."

"I've brought word that one Margaret Ferrie has delivered a baby girl."

Frank's face lit up.

"That's my good man!!!" He gave the lad sixpence, grabbed his cap and coat, and headed out to Cowdenbeath on his bicycle. He parked in front of Greenbrae House and rapped on the door. Mrs. Ferrie opened the door to him and then quickly got back to the bustling household. Several women were helping the midwife clean up.

"Mrs. Ferrie, may I see Margaret?"

She turned to one of the women. "Is Margaret fit fer a visitor?"

"Aye, Annie. Cleaned up an' wi' the wee bairn."

"Gae on up, then, lad."

Frank took the stairs two at a time. Margaret was in bed, nursing her new daughter.

"Margaret! Ye luik well, lass. An' the bairn…"

Margaret smiled broadly. "She's sae bonnie, Frank!"

Margaret gently stroked the babe's head, and soon the babe unlatched and fell asleep. Margaret lifted her gently so Frank could see.

"She is a bonnie one, Margaret. Have you chosen a name? I will go register her for you."

"Ah'd lik' tae call her Martha. Martha Ferrie. No many Martha's aroond – she'll no be mistaken fer anither in school wi' a name lik' Martha."

"Martha it is. I will go to the registrar directly Monday morning. I'll send word to Mr. White that I'll be a bit late into work. She really is bonnie, Margaret. Just like you."

It was true. Little Martha had dark, curly hair and porcelain skin. Her eyes were sure to be blue, like everyone in both Margaret's and Frank's families. Her cheeks had a rosy blush – round, cherub cheeks. Frank thought he had never seen such a beautiful newborn.

"And you, Margaret…you are well? Things went well?"

"Aye, Frank. Ah'm just fine. No as hard as ah thought."

Frank sat on the side of the bed and gently brushed a stray damp curl from Margaret's temple.

"I won five shillings today, Margaret. Here, take it." He reached into his trouser pocket and brought out the money. "For you and our bairn."

"Gie it tae me mum, Frank. Ah'll no be getting' up fer a wee bit. Mum wull tak' care o' it." She handed it back.

Frank rested his hand on the baby's head. "Pity we can't give her the name Sharp. When we marry, we will. Martha Sharp. Martha Ferrie Sharp, unless you want a different name."

"That'll do, Frank." Margaret suddenly sounded very tired. "Ah'd lik' tae sleep, Frank. Ah'm worn oot more than Ah thought. Kin ye gae noo?"

Frank stood, leaned over, and kissed Margaret on the forehead. He then placed a gentle kiss on his new daughter. "Aye, Margaret. You need your rest. I'll come calling t'morra."

Frank went downstairs and found Mrs. Ferrie.

"Margaret asked that I give you this, Mrs. Ferrie. For Margaret and the bairn. I will go register the bairn Monday morning."

Mrs. Ferrie took the money.

"Guid. One less thing tae worry aboot."

"I'll come calling again tomorrow."

Mrs. Ferrie didn't answer, merely waving Frank off as she turned back to helping the busy women.

Frank took his leave. When he got back to Wellsgreen, he called upon a message boy to go to Pittenweem first thing Monday morning to tell Mr. White he would be late, and then he went to the pub to celebrate.

"Aye, Frank! Yer in a guid mood, aye? How come?"

"Ah won five shillings on th' whippet! Barkeep – a pint fer mah laddies, aye?"

"Wull, if yer buyin' pints aroond, here's tae ye winnin' every week!" They all laughed and raised their mugs to salute Frank.

And here's to you, my wee Martha. Would that I could openly celebrate your birth. Frank took a deep swig.

* * *

"Frank, wull ye consider bein' mah slipper? Th' lad ah had is off tae America, an' ah need a lad tae replace him."

"How often, Mr. White?"

"Most weekends, but fer rain. An' no in the winter. Ah'll pay ye two shillings fer yer work."

"How big are the purses?"

"An' how come are ye askin'?"

"I'm wondering whether I should get my own dog and race it. If the purses are big enough."

"Takes an investment, laddie. Takes a guid year tae win back th' cost, an' tha's if ye win aw yer races."

"So, what's an average purse?"

Mr. White fidgeted a little.

"No matter, Mr. White. Next time I go, I'll ask the judge."

"Yer gang tae find oot anyway," White mumbled under his breath. "It kin be ten tae twenty shillings."

"Well, then. I would be more interested in becoming your slipper if I got a cut of the purse, say, twenty percent?"

"Nae, tha's tae much!"

"Well then, I think you need to find yourself a slipper." Frank returned to turning a club head.

It was after lunch when Mr. White came back to the work room.

"Wuild ye settle fer fifteen percent?"

"Twenty."

Mr. White sighed. "Aw right, twenty percent. Dae ye ken howfer tae be a slipper?"

"I've watched enough races, Mr. White. I'll have no problem."

"Yull need tae shaw up an oor afore th' race 'n' check in tae git th' schedule."

"Can I meet Lady before so she can get used to me?"

"Aye." Mr. White picked up a piece of paper and a pencil. "Come by th' hoose a' ten. Here's th' address." He scribbled it on the paper and handed it to Frank.

"See you Saturday, Mr. White."

* * *

Saturday morning bloomed sunny and warmer than normal. Frank pulled out his bike and quite enjoyed the ride to Pittenweem. He was a bit early, so he ducked into the greengrocer and bought an apple before heading over to Mr. White's.

He was about to knock on the door when he heard Mr. White around back, working with Lady. Frank walked around back.

Lady turned her head when she heard footsteps and ran to meet him. At Frank's feet, she ducked her head, crouched slightly, and tucked her tail. Frank reached out to pet her, and her tail started to wag just a little. Frank crouched down in front of her.

"It's all right, girl. I am not going to hurt you." He continued to pet her gently until she licked his hand. Frank then scratched her ears.

"You and I are going to win today, you know that? I'm going to get you ready, and then you're going to run like the wind to your owner. You and me, Lady – we're going to get you down the course in record time."

Lady curved her body to the right, wiggling, and wagged her tail enthusiastically.

"Come 'ere, Lady." Mr. White patted his hand on his thigh. Lady took off straight away and jumped up on him.

"Yer ready, Lady. Ah kin see tha'. Let's be off, then." Mr. White put Lady in a wooden crate in the back of his cart.

"Up ye go, Frank. Sit wi' me." He motioned for Frank to climb up on the driver's bench and then picked up the reins. Once Frank was settled, Mr. White snapped the reins, and they were off.

They got to Kingsbairns at noon.

"Here, Frank. Help me wi' th' crate." Mr. White climbed over the bench to the back of the cart and unlashed Lady's crate. Frank went around back and lifted the crate out once it was free. Then he placed it next to the line of dogs in crates. Mr. White pulled out a water bowl, filled it at the trough, and placed it in Lady's crate. He put a blanket over the crate and turned to Frank.

"Come wi' me – we need tae check in." Mr. White led the way to a table set up on the side of the starting line. Two men were sitting there, checking in the race hopefuls.

"Alexander White, racing mah whippet Lady. Mah slipper is Frank Sharp."

"Sixpence tae enter, Mr. White."

White handed over the coins.

"Yer in th' second heat, White. First gate."

"Thank ye."

Frank and Mr. White headed back over to Lady.

"Noo, ye pick up Lady by th' scruff o' th' neck. Dinnae pick her hind end by th' tail; it's nae as guid as puttin' yer hand just under her tail sae ye can gie her an extra push tae start."

Frank brought Lady out of her crate and knelt down beside her. He grabbed her neck by the scruff and placed his right hand under her tail.

"Like this?"

"Aye, tha's guid. When ye toss her, push her oot hard wi' your right hand. She's used tae it, sae dinnae change th' routine. Dinnae want tae confuse her."

Frank rubbed Lady's ears before putting her back in her crate.

"First gate – the one closest to the check-in table?"

"Aye. Are ye gang tae place a bet on mah girl? I'm headed ower to the bookmaker."

"I'll stay with Lady until you get back. Then I'll go."

Frank knelt, talking to Lady and scratching her ears. "You're going to win today, aren't you, good girl? Aye, you are a pretty one.

And fast! You are so fast!" He bent his head down so his forehead touched hers, and Lady's tail started to wag.

"Such a good girl!"

And for that, Frank got a kiss on his cheek.

"You and I will get along, won't we, girl?"

Mr. White returned, and Frank put Lady back in her crate. The slippers were setting up for the first heat – Frank rushed off to place a bet and got back just as the first heat was ending.

"Ah'll be gang tae the end noo, Frank. Git Lady ready – first gate."

"Aye, Mr. White."

Frank brought Lady out and led her over to the first gate. He knelt next to her as the other slippers were getting ready. He grabbed Lady by the scruff of her neck with his left hand and placed his right just under her tail. As he watched for the starting signal, he leaned close to Lady's ear.

"Run like the wind, pretty girl."

Just then, the hand dropped, and Frank hurled Lady. She landed a good ten feet beyond the next furthest racer and won by a good two lengths.

Mr. White came running down the sideline with Lady. He was all smiles.

"Frank! Tha's th' best time ah've ever seen! Yer a braw one... Ah dinnae ken how braw!"

Frank knelt in front of Lady, smiling and petting her.

"You did it, girl! You're the best!"

She licked him, wiggling in excitement and happiness.

Frank stood. "Do I need to do anything between now and the next elimination?"

"Gie mah Lady some water 'n' let her rest."

Frank took out a bowl, filled it, and took Lady over to a sunny spot on the grass. He sat down, placing the bowl near her. When she was finished drinking, he called her over and patted his lap.

"Bide here a while, little girl." Lady lay down and put her head on Frank's lap. He petted her, all the while speaking to her in soft tones.

"You're going to take the purse today, little pup. You are the best!" And Frank was right.

"How much is the purse, Mr. White?"

"Twenty-five shillings! A guid purse t'dee. An' ah won anither five shillings wi' the bookmaker. A guid dee!"

"Five shillings for me, Mr. White."

Mr. White handed over the twenty percent. "Ah dinnae mind, lad. Wi' yer arm, Lady wull win aw ways."

Frank didn't tell Mr. White that he had won eight shillings on his wager. It was a good day.

* * *

The first rainy Saturday, Frank took the bus into Edinburgh. He had saved several pounds and headed into a jeweler. He walked up to a salesman at the far counter.

"I am looking for a wedding ring."

"I would be glad to help you, sir. What might you have in mind?"

Frank looked at the display case. "I want something dainty. My intended's name is Margaret... Do you have anything that might resemble a Margaret?"

The salesman assessed Frank's clothing and brought out a ring with six garnets set around a very small diamond. It looked very much like a flower on a very thin gold band.

Frank peered at it. "That is perfect! Can you tell me the price?"

"It's five pounds sterling, sir. That includes engraving."

Frank held it up. "I don't have a date yet for the engraving. Can I give you two pounds and have you hold it for me until we set a date?"

"That would be fine, sir. This ring is nine-carat gold, set with garnets and a diamond. It is a fine ring."

Frank pulled out two pounds. "My name is Frank Sharp, Wellsgreen, Fife."

The clerk wrote out a receipt and gave it to Frank.

"How long does it take to complete the engraving?"

"We would like two weeks, sir."

"I will be back in a fortnight, then, with a date. Thank you."

Frank turned and left, not knowing – or caring – whether he had made a good deal. He knew nothing of gold or stones. He just knew that the ring was perfect for his Margaret. Very proud of himself, he headed over to Garden Close.

When Margaret opened the door with Martha in her arms, he couldn't miss the distress on her face.

"What's wrong, love?"

"'Tis 'Martha, Frank. She's taken tae coughing aw nicht lang, an' her wee heart is beatin' hard. Ah kin see it through her wee chemise."

"Let me see her." Frank gently lifted the babe out of Margaret's arms. The movement made Martha cough – a rattle from deep within her chest – so fiercely that her sternum contracted. It was obvious she was having a difficult time breathing.

"Margaret, did you call the doctor?"

"Aye, he came once tae see th' bairn. Said she has bronchitis. Ah'm tae gie her a drop o' whisky in some honey. We dinnae hae honey, sae ah dipt mah finger in some whisky an' put it on her tongue. Dinnae dae much…calmed her a wee bit, but th' cough aw ways comes back."

"I think we should call him again, Margaret."

"Me mum says we cannae afford anither call. Th' doctor was nae help."

Frank rocked the babe in his arms.

"Margaret, she doesn'a luik guid."

The coughing reddened Martha's face and racked her little

body, and her hands and feet were cold and a bit blue. Frank took off his jacket, wrapped her in it, and held her tightly against his warm chest. She snuggled in and settled down.

"Mibbie it's just a spell, Frank."

"Go fetch the doctor and have him come back. I'll pay his fee. Puir wee one here. I cannae bear tae see her suffer."

Margaret grabbed her coat and walked out the door.

"Ah'm off, then. Watch th' bairn, Frank."

Frank rocked Martha in his arms as he headed into the front room. Mrs. Ferrie was busy sweeping.

"Th' bairn's puir sickly. Nae guid."

Frank headed over to the table and poured a drop of whisky onto his finger. He let Martha suck it, and she nodded off to sleep shortly thereafter. Frank held her in his arms quietly until Margaret returned with Dr. Nairn.

"The bairn is still coughing?"

"Aye, and she is breathing hard at times. Her hands and feet won't warm."

Frank unbundled Martha for the doctor, who took out his stethoscope and listened to her heart and lungs. He shook his head.

"She has a weak heart, and her lungs are laboring for it. There is nothing I can do for her. I'm sorry. Perhaps she can pull through – if she were only larger. Keep her warm and quiet. Try to get her to nurse more. Maybe, with time, her heart and lungs will become stronger."

Frank moved Martha to one side and reached into his pocket for several shillings. After giving them to Dr. Nairn, he again wrapped Martha up in his jacket and sat back down. His shoulders slumped forward, and his head bent low. He curled around his little baby girl as if he wanted to become her cocoon, creating a healing environment for her and trying to pass his health and strength to her.

"Frank, is she awake? Mibbie ah shuid hae a go nursing her."

Frank gently uncovered Martha's face and passed her over to

Margaret. He then stood, picked up his cap, and fingered it uncomfortably.

"Margaret, if there is anything I can do. I'll be back tomorrow." He kissed her gently on the forehead and placed his hand on Martha's head before leaving. He didn't go straight home – he headed to the pub. He went to the farthest bar stool, away from the handful of patrons gathered at the center of the bar. Straddling the stool, he raised his hand to the barkeep.

"A pint fer ye, Sharp?"

"No, not tonight, Callum. Give me a whisky, neat."

* * *

It rained on and off for the next two weeks. Everything was sodden and gray. There were no dog races and no bike-riding into Pittenweem. There was only gray and mud and wind, matching Frank's temperament exactly. He traveled back to the jeweler in Edinburgh.

"I would like to pick up the ring you have on hold for me."

"I'm sorry, sir – didn't you want engraving with that?"

"Please take off the cost of engraving. I will come back with it so you can engrave it when we know the date. We have a family issue which has postponed our date indefinitely."

"Sorry to hear that, sir. Without the engraving, the cost will be four pounds twelve shillings."

Frank paid the clerk and quietly took the boxed ring. When he got back to Wellsgreen, he placed it in the toe of one of his Sunday shoes. He then headed to Garden Close, as he did every night.

Frank knew the moment he entered that Martha's condition was not good. The heaviness in the home was palpable. Margaret's entire family was there, and everyone was hushed and somber. Margaret was in the front room, slowly rocking a listless and shallow-breathing Martha, whose coloring had lost all rosiness. She was grimacing in pain but didn't have enough energy to cry. Margaret didn't acknowledge Frank – didn't offer to have him hold Martha – didn't even raise her head.

Frank stood by the door, not speaking a word, ignored by all as Margaret rocked her infant child. She rocked until Martha was totally blue and developed the splotches from pooled blood that no longer coursed through her delicate veins. She rocked until her mother finally came over and tenderly put a hand on her shoulder.

"She's gang, Margaret. Gie the wee bairn tae me."

Margaret kissed her baby one final time and burst into tears. She passed the dead child to her mother and wailed in grief. Frank went over to comfort her, but she pushed him away. She pushed everyone away. Frank tried again a few minutes later, but Margaret would have none of it.

"I'll be going, then, Margaret. I'll come back tomorrow." He showed himself to the door.

* * *

"Ye've been in a mood, Frank. Yer no yersel."

Frank was quietly eating a late dinner as his da sat by the stove, reading the paper. Bess was cleaning up the dishes in the scullery, Andrew and Lill were out back, enjoying the last rays of the day while they tended the garden, and Maggie was darning an old sock by the window.

Frank didn't respond, keeping to his food.

Da put down the paper.

"Th' lot o' us are gang to Canada wi' Jimmy. Next year. Ye kin hae th' hoose if ye kin afford th' rent. Or ye kin come wi' us."

Frank dropped his fork and turned away from the table. "When did you decide that? You and Mum? And Maggie, Jock, Andrew, and Lill?"

"Aye, th' lot o' us. Gang tae git a land grant an' farm. Land is free for farmin' in Winnipeg. Wuid ye come wi' us?"

Frank thought for a moment.

"Not right away, but maybe later. I've things I need to settle here before I think of leaving. I don't think I'll be ready by next year."

"Rob's nae comin' noo, ither. Mibbie later. Ness is expectin' anither bairn an' doesn'a want tae travel wi' a newborn. An' Jeannie's stayin' here wi' her husband. Yull hae some kin here efter we're gang."

"I'll take the house after you're gone. And maybe take one of your jobs at the Rosie. What's the wage now?"

"Thair payin' sixteen shillings a week noo. No a bad wage."

"Are they hiring yet?"

"Ah cannae say, but thair's many a miner tha's leavin' fer land in Canada. An' work in America...th' factories ur offerin' passage fer two year's work, ah hear. Fer those tha' kin read an' write English."

"Da, do you know what pub Mr. Low frequents?"

"Nae, but he bides in Dysart."

"Think I'll go over to Dysart Friday and visit some pubs."

Frank got up and headed for his cap and jacket. "I'm off to Cowdenbeath."

He hopped on his bicycle and headed over to Garden Close, as he did most nights. When he knocked on the door, it was promptly opened by Daisy Ferrie, one of Margaret's younger sisters.

"Is Margaret in?"

"Aye. Wait here."

Daisy closed the door and returned a short time later.

"Ah'm sorry, Frank, but Margaret's no acceptin' visitors t'nicht."

"She hasn't accepted visitors for three weeks, Daisy. Do you know when she might?"

"Nae, Frank. Ah'm sorry." With that, Daisy shut the door.

Frank shook his head, got on his bicycle, and headed back to the corner pub in Wellsgreen.

"A pint, Callum."

"Comin' up, Sharp." Callum poured an ale and brought it over to Frank.

"Yer no sae chipper, Sharp."

"A lot on my mind, Callum. That's all."

Frank took a long swig and looked around the room. There were maybe a couple of dozen men there... Several were playing darts, a few groups were laughing at the two corner tables, and the rest were silently nursing their drinks at the bar. Frank was one of the men nursing his drink as he considered his future and what to do to break through to Margaret. He lit a cigarette and smoked it as he finished his pint. When he was finished, he put several pence on the bar and left.

The following Friday, Frank cycled into Dysart. He found Charles Low at the fifth pub he visited – Low was sitting at the bar alone, smoking a cigarette and downing the whisky sitting in front of him. This pub, like most, was wood-paneled, filled with a smoky haze, and poorly lit. There were a couple of dartboards on the side wall, several small, square, varnished pub tables in the middle of the room, a few booths on one side, and a bar across the back wall. Frank walked through the haze to the bar, and he stood at the barstool directly to the left of Low.

"Barkeep, I'll have a Haig's, neat." Frank swung his leg over the stool and sat down.

Low looked up briefly, but not recognizing Frank, he turned his attention once again to his glass.

The barkeep placed Frank's whisky on the bar. After lighting a cigarette, Frank picked up his glass and toasted Low. "Here's tae ye." He took a gulp.

Low looked again at Frank. "Ye luik a bit familiar, but ah cannae place ye."

Frank smiled. "You are Charles Low, overseer at the Rosie. I worked there as a lad. Frank Sharp."

Low smiled and reached around to shake Frank's hand.

"Noo ah remember ye! The lad wha' lifted th' coal cart off Crawford! Ah'll ne'er ferget tha'. An' ye whair just a lad!"

Frank smiled. "How are things at the Rosie now? I hear a lot of men are leaving for Canada and America."

"Aye, thair resignin' weekly. Ah still hae a waitin' list, but it willn'a last forever. An' how ye be? Whit are ye daein' noo?"

"I'm still working with your cousin Mr. White, over in Pittenweem. And he and I are racing his whippet on the weekends. I'm his slipper. I wanted to thank you for sending me his way."

"Guid tae hear tis workin' oot, Sharp."

Frank raised his glass again and took a sip.

"You didn't hear it from me, but you're soon to lose another several men. My da, Jock and Jimmy are leaving to find their fortunes away to America. They tell me there's a flock of men leaving."

Low stopped. "Dae ye ken when? Thair some o' mah best men."

"Next year. Jimmy's staying back, but not forever. You know, Low, I've a strong back… I'd consider taking one of their places. If you think you could use me, let me know. I'll be taking over my da's place when he leaves."

"Yur no leavin' wi' them?"

"No. I have a girl that I want to marry. She's not wanting to leave her family here and go so far away. She won't marry me if I tell her we're leaving."

"Dae ye ken who else is set tae leave?"

"Sorry, no. But maybe I can ask."

Low finished his whisky and snuffed out his cigarette. "Ye dae tha' fer me, an' ah'll see ye a place a' the Rosie. Sooner than later." He patted Frank on the shoulder as he got up. "Ah've tae leave afore th' missus gets in a dither. Guid tae see ye, Sharp."

Frank raised his glass. "And you too, Low."

He waited several minutes after he watched Low leave, and then he gulped down the rest of his whisky and headed to the pub in Wellsgreen.

"A pint, Callum." Frank put several pence on the bar and perched with one leg down, turning to survey the crowd. He caught the eye of his old friend Jamie Campbell, who came over and took the next barstool.

"Aye, Frank! We dinnae see ye much aroond here. Howfer ye be?"

"Fine, Jamie. I've been working in Pittenweem and getting back too late to stop here much. How are you?"

Jamie grinned. "Ah'm guid. Ah'm set tae be merrit tae Kate Blyth."

"Good for you! Glad to hear it. I'm sure she's a fine lass."

"Aye, tha' she is. Ah'm a lucky lad."

"Are you still at the Rosie?"

"Aye. 'Twas a guid thing fer work, the war. Wages up."

"I hear that men are leavin' to America… You might see higher wages yet."

"Yur no only sayin' it, Frank. Loads o' the Wellsgreen lads hae gang o' are thinkin' on it."

"I haven't seen most of them in quite a while. Cunningham? Paton? MacIntosh?"

"Cunningham an' Paton gang aw ready. Kilgour an' Broon are gang soon."

"Won't be many left here."

"Most o' thair folks ur stayin'. Better fer us wi' fewer men."

"I imagine. So, when's the big day?"

"Six weeks. Ah'll be a merrit man." Jamie laughed and picked up his ale. "Here's tae me!"

Frank laughed and toasted his childhood friend.

* * *

It wasn't two weeks later that Low sent word to Frank to come to the Rosie. Frank sent a messenger to Mr. White, and then he walked through the mine's long-familiar gates and over to Low's office.

"Sharp! Ah kin tak' ye on in a month. Are ye still interested?"

"Yes, Mr. Low. Where will you put me, and what will be my wage?"

"Ah need tae start ye a' the pithead. We're payin' fifteen shillings a week."

Frank hesitated, pained and a bit crestfallen.

"I was hoping for sixteen shillings, Mr. Low. That's the going wage, isn't it?"

"Ah'm payin' fifteen, lad."

Frank reached over to shake Low's hand. "Thank you for the offer, Mr. Low. You did say sooner than later, and you are a man of your word. But I must decline your offer."

Frank put on his cap and turned to leave. His hand was on the doorknob, pulling open the door, when Low said, "A minute, Sharp. No many a braw man as yersel'. Tell ye wha'… Ah'll gae sixteen, but ye cannae tell yer wage tae others."

Frank turned and headed back.

"I accept your generous offer. I need some time so your cousin can find a replacement for me. When might I start?"

"Come th' first o' the month."

"Perfect! Thank you. It will be good to be back." Frank shook Mr. Low's hand again and left.

* * *

Frank knocked on the Ferries' door in Garden Close.

"I've come to call on Margaret." It was a very familiar statement to Mrs. Ferrie.

"Ah've told ye afore, Frank. Margaret's no takin' visitors."

Frank pulled the ring from his pocket and held it out in front of him.

"Ma'am, this time, I'll not take no for an answer. Please send Margaret down."

Mrs. Ferrie examined the ring and shook her head a bit, but she headed into the scullery. Frank heard voices: Mrs. Ferrie sounded determined; Margaret sounded adamant and agitated. While the words were muffled, Frank was sure that Mrs. Ferrie was determined to get her oldest daughter married, and she finally ordered Margaret out into the front room.

"Margaret, I've come to ask for your hand in marriage." Frank held out the ring for her to see.

"Noo yull tak' th' ring an' say aye." Mrs. Ferrie shooed Margaret towards Frank. "Tak' it!"

Margaret reluctantly took the ring from Frank and slipped it on her finger.

"I'll get it engraved before the wedding – once we set a date."

"Margaret, ye kin git a dress in a month. Nae use waitin' past tha'." Mrs. Ferrie was pushing hard.

"Margaret, would you walk with me?" As Frank extended his arm to Margaret, he glanced at Mrs. Ferrie, who nodded approvingly.

"Noo ye gae, lass. Gae wi' yer laddie."

Margaret took Frank's arm, and the two walked out the door.

"Margaret, I start at the mine in a month. My parents and most of my family are leaving for America soon and say I can take over their house. They will be gone in six months, and then we can have the house to ourselves. My wage is sixteen shillings. I told you I would marry you when I could, and now I can."

"Ah dinnae deserve tae wed. God punished me fer havin' relations afore I was merriet."

Frank stopped and turned Margaret towards him. "Margaret," he said quite sternly, "stop talking that foolishness. Many a bairn passes in infancy. Ye ken tha'."

Margaret hung her head in sadness and shame. "I dinnae deserve tae be wed."

Frank let go of her shoulders and took her arm once again. As they walked, he said, "Well, you will be wed, deserving or no. To me.

In a month. You will be Margaret Sharp, living in Wellsgreen, married to a coal miner."

"Ah cannae show mah face thair, Frank."

Frank lowered his voice to a whisper. "I told no one about the bairn, Margaret. Not even my parents. Nobody knows now, and they won't – ever. We will never speak about her. Ever. Your parents never come to Wellsgreen, and even if they did, they would never discuss the bairn. You know that. You and I – we will start fresh."

"Ye tellt nae a soul?" Margaret looked hopeful and relieved.

"Nary a one. It is our secret. And you and I – we will take it to our graves."

The two walked in silence to the edge of Cowdenbeath.

"But now you need to meet my parents, Margaret. When can I bring you to Wellsgreen?"

"Mibbie end o' week? Ah need tae press mah Sunday dress an' polish mah boots."

There was a lightness in Margaret's step on the way back that she hadn't experienced in several months.

* * *

Mr. White was none too pleased with the news.

"Yer quittin', are ye?"

"I've a job at the Rosie, Mr. White. I'm settling down and getting married. I need to get home at night earlier."

"Wull ye still be mah slipper?"

"No, not anymore. I'm giving up the racing, too."

"Yer gang tae gie up th' wagerin' money?"

"Yes. I'm very sorry. Thank you for taking me on when you did. I've learned a lot, and it's been a pleasure working with you."

"Lady wull miss ye, tha's fer sure. You've a way wi' dogs, Sharp. Best o' luck tae you an' the missus."

"I'll miss Lady, too. I'll give you two weeks' notice. You'll find a lad by then."

* * *

It was a very small wedding, held in the Ferries' front room. Banns had been published within a week of Frank's proposal, and the ring was back in Edinburgh, getting engraved – "R. S. and M. F., 20-6-1920." The local minister officiated. Jimmy witnessed for Frank, and Daisy for Margaret. After the ceremony, Margaret took off the ring to read the inscription.

"R. S.?"

"Aye. My full name is Robert Funkie Thomson Sharp. I used 'R' because I will take back my name. One day."

"Dinnae ye hae a brother Robbie?"

"Aye. My da registered my birth after a trip to the pub. He was always very fond of the name Robert."

Margaret laughed. "Well, ah'll aw ways ken ye as Frank."

Frank lifted a glass of scotch. "Tae mah wee wifey – Margaret Sharp."

* * *

Six months later, most of the Sharp family left from Glasgow and sailed to Montreal, and Frank and Margaret experienced living without a gaggle of others for the first time in their respective lives.

CHAPTER SIX

Margaret greeted Frank with a kiss at the back door.

"Ah've yer clean clothes, Frank." She handed over a freshly washed set of clothes for him as he put his grimy, coal-covered shirt and trousers in the laundry basket by the back door. He smiled at her and leaned over to give her a kiss after he pulled on his clean trousers.

"A letter came th'dee from yer da." Margaret went into the front room and picked up a letter off the table.

Frank tore into it, reading.

"He says the weather in Winnipeg is awful! Never saw so much snow and wind – up to the windows!"

Frank read a bit more.

"Not worth the land offer, he says. Poor rainfall in the summer – hard to grow crops."

Frank read some more. Then he looked up.

"The lot of them are leaving to move to the United States. They're going to Detroit. He says it's the richest city in the world. Always looking for men to work in the motorcar factories."

Margaret smiled as she put the dirty clothes by the washboard.

"Ah've made shepherd's pie fer dinner. It's ready an' on th' table."

"Shepherd's pie! That's a treat!"

Margaret smiled again. "Ah ken ye lik' it, Frank."

Frank grinned broadly and lifted Margaret up in his arms.

"You take such good care of me, wee wifey."

"An' noo ye kin put me doon, Frank. Gie an' eat yer dinner afore it gits caud." She shooed him to the table.

"Did you hear? Winston Churchill lost his MP seat. Dundee was taken by a Prohibitionist and the Labour Party. Strange times, Margaret...strange times."

"Ah dinnae follow politics, Frank. But did ye ken tha' the butcher cut his arm an' closed th' shop fer th' week?"

Frank scooped up the last of the mashed potatoes topping the chopped lamb and onion hash beneath them.

"Wonderful, lass. Really delicious." He pushed the plate away.

"I hear that Lochgelly Coal and Iron is looking for a turner. They are paying two pounds eight a week. I think I might go up and apply... I think it can't be much different than turning golf club heads."

"Tha' wuld be a nice raise, Frank! But 'tis a bit further awa'."

"For a higher wage, I will make the trip. I hope Mr. White thinks to give me a good recommendation if he's asked. It's supposed to rain all night. Chances are the mine will be shut down tomorrow. I'll go to Lochgelly in the morning."

"If ye think it's fer th' best, Frank." Margaret busied herself with cleaning the table, then the dishes, and then the clothes.

Frank sat down next to the radio he had recently purchased and, pulling out a pipe, started to listen to the 5MG broadcast from Glasgow – the first radio station in Scotland, only three months old. Frank was obsessed with this newfangled radio and never missed an evening.

"Margaret, do you want to come listen?"

"Frank, ye ken ah've cleanin' tae dae. Mebbie efter ah'm done." Margaret was scrubbing Frank's work clothes on the washboard. She rinsed them, wrung them, and hung them on the drying rack by the cast iron stove. By the time she had finished her chores, the station had signed off for the evening.

Frank turned off the radio and glanced up at the pendulum clock on the wall. "Nine o'clock. Are you about ready for bed, my bonnie lass?" He got up, walked over to Margaret, pulled her close, and gave her a kiss. His hand wandered down her back, and as it rested on her behind, he pulled her even closer. "I've some business I would like to attend to," he whispered in her ear.

Margaret smiled and untied her apron. Hanging it on a peg near the scullery, she headed towards the stairs and held out her hand. Frank took it, and the two headed upstairs.

* * *

Frank boarded the bus to Lochgelly, pulling his cap down low over his eyes and hunching over against the chilling rain, which was being driven by a gusty wind. The bus stopped at the company gate. Frank was the only one that got off – the day shift had started hours ago. He walked through the gate and stopped, looking around to determine where he should go. Lochgelly was large and varied, with coal pits, brickworks, and decommissioned blast furnaces. He decided against the three-story building, which was feeding coal down a conveyor to a receiving train car. He headed to the right, towards a one-story building that most likely held the offices. He walked down the side of the building until he found a shingle hanging over a windowed door: "Offices." He walked in.

There were four offices off a center hallway – two right and two left – and a larger office at the end. The offices had half-windows facing the hallway, which was paneled in dark wood and had a linoleum floor. Behind the offices' closed doors, clerks busily entered data into large ledgers. The door at the end, however, was open. Gaslights, spaced between each side office, lit the hallway. Frank walked down to the end and knocked on the door jamb.

"Yes?"

"Are you the hiring manager, sir?" Frank didn't enter or peek around the corner. "I noticed you placed an advertisement for an iron turner, and I would like to apply for the position."

"Come in, young man."

Frank walked into the office. The man sitting at the desk to the right was middle-aged and somewhat overweight – something that Frank rarely saw. Frank walked over to the front of the desk as the man stood up to shake his hand.

"And you would be…?"

"Frank Sharp, sir. I have this ad…" Frank pulled out a half-page of the newspaper with the help wanted ads from his pocket. "It says you are looking for a turner." He held the paper out to the man behind the desk. "Is the position still open?"

"Aye, it is. Thomas Drummond."

"Nice to meet you, sir."

"You are interested in the iron turner position? What experience do you have?"

"None with iron, sir. However, I turned golf club heads for a few years over in Pittenweem. After the war. I worked for Mr. Alexander White. I am sure he would give me a fine reference. He often said I was good with my hands."

"How old are you, lad?"

"I'm twenty-three, sir."

"Married?"

"Yes."

"Family?"

"Not yet, sir. Margaret and I married last year and have been busy setting up house."

"Won't be long, lad. Won't be long. Where are you employed currently?"

"I am working the coal face at the Rosie."

"And how long have you been doing that?"

"My entire family worked there. I started as a messenger at twelve and worked until I joined the Forty-Second Blackwatch in 1914. When I returned from the war, there were no open positions there, but the overseer recommended me to his cousin, Mr. White. I worked for him for nearly three years and then returned to the Rosie, where I have been for the past two years."

"Have you ever worked an iron lathe?"

"No, sir. Just a wood lathe."

"Why did you leave Mr. White?"

"For the wage, sir. I wanted to marry, and I needed to provide for a wife."

"And why do you want to leave the Rosie?"

"Two reasons: for the wage, because it won't be long before the bairns come and I'll need to provide for them, and to get back to using my hands. I miss that."

Drummond studied Frank closely. "You are certainly a braw lad. What did you do in the Blackwatch?"

"I was calisthenics instructor for a longer time than anything else, but I was a sniper on the Western Front. I made lance corporal."

"You entered the war quite young."

"That I did. Along with many others."

"Come with me." Drummond came around from the back of his desk and headed towards the door. For his age and weight, he moved surprisingly gracefully. Drummond grabbed his cap and coat from the coat rack next to the door and headed down the hallway and out the door. Frank followed. Drummond headed over to a nondescript one-story building several hundred yards away. He and Frank walked into the ironworks, where several men were making various mechanical parts for the plant.

Drummond walked up to an unmanned lathe. "Wait here a minute."

He then walked over to a man turning a piece of iron into, perhaps, a lever – too early in the process to tell. He picked up the engineering drawing next to the man's lathe, grabbed an unfinished piece of stock iron, and walked back to Frank.

"Can you read this drawing?"

Frank studied the drawing. "These are the dimensions of a lever, three feet long, three inches in diameter at one end, and two and a quarter inches at the other." He studied the drawing again. "It's cylindrical along the shaft and reduces slightly to one and three-quarter inches six inches below the end in a gentle slope before opening up six inches from the smallest diameter, gaining diameter gradually until it reaches three inches."

"Good. Now turn it." Drummond turned on the machine by engaging a gear that connected the drive to a crankshaft that ran across the ceiling and powered all the lathes.

Frank took the piece of metal and studied it carefully. He watched the man working the lathe next to him for several moments before gingerly placing the piece of iron against the rotating lathe to feel the interaction and assess how hard he had to push and how quickly the iron would mold to his will. He moved the piece of iron back and forth several times and then pulled back, measuring with calipers the diameters at both ends. He marked the shaft six inches down and defined the narrowest part. As he worked the piece, stopping and measuring, assessing the smoothness of the grind, he was lost in time, focused on the lever.

After ninety minutes, he was finished. He hadn't noticed that Drummond had left quite a while ago. Frank left the ironworks and headed back to Drummond's office, lever in tow. He again knocked on the door jamb of Drummond's office.

"Mr. Drummond?"

"Is that you, Sharp?"

"Aye. I've finished."

"So, let me see how you have done."

Frank walked in and handed over the completed lever to Drummond, who took out calipers from his side drawer and thoroughly measured the piece.

It seemed like hours to Frank, but finally, Mr. Drummond said,

"A fine job, Sharp. You're hired. When can you start?"

"I need to give two weeks' notice, sir. And thank you."

"Two weeks it is, Sharp. Welcome to Lochgelly Coal and Iron."

* * *

Frank burst through the back door and quickly slipped off his boots.

"Margaret! Margaret, are you here?"

"Aye, Frank." Margaret came from the front room, broom in hand.

"I got the job! Two pounds eight a week! I start in two weeks."

Frank headed to the small bureau in the front room, grabbed two glasses, and poured out some single malt. He handed one to Margaret. "We need to celebrate!" He raised his glass. "Slainté!"

"No, Frank. No afore supper. Salmon, fresh caught. The salmon ur runnin'. Mah cousin Callum went up th' Tay an' brought a load back."

Frank emptied his glass and put it on the table. He grabbed Margaret by the waist.

"It's going to be so much better, lass. Wait and see." He kissed her, but she pushed him back a bit.

"If ah dinnae git tae dinner, it wull be spoilt." She grinned, kissed him on the cheek, and headed for the scullery. She came out with two plates and set them on the table.

"Anither letter came from yer folks." She sat down to eat.

"After dinner, Margaret. This looks delicious!"

Mah friend Jeannie Wilson is off tae Canada wi' her husband."

"Who'd she marry?"

"Willie Brant. Thair gang tae Hamilton. Ah'll sairly miss 'er."

"Seems like the whole of Wellsgreen is leaving. Glad that Jimmy is here. Most of your family has stayed, though."

"Aye. Ah'm glad o' tha'."

They finished the rest of their dinner in silence. Then Margaret got up to clear the table while Frank went to the front room and over to the chair next to the radio.

"Th' letter's on th' front table," Margaret called as she headed to the scullery. Frank picked up the letter before he sat down and turned on the radio.

Dear Frank –

Hope this finds you well. We have left Winnipeg and landed in Detroit. Robbie has found a position as a clerk at the Ford Motor Company, and Andrew has started on the line. We have a lovely home on a boulevard with a large park right across the street. Scots have settled here in Clark Park, and it feels a bit like home – except that the houses here are so big!! Everyone has their own room upstairs! Jimmy Hooks lives next door – you remember Jimmy? He's also working at Ford.

Maggie is working at a laundry. There are many jobs here for the asking. That part is very different from the old country. And the city is so big! There is a trolley car that runs up and down Woodward Avenue, right to the ferry docks on the river. It is lovely.

We were wondering if you might come when Jimmy does. We miss having the whole family here. It's hard getting used to all of the different kinds of people. They speak different languages and eat different foods. Half the time, I can't understand what anyone is saying. There's a city right next door called Hamtramck. It is filled with Polish people. They make the most delicious sweets for Lent. I hear there are lots of Italians around a neighborhood by Lake St. Clair, but I've never been there. And the Irish live in a place called Corktown.

I mainly stay around Clark Park. I've never lived in such a big and busy city, and it's a bit much at times. There is this huge store downtown called Hudson's. It sells everything you could imagine except groceries. It has mechanical boxes that go up and down to all of the floors – they are called elevators. The elevators are needed because there are dozens of floors. I have never seen anything like it at all. You must come see.

There are more Scots immigrants in Windsor now than here. I take the trolley down to the ferry and cross over to buy meat pies and shortbread at a Scottish bakery there. I do miss Wellsgreen at times. It was quiet, and everybody knew everybody. There is good and bad here, but life really is easier.

Please think about coming. We miss you, Frank.

Love, Mum

Frank finished the letter and handed it over to Margaret, who had come in with some socks for darning. She sat down and read it silently.

"Wuld ye leave Wellsgreen, then, Frank?"

"I just took a position at Lochgelly! And I'm making a much better wage. I want to make a go of it here. I think I can work up to a responsible position – maybe even engineer. I think we will be comfortable here, Margaret."

Margaret let out a deep breath. "Tha's guid tae hear, Frank. Ah'm nae sure ah'd fancy a big city."

Frank turned on the radio and lit up a pipe, and he listened to the crackling broadcast as Margaret deftly darned the hole in one of his socks.

* * *

It was an unusually warm September evening as Frank stepped off the bus from Lochgelly and walked around back, as he had done since childhood. He slipped off his shoes by the back door.

"Margaret! I'm home!" Margaret wasn't in the scullery, which was unusual at this time of day.

"Margaret?" Frank called as he entered the front room. There sat Margaret, leaning into a bucket.

"Are you ill?" Frank rushed over, the concern in his voice undeniable.

She looked up and smiled wanly. "Nae th' best way tae tell ye ah'm pregnant."

Frank lit up. "A bairn! Wonderful! How far along?"

"Aboot three months, ah think. I wasn'a sure. Ah visited th' midwife this mornin' – tha's wha' she said."

Frank went into the scullery and brought back a glass of water. "Here. Are you feeling better?"

"Aye, ah am." Margaret drank the water slowly. "Thank ye." She stood up and took the bucket out back, where she washed it out.

"Supper wull be a wee bit late."

Frank smiled and came up behind her, wrapping his arms around her waist and nuzzling her neck. "For the best reason ever." He let go and went into the front room.

* * *

John Paton Sharp was born on April 24, 1923, and was named after his grandfather, as was the custom.

"Ye kin come in, Mr. Sharp. Margaret an' the bairn are fine." The midwife was wiping her hands on her apron after setting down a bucket of pink water. She picked it up again and went to dump it out back.

Frank walked into the room and right up to Margaret, who was sitting up against plumped-out pillows, her baby at her breast. She smiled. "A braw one, aye?"

Frank came over and gave Margaret a kiss on her cheek. "He's healthy?"

"Aye. An' hungry."

Frank laughed. "Just like his da, I'd say. When can I hold him?"

"Whin he's done. Wull ye go doon and register him?"

"Aye, straightaway if you like. Name's John Paton Sharp, aye?"

"It's a guid name, aye." She smiled down at the babe and then back up at Frank. "Wull ye tell Ness? She said she'd bring supper in fer ye."

"Aye. I'll let you and the wean rest. I'll go to the registrar and then to Ness and Jimmy's. I'll be back – maybe then wee Jack will be ready to meet his da." Frank kissed Margaret again and left.

* * *

"How's the bairn, Sharp?" Frank and Drummond happened to be walking into the works at the same time.

"He's fine, Mr. Drummond. Getting big! He's already six months old. Healthy, too – Margaret swaddles him tight and lets him sleep outdoors when it's not raining. He's kept healthy."

"Glad to hear it, Sharp. Say, can you stop by my office before you leave this evening?"

"Yes, sir. Of course." Frank reached over to shake Drummond's hand, and then he headed over to the ironworks.

Frank smiled to himself throughout the day. *Wonder if I'll be getting more wage? Maybe get promoted? Drummond likes my work. Wait until I tell Margaret!* As busy as Frank made himself, the day dragged on and on. Finally, the whistle blew, and Frank hung up his apron and went to see Drummond. The clerks had already left for the day, and Frank walked past the dark and empty offices to Drummond's open door. He knocked on the door jamb.

"Sharp? Come in."

Frank walked in, cap in hand.

"Have a seat, Sharp." Drummond got up, walked around to the front of his desk, and leaned up against the edge.

"You've been doing good work, Sharp."

Frank smiled. "Thank you, sir."

"Good work. And that makes this difficult for me. I have to move you to the coal face. We've lost too many miners, and you are the last one into the shop."

Frank stopped smiling.

"Sir, I've never worked the coal face."

"I know, Sharp. That's why I have to start you as an apprentice. You'll learn it fast enough, I'm sure. I'll move you up as soon as the foreman tells me you've advanced."

Drummond pulled out a cigarette and lit it. He offered the pack to Frank, who turned it away.

"I know you have a young family, but an apprentice coal miner's wage is less. Fifteen shillings. I can't give you more than a pound a week – that's a shilling more than most apprentices."

Drummond paused, stood up, and walked around to the back of his desk.

"I'm sorry, Sharp. Worst part of my job. You'll start at the coal face Monday." He busied himself with some papers on his desk, not looking up.

Frank stood, waiting for Drummond to look up and continue. After several silent and uncomfortable moments, he turned and left. Drummond didn't look up until Frank was halfway down the hall.

* * *

"We're leaving, Margaret. As soon as I can raise passage. I'll leave you here until I have a job, and then I'll buy passage for you and the bairn to come. Scotland's not done me any favors."

Margaret looked at Frank in disbelief.

"We're leavin'? Tae gae whair?"

"Canada. The United States. Australia…New Zealand. Somewhere else."

"Whyfer, Frank? Wha' happent?"

"Drummond is moving me to the coal face as an apprentice, at a lower wage. He says I'm the last one in and he's lost too many miners. I will suffer through it, but as soon as I can manage it, we are leaving."

CHAPTER SEVEN

"She sails April twenty-fourth. And what class of ticket do you wish?" The Cunard clerk shuffled papers as he spoke through the glass.

"Third class." Frank had never spent eighteen pounds sterling all at once on anything in his life, and it was a bit daunting.

"That will be eighteen pounds, sir." The clerk waited for Frank's money and then shoved a few papers through the window. "Please fill these out." He passed a pen through the window.

Frank walked over to one of the wooden desks lined up along the west wall, sat down, and started to fill out Immigration Form 30A, required by Canadian Immigration authorities. When he had filled out what he was sure was correct, he headed back to the clerk's window with the partially completed form. He shoved it back through the window and waited.

"You haven't completed everything,"

"That's correct. I have some questions."

The clerk read the form and then picked up a pen.

"You don't have a job lined up?"

"No. I will look for work when I get there."

"Then I suggest we add 'anything suitable' for your intended occupation."

The clerk read on, correcting where needed.

"Do you intend to permanently stay in Canada?"

"Yes."

The clerk wrote "settle" in the space for "Object in going to Canada."

"How much money do you intend on taking?"

"I'm not sure. I need to leave most for my wife and son, who are staying here until I find work and a place for us to live."

"The Canadian government likes to see at least fifteen pounds," the clerk said as he entered that on the form. "You paid for this ticket yourself?"

"Yes."

"Good. The *Athenia* debarks in Montreal. Will you stay in Quebec?"

"No. Perhaps Ontario."

"I'll put Windsor. That's the hub of most manufacturing. Officials like to see that for someone without a job in hand."

The clerk studied the rest of the form. "Everything else looks in order." He signed the form and gave Frank a ticket. "Have a pleasant voyage."

"Thank you." Frank carefully put the ticket into his deepest pocket and left the ticket office. He grabbed the next bus from Kirkcaldy back to Wellsgreen. He was heady with excitement.

Frank walked in the back door of his rowhouse and searched out Margaret. She was busy changing the baby's diaper. Frank pulled out the ticket and walked up to her.

"April twenty-fourth, Margaret. That's when I'll be gone."

"Tha's the bairn's birthday! Yull be leavin' on th' bairn's first birthday?"

"That's when the ship sails, Margaret. I don't control the dates." He showed her the ticket. "Eighteen pounds. I never spent that much all at once on anything."

Margaret started to tremble. Frank walked over, took Jack, and placed him in his cradle. Then he turned to Margaret and hugged her.

"It will be fine. I'll take you to your parents until I'm ready to send for you. I've saved up twenty-five pounds for your upkeep. I've already spoken to your brother Alec – he'll escort you and Jack when the time comes."

Margaret started to cry.

"We'll be fine, Margaret. Better off than here. We can buy our own house and have a much bigger garden. My brother Rob has a house AND a motorcar! You'll see. We will be fine. Not much of my family left here. You know that – Jimmy left several months ago. We will have lots of family around. Wee Jack will have lots of cousins to play with."

Margaret buried her head in Frank's shoulder but broke off when Jack started to cry. She pushed herself from Frank and picked up their son.

"He needs to eat." She sat down and bared her breast for the baby, who immediately stopped crying and started to nurse.

"Margaret, we..."

"Nae noo, Frank. Th' bairn's nursin'."

Frank headed towards the stairs but turned halfway there and looked back at Margaret. He hesitated a moment, but then he turned back to the stairs and left her with the baby, not saying a word.

* * *

Frank's packed suitcase was downstairs, by the door. He looked around one last time at the now-empty row house as the carters took the last of the furniture and piled it onto their cart to take it to the church for someone less fortunate. Frank picked up his suitcase, closed the door, and headed to Cowdenbeath, where Margaret and baby Jack were already settled. Frank knocked on the door.

"Wull, Frank – ah see yur ready tae sail." Mr. Ferrie was not smiling.

"Th'morrah, Mr. Ferrie. I've brought twenty pounds for Margaret and the bairn."

"Come in, then." Mr. Ferrie turned sideways so Frank could pass. Margaret and her mother were busy while the babe slept in a small cradle. Margaret turned as Frank entered and hurried over to him.

"Ah'm gang tae miss ye sorely, Frank." Her voice trembled.

Frank took Margaret into his arms and cradled her head against his shoulder.

"The trip's two weeks, Margaret. As soon as I land, I'll write. And as soon as I find employment and somewhere to live, I'll send for you. I'll save every penny for your passage. I hate to leave without you. I will miss you so." He kissed her on the forehead. "We need to look to a better future for us and the bairn. We owe it to ourselves and our family. Please don't be sad. This is the best for us. We can send money home to your family – it will be better for everyone."

Frank reached into his pocket. "Here's twenty pounds. I'll send more when I can. Hopefully, I can send for you in a month or two. Have you talked to your brother Alec? Will he still accompany you?"

"Aye, Frank. He's ready tae leave wi' us." Margaret went over to the baby and picked him up. He fussed a bit at being awakened. She walked back to Frank, holding Jack in one arm.

"Jackie, yer da's leavin' fer America. Kin ye gae him a kiss an' wave bye?"

Jack smiled at Frank and reached for him. Frank picked him up and kissed him.

"Aye, Jackie!" Frank bounced the baby up and down. "We'll have a great time in America, aye? Will you be a good bairn for your mum while I'm away?"

Jack grabbed at Frank's face, laughing. Frank turned his face away a bit and laughed with him.

"We'll have fun, son. Soon. Can you say bye?"

Jack just laughed, and Frank reluctantly gave him over to Margaret.

"I need to go, Margaret. I need to be in Glasgow by tonight. Callum Fraser's folk have agreed to put me up for the night. We set sail early tomorrow morning."

Margaret gave Jack to her mother and hugged Frank tightly. "Hurry tae bring me o'er, Frank. Hurry," she whispered into his shoulder.

Frank wiped a tear from her cheek. "As soon as I am able, Margaret. I can barely stand the thought of being away from you a day, let alone a month." He squeezed her tightly and then broke off brusquely.

"I love you, Mrs. Sharp." There was a catch in his voice. He turned quickly and left Garden Close for the last time.

* * *

The ship *SS Athenia* was moored along a dock in the middle of the port. Frank walked down the long dock and stopped at the gangway to show his ticket to the Cunard employee on duty. Ticket verified and passenger list completed, Frank walked up the gangway with his suitcase. He took a place on the railing, where he watched as other passengers approached and boarded. It didn't take long until the entire railing was crowded with voyagers. The ship let out three blasts on its horn, and the last of the passengers scurried aboard. Three more blasts, and the gangway was removed. Dockhands unlashed the moorings and threw them up to waiting deckhands fore and aft. With one long horn blast, the ship left the dock. Frank was on his way.

Frank grabbed his suitcase and followed the crowd heading below deck to third class. He found his cabin: a small, dark nook with four narrow berths, two on each side, one up, one down, separated by an aisle no wider than thirty inches. Frank placed his suitcase on a lower berth as two men entered. Shortly after, a third man appeared. They claimed available berths and set about to get organized, no one saying more than "Aye, guid mornin'." Frank simply nodded acknowledgment.

Shortly, a crew member arrived at the door and leaned in.

"Guid mornin' tae ye, lads. Ah see tha' ye'v found yer berths. Th' loo is doon the hall." He pointed left. "Th' mess is up – gang up th' companionway aft. Breakfast served from six tae seven. Second meal served from three tae four. Only two meals. Aboard, 'tis one hand tae yersel', one hand tae th' ship. Aw ways. Dinnae gae tae th' deck in rough seas. Stay in yer berth. Th' bucket thair" – he pointed to a tin bucket on the floor – "tha's fer whin yer peely-wally. Dinnae gae on deck tae boak."

One of Frank's cabinmates said, "Sorry…I'm not Scottish. To be clear, if we need to vomit, we all use that bucket?"

The crewman laughed. "Aye. Dinnae ye gang tae th' deck. We dinnae wan' tae lose ye, ye ken? One hand" – he lifted his right hand and grabbed the door jamb – "tae th' ship. Aw ways. We dinnae wan' tae lose ye. Ye ken?"

The crew member leaned back out a bit. "Oh, ye cannae smoke below deck. We dock in Montreal on May fifth. Hae yersel' a bonny passage." He left to pop into the next cabin.

Frank sat on the edge of his berth, his legs hanging uncomfortably over the wooden rail meant to keep a body from falling out in rough seas. There was barely room for him to sit upright. Not satisfied, he got up and went out to speak to the crew member.

"Excuse me, is there anywhere we can play cards or write a letter?"

"Aye. Th' mess is open whin thair's nae a meal bein' served."

"Thank you." Frank started to explore. He went up the companionway aft to find the mess hall. The floor above had steerage cabins, like below, but at the end was a large room. He entered the mess hall and found rows of tables bolted to the floor, with benches on both sides, also bolted. It was extremely spartan. He turned around and headed astern. Midship he found another companionway. He went up it, but at the top, he was stopped by the crew.

"I'm sorry, sir. Steerage passengers are not allowed to use this companionway. This floor is reserved for second-class passengers."

Frank quickly surveyed the hall before he turned and left. The lighting was better, and the floor was carpeted. Beyond that, the hall looked the same. He turned, went back to steerage, and found his cabin.

"Any of you lads have a deck of cards?"

Before anyone could answer, a crew member called out loudly from the hall, "Please head up the aft companionway and go up to the deck for a safety briefing. The briefing starts in five minutes."

The third-class passengers crowded in the narrow hall and slowly filed up the gangway and then up two more to the aft deck. There they circled around several crew members who were pointing out features of a lifeboat that had been turned over. Frank couldn't hear much of what was being said, but it didn't seem too complicated. His attention was diverted by another crew member passing out life jackets.

"Please practice putting your life jacket on."

Frank pulled the collar over his head, as did everyone watching the demonstration.

"Pull this long tab through your legs and buckle it in front. Secure the crossties... No, like this." The crew member walked over to a young man who had gotten it wrong and corrected him. Frank had no problem with it and stood with the others as several crew members walked around and inspected the passengers.

"Very well. Please remove your life jackets and stack them over here," said the lead crew member, pointing to an empty spot near the aft bulwark of the pilothouse. "In case of emergency, we will pass these out as you reach the deck. Thank you. Please return to your cabins."

The ship was just leaving the River Clyde and heading out to open sea. Frank fell back and stood at the aft rail to watch Scotland slowly fade from view past the churning wake of the powerful propellers ratcheting up to full speed.

* * *

The cruise across the unusually calm North Atlantic was uneventful. Frank and his cabinmates passed the time playing cards, chatting, and passing around a book one of them had brought. On the tenth day at sea, there was an excited commotion in the hall.

"Go up aft! You can see land!"

Frank leaped to his feet and headed up one of the two gangways as quickly as the crowd allowed. The *Athenia* had entered Cabot Strait and was sailing smoothly past fairly far islands on either side. The land resembled the western coast of Scotland, which Frank had watched fade into the distance only ten days ago. The land then fell off, and it appeared as though they were again in the open sea. It wasn't until the *Athenia* headed into the Gulf of St. Lawrence that Frank could again see land from the aft deck.

The ship didn't roll at all in the St. Lawrence Seaway. After ten days at sea, Frank felt as if the ship was still rolling with the swells. He headed back to his cabin, excited.

"Aye, lads. Best be packing up. We look to be in a river – can't be long now." Frank started packing up his suitcase, but he stopped at the sound of crew instructions being bellowed in the hall.

"First stop, Quebec City – two days. Then another two days to Montreal. Please head to the mess hall to pick up your -documentation for entry. You should have completed it prior to boarding – Form 30A. Welcome to Canada."

Frank filed up the companionway to the mess hall and stood patiently in line for fifteen minutes. *Just like the army.*

"Name?"

"Frank Sharp."

The clerk wrote Frank's name in a large, bound passenger log and then rifled through a stack of papers until he found the one he sought. He handed it to Frank.

"Is this your form?"

Frank glanced at it. "Aye."

"Don't lose this. Next!"

Frank turned and went back to his cabin. He took his paper and placed it carefully in the bottom of his suitcase, next to his photo of

Margaret. Then he picked up the photo and smiled as he gazed at his love. Finally, he put the photo on top of his papers, put his belongings on top of both of them, and shut the suitcase.

* * *

After navigating the Canadian immigration officials, Frank headed straight to the train station and bought a ticket to Windsor. He settled in his seat, choosing one across from an elderly woman who was already nodding off. He looked out the window at a thriving city, larger than any he had ever seen, with wires held high on wooden poles that ran the length of the street, which puzzled him. He shook his head slightly and reached into his pocket to pull out the last letter he had received from his mother. Re-reading it, he wondered how he would find Clark Park. He folded it and put it back into his pocket. As he looked out the window at the passing scenery – nothing but fields and forests, all uncultivated – he was amazed that it was the same for hours on end.

The train eventually stopped in Toronto, where several people disembarked and a few got on. Frank was astonished at how different the city looked from those in the old country. The buildings were taller, many simply huge cubes with windows. These were nothing like those back home. There was also much more hustle and bustle. Frank was enthralled.

He gathered his belongings and hopped off the train in Windsor. There he followed the remainder of the passengers into the large terminal and headed up to a clerk manning a window.

"Excuse me…can you tell me how to get to Detroit?"

The clerk, busy with some paperwork, didn't look up. "Catch the ferry – fourteen blocks east, down Riverside, at Devonshire."

"Thank you." As Frank headed out the same doors he had entered, he stopped. He hadn't realized that the Detroit River was on the other side of the tracks. He headed back in, walked through the terminal, and went out the south doors. Then he turned left and started walking.

It was a very pleasant, sunny May day, and Frank didn't mind the two-mile walk. It was already warmer than most Scottish summer days, and he took off his jacket and threw it over his shoulder after rolling up his shirt sleeves. He started quietly whistling a little ditty. It was a very good day.

When he arrived at the ferry, he walked up to buy a ticket.

"How much for a ferry ticket?"

"Twenty-five cents US, thirty cents Canadian."

Frank was taken aback – he hadn't thought of currency issues. "I only have British currency."

"You have to go over and apply for permission to visit." The clerk handed Frank a form to complete. "Fill the front of this out and bring it back to me."

Frank took the index card and went to a bench to fill it out. Five minutes later, he was back at the clerk's window.

"Just a one-day visit? That shouldn't be a problem. The currency will be, however." The clerk paused as he finished reading the form. "You just arrived two days ago? No wonder you haven't Canadian currency. Tell you what – give me sixpence, and I'll worry about getting it converted. If I send you to the currency exchange, you'll not have much time in Detroit. You going to visit family?"

"Aye, I am. Thank you." Frank handed the clerk six pence and took his ticket.

"Don't forget your card. You'll need it on the other side."

Frank picked up the index card and headed to the dock. The clerk put the sixpence in the drawer and pulled out a quarter. He smiled to himself; he made a tidy little profit from these hapless foreigners.

* * *

Frank got off the ferry and headed to the ticket office.

"Excuse me – where can I get a map of the city?"

"We have them. They are a nickel."

Frank paused.

"Is there somewhere I can exchange pound sterling for dollars?"

"A block and a half east. You can't miss it. There's a big sign that says 'Currency Exchange.'"

"Thank you." Frank walked down, exchanged a pound, and returned to the ticket office.

"A map, please."

"That'll be a nickel."

Frank handed the clerk the biggest coin he had and received two small coins in return, along with a map. He went over to a bench and pulled out an address from his pocket – 7744 Pitt Street. He was dismayed – five miles away. As he walked away from the river, he spotted a trolley. After looking at his map again, he took the trolley to Vernor Avenue, watching busy people get on and off in front of more stores and offices than he coule ever have imagined. He hopped off at Vernor and walked the several blocks to Pitt Street. He stopped on the sidewalk and pulled out the address again. Once he'd double-checked that this was the right place, he walked up and knocked on the door.

Bess Sharp could barely contain her happiness. "Frank! Yer luikin' well, lad! Ah dinnae ken whin you'd get here! Guid tae see ye! Come in!" She stepped aside a bit so Frank could enter, and then she gave him a big hug. "Are ye hungert?"

"I could use a meal, Mum. I've not eaten since early this morning."

Bess hurried Frank to the table. "Sit here. Ah'll bring ye a guid supper." She hurried into the kitchen and returned with a big bowl of rich beef broth soup and a hunk of bread.

"Here ye go, lad. Eat up." She put the food down and sat at the table.

Frank ripped off a piece of bread and dipped in into the soup. "Delicious, Mum! I haven't had a decent meal since I left Scotland." He turned to the serious business of finishing the soup while it was still hot.

When he was finished, he sat back and sighed contentedly.

"Whair ye bide, lad?"

"I am in Windsor. I've only been in Canada a couple of days. I have a room with Dan Wells – a lad I met while in the army. He's been kind enough to let me a room." Frank looked around the house. "Big house! Is everybody here?"

"Nae. Rob, Jimmy, an' thair broods live on Central, aboot a block or two awa'. Th' rest bide here. We've three rooms upstairs an' a washroom! An' ye kin see, thair's a parlor an' a room fer eatin' here. Nae made o' stone, an' the wood makes a drafty hoose. But th' space is guid."

The grandfather clock chimed. "Four o'clock. When does Da get home?"

"He shuild be hame any time."

Bess picked up the dirty dishes and headed into the kitchen while Frank went into the parlor and looked around. The room was tidy, even though the obviously second-hand furniture was well worn. Bess had crocheted some intricate doilies with cotton string and placed them on the backs of the chairs, the settee, and the end tables. Da's beloved radio was sitting on an end table – probably the only household item that had come with him from the old country.

Bess returned from the kitchen and sat in a chair by the window. "How's th' bairn? An' Margaret?"

"They're wonderful, Mum. Little Jack is a year old – I left on his birthday. Once I get settled, I will send for them. Margaret's brother Alec already agreed to chaperone them across." Frank let out a small sigh. "I miss them so. I can't wait until they get here. I've got to find work so I can send for them."

Just then, the front door opened, and in came Frank's father. "Laddie! Yer here! Whin did ye git in?"

"The boat got to Montreal just two days ago. I took a train to Windsor and got settled yesterday. I have a visitor's pass for just one day. I thought I'd ask you about work here."

Da Sharp hung his jacket on the coat rack by the door, took a pipe out of his pocket, placed the newspaper that was under his arm on an end table, and sat down.

"Jobs fer th' askin', lad. Ford Motor line jobs. Jimmy's a machinist. Rob's a clerk."

"A machinist? Is that like an iron turner? I was an iron turner at Lochgelly Works."

"Aye, laddie. You cuild join yer brother as a machinist. Ye kin ask 'im. Or ye kin claim yer 160 acres in Canada, if ye kin stand bitter cauld 'n' loads o' snow." Da laughed as he turned on the radio to hear the news. "Ah cuidn'a stand it. Ah gave back mah land. But ye might think o' stayin' in Windsor, fer the whisky if nae else. Cannae git a legal dram here."

Talk paused as both men listened to the radio announcer.

And in Washington, the Immigration Act passed by the House last month is headed to the Senate for a vote. If passed and signed into law, the number of immigrants allowed in will be significantly reduced.

Frank waited for more details, but none were coming.

"Da, what is that all about?"

"Ah hear 'tis fer keepin' Jews oot. Ah wuildn'a worry."

Frank reached into his pocket and brought out his American money. "Da, can you tell me what's what?"

Da laughed. "Aye, laddie." He picked up the coins and laid them out in order. "This big one – 'tis a quarter. Twenty-five cents. This wee one – 'tis a dime. Ten cents. An' this middle one – 'tis a nickel. Five cents. This wee copper one – a penny. A cent. One hunnert cents in a dollar. Canadian's aboot th' same."

The pendulum clock struck five.

Da looked at the clock and stood up. He walked over to a candlestick telephone on an end table, proudly picked it up, and showed Frank. "We've oor own telephone, Frank. We kin call Jimmy or Robbie fae here. Jimmy's number is Hemlock 0654."

Da dialed the number and waited a moment.

"Aye, Jimmy! Tis yer da. Yer brother Frank is here! Mibbie you an' yer brothers kin come an' visit? He bides in Canada noo – jus' arrived Monday. He has but a one-day pass. If ye cannae see him tonicht, yull need wait til next time."

Da paused for an answer.

"Next time, then. Bye." Da hung up the phone.

"Yer brothers cannae come tonicht, Frank. A bairn's got th' croup."

"That's fine. Do you know when the last ferry leaves for Windsor?"

Da glanced at the wall clock. "Ye cannae mak' it tonicht – th' trolley cannae git you thair in time. Th'morrah. Hae som' supper wi' us. Andrew an' Lill wull be home soon."

"What are they up to?"

"Maggie's merriet an' didn'a leave Winnipeg. Lill works in a laundry. Andrew is a window washer. The lot o' them wull be home by half past." Da sat back down. "And Margaret an' the bairn?"

"I left them in the old country and came alone to find work. Margaret's brother Alec will accompany them over when I am settled. The bairn's braw, Da. A good lad."

Bess came in, wiping her hands on her apron. "Wull ye be stayin' fer supper then, Frank?"

"Aye, Mum. Happily. I'm not much in the kitchen."

Bess laughed. "Nae many men are, Frank. Nae many."

She went over to the sideboard and brought out six plates and placed them on the table. She rearranged a couple of chairs to make room for a sixth plate. Then she headed back to the kitchen.

"I'd like to settle here in Detroit, Da. Such a big city! It's a sight to behold."

"'Tis a guid place, Frank. Luik a' wha' we have here! Work's easy tae find, an' wages are guid enough fer a telephone an' a big hoose. 'Twas a guid move. Aw but Prohibition. Ah cannae git a dram. Nae legally." Da grinned. "Wi' Windsor a wee boat ride awa', it's nae hard tae find a dram here o' thair. Or tae tak' a wee trip on th' ferry."

Da looked out the front window, thinking. "'Tis fierce hot here in summer, though. An' winter's bitter cauld. No as bad as Winnipeg, mind ye, but nae like the auld country."

The door opened, and two siblings entered. Lill squealed when she saw Frank and rushed over to give him a hug. Andrew smiled broadly as he came over to shake Frank's hand.

Hearing the commotion, Bess called to Lill, "Lass, come an' help wi' getting' dinner on th' table."

Lill headed for the kitchen as the four men headed to the table.

* * *

Frank spent the night on the settee and left after breakfast. He caught the trolley back to the ferry dock and headed back to Windsor. Dan hadn't yet left for work.

"Frank, are you interested in working with me until you get settled in Detroit? I could use a hand."

"I've never been known to turn down a chance to earn some money, Dan. What's the job?"

"I deliver metal parts for Jos. Rowley, and Company. Yesterday someone asked if I knew another driver."

"Can you teach me? I've never driven before."

Dan laughed. "It's easy. I promise. I don't start until ten. Come on out. I'll show you."

The two went to the curb, where stood a doorless 1923 Ford pick-up truck.

"Here, you get in the driver's seat." Dan climbed into the passenger seat. "Okay. See those three pedals on the floor? The one on the right is for gasoline. The one in the middle is the brake. The one on the left is the clutch. The gear shifter is that long lever on your right.

117

Push the clutch in with your left foot and push this button." Dan pointed to an ignition button on the dash.

Frank did as he was told, and the engine began to rumble.

"Now pull the lever towards you." Frank engaged the transmission. "Now, slowly lift your foot off of the clutch."

The truck slowly rolled forward.

"Your right foot is for both the fuel and the brake. Push the gas pedal to go faster. Push the brake to stop. Depress the clutch to switch gears – there are only two. And, of course, steer the truck. The hardest part is watching for traffic at corners. Oh: and mind the stop signs."

Frank slowly drove the truck straight. At the corner, he stopped."

"Traffic rule, Frank: the vehicle on your left always goes first if you arrive together. Otherwise, first come, first served. Turn right here. Stick your left arm out of the truck straight to signal a left turn. Stick your arm out bent at the elbow, pointing up, to signal a right turn."

Frank stuck his arm out, bent at the elbow, and turned right. His little driving lesson took him around the corner and back to Dan's place.

"That's not very difficult." Frank stepped on the brake.

"Push in the clutch, move the clutch lever to the neutral position – that's straight up – and push the ignition button to turn the engine off. There you have it – your first driving lesson."

"Dan, I'd not be very comfortable driving a truck without a bit more practice."

"You'll need to get a driver's license. Don't worry – it's simply an identification card. Costs a quarter. It'll come in the mail in about a week or two. Then you can take the job. Until then, you can ride along with me. I can show you the ropes."

"Thanks, Dan!"

Frank spent the next couple of weeks practicing his driving and helping Dan with his route. He went to visit his parents Saturdays. And it was on a Saturday a couple of weeks later, as he was listening to the radio with his da, that he heard the news.

President Coolidge signed the Johnson-Reed Act today, placing strict quotas on immigration based upon country of origin. The law goes into effect this coming Monday, May 26."

Frank looked at his da, in a minor panic.

"I haven't applied for immigration! I've got to go down to the docks and pick up a form. Right now! Come on with me, Da. I might need you to vouch for me."

"Are ye sure, lad? Ah dinnae think thair be much problem."

"Please, Da. Let's go."

"Aw right, then." Da got up and grabbed his cap. "Bess, Frank an' ah ur gang tae th' ferry fer a bit."

The two hopped on the trolley and went down to the docks at the foot of Joseph Campau. Immigration workers were there every day, as long as the ferries were running. Frank walked into the office ahead of his father. Quite a line had formed, and it took about twenty minutes to get up to the window.

"May I help you?"

"I'd like to apply for immigration."

"Nationality?"

"Canadian."

"Birthplace?"

"Scotland."

"Name?"

Frank pulled out his Ontario driver's license and handed it over. "I think this has most of what you need."

The clerk took the license, turned to a typewriter, and added Frank's name to the log of persons applying to immigrate. He gave Frank back his license and an index-card application.

"Here. Fill this out. Bring it back Monday – we don't take immigration applications on the weekend."

"Thank you." Frank turned to his father. "Thanks for coming with me. Hopefully, I will get in under the wire."

The two hopped the trolley and headed back to Pitt Street.

Frank took the first ferry Monday morning, card in hand, and headed to the immigration office by the ferry docks on the Detroit side of the river. The office wasn't yet open, but already there was a long line of waiting hopefuls.

An hour later, Frank was standing at the clerk's window. He shoved the card across the smooth wooden surface to the clerk.

The clerk took it and read it carefully, front and back.

"You have no quota number?" The space on the back was empty.

"No, I don't. But I came to apply Saturday. The law went into effect today, didn't it?"

"At 12:01 AM." The clerk took a stamp, inked it, and then forcefully stamped the word "DEBARRED" twice on the front and once on the back.

"I'm sorry, but your application is denied. Without a quota number, you are not eligible for entry. Shall I place you on a waiting list?"

"Yes… please. Do you have any idea how long it will be before I can enter?"

"I will request a quota number for you. That's handled by Washington… I have no idea. These applications come in from every port of entry. You will get a letter with your number."

Frank hung his head and headed back to Windsor.

* * *

26 May 1924

My dearest Margaret –

I am heartbroken. The United States passed a law that was signed on this past Saturday limiting immigration. I applied Saturday, but the office doesn't accept applications on the weekend. The law went into effect today, and even though I was in line before the office opened, I was denied entry. I have to wait for a quota number.

I have a job driving a truck, delivering orders. I will get us a place in Windsor and send tickets for passage for you, Alec, and the wee bairn. It's quite easy crossing the river to visit family. And at least here in Windsor, we can get a wee dram – it's not legal in the States.

Wages are much higher here, so it shouldn't take more than two or three months before I can send for you. I miss you so. I find myself hugging my pillow in my sleep.

Keep safe, my bonnie lass.

All my love, Frank

* * *

It took Frank ten weeks to purchase three third-class tickets on the *Athenia* and secure a bungalow on Francois Street. He took the train to Montreal on August 15 to meet the ship as it docked, and there he eagerly watched the trail of weary Scots disembarking and trudging headlong into their new lives. Halfway through the crowd, he spotted Margaret. She was wearing a broad-brimmed straw hat and a dress too heavy for Canadian August weather. Walking in back of her was Alec, carrying little Jack on one arm and a suitcase in the other. He towered over most everyone on the gangway.

"Margaret!! Margaret!!" Frank waved his arms wildly as he shouted her name.

She searched the waiting crowd, and then her eyes landed on him. She smiled broadly and waved back. Then she turned to her brother and pointed out Frank in the crowd. Alec raised the arm carrying the suitcase a bit in acknowledgment.

Frank cut through the crowd to reach them, and by the time he got to the bottom of the gangway, Margaret, Alec, and the bairn were waiting for him. Frank grabbed Margaret around the waist and spun her around, and then he kissed her passionately.

Frank let her go and turned to pick up his son. Baby Jack didn't immediately recognize his father and pulled back a bit.

"Jack, it's your da! Don't you recognize me?" Frank chucked his finger under Jack's chin. "It's your da!"

Frank reached under Jack's arms and lifted him up far over his head, which made Jack laugh delightedly. "That's right, laddie. I'm your da! Now remember me?" He brought Jack back down and gave him a kiss on the cheek. He then turned to Alec, moving Jack to his left arm so he could shake Alec's hand.

"Thank you so much for bringing Margaret and Jack, Alec. I am eternally grateful."

Alec took off his cap and wiped his brow. "Aw ways sae hot here?"

Frank laughed. "I hear winter is fierce, but we will see. Summer's definitely steamy, I agree."

Alec took off his tweed jacket and pinned it between his knees as he rolled up his sleeves. He slung the jacket over his shoulder and picked up his suitcase.

"Margaret, you take the bairn and let me have your suitcase." Frank gave Jack to his wife and picked up her suitcase. "We need to catch the train to Windsor. It leaves in ninety minutes."

* * *

Frank walked up to the front door and unlocked it. He pushed the door open to let Margaret and Jack enter into their new home. Alec followed.

"Aw this just fer th' three o' us?"

"Aye. And Alec can stay here until he finds work. We have the room."

Margaret walked around the parlor and dining room and then entered the kitchen. She peeked out back to the fenced yard and then went upstairs. She came down and then headed down to the basement. Walking back up, she stopped under the archway to the kitchen.

"Tis sae big, Frank! Ah cannae believe tis fer just th' three o' us."

Frank turned to Alec. "You can have the room on the right, up the stairs. The three of us will take the other." Frank turned to Margaret. "I stocked the icebox with food for supper tonight and breakfast tomorrow."

"An icebox?"

"Aye. Come and see." Frank led Margaret into the kitchen and over to a wooden box with two doors, firmed latched. He opened the top door to reveal a large block of slowly melting ice. He then closed that door and opened the bottom compartment.

"Put your hand in there, Margaret." She reached in and pulled her hand back out.

"It's cauld!"

"Aye. Food keeps well. There's a chicken in there for dinner, plus some tatties and greens. And eggs and sausage for the morning."

Margaret shook her head in amazement. "Will wonders ne'er cease?"

"We have a coal furnace in the basement." He pointed to a large, ornate iron grate in the floor. "The heat rises up through these grates in the winter, all the way upstairs. I hear, come October, the coalman comes around and pours a load of coal down the chute. I'll have to figure that out. When the time comes."

Frank stood firmly in front of Margaret and grabbed her hands. "Well, do you like it? Will you be happy here?"

Margaret looked up at Frank. "'Tis more than I imagined, Frank. 'Tis wonderful. Aye, we kin be happy here." She kissed him gently.

Smiling, she let go of his hands. "Noo, ye tak' th' bairn whilst ah cuik dinner. In mah new kitchen."

CHAPTER EIGHT

"Ah tuik Jackie tae school t'day. They testet him. He's guid wi' aw his numbers an' letters, sae he's gang inta class wi' the fives." Margaret looked proudly at her son. "Aye, he's a clever lad. They said sae."

"You taught him well, love." Frank kissed Margaret's cheek as he put down the paper on the end table and went to wash his hands for supper. Margaret set the shepherd's pie and beans on the table, sat down, and spooned out supper onto Jack's plate before filling Frank's – leaving her own plate for last.

Frank sat down. "Jack, would you say grace?"

Jack bowed his head. "Thank ee, Lord, fer th' food on th' table, th clothes on oor backs, an th roof o'er oor haids. Amen."

As he picked up his fork, Frank said to his son, "Jack, are you excited to be going to school? I hear you will be with the fives, even though you're only four. Big for your age, though. I don't think the fives will know unless someone tells them."

"Ah'm nae skeert, Da."

Frank looked directly at his son. "You know, son, there will be many children that will be speaking Canadian English. They might not understand you well. I think it will be easier for you to speak more like I do. Suppose you can try to do that?"

Jack sat up straight and pulled in his chin a bit. He did his best imitation of his father, even lowering his pitch as much as he could. "Son, do you suppose you can speak like me?"

Margaret and Frank let out peals of laughter.

"Yes, Jack. Just like that. That was fantastic." Frank reached over and patted Jack on the head.

After supper, the dishes were washed and put away, and Jack was put to bed. Then Frank and Margaret relaxed in their respective chairs in the parlor. Margaret picked up her mending, but Frank put off picking up the newspaper.

"Margaret, I think it would be best for you to try and speak as you learned in primary. It will help Jack going forward. Do you suppose you could try and do that?"

Margaret looked up at Frank, considering his request. "Ah dinnae see a problem, Frank."

Frank leaned forward a little. "Margaret, now that I have my own truck, I can pick up new customers. There might be times where we need to entertain new clients. Non-Scottish clients. It will be important to our family for us to fit in. I am asking you not just for Jack, but for me. We will speak the King's English in this house. It is the language of Canada."

"Are you tellin' me howfer tae speak?"

"Yes, Margaret, I am. You and Jack, too. We are Canadians. We will speak Canadian English."

Just then, the German Shepherd, Cae, barked. Frank got up.

"I need to feed Cae, take her for a walk, and put her to bed in the truck."

Margaret was still up when Frank returned.

"Yer th' man o' the hoose. Ah'll...I'll try mah best tae...to...do wha' ye ask."

Frank kissed her. "Thank you, Margaret. It's for the best."

* * *

Frank knocked on his brother Jimmy's door at midnight.

"Happy Hogmanay! Thought I'd be your first footer."

"Welcome, and come on in! Happy Hogmanay, Margaret!"

It was a cold, still night. There was no cloud cover, and the quarter moon was bright against the sky. Frank, Margaret, and a rather sleepy Jack walked into the brightly lit house, full of the Sharp clan, animated with the joy of the new year. The children went into the basement to play for a while, but soon sleep overtook them. Margaret and Ness went down to check when the basement went silent and found the cousins curled up on the floor, each wrapped in a blanket that had been thoughtfully left for them.

Margaret put her finger to her lips and smiled as the two women quietly went upstairs and closed the basement door.

"A wee dram fer th' New Year, then." Da Sharp was in a jovial mood. "Here's tae 1925! A guid New Year to one an' aw, and many mair may ye see!" He walked around, pouring a few ounces of single malt into everyone's raised glass.

"An' a guid New Year tae ye!"

The lively chatter ended after a couple of hours, and all but Frank and Margaret went back to their houses.

"Ye kin tak' the bairn's room, Frank. The weans wull sleep doonstairs, as they are noo."

Margaret spoke up. "Very kind of you. We will take up that offer. Guid nicht." She had slipped into broad Scots, but realizing what she had done, she lowered her head and glanced briefly at Frank. She reached over, took Frank's hand, and led him over to the stairs. "We'll be headed up now. The first ferry comes early."

Frank and Margaret went up and took the bairn's bed. Several minutes later, they heard Jimmy and Ness enter their room and close the door.

Frank rolled over to Margaret, placed a hand on her breast, and whispered, "Let's start the new year off with a bang, Margaret."

She stifled a laugh, rolled on her side, and kissed her husband. "I think that would be a fitting start."

* * *

"We've been invited to Rob and Jess's for Independence Day,

Margaret. Shall we go?"

Margaret wiped her brow with her apron. It was a sweltering July first, and Margaret, seven months pregnant, was very uncomfortable.

"If the weather is like today, I'd say no. Ask me later, when I feel better." She rested her hand on her distended abdomen and then headed for a glass of water. "Would you mind if I took some ice for my water?"

"My lord, no. In fact, you sit. I'll bring it to you." Frank brought a glass of ice water and a wooden expanding hand fan. "You are so flushed. Please rest."

"Jackie, want to come with me and Cae to make a delivery?" School was out, and Frank wanted Margaret to rest.

Jackie jumped up excitedly. Next to riding in the back of the ice wagon, Jackie liked nothing better than to be going with his father on a delivery run.

"Get your cap then, laddie." Frank headed out to fetch Cae from the backyard, and they met Jack at the truck.

"Up you go, then. Mind you sit proper and stay in the truck while I carry the load in."

The threesome – man, lad, and German Shepherd – headed to Ouellette Avenue. Frank stopped in front of a hardware store, where he got out and carried in several cartons of merchandise. After pocketing his cartage fee, he started the truck and headed east on Wyandotte Street, towards home. They were crossing McDougall after making the four-way stop when a young man in a sedan ignored the stop sign and ran into the back end of the truck.

Frank instinctively reached for Jack, pushing the child against the back of the seat with an outstretched arm. Cae flew towards Frank, but between the man and the steering wheel, he stayed unharmed in the cab.

"Jackie! Are you hurt?" Frank took his son by the shoulders, his eyes anxiously scanning his son for any signs of injury. Jack's eyes were huge, and his mouth a bit agape.

"Nae, ah dinnae think so."

"Okay, you stay right here. Understand?"

Frank got out and headed for the other driver.

"You ran the stop sign. What were ye thinking? You've crashed my means of support!! I cart and deliver items for people, and now I can't!" Frank was angry as he inspected his truck bed. The rear fender had been bent sharply into the wheel, crushing the wooden spokes. The truck was not drivable. Cae growled from the truck cab. Frank turned to his dog. "Down, Cae! Stay." The dog, very well trained, did what was asked of her.

The young man was visibly shaken and quite apologetic. "I...I...I am so sorry! I was thinking of something else. This is my parents' car. We will cover your damage." He went into his car, brought out a pencil and a piece of paper, and started writing.

"Here is my name and address. Please send me the bill. I am very sorry."

"Well, help me push the truck out of the way." Frank pulled the fender back, and the two men pushed the truck to the side of the road, away from the intersection.

"I will get the truck fixed and send you the bill. You best pay promptly. I'll not be making any money until this truck is repaired, and I have a family to feed."

Frank lifted Jack out of the truck and patted his thigh to summon Cae, who jumped down and heeled next to Frank.

"We'll have to walk home, Jack. Can you do that with me?"

The three started home, keeping in the shade from buildings where possible and then staying in the shade of the trees when they got to the residential area. By the time they got to Francois Street, Cae was panting heavily, and Frank and his son were drenched in sweat. The first thing Frank did was get some fresh water for Cae.

"Did you get delayed? I was expecting you a while ago."

"No. We had to walk home from Wyandotte and McDougall. The truck was hit by another car, and it can't be driven."

Margaret gasped. "Oh no! Can it be fixed?"

"I think so. I need to find a mechanic to fetch it and repair the wheel, tire, and fender. I hope that's all that's wrong."

Frank went to the phone book and found a mechanic.

"Hello? My name is Frank Sharp, and I am looking for a mechanic to pick up my damaged truck and repair the rear wheel and fender. We were hit by another car." ... "No, it's not drivable. The spokes are broken." ... "At the corner of Wyandotte Street and McDougall. Pulled to the side, on the south side on Wyandotte, east of McDougall." ... "Frank Sharp, 1041 Francois. I have the name and address of the driver that hit us. He said he would pay for damages." ... "Thank you. Please call when you take a look at what needs to be done. Thank you."

Frank hung up and turned to Margaret. "I don't think we'll be going for Independence Day, Margaret. I can't work without my truck. We have to watch our pennies."

* * *

The mechanic called the next day.

"I have some unfortunate news, Mr. Sharp. The rear axle was damaged also."

"But it can be fixed, right?"

"Yes. If you give me the go-ahead, I can order the parts. It usually takes two weeks to get them."

"Two weeks? Is there any way to get them sooner?"

"No, I'm sorry. Especially with the American holiday in a few days. The factories shut down for inventory and model change re-tooling in July. We'll be lucky to get everything in two weeks."

"Please order what is needed, and if you can, please expedite. Without my truck, I have no income."

"I understand, Mr. Sharp. I'll do what I can. I'm sorry for you."
Frank hung his head.

"What's wrong, dearie?" Margaret came over and placed her arm around him.

"The truck won't be back for two, maybe three weeks. Margaret, that means no income for that long. That and I just might lose some customers who can't wait."

Frank turned out of Margaret's hug, grabbed his cap, and headed toward the door.

"I'll be back later," he said quite gruffly, and he left to see if he could find Dan Wells.

Dan wasn't home, but Frank saw his truck in front of a corner bar. He walked in and waited a few moments for his eyes to get accustomed to the dimly lit, smoky bar. This bar had seen better days. Every item in it was weary with use. The leather on the bar stools was cracked, and the finish on the legs was dull and scratched. Even the bartender was worn. His balding head was fringed in dirty gray, and his shirt was pulled open above his belt, revealing a threadbare, stained undershirt stretched tightly across his distended belly. His eyes were glassy with boredom as he mechanically filled drink orders, shunning conversation. Frank took it all in. Then he spotted Dan at the far end of the bar.

He walked up to Dan and pulled up the barstool next to him.

"How you doing, Dan?"

"Well, hello, Frank! It's been quite a while! How ya be?"

"Could be better, could be worse. And you?"

'Not bad, not bad. You live in these parts now?"

"No, we're still over on Francois Street. But I needed to talk to you. My truck is out of commission for two, maybe three weeks. Accident. I was wondering if I could interest you in picking up my deliveries for a few weeks."

Dan was silent as he considered the request.

"Good time to ask, with the factories being shut down. If it was any other time, I'd have to say no. I keep all the fees, right?"

"You can keep all the fees, but I get all my customers back when I have my truck. I'll not take kindly to you angling for my customers."

"When the factories are back up, I have my hands full. I couldn't take them all on if I wanted to. Hope you are back in commission by the end of shutdown – I'll have difficulty making both yours and mine."

"We have a deal, then. Will you be home later? I'll go get my delivery schedule and bring it to you. I have the next three days booked. I'll have to get new deliveries to you as I get orders. Can I call you with them?"

"Sure. Stop on by the house after supper."

"Thanks, Dan. See you later."

Frank left and headed home.

* * *

Margaret woke up in the wee hours of July 6. "Frank... Frank!" She shook Frank awake. "I think I'm having contractions. It's too early! The babe's not due for two more months." She stopped and gasped a little. "Another one. Can you call for the midwife or the doctor?"

Frank was still groggy. He shook off his drowsiness and sat up. He looked at Margaret and then got up and walked around to her side of the bed.

"Has your water broken?"

"No, not yet."

Frank sat down on the edge of the bed.

"Margaret, I'm not calling for anyone. We can't afford to call anyone. We can't even afford another bairn right now. Just rest. Maybe the heat is too much for you. Just rest here. Maybe they will stop." He placed his hand on Margaret's large, round belly and let it sit there for several minutes. "Just rest quietly. I'll bring you some water." Frank stood and went into the kitchen.

When he returned, he looked anxiously at his wife. Margaret's face was beet red, and she was grimacing in pain. "'Tis nae guid, Frank. Something's very wrong." She could barely speak. "Wull ye call th' doctor?"

Frank went to the side of the bed and put his hand on Margaret's forehead. "You're burning up, Margaret. Is it the bairn?"

"Ah dinnae ken, Frank."

"I'll nae lose ye, Margaret. I'm gang tae th' firehouse – cannae find a doctor a' this hour. Maybe they can help." Frank grabbed his cap as he bolted out the door.

Frank returned in an hour or so and went straight to Margaret's side. Her condition hadn't improved.

"Did ye find a doctor?"

Frank hung his head. "No. The best the firemen could do was take you to the hospital. They thought that the baby should be delivered. You and I can do that, Margaret."

"Th' bairn's nae ready, Frank."

"I'll nae lose ye, Margaret. Ah'd rather lose the bairn. Little Jackie an' I – we need ye."

Frank stood up, went to Margaret's knitting basket, and pulled out the longest knitting needle.

"Come with me, Margaret. Come into the bathroom."

Margaret's eyes got wide with fear. "An' wha' ye meanin' tae dae?" She slipped back into her native brogue.

"Come with me, wife. We are going to break your water and deliver this baby. Come get into the tub."

"Nae, Frank! Nae! The babe might die! Nae." She started sobbing uncontrollably.

"Now, Margaret! You come with me, now!" Frank grabbed Margaret by the elbow and guided her up. "If the baby lives, it's meant to be. If the baby dies, it's meant to be." He pulled her into the bathroom and lifted her into the tub. Lifting her nightgown, he spread her legs and inserted the knitting needle into her vagina carefully, prodding ever so gently to find an opening in her cervix. He was finally successful, and water gushed out.

Margaret was in labor for another two hours before their child was born. It was a boy. He was alive, but his breathing was labored. The child's sternum rose and fell a good inch with every labored breath. Frank rested the boychild between Margaret's breasts.

"I don't think he's going to make it, Margaret. Hold him, keep him warm, and say your goodbyes."

Margaret was no longer sobbing, but her tears were a never-ending stream down her cheeks.

"Shall we name him now? Before he passes?"

Frank's voice turned hard and cold. "No. Names are saved for the living. He shall die Baby Boy Sharp. His life for yours." Frank left the room.

Margaret cooed to her newborn son, talked to him, and sang to him in a voice broken with heartache. "Ah'm gang tae miss ye sorely, laddie, I wisht ye's bide a while wi' us. Ye hae an older brother, ye ken? He was hopin' fer a boy tae play wi'. Ye'd lik' him, ah'm certain. He's gang tae sorely miss ye, tae. Ah, mah wee little laddie. Ye luik lik' yer da, ah think. Yer th' first tae nae be born in Scotland, ye ken? Th' first Canadian! Kin ye nae breathe a bit better? Kin ye nae try tae stay wi' us?"

Margaret leaned over and, covering her child's mouth with hers, blew in a gentle breath. After several of those, the baby was not quite as blue, but he went back to his labored breathing when on his own.

"Och, wee one. I dinnae ken if ah kin bear tae lose anither bairn. Nae anither one. Stay wi' us, laddie. Be mah miracle." Margaret wrapped the baby in a towel and laid him on the floor as she washed herself and the afterbirth down the drain. She stepped out, dried herself off, and went for a clean nightgown. When she came back to her child, he had stopped breathing. She dropped to her knees, picked up his lifeless body, and rocked him back and forth, moaning in abject grief. When Frank heard that, he called for the coroner.

Margaret, still feverish but less so, took to her bed for several days. Frank tended to Jack and brought Margaret porridge, which was all he knew to make. Margaret refused to eat, but after several days, her fever broke, and she regained her appetite. And that night, when Frank came to bed after sleeping on the settee, Margaret stood and left the bedroom.

CHAPTER NINE

"Andrew, you don't look well."

"Ah dinnae feel well, Frank. 'Tis mah stomach wi' pains."

Margaret stopped clearing the table to look at Andrew. "You should go to the doctor, Andrew."

"Ah cannae, but fer Agnes. She's wi' child, an' ah need tae save fer the bairn an' th' midwife."

"You won't do your wife or bairn any favors if you don't take care of yourself."

Frank broke in. "Your face is puffy, Andrew. Let me call a doctor."

"Nae. Cannae afford it."

Andrew got up and went to the parlor to lie down. "Ah'm sae tired. Mind if ah lie a bit?"

Frank went into the kitchen with Margaret. "Andrew looks bad, Margaret. Maybe we should send for Agnes?"

"They don't have a phone, Frank. We'll have to send a messenger."

Frank paused. "I'll go over tomorrow and bring her back. Andrew looks terrible – I noticed that his legs are swollen, too. There's something quite wrong."

Just then, Jack came in. "What's wrong with Uncle Andrew?"

"He's not feeling well, Jack. That's all. Now, why don't you run along and play with Peter and Jeff? They're out on the swing."

Jack dashed outside, and a moment later, Andrew began to moan. Frank and Margaret rushed into the parlor to find him holding his stomach. His trousers were soaked in bloody urine. Frank went to the phone and called for a doctor while Margaret knelt beside Andrew.

"We're calling for a doctor, Andrew. You're very sick and need help. I'll have no argument from you." Andrew was in too much agony to protest.

It was dark when Dr. Agnew arrived. Jack was in the parlor, both fascinated and horrified by the scene unfolding.

"Jack, go to your room. The doctor needs to tend to Uncle Andrew, and you shouldn't be here."

Dr. Agnew got to work, taking Andrew's temperature, looking into his eyes, examining his extremities, and palpating his abdomen. Each time he did that, Andrew cried out in pain. He was slender, but his abdomen was distended.

Dr. Agnew stood and called Frank and Margaret aside. "Can we speak in the kitchen?"

The three left Andrew's side.

"This is your brother?" Dr. Agnew asked Frank.

"Yes – my youngest brother."

"He's young... I take it he's single?"

"No, he's married. Been married for two years. His wife is in Detroit: she's three months pregnant with their first child."

The doctor hung his head. "Your brother is dying, Mr. Sharp. He is bleeding internally, and from the look of his abdomen, he's been bleeding for quite a while. There is nothing I can do to save him at this late stage. I can administer laudanum if you wish – enough to put him to sleep."

"Do we have enough time to fetch his wife?"

"I'm sure you don't want Andrew to suffer needlessly."

Frank turned away from the doctor, thinking.

"Ease his pain, doctor. But don't give him too much. I will go fetch Agnes. Please make Andrew comfortable, but let his wife say goodbye."

Frank took his truck keys and left for the ferry docks. He returned an hour later, alone.

"Missed the last ferry. Damn that the tunnel isn't finished – damn that the bridge isn't, either."

The doctor had left by the time Frank returned, but he had left a small bottle of laudanum with Margaret.

"What do you think, Frank? Shall we try and fetch Agnes tomorrow?"

Frank looked at his brother, lying unconscious on the settee. Then he looked at the bottle of laudanum on the end table.

"Why, Margaret? Why put him through this? We should end his misery here and now. But I will promise Agnes that we will always be here for her." Frank picked up the bottle.

Margaret gasped. "I cannae watch ye dae this, Frank. Nae." She ran into the kitchen.

Frank knelt next to Andrew. He took his brother's hand in his. "Andrew, you always were my favorite. I have loved you dearly. I can't stand to watch you suffer. Goodbye, laddie. May the good Lord take you, and may you never feel pain again." He kissed his brother on the forehead before opening his mouth and emptying the bottle into it. He then sat there, holding Andrew's hand, and watched as his brother's breathing got lighter and lighter, lighter and lighter, until it stopped altogether. He then called the police to report a death. The coroner's report read: "Cause of death, nephritis; date of death, March 29, 1929."

* * *

Frank and Margaret stood on either side of Agnes as they laid Andrew to rest in Windsor Memorial Gardens.

"Will you stay with us, Agnes? You are welcome to stay as long as you want."

"Nae, thank ye. Ah'll bide wi' mah parents. Kind o' you tae

offer."

"We will come visit you, Agnes. You will always be our sister-in-law. If you need anything, please just ask."

Agnes's parents came up from behind and guided Agnes away. "Come noo, lass. We shuild be gang hame."

Margaret placed a rose on the mound of dirt. Then she and Frank left for home.

Frank picked up the mail before he unlocked the front door and went inside. He flipped through rather absentmindedly until he got to a letter from U.S. Immigration. He tore into it and read it rapidly.

"Margaret! Margaret! We have an immigration number! Or, we will have one this year. This says that we should be allowed entry in about six months!"

"Are you sure you want to leave Windsor? We have a nice little home, and Jack is in school. You have a carting business that's keeping us well. Are you sure?"

"I am perfectly sure, Margaret. There is so much opportunity across the river! Wages are higher. It's the most important center of industry in the world! I can work with my hands again. I can be an iron turner and earn far more than being a carter in Canada. And you can have family nearby – and Jack can have cousins to play with more than once in a while. We can find a home on Pitt Street or Central – or any of the close streets. You'll see. It will be much better."

Margaret demurred. "You're the man of the house, Frank. If you say so." She went into the kitchen to start fixing an after-school snack for Jack, who was due home any minute. It would be nice to have family around. She didn't have many friends in Canada – Jeannie Wilson, but she lived in Hamilton. Margaret didn't get a chance to see her very often.

Frank jotted down a list of things that he had to do... He had to get his truck across. He also needed to find out about getting Cae across. He imagined that there was some sort of quarantine procedure.

Oh – and furniture. Should he sell it and buy new in America or have it ferried across? He also needed to understand how much all this would cost. He had a lot of work to do. In the back of his mind, he wished Margaret was as excited as he was. She had been quite distant since the baby had died – obedient, quiet, respectful, dutiful…but distant. She had been sleeping in the second bed in Jack's room ever since July 6, 1926.

Frank had tried to ease her pain. About a month after the truck was back and his customer base was once again stable, Frank came home with a box wrapped in pretty floral paper.

"Margaret, I have a present for you!"

"A present? For what?"

"Just because." Frank grinned. "Here – open it."

Margaret took the box and unwrapped it. Inside she found an exquisitely ornate teacup and saucer. It was the palest, softest green – Margaret's favorite color. Around the rims of both the cup and saucer were intricate gold foil designs.

"Frank, these are beautiful!" She placed them very carefully in the sideboard. "Not for use, these. Too special. Thank you, Frank. That was quite thoughtful."

Frank thought she might come over and give him a hug. He thought that maybe the ice that seemed to have surrounded her heart might thaw a bit. He thought that at least she would smile. He was disappointed. *She just needs more time.*

"I'll have supper on the table shortly, Frank." She left for the kitchen. "Can you please call Jack and have him wash his hands?"

After supper was over and dishes were washed, after Jack was put to bed and the evening was quiet, Frank stood up from his second-hand, well-worn leather reading chair and turned to Margaret.

"It's a bonnie evening, Margaret. Let's go for a little stroll."

Margaret looked up from her needlework. "We shouldn't leave Jack alone, Frank."

"I'll bring Cae in to protect him, and we can lock the door. We needn't be gone very long. Come, Margaret. We used to so love our walks. Can we give it a go?"

Margaret hesitated. "No, I think not, Frank. I've still work to do."

Frank came over and squatted down beside his wife. "Margaret, we have become so distant. I want us to be like we used to be. Can we be in love again?"

Margaret put down her handwork on her lap rather quickly. She looked directly at Frank. "Frank, yer nae th' man ye wurr afore. Ye killt yer bairn, an' ye killt yer brother. Ah think ye love yer money more than yer folk. Yuv a hard side ah ne'er seen afore, an' ah dinnae lik' it. Ah dinnae lik' it at aw."

She stood, shoved her handwork into the small basket next to her chair, and stormed out of the room.

Frank rose, looking after her. He just stood there, thinking, for several moments. Instead of following his wife, he went back to his old leather chair, sat down, and turned on the radio.

* * *

On October 5, 1929, Frank, Margaret, and Jack immigrated to the United States. The entire Sharp clan celebrated at Da and Bess Sharp's house that night, and to liven the festivities, Frank had smuggled over a fifth of single malt.

"Hae ye foond a hoose yet, Frank?"

"There's a for rent sign on Central, three blocks from here. I'll go and see if we can get it tomorrow. With any luck, it is empty... Our belongings won't be here for several days. If we can move everything right in, that would be the easiest."

"Wee Jack kin gang a' school wi' his cousins! Whair are th' bairns, anyway?"

"Doonstairs playin'." Ness turned to Margaret. "Cannae wait tae hae ye here, Margaret! Ah'm sae pleased!"

Margaret smiled at Ness. "It will be good to have family so close. No more waiting for the ferry."

"Puir a dram fer us, Da. Here's tae Frank an' Margaret – in America!"

"An' Frank. Say guidbye tae yer whisky." Jimmy laughed heartily as he raised a glass.

* * *

The loud horn bellowed at the Studebaker assembly plant on Thursday, October 24, as it always did at quitting time. Frank finished tidying up his work station then headed home. After supper, as usual, he turned on the radio.

The New York Stock Exchange experienced wild swings today, falling eleven percent before recovering nine to close two percent down. Trading was at a feverish high.

Frank listened for a while longer before turning off the radio and picking up the paper.

"I don't know why rich men's gamblings make so much news," he mumbled to no one in particular.

The house fell comfortably silent as Frank finished reading the paper and Margaret continued to knit a sweater for Jack – it was getting chilly out.

Frank folded the paper and lit a pipe. "Margaret, I heard today that I can't apply for a skilled trades apprentice job for at least six months. I think I would like to learn machine repair. The job pays well – ten percent higher just to start."

"If that's what you want, Frank. I'm sure you will do well at it." Margaret didn't look up from her deft fingers as she answered.

"If you don't mind, I think I'll head over to Rob's for a bit."

"That's fine, Frank. Say hello for me to him and his wife."

"I will." Frank stood, grabbed his jacket and cap from the coat tree that stood faithfully by the front door, and left.

It was a damp and blustery evening. The young trees lining the

143

streets had lost a good half of their gold, red, and orange leaves. The streetlights obscured the stars, but the bright quarter moon was vivid, high in the sky. Frank stood his jacket collar up, pulled his cap down low, and shoved his hands into his pockets, and then he pulled the jacket tightly across his back as he walked the three blocks to his brother's house. The porch light was on – Frank knocked and was let in.

"Come on in, then... 'Tis cold an' damp oot. How ye be?"

"Hi, Jess. Robbie home?" Frank removed his jacket and cap and hung them on the coat tree. "Margaret sends her love."

"Aye, he's in the parlor. When ye git hame, ask Margaret if she wants tae gae ta Hudson's Saturday."

"Aye, I will."

Frank walked through the arch leading into the parlor. "Hello, Rob. All's well?"

"Aye, just fine. What brings you tae visit?"

Frank took a seat. "I wanted to ask you what you thought of all of the news about the stock exchange. You've an office job and know more about business. What do you think?"

Just then, Jess stuck her head in. "Can ah git ye a cup o' tea?"

"Yes, please. Sounds delicious. Thanks, Jess."

Rob sat back and puffed on his pipe. "Folk in the office don't see it as much tae worry aboot. It came back."

"I don't know much about such things, Rob. Seems to me just a bunch of rich men gambling. Why is it getting so much coverage?"

"Ah'm nae an expert, but ah hear tha' th' swings make people worriet. An' if people are worriet, they dinnae spend thair money. The economy cuild slow doon."

Frank considered what Rob said.

"Are you worried?"

"Nae much."

"Then I'm not worried, either." Frank took the cup of tea that Jess had just brought in and took a sip. "Say – are you planning on going to any hockey games this season? First game is in three weeks."

"Aye, mebbie. Hope the Cougars go further in the playoffs this year than last. Losin' tae Toronto in th' quarterfinals was disappointin'."

"Well, if you decide you want to go, let me know. I might even get Margaret to join us."

Frank finished his tea and stood. "I best be going." He took his teacup into the kitchen, kissed Jess on the cheek, and went into the foyer for his jacket and cap.

"Would you like to bring the family over Saturday for supper?"

"Love tae! See ye then!"

* * *

On Monday the newsboys were on every corner shouting out the headlines as the day came to an end and factory workers streamed out onto the sidewalks and street crossings.

"Get your paper! The Dow drops thirteen percent! Read all about it!"

Frank pulled out three pennies and bought a copy, and he tucked it under his arm as he caught the streetcar home. After supper, he read the troubling news about the stock market and called Rob.

"Rob, what do you think about the stock market today?"

"'Tis nae a guid sign, Frank. Ah'm gang th'morrah an' take mah money oot o' th' bank."

"Makes me glad I didn't open a bank account. What might happen? Do you know?"

"Nae, I dinnae ken. Better safe than sorry, though."

"Thanks. Maybe it will swing back tomorrow, like it did last week."

"Mebbie."

"All right. Thanks, Rob. Bye."

* * *

The newsboys were out in force Tuesday after work.

"Get your papers here! The Dow drops another twelve percent! Bank deposits being withdrawn! Read all about it!"

Frank grabbed a paper and headed home, worried.

"Margaret, something bad is happening. The stock market is crashing."

Margaret stared at him blankly. "What's a stock market?"

Frank kissed her on the cheek. "Of course you don't know. It's business, Margaret. I shouldn't have even said anything. What's for supper?"

"Ah've made a roast chicken."

"Sounds delicious. Where's wee Jackie?"

"He's out back on the swing. Ever since you hung it on that tree branch – he loves it." Frank headed out back to say hello to Jack. He stood by the back door, watching his redheaded son swing back and forth. The lad's freckled face beamed as he timed his swing to push himself higher and higher. As he reached the zenith of the arc, he pulled hard on the rope and moved his legs skyward, increasing his momentum. He was a bit off-center though, and he started to rotate. He slowed down and tried to plant his feet on the ground before he lost control. It took him several passes before he could stop. When he finally came to a halt, he noticed his father watching. He jumped off the swing, ran over, and hugged his father.

"Time to come in, Jackie. Supper's almost ready. How was school today?"

"Fine, Dad."

"Do you like second grade?"

"Aye, it's okay. I like arithmetic – I'm good at it, teacher says. And science. Science is fun. We're learning about hills and mountains and rivers."

"That's fine, son. Do your best, aye?

"I do, Papa."

Frank let Jack enter first. "Go upstairs and wash your hands, now."

* * *

Frank was feeling much better Wednesday, as the newsboys crowed that the market had recovered almost all of the prior day's loss. After supper, he headed over to Rob's, taking Jackie with him so he could play with his cousins.

"So, Rob – did you take your money out of the bank?"

"Aye, ah did. But ah see th' market's back up. Mebbie I'll put it back."

"Maybe you should keep it out. This up and down is unsettling. I'd keep it out until things settle down a bit. You never know about these things. I've a feeling that this is not settled. The radio says that people don't spend when things are uncertain. If that's the case, they won't be buying cars much. I'll tell you this much: I certainly won't be putting my money in a bank anytime soon."

Rob thought about that and then changed the subject. "How's th' job?"

"Not bad. Good money. I want to work my way up to skilled trades. I can't get into the apprentice program, though, until I have a good year under my belt. It'll do. The pay keeps us well. We're even able to save a little every week. I haven't told Margaret, so don't let on. I want to surprise her with something – maybe even buy our own house one of these days."

"Wouldn'a tha' be guid! Yur Margaret wuid be happy wi' tha, ye ken?"

Frank grinned. "I think so. We'd better be going – wee Jackie has school tomorrow. Good to talk with you, Rob."

"An' ye tae, Frank."

Frank walked over to the basement stairs. "Jackie, we've got to leave. You've got school tomorrow."

* * *

By the end of the year, the Dow Industrial had drifted down another nine percent, but by the end of January 1930, it crept up again. By the end of April, the Dow was higher than it had been at the end of the previous October. The line at Studebaker had slowed down, but Frank and his brothers still had jobs. With little worry, the extended Sharp family got together on Belle Isle for 1930's Fourth of July.

"Jackie, we've got sparklers for you and your cousins! Here, let me show you." Frank brought out a sparkler and lit it, holding it out from his body. Jackie was transfixed.

"Now take care because it's very hot, so don't touch it! It's only for lookin' at. And hold it out from you – if those little flyin' sparks land on your clothes, they can make holes. Your mum wouldn'a be too pleased."

After a picnic, the children went with their mothers to play while the men lit cigarettes and sat on the grass, chatting to the sound of a band playing by the Grand Canal.

Rob was somber. "Laddies, th' numbers dinnae luik guid fer cars. We're nae sellin' many. If this keeps up, thair gang tae close plants."

Frank had heard some similar rumblings at Studebaker. "I've not been on the job for a year. If things keep slowing down, I'm afraid I'll be let go."

Da Sharp spoke up. "Ah nae wan' tae change th' subject, but yur mum an' ah are nae getting' along. Nae fer a lang time. Ah'm gang tae Winnipeg tae bide wi' Margaret an' her man."

The talk of the economy stopped dead in its tracks.

Frank, Rob, Jock, and Jimmy looked at their father in surprise and disbelief. Frank spoke first. "Da, you've never mentioned anything before. Are you sure? What's going to happen to Mum?"

"Lill works. She wull be stayin' wi' her in th' hoose. Her wages ur enough tae pay th' rent. Th' rest o' you kin help if need be…" Da's voice drifted off, but with a tone that definitely did not invite discussion.

"When ye leavin', Da?" Jock seemed resigned to the situation.

"Margaret's comin' tae git me in a fortnight."

There was not much more that could be said. Finally, Jimmy stamped out his cigarette and stood up. "God speed, Da." He left to find his wife.

*   *   *

Frank came home early one night in late September.

"You're home early, Frank." Margaret was ironing. She barely looked up as Frank entered.

Frank's head sagged as he hung his jacket and cap on the coat rack. "I've lost my job, Margaret. About two hundred of us. Cars aren't selling."

Margaret set the iron on the trivet. "You will find another job, Frank. Won't you?"

"More and more men are off work, Margaret. Not as easy as it used to be. I'll start looking first thing in the morning. But we can do this. We had it worse back in the old country. We know how to do with very little. Do I have time to check on Rob and Jimmy?"

"Be back in two hours." Margaret picked up the iron and heated it on the stove before starting again.

Frank walked over to Rob's house and found him and Jimmy on the front porch.

"You're both home early, too," said Frank as he climbed the stairs. "A bad sign?"

Jimmy was the first to speak. "They've cut mah hoors in half. Ah'll only get twenty hoors a week." He snuffed out his cigarette with the sole of his foot in disgust.

"And you, Rob?" Frank lit a cigarette himself.

"They've sent everybody home early t'day. Told us tae be in th' office t'morrah at eight o'clock fer a big meeting. Yer hame early yersel', Frank."

Frank took a long drag on his cigarette. "Won't be buying these

149

much anymore," he said as he stomped it out on the porch. "Got laid off today. Me and two hundred others. Cars aren't selling, and I didn't have enough time in."

"Wha' will ye do, then, Frank?" Rob showed genuine concern. "Jobs are scarce nowadays."

"Anyone heard from Jock?"

"Nae, no a word," replied Rob.

"I am going over to Windsor tomorrow. Look up Dan Wells. Maybe he can take me on as a driver again. I still have my truck. Or maybe he knows someone. I'm still strong, aye? Stronger than most. Maybe it's better in Windsor. What will you two do?"

"We're talkin' aboot movin' oor families in t'gether. These hooses are big enough, an' we can split the rent. Still better off than in th' auld country, aye?"

"Aye, for sure that. Glad that the two of you still have half a job each, at least. Wonder about Lill. And Mum."

"We'd have heard, ah think. Must still be fine." Rob stood. "I best speak tae Jess aboot sharing th' hoose. Think here, Jimmy?"

"Aye – yur hoose is better, Rob."

"Still better than th' auld country," said Rob as he opened the front door and went in.

Frank turned to Jimmy. "Have you told Nessie?"

"Aye, had to, comin' home early lik' ah did. Didn'a tell her aw th' bad news, though. She doesn'a know aboot all th' men losin' their jobs nowadays. She jus' thinks it's a slowdown."

"Margaret doesn't understand, either. Too busy tending to the bairn and the house. Not even interested, I think. Hopefully, Dan can set me up. I can take the bridge back and forth now that it opened. Easier than the ferry, and I don't have to worry about ferry schedules. I'll find something – we'll scrape by."

Frank reached over and patted Jimmy's shoulder. "We're strong stock. We'll make it. I'd best be getting home. Margaret said I couldn't be gone that long. Good to see you, Jimmy. Say hi to Nessie." With that, he walked down the steps and headed home.

The next day, Frank drove across the new bridge to Windsor and headed to Dan's house. Dan being home would be a bad sign...and Dan was home. Frank knocked.

"Hello, Dan. How you be?"

"Hi Frank. Come on in. Haven't seen you in a while."

Frank stepped over the threshold and into the small parlor. He took off his cap.

"Times are nae guid, Dan. No jobs. How are things here?"

"The same, Frank. I still have some deliveries, but they are half what they used to be. I only run every other day now."

Frank sighed. "I was afraid you'd say that. I've been looking for work since Studebaker laid me off. No takers. We have meager savings, and the wife and bairn need taken care of."

"Wish I could help you, Frank... I do. But as far as I can tell, there are no jobs here in Windsor, either. I'd take you on, but I can barely make ends meet myself."

"Have ye any ideas for me?"

Dan paused and thought for several seconds.

"You still have your truck?"

"Aye."

"You might see if you can scavenge bricks and lumber. Not everyone can load up materials like that. You take the nails out of the lumber and knock the mortar off the bricks, and maybe you can sell the material. Make sure you tell the owners you'll remove their debris for free. Save them money. Turn around and sell it, delivered."

Frank considered the idea and then brightened up.

"Aye, there's an idea! I'll give it a go. Suppose I can scavenge in Windsor, too?"

"I don't know, but you can ask. There are old buildings coming down by the river... I've seen piles of bricks and lumber. Maybe you

151

can start there. If you can't take the supplies across the river, you might be able to sell them here. They're building a distillery upriver. Worth asking."

"If I can't take it across the river, I'll need somewhere to work. If I give you ten percent, can I use your backyard to yank the nails and chisel the mortar off the brick? I'll clean up after myself, that's a promise."

"Get the work first and try and take the materials to the States. If all else fails, then you can clean the wood and bricks here. Keep me posted."

Frank shook Dan's hand. "Thanks, Dan. You've always been a good friend. I will pay you back someday."

"I'll remember that, Frank." Dan grinned as he showed Frank the door.

Frank headed out and took Riverside east. After a few miles, he saw the distillery construction site mentioned by Dan, with piles of debris on either side. He drove by slowly but saw no one on site, so he turned around and headed back home. He was stopped at the border.

"Name?"

"Frank Sharp."

"Citizenship?"

"Canadian."

"You have quite an accent, Mr. Sharp. You live in Canada?"

"No, I live in Detroit."

"May I see your green card?"

Frank pulled out his wallet and handed over his green card, which the guard studied.

"You wouldn't be bringing over any whisky in this truck, now, would you?"

"No, sir."

"Mind if I check?"

"Go ahead."

The guard walked around to the back of the truck and peered in. "An empty truck?"

"Yes, sir. I was visiting a friend, looking for work."

The agent paused. "Ah, tough times, I know. I have two brothers on the same boat. Good luck to you, Mr. Sharp." He gave back the green card.

"Thanks." Frank engaged the clutch and slowly rambled off. Instead of driving straight home, he drove around, looking for building materials he could reclaim. He started on the Southwest side, near the bridge. As he drove street after street, he realized there was no new construction. He made his way slowly downtown...and there it was. Demolition of the old federal courthouse to make way for a new structure. He pulled over on Fort Street, got out of his truck, and headed over to a couple of construction workers on site.

"Excuse me, is there a supervisor I can speak with?"

"No work here, buddy." The answer was curt as the worker snuffed out his cigarette and turned to get back to work.

"Not looking for a job. I was wondering if I could haul away the debris. I have a truck."

The worker stopped and turned. "That man over there in the yellow hat? Jones. He's the one you should talk to."

"Thanks." Frank walked briskly over to the man in the yellow hat and stood quietly to the side as Jones finished a conversation.

"Sorry, we have no work." Jones had probably said that a hundred times a day.

"Not looking for that, Mr. Jones. I would like to haul away your debris. I have a truck."

"We have someone for that."

"But I see there's a large pile. I can start today. I can start now. I will take it for free. No need to wait – no need to pay someone."

"I have no one to load it."

"I will load it. I figure I can move three loads before the day ends… I can move five tomorrow."

"What materials would you want?"

"Wood. Bricks. You probably want the copper. You can get a pretty penny for that."

Jones took a deep breath. "Free?"

"Yes."

Jones looked around and then lowered his voice. "I don't want this out in the open – I can't have hundreds milling around, clamoring for work. Come tonight after dark. If you can level that pile" – he pointed over his shoulder to the right – "in a week, you can get the job for the rest. But at night, mind you."

Frank grinned. "I'll start tonight. I'll do a good job. Thank you, Mr. Jones." He nearly ran back to his truck and headed home. Before he walked in the door, he went to the backyard and surveyed it.

"Margaret! I'll be loading up the backyard with brick and lumber. I start tonight."

"Whatever will you do with it, Frank?"

"Clean it up and sell it, I hope. I get it for free. I'll be gone all night until I've cleaned out the site."

"The site?"

"I'm cleaning up the debris from the old courthouse downtown."

"Who will buy it, Frank? People have little money."

"The rich folk still have money. Still building houses, labor so cheap. Boston Edison, maybe. Indian Village. Grosse Pointe. I'll talk to contractors. They can buy at a discount and still charge full price."

Margaret sighed. "You always were enterprising, Frank. I hope it works out. Can you use some to build a little coop? We can get some chickens – we'll need them for over winter. I've canned most of the garden already."

"I'll build us a coop, Margaret. And with the first sale, I'll buy some chicken wire and a few chickens. It can't be big, mind you – I'll need the room for the material."

"Just enough to get by over winter, Frank. A half-dozen chickens. We can eat the eggs, and I'll can a chicken a month. That'll take us to spring."

Frank walked over and gave Margaret a kiss on the cheek. "We'll pull this off, Margaret. Now I'm off to take a nap – I'll be up all night."

That evening, as the sun was setting, Frank put Cae in the passenger seat and took off down Fort Street. He pulled up next to a pile of wood and started loading the truck. He was able to get three loads in before the sun started to rise. When Margaret woke up, she saw quite a pile of lumber in the backyard.

Frank slept until noon. Then he woke up, went outside, and started pounding the nails out of the lumber. He placed them in an old, large tin can. He hadn't gone through the entire pile by the time Margaret called him in for supper. When the sun set, Frank set off again to the courthouse with Cae.

Frank cleared out the pile Jones had pointed out within the week, as promised. The backyard was filled to capacity with stacked lumber and bricks. Frank headed out during the day to find Mr. Jones.

"I see you cleared out that pile of rubbish."

"Yes, sir. And thank you. I can't start on that second pile at the moment; I've run out of room to store it. Can you wait a while to clear out the rest?"

"I can't wait on you. You come back when you're able. If it's gone, it's gone." Jones walked away, clearly irritated.

Frank went back home, took his hammer out, and continued to remove nails. When that was done, days later, he knocked off the mortar from all the bricks. When he had finished, there were neat and orderly stacks of clean lumber and stacks of clean bricks – enough for three, maybe four bungalows. His next step was to pull out the telephone directory to find general contractors. Armed with a list of addresses and with samples of both the brick and lumber in his truck, Frank took off to market his materials.

"No, sorry – we aren't starting now. Winter's too close."

"No, sorry."

Time and time again, "No, sorry."

After an entire day of rejections, Frank pulled into a gas station to fill his tank, probably for the last time in a while; he needed to start walking. He had promised Margaret a chicken coop and half a dozen chickens.

"Hey, Scotty. How ya doin'?" Buddy said to Frank as he stuck the nozzle into the gas tank. "You've got a load. Hey, Cae – good dog."

"Just half this time, Buddy. Tried to sell this lumber and brick. No luck. Bad time of year."

When Buddy had finished, he turned to Frank. "Times are tough, that's for sure. Listen, pay me when you can. You looking for work?"

"Aye, I am. I haven't found anything."

"I have a proposition for you, then. There's a corner off Warren, over near Dearborn. The busses run back and forth. I can get a fuel tanker there – we can pump right from the truck. Want to help run it for me? Take shifts. I can't be there every minute. At least over the winter. We can split the profits seventy-thirty."

"If I'm there as much as you, can we make it sixty-forty?"

"Tell you what. I want to do this, but I ca`n't do it alone. Can we start at seventy-thirty? If all goes as I planned, I will move to sixty-forty in the spring. I need to put up the money to buy the tanker of gas and won't ask for anything from you. Give me six months."

Frank extended his hand. "Deal. Tell me when the tanker gets here, and then tell me my hours."

Buddy shook his hand. "Do you have a telephone?"

"We gave up the phone – needed to save the money. I'll stop by every week."

"It's a deal. See you soon, Scotty."

Frank left for home, unloaded his truck, and started building a chicken coup.

* * *

"Margaret, I found employment."

"That's wonderful, Frank! Where will you be working?"

"I'm going to pump gas in Dearborn. Not a steady wage, but I get a portion of the profits."

Margaret scowled. "No regular income?"

"Better than nothing, Margaret. Couldn't sell any building materials. Wrong time of year. No one starts a new house in the fall. This work should keep us until spring."

"I see you've started on the coop. When can we get some hens?"

"I probably can't buy them until spring. Not until some money starts coming in."

Margaret went over to the side table in the front parlor and returned with a newspaper. "Frank, I was talking to the neighbor. She works at Banner Laundry. She said a laundress just quit because she is pregnant. She says the company likes women from the old countries. I think I need to go there tomorrow… I can't see how we can hold out without more money. I can take the streetcar with Ludmilla and see."

"My wee wifey shouldn'a have tae work!"

"Frank, put that aside. We do what we have to do to get by. I've worked before; I can work again. Until you – we – get on our feet again. These are tough times, but not as tough as in the old country. Do you nae remember? Just for now…just until spring, maybe. We need to eat, Frank, and winter's coming. No garden to tide us over. I've canned all the vegetables – maybe enough to last the winter. Maybe not. It will be close. We can get those chickens before winter if I get a job."

Frank hung his head dejectedly for several moments. Then he

raised it. His jaw was set with determination. "You are right, of course. I will make it up to you, Margaret. I will make it so you will not need to work for long. I promise you that. I will do right by my wife – and son."

CHAPTER TEN

"Jackie, have you fed the chickens?" Margaret didn't even turn around from the stove, where she was fixing a stew from the 1/8 pound of bacon she had gotten as a Christmas present from work.

"Yes, Mum. I did it right when I got home from school. That smells so good! Is that bacon?"

"Yes it is! A special treat – a Christmas present from work. Were there any eggs?"

"I brought the eggs in before school – right after I got the clinkers out of the stove. Want me to check again?"

"No, that will be fine. Are you still doing well with your lessons?"

"Yes, Mum. Like always."

"That's a good boy. Your da should be home soon. Get your homework done before he gets here so you can help him if he needs it."

"Yes, Mum." Jack took a seat at the table and started working on arithmetic.

Frank didn't arrive home until after dark – which wasn't terribly late, as it was winter solstice. He hung up his hat, scarf, and coat, removed his boots and gloves, and headed over to the coal stove, where he rubbed his hands close to the unit to warm them.

"Bitter cold out there." He coughed several times. "Smells wonderful, though. What's that you have? Bacon?"

"Aye. We got one-eighth pound from work as a Christmas present. I'm making a stew – it should be ready shortly."

"What a treat!" Frank coughed again. "Do we have any tea?"

"No – we ran out last week."

"My throat is a bit raw… Can you get me a little hot honey water?"

Margaret stopped stirring the stew and put the teapot on the stove. "I'll have it for you in a few minutes. Frank, you've been coughing a lot lately. Are you sure you aren't coming down with grippe?"

Frank tried to answer but was struck by a coughing fit. He shook his head and leaned over the coal stove. The teapot was starting to steam, and he took several deep breaths, which calmed his coughing spell. Margaret came over with a cup and poured some boiling water into it. She then put in a teaspoon of honey, stirred it well, and gave it to Frank.

"Care with this now, Frank. It's boiling hot."

Frank put it under his nose as it cooled, breathing in the steam.

"You might want to call the doctor, Frank. Before that cough gets worse."

"Nae, Margaret. We've no the money – not now, at least. I won't get paid until the end of the month. If I still have the cough by then, I'll go. I promise. Jackie! How are you, son?" Frank walked over and tousled Jack's hair.

"I'm well, Da."

"No trouble at school?"

"No, Da. I'm doing well."

"That's a good lad." Frank took a deep drink of the hot honey water and sat down. "Jackie, could you run and get me my warm jumper? The one on the back of the chair? I've taken a chill."

Jack got up promptly to fetch the sweater on the back of Frank's chair in the parlor and brought it back.

"Jack, time to put your schoolwork away and set the table. Supper's ready." Margaret moved the pot of stew off of the burner, ladled out three bowls and set them on the table. "We have no bread tonight, but we have a very special treat!" The bowls were filled with potatoes, leeks, some chopped parsnips, carrots…and very sparse pieces of pork. There was silence around the table as everyone quickly ate.

"Is there more, Mum? This is so good!" Jack lifted up his bowl.

"Are you not full? I would like to give you more, but what's left is meant for dinner tomorrow. But I did take the stale bread we had and made a small bread pudding. Would that do?"

Jack grinned broadly. "My favorite! Aye, Mum. I'd love that."

Margaret smiled and got up to bring the pudding to the table.

"This is another treat, Margaret! Wonderful dinner. You are such a good wife and mother." Frank leaned over and gave Margaret a kiss on the cheek. She froze just the slightest bit and changed the subject.

"You look a bit flushed, Frank. Are you sure you've not a fever?"

"I might have a touch. More honey water?"

Margaret got up and poured Frank another cup of hot water, adding a scant teaspoon of honey.

"We need the end of the year to come, Frank. We have no flour for bread and are nearly out of honey. And I am out of lard for soap. The month can't end soon enough."

Frank sighed. "I know things are scarce. But we have a roof over our heads, food to sustain us on the table, coal in the stove, and a good son." He smiled at Jack. "It could be so much worse." He suddenly coughed again. "I think I need to take to my bed early tonight. Jack, make sure you do everything your mother asks now… I need to try and sleep this off."

Frank got up, patted his son's head, gave Margaret a peck on the cheek, and headed to bed.

* * *

"Jack, let's go cut down a Christmas tree." It was Christmas Eve morning, and the day was calm and sunny but cold. Frank bundled himself up to guard against the weather. Jack excitedly grabbed his hat, coat, scarf, and gloves and headed out to the truck. Frank laughed as he watched his son.

"Margaret, he's such a good lad. We'll be back soon."

Frank and Jack headed out of the city and on toward the Irish Hills. Before they got there, however, they saw a farm with a "Free Christmas Trees" sign. Frank pulled in and drove up to a barn where several people had gathered.

"Jack, you stay here until I find out what's going on."

Jack nodded, and Frank headed over to a man encircled by people.

"My trees are free," the man was saying, "but they are not small. I want to clear a plot of land for corn, and there are several pine trees there. If you fell a tree, you can take the top of it. Free."

"Do you have tree saws?" someone asked.

"I have a couple...one- and two-man." The saws were at his feet.

Frank spoke up. "I'll take the two-man... Who wants to help me cut down two trees? One for you, and one for me."

The man across from Frank, wearing a rather threadbare coat and gloves with holes in them, said, "Can we take some wood for fires?"

"Six feet of trunk, but no more. Unless you take out the stump."

The man in the tattered coat looked at Frank. "I'll partner up with you on the saw."

Frank picked up the big saw. "Where do you want us to cut?"

"That stand of pines past the barn, on the right."

Frank had a coughing bout, but he waved it off and motioned to the man who had volunteered. "Let me get my son... He's in my truck." Frank walked halfway to the truck and motioned for Jack to follow him. Then the three headed off to the stand of pines. They picked two trees on the edge of the wooded area. It only took about a half hour to cut both trees down. They were maybe twenty feet tall, so their trunks were not too thick. They cut the top six feet off for the two Christmas trees, then the next six feet for firewood.

"You can have my section for firewood. We burn coal, so I have little use for the wood."

"Are you sure? That's mighty fine of you, foreigner."

Frank let the slight roll off his back. "Happy Christmas to you. But can you see that the saw gets back to the farmer? Thanks." He motioned for Jack to pick up one end of the treetop, and then they headed to the truck and threw it into the bed.

Back home, Frank sawed a couple of strips off one of the pieces of reclaimed lumber and fashioned a tree stand.

"Here, Jack. Take the hammer and place a couple of nails into the tree trunk…here and here." Frank held a wood strip in place. "Mind you to hit the nail, not my hand. Take two hands. Hold the nail in one and the hammer in the other. Hold the nail straight and tap it in until the wood grabs it. Then you can let the nail go and pound the nail in."

Jack did as his father instructed, but he stopped when Frank interrupted.

"No, Jack. The nail is not straight. Wiggle it out and try again."

Jack didn't get it straight time and time again. Finally, Frank took the hammer and nail. "Here then, Jack. You hold the wood and watch me." It took two taps to sink the nail halfway and then just two more to sink it in entirely. He stopped for a bad bout of coughing and then got back to the task at hand.

"Now, do you want to try again?"

Jack held his head. "No. I cannae do it, Da."

"Maybe next year, then, Jack. You're still a bit on the wee side. We'll try again next year. Now let's finish this and get it inside."

The tree stood proudly in the front parlor. Margaret showed Jack how to make chains out of paper, which kept the child happily occupied for quite a while. Frank lifted Jack so he could string the chains high on the tree, winding them down to the bottom. Margaret had crocheted little white lacy snowflakes out of cotton string, which they placed all over the tree. She had also made a big, lovely bow out of some pretty gingham scrap she had left over from a dress she had made for herself, and Frank lifted Jack so he could place it on top of the tree. When all was said and done, the trio stepped back and admired their Christmas tree.

"It's beautiful, Da, isn't it?" Jack was beaming.

"Aye, laddie, that it is."

Margaret walked up behind Jack and put her hands on his shoulders. "Now, Jack, you and I need to go get a chicken for Christmas dinner. Will you help me catch one?"

"Aye, Mum. But can I choose which one? I have a favorite that I don't want harmed."

Margaret smiled at Jack. "You pick, Jack. But even though you tend to them, you know they're for feeding us with their eggs and meat. Don't get too attached to 'em."

"Yes, Mum." Jack followed Margaret out to the chicken coop, where he easily caught a chicken. Margaret deftly broke its neck with a sharp twist and started plucking its feathers. Jack, disturbed by the sight, quickly went indoors.

"Why the glum face, laddie?"

"Mum just killed a chicken. I just fed that chicken this morning. Poor bird."

Frank squatted so he was at eye level with his son. "Jack, that is nothing to be sad about. It's nature… Does a lion eat a deer? Does a big fish eat a little fish? It is the way things work in this world. We have fed and sheltered our chickens, even in winter. When their time comes, we will be repaid with the food they provide us."

Jack looked down at the floor. "But I just fed her this morning." He pulled away and ran up the stairs. Frank, caught in another fit of heavy coughing, let him go.

When Margaret finished plucking and gutting the bird, she came in.

"Our lad is too soft, Margaret. He needs to toughen up, or he'll have a hard time making it."

* * *

It didn't snow Christmas morning. It was overcast and rather dreary, but that didn't dampen the spirits in the Sharp household. Frank had made a little wooden car for Jack out of some of the lumber in the back. It had been carefully sanded and decorated using a red-hot piece of metal to make dark burnt-brown door handles and wheel spokes. Margaret had knit Jack a new sweater in his favorite color – blue. Frank had also made a wooden box for Margaret with carved roses on the hinged top. It was perfectly crafted and obviously a labor of love. Margaret had knit Frank a pair of gloves and a new pair of thick wool socks. It was a fine Christmas.

* * *

Frank doubled over, coughing, while pumping gas between Christmas and the New Year. It wasn't horribly cold – somewhere is the mid-thirties – but it had been overcast, wet, and windy for days, the type of damp, cold air that manages to chill a body to the core. Frank recovered, put the gas cap back on the Model T, and went to the window to collect what was due.

"That'll be a dollar seventy-five. You were nearly empty." The driver handed over two one-dollar bills, and Frank gave back a quarter. "Happy New Year to ya."

"And to you, too, Scotty."

The driver pulled out, and Frank went over to the stool by the tanker truck to wait for the next customer, huddling against the weather, cap pulled down tight and arms wrapped around his body to try and contain what little heat he could generate. It was a boring, miserable job...but it was work.

Several minutes later, a shiny new Packard pulled up. Frank rose quickly and rushed to the river-side window.

"Help you, sir?"

The driver was very well dressed – but flashy – maybe thirty years old or so. Sitting next to him was an attractive younger woman dressed to the nines. They were laughing and flirting.

"Fill 'er up." The driver ended the directive by taking out a cigarette and lighting it." Frank filled up the tank and returned to the car window.

That'll be a buck fifty, please."

The man looked Frank over and then glanced at Frank's truck, where Cae stood guard in the driver's seat.

"That your truck?"

"Aye, it is."

"Are you Irish?"

"Nae, Scottish."

"Your truck in good working order?"

"Aye, I keep it up."

The man reached over and shook Frank's hand. "Peter."

"Frank Sharp"

Peter Caravaggio pulled a business card out of his vest pocket. "If you ever get tired of standing in the cold, pumping gas, give me a call. We can always use men with trucks. The pay is good, I promise. Probably a lot more than you're making now." He gave the card and two dollars to Frank. "Keep the change." He wheeled out quickly onto Warren.

Frank stayed until six, towards the end of rush hour, and then closed up shop and left for home.

"Yer coughin' quite a spell, Frank. You've been at it for weeks. You need to see a doctor."

"I'll be fine, Margaret."

"You've had that cough for weeks, and it's not getting better.

What will Jackie and I do if we lose you?"

Frank scowled. "Do we have tea?"

"Aye, we do. I'll fetch you a cup." Margaret got up from the table and headed to the kitchen. She was halfway there when there was a knock at the door. She went to answer it instead.

"Aye, Jess! Come in! What brings you over? Can I get you a cup of tea? Let me take your coat."

Margaret busied herself with hanging up Jess's coat and hat. She turned around with a smile, but it faded quickly when she saw Jess's face.

"What's wrong, Jess?"

"It's Rob. He's no well, Margaret. No well a' all. De ye ken a doctor? We've nae gone tae one here an' don't have a name."

Aye, I know a good one. Dr. James MacIntosh. I'll fetch his number. Ye can use our phone. There, on the side table." Margaret hurried into the kitchen and returned with a business card. "He dinnae mind late hours for an emergency. Let me dial him fer ye."

Margaret went to the phone. "Operator, please connect me with Hemlock 7717. Dr. MacIntosh. Thank you."

She waited several minutes for the connection to go through.

"Dr. MacIntosh? This is Margaret Sharp... Yes, fine, thank you. Hope you are well... No, little Jackie's fine. It's my brother-in-law, Rob Sharp. His wife, Jess, came over. Says Rob is doing quite poorly. Could ye manage a visit?"

Margaret turned to Jess. "What's wrong wi' him, Jess?"

"He's a bad fever and great pains in his stomach. Tae double o'er."

Margaret relayed that into the mouthpiece and waited for an answer.

"An' how long, Jess?"

"It started aboot a week ago. It's only gotten worse."

Margaret again relayed the information.

"Aye, thank you, Doctor. Their address is 4799 Pitt... An hour, you say? Thank you." She hung up the phone.

"Do you have enough money to pay the man, Jess?"

Jess bowed her head in shame. "We cannae pay until Friday next, Margaret. Things are tight, wha' wi' th' company cuttin' Rob's wage. Ah cannae e'en buy groceries now."

Margaret went over to her purse.

"I've no much, Jess, but here's a dollar. Pay me back when ye can. The doctor will take the rest when ye can pay, too, as long as you can give him something."

Jess bowed her head and gratefully took the money. "I thank ye kindly, Margaret. I'll ne'er ferget it. I'll pay ye back next payday."

Margaret gave Jess a hug. "Best get back tae yer man then, Jess. Godspeed."

She went into the kitchen and returned with Frank's tea.

"That was generous of you, Margaret."

"We don't have much, but nae guid'll come of it if Rob cannae work." She put down Frank's cup in front of him. He took a swig and then went into another coughing fit.

"And Frank Sharp – if that cough is not better by next week, you'll find Dr. MacIntosh waiting here in the parlor for you when you come home from work."

* * *

Frank stopped off at Rob's before going home from work the next day.

"Hi, Jess. I just stopped by to inquire about Robbie. How is he?" The look on Jess's face said it all.

"He's nae well, Frank. Nae well a' all. The doctor said he's a bad infection in his innards. I'm to keep him quiet and make sure he drinks lots of water. Nae more tae do but pray an' hope he can fight it off." Jess's voice was emotionless. She was wan, and Frank could tell she hadn't slept in quite a while.

"He cannae work, Frank. He's lost his job wi' the sickness."

Frank studied his hands. "When's your rent due, Jess?"

"First o' th' month. An' we dinnae hae it."

"How much are you short?"

"Aboot five dollars. And that's if I buy no groceries."

"Tell you what, Jess. Save as much as you can. Then call me at the end of the month. I will try to get you the balance. No promises, but I will try."

"Thank you, Frank." Jess reached out and squeezed his hand. "Dae ye want tae see yer brother?"

"Aye, Jess, if he's up to it."

Jess led Frank up the stairs to the bedroom where Rob lay still.

"The doctor gave us tonic to help him sleep." Jess pointed to a small vial on the nightstand.
"Laudanum."

Frank walked over to the side of the bed. "Rob?" he said softly, taking Rob's hand. That was enough to rouse Rob out of his stupor somewhat.

"Frank?"

"Aye. Frank. You've looked better, my good man."

Rob gave a feeble smile. "Aye, I'll not argue tha." He let out a deep sigh. "Frank, I'm feeling quite puirly. I'm nae sure I'll pull through. Wull ye tak' care o' Jess and the weans if I dinnae pull through?"

"No talk of that, Rob. You need to pull through. Your family needs you. Now, you do what the doctor said, no argument! I've already told Jess that I will try to cover what's needed for rent come the first of the month. That should ease your mind for now. You concentrate on getting better. Ye ken?"

Frank was suddenly stopped by another bad coughing fit.

Jess looked at him with alarm. "An wha's tha', Frank? Yer nae well, either?"

Frank waived her off until the attack ended. "It's just being

169

outside all the time, pumping gas in this weather. Nasty. It'll pass." He coughed a few times more. "I'd better go before both of you start coughing, too. Last thing you need." Frank squeezed his brother's hand. "See you soon, Rob – standing. Take care. Jess…" Frank gave a quick nod to Jess in acknowledgment and headed home.

* * *

"He's dead, Frank. He passed last night."

Frank stared at his broken sister-in-law, head bowed and shoulders slumped, standing in the parlor. "Can we bury him in Windsor Gardens, next to Andrew?"

"We can do that, Jess. But we can't afford a headstone. Not for Robbie, not even for Andrew."

Margaret interjected. "What will you do, Jess? You and the bairns?"

"We're gang back tae Scotland. Ah can work wi' mah mither tending the weans. Mah da an' brothers are sending the fare fer us. Ah cannae stay here."

Margaret walked over to her and grabbed both of her hands. "We are so sorry, Jess. We will miss you sorely." Margaret brushed Jess's cheek with a kiss. "Do you and the bairns want to stay here until the ship leaves? Maybe your landlord will refund some of your rent, being you're a widow now."

"Nae, tha's very generous, but we'll stay fer now at oor hoose. Th' landlord's nae willing tae give us a break. Might as well get oor money's worth. If our fares come in time, the next ship sails on the third. Mebbie we'll stay wi' you fer a day or two afore the ship leaves. Or mebbie just stay in th' hoose – it'll take longer than tha' fer the landlord to get the police to kick us oot."

"Well, just keep it in mind, Jess. Don't end up on the street."

"Och, noo. We'll manage."

Jess would not be broken for long.

* * *

Dr. MacIntosh was waiting in the parlor when Frank returned home the next day.

"Your wife tells me you've been bothered by a bad cough for weeks, Mr. Sharp."

Frank tried to answer but fell into a coughing spell.

"I see. Well, take off your coat and let me have a listen." Dr. MacIntosh lifted his stethoscope and listened to Frank's heart and lungs, front and back.

"Take a deep breath for me." That made Frank cough all over again.

"Your lungs have quite a bit of fluid in them, Mr. Sharp. How long have you been coughing like that?"

Margaret quickly answered, "Since before Christmas."

"Your wife tells me you work outside. Are you outside all the time?"

"Aye."

Dr. MacIntosh took the earpieces out and wrapped the stethoscope around his neck. "You're working on a moderate case of pneumonia, Mr. Sharp. If you keep working outside, it will only get worse. You need bed rest. I want you to sleep propped up with pillows. Mrs. Sharp, I recommend you boil a little camphor in water and have your husband inhale the steam several times a day. Stay as warm as you can manage – all of the blankets you can stand. Mrs. Sharp, he needs plenty of fluids – hot fluids. Hot tea. Hot broth. And keep him bundled up and in bed as much as you can. Mr. Sharp, you run the risk of severe illness – maybe even death – if you do not follow these directions. Stay in bed until that cough clears up. And that's an order! Understand?"

"Margaret looked piercingly at Frank and then said, "Thank you, doctor. How much do we owe you?"

"Three dollars."

Margaret looked inquiringly at Frank.

"There's fifty cents in my right coat pocket. Can we pay you the rest on time?"

The doctor sighed. "I don't have much choice, do I? Pay me when you can." Dr. MacIntosh took the fifty cents from Margaret and excused himself.

"Now, Frank, you need to go right upstairs and to bed. I'll heat up some broth for you. You've already lost two brothers...please. For our sake – don't join them."

"I will. I promise. But before I do that, I need to make a phone call." Frank pulled out the business card and headed over to the phone. His first call was to Buddy, telling him he needed to quit immediately. The second call was to the flashy young man who drove a brand-new Packard.

"Mr. Caravaggio? This is Frank Sharp from the gasoline tanker. I am interested in what you might have in mind for work. Can we meet, maybe in a week or two? I need to lay low for a while – doctor's orders... No, I just need to get rid of this cough. Doctor said it's working into pneumonia.... Great. I'll call you as soon as I am able."

Frank closely followed the doctor's orders, and in a little more than a week, he called Mr. Caravaggio once again.

* * *

Frank paused when he entered the 2 Way Inn shortly before one in the afternoon to allow his eyes to adjust to the darkened room. He spotted Caravaggio sitting with a couple of men at a table near the back. Caravaggio motioned for Frank to join them.

"Welcome, Mr. Sharp. Have a seat! Here – order some lunch. We've just started." Caravaggio signaled for a waiter.

Frank looked cautiously at the men. He had never eaten at a restaurant before. Caravaggio said, "Whatever you want, Mr. Sharp. It's on me."

Frank looked up at the waiter and said, "I'll have what he's having." He pointed to the plate of pasta in front of Caravaggio.

"Good choice! It's my favorite." Caravaggio raised a glass of water in a salute and took a drink. Using a soup spoon, he curled some spaghetti around his fork while he spoke to his companions. "Sharp – the man with a truck and a German Shepherd." He stuffed the fork into his mouth.

"Here – take a piece of bread while you wait," he said while his mouth was full, motioning to the breadbasket on the table. "Eat. The bread's from the Detroit Italian Bakery. Best bread in the city."

Frank ripped a piece off of the Italian long roll, spread a little butter on it, and started to eat.

"You want good-paying work, Sharp?"

"Aye, sir."

We have a proposition for you, then. You and your truck – the dog is an added bonus. We would like you to move materials from Grosse Ile into Wyandotte, maybe three or four nights a week. Are you interested?"

"You want me carting?"

"Yes – is that a problem?"

"No, not at all – that's what I bought the truck to do. I used to do that when I lived in Windsor."

"Excellent!!! You told me you were Scottish, right?"

"Aye, sir."

"How long have you been here?"

"I've been in the States two years now."

"You know your whisky, then," laughed Caravaggio. "Here's the job: I have a little place on Hickory Island – at the tip of Grosse Ile. It's very, very quiet. I will pay you twenty-five dollars a trip. You pick up the load on Hickory Island and drive it to Biddle Street. No questions. Are you interested?"

Frank's mouth fell open at twenty-five dollars a trip. One trip would net as much as Frank had been making in a week.

Frank lowered his voice. "These, um…materials I will be hauling…"

Caravaggio interrupted. "I believe we both understand the nature of the product, Sharp."

Just then, Frank's plate of pasta appeared in front of him. He had watched Caravaggio use his fork and spoon and did the same. After his first forkful, Frank paused.

"I am very interested, Mr. Caravaggio."

Caravaggio smiled broadly. "I thought you might be. Tommy here will meet you at Fort and Van Horn – is tomorrow night good?"

Frank looked intently at Caravaggio. "Hickory Island…. Do you have a cottage there?"

"There's not much there, actually. A house or two. Quite a bit of empty land."

Frank paused. "I would think that a truck crossing the bridge in the dead of night would be an easy target to spot. How much commercial traffic crosses that bridge?"

"Basically, the only commercial traffic is for the yacht club and naval base."

"Hmmm… Trucks in full; trucks out empty. And a naval base. What might people be hauling in and out?"

"Supplies in, that's for sure. Rubbish out, perhaps. I can't think of anything else offhand."

Frank slapped his hand on the table. "That's the answer, then. Not at night – in broad daylight. I need to be taking rubbish out."

Caravaggio looked at his lieutenants. "What do you think, gentlemen?"

Tommy said, "It would be easier to get lost in a stream of traffic. If Scotty here is willing to give it a go, I think we should try it."

Caravaggio looked at Frank. "You've got a head on your shoulders, that's for sure. Okay, then. Not tomorrow. Thursday – meet Tommy at two in the afternoon, Fort and Van Born. Your idea, Scotty – you come up with the camouflage. Tommy here will pay you when the load is delivered."

Frank quickly finished his pasta and stood.

"Thanks for the job and thanks for lunch, Mr. Caravaggio. Tommy, I'll see you Thursday. two PM sharp, Fort and Van Born." Frank shook hands all around and left.

* * *

Frank got up early the next day and went downriver to watch traffic across the Grosse Ile Parkway Bridge. When he spotted a truck with trash leaving the island, he followed it to Zug Island, where the trash was dumped as fill in the marshy area. He had seen enough – he went home with a plan in mind.

Frank was helping Jack with his homework at the kitchen table when Margaret got home.

"How was your day, Margaret?"

"Fine, Frank," Margaret answered while hanging up her coat and taking off her hat. "Mariska and her husband are going to the Cougars game this weekend. Asked if we wanted to go. Of course I said no, but it was nice for her to ask."

"Maybe next time, Margaret. Say, do we have any muslin? Enough for a truck bed cover?"

"Let me go look – I might have something you can use. But let me get supper started first. Jackie, will you please run down to the cellar and bring up a couple of potatoes and jar of beans?" Margaret threw on an apron, pulled out some pots and pans, and put them on the stove.

"Margaret, I think I've found work. Carting. I've been asked to haul rubbish to Zug Island. They are using it to fill in the marsh there. That's why I need a truck bed cover."

"Does it pay well?"

"Fair to middlin' – better than nothing. And better than the gas tanker… I don't need to wait to get paid. I get paid upon delivery."

"When do you start?"

"Thursday. Probably not every day, but it's still better than manning the tanker. I'm going to try and get several trips a week. If I can do that, I can maybe double what I was making."

"That's good, Frank, but it doesn't sound all that steady. Still, it's hard enough to find work nowadays. I'm happy for you. Happy for us."

Frank stood, walked up behind Margaret, and wrapped his arms around her waist. "If this works, you can quit your job, Margaret. Wouldn't that be nice?"

"We'll see, Frank. Let's not count our chickens before they hatch."

Just then, Jackie came up from the cellar. "Now, Jackie, have you fed the chickens?"

"Not yet, Mum. I needed to do my homework. Da said."

"Well, go tend to them. Then come back and set the table."

"All right."

Supper come and gone, Margaret went into the closet to look for some muslin.

"Will this do?"

"I think it will, Margaret. Let me go and measure the truck bed."

Frank left for a short while. When he came back, he said, "Can you make it five feet long and three feet wide?"

Margaret held up the fabric, turning her head far to the left and extending her right arm out to the side. She held the fabric up with one hand touching the tip of her nose. "That's three feet." She moved the fabric to measure the rest. "It's just short of five feet, Frank, but it is three feet wide."

"That will do just fine, Margaret. Do you mind me using the fabric?"

"If it'll bring in a wage, it will go to good use." She handed over the muslin. "Now I need to clean up the kitchen."

* * *

Thursday morning rose cold and clear. After Jack was off to school and Margaret off to the laundry, Frank piled Cae and the piece of muslin into the truck cab and headed out to scavenge some appropriate trash. When the truck bed had a three-to-six-inch layer of cans, glass, and cardboard, he covered it over with the muslin and tied it down with twine. He was at the corner of Fort and Van Horn five minutes early, waiting. Tommy was five minutes late.

"A dog? I won't sit squished with a dog."

"He's great protection. I'll follow you, then – will that work?"

Tommy shrugged, not hiding his slight irritation. "That'll have to do. Just follow me." He took off, and Frank followed. It wasn't far to the bridge, and after crossing, the two vehicles slowly meandered south, through Grosse Ile and then through Mesco Island, down to tiny Hickory Island. It was mostly wooded, with only a single road on one side. The Grosse Ile Yacht Club was to the left after crossing the low concrete bridge between Mesco and Hickory Islands. Tommy turned away from the club and headed down Bayview Road, which wasn't more than a couple of dirt tracks through the heavily wooded area. Halfway down, he turned into the trees on another set of dirt tracks and stopped. When Frank got out of the truck, he could see Gibraltar Bay through the branches. As he approached the waterfront, he could also see the naval air station, busy with servicemen and airplanes.

"Right across from the naval air station? Bold."

"That's why it's such a great place. With the yacht club, people are used to boats coming and going, and no one would think us brazen enough to do this." Tommy headed into the woods to a small clearing that was piled with several wooden cases covered in pine brush.

"This is the payload. I'll help you load it."

"Give me a minute: I need to get the truck bed ready." Frank pulled off the muslin and piled the trash on top of it. He and Tommy then loaded the cases into the truck. Frank arranged them flat and covered them with the muslin – then he piled on the trash. When he was done, his modest truck looked quite innocent.

"Clever." Tommy was impressed.

The two vehicles slowly made their way to a nondescript two-story house on Biddle Street, where the two pulled around back. Tommy looked around to make sure the alley was empty and then knocked on the back door while Frank wrapped the muslin around the trash and pulled it off. Several men came out of the house and quickly moved the cases in.

"Here, Sharp." Tommy handed over twenty-five dollars. "I'll tell Mr. Caravaggio that the transport went smoothly. Have you given him your telephone number? I think he'll want to use you again soon."

"I have. Pleasure doing business with you, Tommy. Hope to see you soon." Frank tipped his cap while he shoved the cash into his pocket.

He got home in time to meet Margaret at the bus stop.

"And what's the occasion that you pick me up?"

Frank grinned. "I got paid today, Margaret." He reached into his pocket and pulled out twenty dollars. "Here – Saturday let's buy some more chickens. And groceries. And replace that muslin I used."

Margaret looked at the cash in amazement. "For one day's work?"

"Aye. Margaret, my love…. This is good. This is very good."

CHAPTER ELEVEN

"Jock's nae guid." Bess was standing at Frank and Margaret's door, and the words came out the minute the door opened. "Will ye come?"

"What's wrong, Mum?"

"He's a frightful cough. Doubled o'er wi' it. And he's burnin' up wi' fever. We cannae afford a doctor."

Frank sighed as he grabbed his cap and a light jacket.

"Margaret, I'll be back as soon as I'm able."

He escorted his mother to the truck. "How long has he been sick?"

"April."

"Mum, that's weeks ago."

"We couldn'a afford a doctor, Frank."

"You should have called me."

It didn't take long to get back to where Bess lived with Lill. Jock was set up in the parlor, on the sofa. Frank walked over to him and pulled up a chair.

"Hello, Jock. I hear you've been feeling poorly."

Jock turned his head. "Aye, Frank. Guid tae see ya. Nae, I'm terrible weak an' feverish." He coughed violently. Frank could hear his chest rattle as he tried to breathe in – able to manage only very shallow, rapid breaths.

"Mum, you should have called me earlier. I'm off to fetch a doctor."

"We cannae pay fer him."

"I'll pay."

Frank abruptly left, and he returned in an hour with Dr. MacIntosh. As they approached the house, Frank said quietly, "I think he's got pneumonia, and I think he's far into it."

It only took a quick examination to determine that Frank was right.

"Mrs. Sharp, your son needs to go to the hospital. He's very ill, and his recovery is not assured."

"We cannae afford it."

Frank interrupted. "I'll take care of it." He turned to the doctor. "Shall I take him right now? I'll carry him to the truck right now."

"You should."

Frank handed the doctor five dollars and then went over to Jock. He wrapped him up tightly in a blanket and easily carried him. "Open the door, Mum."

"Ah dinnae ken whair ye get yer money, Frank, but it's welcome. Jock, be well an' haste ye home, now."

Frank piled Jock into the truck and drove to Detroit Receiving Hospital. He pulled into the emergency entrance, got out, and carried Jock through the doors. An orderly saw what was happening and quickly rolled over a gurney.

"This is my brother, Jock Sharp. He was just seen by Dr. MacIntosh – we were told to bring him here immediately. You can see he's having a hard time of it."

Jock was whisked away while Frank provided admitting information.

"Can I say goodbye?"

"It's getting late, Mr. Sharp – after visiting hours. You can come on by tomorrow to visit with your brother."

"Tell him God speed for me if you see him. Tell him I'll be here tomorrow."

Frank had a whisky run the next day. He had been moving cases for several months and was no longer escorted. He stopped by the hospital before heading for Grosse Ile.

"Can you tell me what room my brother has? Jock Sharp."

The nurse at the desk looked at her inpatient listing and shook her head sadly.

"I'm sorry, but Mr. Sharp can have no visitors. He's in isolation in a steam tent. He is in serious condition, I am afraid to say. Are you his next of kin?"

"I'm his brother. I would say our mother would be next of kin. Bess Sharp."

"Shall we call her in case of emergency?"

"No – call me. My mother doesn't have a phone. I gave my number last night when I brought Jock in. It should be in his record."

"We will call you with any new developments, Mr. Sharp. You might want to call before you come tomorrow – it might save you a trip."

"Thanks. Have a good day." Frank left for his run – and his twenty-five dollars.

He returned home later than usual, after five... The drop had moved – again – and the load had been a bit larger than usual. On top of that, the destination had been on the east side.

He opened the front door to see his mother crying, with Margaret doing her best to console her. Margaret looked straight into Frank's eyes, saying nothing but shaking her head and frowning. That stopped Frank in his tracks.

"It's Jock, isn't it?"

"Aye, Frank. He passed early this afternoon."

"I tried to visit him this morning, but he was not allowed visitors. I'm sorry, Mum." Frank went over to his mother and put his arm around her. "I know he was your favorite bairn. You always had a sweet spot for him."

That caused Bess's weeping to escalate into a harrowing wail of grief.

"I cannae tak' this, Frank. This country's been nae guid fer us. It's just me an' Lill noo. I dinnae ken howfer we can make it."

Frank sighed. "I'll help, Mum. I'll take care of Jock's arrangements, too. Don't worry. We'll have him in Windsor Gardens with his brothers, aye? Not alone."

Bess gathered whatever composure she could muster. "Frank, if ye wuid drive me home. Lill will be wonderin' whair I've been off tae." She mechanically smoothed her hair after wiping her eyes with a handkerchief and straightening her dress.

"Sure Mum. Margaret, does Jimmy know?"

"I don't know, Frank. Maybe you should stop by after you drop your mother off and let him know."

"I will. Go ahead – you and Jackie eat. No use waiting on me. I'll eat when I get back."

Margaret quietly nodded.

* * *

Frank pulled up in from of Jimmy's and sat in his truck cab for a few minutes, just taking in the lovely May evening and thinking. It had been nothing but hardship and heartache in Michigan. Would it have been any better if everyone had stayed back in Scotland? He quickly decided no – it would have been hard anywhere.

He got out of the truck and walked up the few stairs to the wide porch. He was about to knock when the door opened.

"I spied you sitting in yer truck, Frank. Did ye need some nerve tae knock?" Jimmy was smiling and joking, but his expression turned somber as he noticed Frank's serious look.

"Wha's th' bad news? I can see it's something nae guid." He stepped back to let Frank in.

"It's Jock, Jimmy. He died earlier today."

Jimmy hung his head. "Puir Mum. She's takin' it hard, aye? What's tae become of her and Lill?"

182

"We'll have to step up, Jimmy. You and me. That's the long and short of it."

Jimmy scowled. "Step up wi' what? We're barely gettin' by, Ness and the bairns and me. Ah cannae find steady work. Day labor is the best I can do, and that's nae doin' th' job. Ness and I are seriously considering gang back tae th' auld country. How are you doing it?"

"I'm hauling trash with the truck. It was the truck that got me the job. But I only make two, maybe three trips a week. Not enough to bring on another – and you don't have a truck."

Frank paused and stared at the floor, as if the grain in that worn plank floor were whispering secrets – or offering answers.

"So, it's on me."

Jimmy said nothing. Frank looked up – his jaw now set with determination, his eyes fiery with resolve.

"No use crying over spilt milk. I'll let you know the funeral arrangements. I'm having Jock buried next to his brothers in Windsor. Give my regards to Ness and the bairns."

Frank abruptly turned and left.

* * *

"My family's fallen apart, Margaret. Jimmy's going back to Scotland. No one left here but my mum and Lill and us. I would have never thought we'd be left alone here. I'm sorry." He hung his head for a moment. His eyes were uncharacteristically soft when he looked up at Margaret. "We will make it, Margaret. Of all of them – us – we will make it. You and me and little Jackie. I will make sure of that. I promise I will give us a nice life."

Margaret dipped her head a bit, blushing slightly. She looked up with a softness Frank hadn't seen in quite a while.

"I know you will, Frank."

"You know, Margaret...new country, new people – I can be whatever I want to be. I'm going to start using my given name. I told Robbie back in the old country I would claim my name someday.

Today's the day. Not Frank… From now on, I am introducing myself as Robert. Robert Sharp."

CHAPTER TWELVE

"Scotty, we've been pushed out of the booze business. Not a very good Christmas present." Caravaggio had summoned Robert to his favorite eastside Italian restaurant. Robert was now an expert in ordering off the menu.

"We knew repeal was coming, Mr. Caravaggio. It was a good run."

"You're a good man, Scotty. We have other, um, interests. We could talk about moving you over."

Robert took an appreciative drink of wine before answering.

"I appreciate the offer, Mr. Caravaggio. I really do. However, I think I'd like to move on. I was very comfortable with the liquor – the law was stupid, anyway. I don't think I would be a good fit with your other interests. I'm moving my family to Garden City. I've bought a piece of property there. Going to build a house for my family. I think it's time we part ways. No hard feelings?"

"None taken, Scotty. I thought you might be interested, that's all."

"I hope we part as friends. I can't thank you enough for what you have done for me. I mean that. It has meant the world to me and my family. Like I said, it has been a good run."

Caravaggio finished what was left of his cannoli and put down his fork.

"Keep my number, just in case. We in the Partnership have

some work to do. We need to discuss how we will replace this formerly lucrative piece of business. If something comes up that I think would fit, mind if I call?"

"Not at all, Mr. Caravaggio."

Robert folded his napkin and put it to the side as he stood.

"It's been a pleasure doing business with you. Really. Merry Christmas to you!"

"To you, too, Scotty."

Robert wasn't sure what he was going to do now that Prohibition was repealed, but he had squirreled away as much money as he could manage for the last twenty-two months. He hadn't told Margaret about the piece of property he had bought – he was waiting for Christmas. He decided to check on his mother and Lill before heading home.

It always broke his heart to see the people in Clark Park lined up for some soup. Although it was December, people in tents were still there, living off the charity of the residents of Detroit. He had made sure neither his mother nor Lill needed Clark Park charity.

"Aye, Frank! Guid tae see ye!" Lill opened the door wide. She smiled broadly as she extended her left hand. "Frank, I'm tae wed Jim Hooks!" She was brimming with happiness.

"I'm happy for you, Lill! But can you not remember I'm going by Robert now?"

"Yer always be Frank tae me. Frank." She grinned.

"So, when's the big day?"

"February fourteenth. Valentine's Day. 'Tis romantic, aye?"

"Lovely. Jim's a good man. Where's Mum?"

"She's nappin' noo. I'll wake her – cannae sleep a day away, anyway."

Lill ran upstairs, and shortly she and Bess came back down.

"A cuppa tea, Frank?" Lill headed automatically into the kitchen. She returned several minutes later with a tray.

"How's work at the laundry, Lill?"

"'Tis fine. Glad tae still have a job, even wi' a wage cut. Better that than the soup line."

Robert reached into his pocket and came out with a ten-dollar bill.

"Here. This should help. Are you coming over Christmas?"

"Oh my! Ten dollars? Are you sure? That's so generous!"

"No worries, Lill. That's for you and Ma."

"Well thank ye, Frank. Christmas? Aye. Lovely. Mind if I bring Jim?"

"Not at all. And could I ask you to call me Robert?" Robert sipped his tea and took a scone off the tray. "Mum, your scones are always my favorite." He finished it and washed it down with the rest of his tea.

"We'll see you Christmas, then. I'd best be going home." Robert hugged Bess and Lill, grabbed his cap, and left.

* * *

Margaret was busy stuffing the goose they had raised for Christmas dinner early Christmas morning when Robert came into the kitchen.

"Can you finish that later? There's something I'd like to take you and Jackie to see."

"Can it wait?"

"Just put the goose in the icebox and you can finish up later. You, too, Jackie! I have a surprise for you."

Jackie's excitement made the request seem so reasonable. Margaret smiled as she stopped what she was doing and put everything into the icebox.

"Whatever do you have up your sleeve now, Fr…Robert?"

"You'll just have to get into the truck and come see." Robert grinned from ear to ear.

The three drove west, down Warren, past Dearborn, out into empty fields. He turned left on Merriman. A few blocks down, he pulled onto a side street and stopped the truck.

"And what's this? A field?" A wave of disappointment washed over Jackie's face, and a hint of irritation flashed across Margaret's face.

Robert got out and walked over just past the edge of the dirt road. He raised his arms, extending them to each side as far as he could, and spun around.

"This, my dear family, is where I am going to build us a new home."

Margaret gasped. "You bought property?"

Robert came over, grabbed Margaret by the waist, lifted her, and spun her around. "Yes, my love. This parcel is ours. Three-quarters of an acre. Room for a big garden and a nice chicken coop, at least. Maybe even room for a sheep or two. Or a goat or two. Merry Christmas!"

"How did you manage that?"

Robert grinned. "I dinnae put oor money in th' bank."

Margaret laughed.

Robert turned to Jackie. "Lots of room for you to explore, Jackie. And you can help build the house!" He continued talking as he headed to the truck bed. "And I saved this present for until we got here…" He reached into the back and pulled out a cloth-wrapped parcel. He turned to his son as he held out the gift. "You can use this out here."

Jackie ripped into the package, untying the string and unfolding the muslin. His eyes opened wide with excitement.

"A BB gun!! Wow!!" He grinned from ear to ear as he examined it. He then held it up and aimed it at a nearby tree.

"No ammunition in it, Jackie. First, I need to teach you how to take care of it and how to use it safely."

Jackie lowered it. Then he lifted it to aim at a different tree.

"Da, this is the best!" He ran over to give Robert a hug. Robert held him off.

"You're nine now, lad. Hugging is for bairns – not for men."

* * *

It was a cold day in February, and Robert was standing on the corner of Fort Street and Clark along with a dozen or so other men early in the morning, looking for a day's work. Soon a Ford Model A pulled up, and a suited man got out.

"You men looking for work?"

"Yes, sir," said an eager young man.

"The Briggs Plant on Mack Avenue will take the lot of you. Get there as soon as you can." The man got back into his car and left.

There was a bit of grumbling – the plant was several streetcar changes and several miles away. Robert turned to the group.

"I have a truck. If you don't mind piling in the back, I can get us there. Fifteen cents a man."

Again, there was a bit more grumbling, but the offer was too good to pass up. Robert ran home and came back shortly. Loaded up, he took off towards the plant. Everyone was shocked to see a picket line. While the men climbed out of the truck bed, Robert approached one of the strikers.

"What's going on?"

"We're on strike. They tried to cut our wages again. We've had enough."

"Didn't know that! It wasn't in the paper."

"Oh, no – the company made sure we didn't make the news. How did you happen to come here?"

"The lot of us were gathered, looking for daywork, and some man drove up and said there was work here."

At that, the picketer stiffened.

"Scab work! I don't think so."

The day laborers were listening to the conversation. A couple tried to push through but were shoved back. Robert wasn't one of them.

"How long have you worked here?"

"Six years. Used to be decent, but lately there's been a lot of wait hours when we don't get paid. Many of us are getting ten, maybe twenty hours of work a week. And now they want to cut that."

Robert looked down at his shoes and pondered what the picketer had said before looking back up.

"I won't be crossing your line. I'd like work, but I'm not of a mind to undercut you."

The picketer relaxed some.

"Thanks. Say – what's your name?"

"Sharp. Robert Sharp."

"Mine's Haupt. Helmut Haupt. When you hear this strike is over, look me up. I'll talk to my committeeman. Maybe we can get you in the union and on the list for a job. We're pushing for forty cents an hour."

"I'll keep that in mind. Good luck to you."

Robert turned to the other day laborers. "I'm not crossing the line, so I'm headed back. If you want a ride back, climb in."

About half the men climbed into the back of the truck, and Robert headed back to Southwest Detroit.

Robert was stacking some lumber when Jackie got back from school.

"Jackie, put your books down and come with me. We need to gather more lumber."

Jack quickly ran in to drop off his books, and then he came back out and climbed into the truck. The two headed out to some of the older neighborhoods, looking for dilapidated, abandoned homes. Anything remotely habitable had squatters – the two were looking for hopeless shells of former homes. They found one just as it was getting dark.

"Quick, Jackie. See those pieces that have come loose? Pull them off and put them in the back." The two worked until it was too dark to continue, filling the truck bed half full before leaving for home.

Margaret was putting supper on the table when the two returned.

"How was your day, Frank?" She caught herself. "Robert. You know, after all of these years, it's going to take me a while to remember."

"That's fine, Margaret. I understand. My day was interesting. A Briggs company man stopped by the corner and told us we could all work. I drove the lot of us over to Mack Avenue, only to find that apparently there's a strike at the Briggs factory. I ended up speaking to one of the strikers. I decided not to cross the picket line, which he appreciated. He took my name. I did get a few hours of work in, heavy lifting. Made some good money on a bet I couldn't lift an engine block. I made more money on that bet than I made actually working."

He spooned some potatoes onto his plate as he spoke. "Once the weather breaks, Jim Hooks agreed to help me dig for footings. Thirty by thirty. I hope to be able to gather enough brick for the entire house. Two bedrooms, with an attic. I've been sketching some plans. After dinner, while Jackie is doing his schoolwork, want to sit down with me and look at it?"

"After the dishes are cleaned, yes. Sounds lovely."

* * *

As soon as the ground thawed, Robert and his brother-in-law Jim started digging for footings on days when they couldn't find work.

"Have you moved in with Lill and Mum?"

"Nae." Jim scowled. "Bess's nae fond o' me. Even though we're marrit, she's nae havin' me live wi' ma wife. Says I need tae have oor own home afore I can live wi' ma wife."

Robert laughed at that. "Well, that certainly sounds like my mother. I'm sorry. Tell you what. I'll ask Margaret if you can board with us in return for your help building. That should help you save money for your own place and help me get this house up."

"If you cuid do that, Frank, I'd be in yer debt!"

"Don't thank me yet. It's got to get by Margaret."

That night, after supper, Robert and Jackie went on their usual scavenger run.

"Tonight we're looking for concrete blocks, Jackie. They're this big" – Robert held up his hands a foot apart – "and this tall." He moved his hands so one was over the other. "They are gray. Okay?"

Jackie grinned. "I love these runs with you, Da." He climbed into the truck, and a few hours later, they returned with maybe two dozen used cinder blocks.

"Now, Jackie, this is what I want you to do." Robert handed Jackie a small hammer and a chisel. "You need to knock off the mortar on these so we can reuse them. Watch me." Robert placed the chisel between a piece of mortar and the block and struck the head of the chisel with the hammer. The mortar flew off. "Here. You try."

Jackie's first try was a failure.

"No – watch. Lay the chisel tip so, when you hit it, it's driven down the side of the block. Not against it – alongside it. Like this." Robert demonstrated once again.

Jackie's second attempt was better, but not elegant like his father's. "That's better, son. Keep at it – you'll get the hang of it."

Robert stacked the cinder blocks next to Jackie. "Now clean all of these up, son. We'll go out again to get more when these are cleaned properly."

* * *

"Jackie, come help me pitch this tent." Robert was laying out the canvas tent and dropping pegs at the tiedown loops.

Jackie came running. "Are we camping here tonight, Da?"

"Yes we are, Jackie. Your uncle Jim and I want to start laying the footings first thing in the morning. With any luck, if we work from daybreak to when the sun sets, we can lay the entire foundation."

Margaret walked over from the truck, carrying a large basket.

"Robert, when Jackie is done, can you send him over to help me plant the garden? A bit of a late start, but that's the best we can do this year." She headed over to the plot that Robert had turned over for her and knelt down and started with the beans.

"Tell you what, Jackie. I'll get Jim to help with the tent – go help your mother. She's right about a late start. We need to get that garden in if we are going to eat well this coming winter."

Jackie hesitated.

"Go on now, son. Go help your mother."

The foursome worked until nearly dark. Robert built a campfire, and they sat around eating sandwiches that Margaret had brought.

"I love camping." Jackie was sitting cross-legged, watching the flames dance in and around the fire logs.

"You've been a good helper today, Jackie. Tell you what. If you keep being such a good helper, I'll take us all camping to the Irish Hills for Independence Day. Would you like that?"

Jackie's eyes lit up. "Oh, yes, Da! That would be so fun!"

"Well then, from now until then, you do everything asked of you. And that starts now. We need to go to sleep because we are getting up very, very early. All right?"

"Yes, Da."

Robert put out the fire, and everyone headed into the tent for the night.

* * *

By the Fourth of July, the footings were set, the sill plates down, and the exterior wall framing up and secure. There was much work to do, and both Robert and Jim worked around any day jobs they managed to get. Nevertheless, Robert took Margaret and Jackie to the Irish Hills like he had promised.

"Robert, this is an extravagance. Lovely, but we have so much work to do." Margaret didn't usually fret.

"Margaret, I made a promise to Jackie. Didn't I, Jackie?"

"Aye, Da."

"And you did what I asked of you, didn't you?"

"I did, Da. I worked hard."

"That you did. Jackie. The only men worth their salt are men who keep their word. There's nothing more important. So, even though we do have a lot of work to do, it's more important that we're men of our words. Understand?"

"Yes, Da."

Now, we can only stay a few days, right? You understand that we have got to get back. But for the few days we are in the hills, we will have a really good time. Did you bring your BB gun, baseball mitt, bat, and ball?"

"Yup!"

"Like I said – we are going to have a very good time, laddie. A splendid time."

Margaret simply smiled.

* * *

By the first of August, the bungalow on Edgewood had a roof, siding, windows, and doors. It was closed to the elements, and that was all that really mattered. Margaret quit her job, and the family moved out of their rented home in Detroit. Without the expense of rent, utilities, or a phone, Robert had enough money left to last until the following spring.

He stopped taking day jobs and devoted his time to building the house. He built furiously throughout August, but when September neared, he sat down on the concrete entrance step and called Margaret over.

"Margaret, I'm not making progress fast enough to have the house fit for you and Jackie in winter."

"What would you have us do?"

"I'll ask my mum to take you in until spring."

Margaret fell silent, thinking.

"If it's all the same to you, I would rather ask Jeannie Wilson if we can stay with her in Hamilton over winter. Your mother and I would have a terrible time under the same roof. All she would do is complain about the extra mouths to feed. Jeannie and Bob have a bigger house, and Jackie can go to school with their son, Will. I'd be happier. Bob has a good job – I think it would be easier for everybody."

Robert stared at Margaret. "I never knew you and my mum had issues."

"It would just be bad, Robert. Trust me. Let me write Jeannie and see if they'll have us. Now, I'd best be getting back to cooking." She got up and went to the stone fire pit where a cast-iron pot was sitting in hot embers.

The last week in August, the letter from Jeannie Wilson came. Margaret waited until she could open it with Robert. A smile came across her face as she read it.

"Jeannie says yes. School starts the first week of September… She asks whether you can get us there this weekend. I'll have to enroll Jackie in school."

"I'll do that. I'll miss you fiercely, though. You and the lad."

Margaret's mind wasn't on Robert's response.

"I'll have to harvest the garden and can as much as I'm able. I'll also can all of the chickens so you have food to eat. Can you manage to take your laundry into Dearborn? And where will you sleep when it's too cold in the house?"

"Don't worry on me, Margaret. I'll get by. I like your idea of canning everything. If you and Jackie could get all of that managed before the weekend, I should have enough food for a long while."

"I hope I have enough jars… Let me go count. If not, have we enough money to buy more?"

"Just tell me what you need."

Margaret left to find the boxes that held kitchen supplies within the stack of belongings covered with sheets in the middle of the unfinished living room.

"Jackie!" Robert called out across the field to his son, who was busy climbing a tree. "Come on in, son."

Jackie clambered down the tree trunk and came running.

"Jackie, you and your mother are going to Ontario for the school year. You'll be staying with Mr. and Mrs. Brand and their son, Will."

Jackie first looked at his father in disbelief, and then waves of sadness washed over his face as he hung his head.

"I don't want to go, Da. I want to stay here with you and build."

"You've been a great helper, son. But look around. The house doesn't have heat or plumbing yet. It's not fit for you or your mother to live in come winter. You spend the school year in Hamilton and come back when school is out. By then, the house will be in fine shape."

"Will you come visit?"

"Of course I will. I will come for Thanksgiving and Christmas and other times, too. And when you come back, we'll have a finished house. I will miss you, son, but this is what must happen."

Robert put his hands on Jackie's shoulders. "We'll be taking you up this weekend. I'll need you to help your mum can all of the chickens and vegetables before then. It's going to be a big job, and she'll need you to get it all done. It's what will feed me all winter long. Can you do that for me?"

"Aye, Da. I will."

"No problems catching the chickens for your mum to can?"

"No, Da. I want you to be able to eat."

"That's a good lad." Robert patted his son's head. "Now, get along."

Jackie ran into the house and helped his mother gather the canning supplies.

* * *

"I've put up everything from the garden and all of our chickens. I've stacked them all in the corner for you. We'll have to buy new chicks in the spring. I've finished the new jumper I made for you – nice, thick wool, it is. Here." Margaret handed over a thick turtleneck sweater she had just finished knitting. "All of your clothes are clean. I've stacked all of our blankets by the bed for you. I can't think of anything else. You'll be fine?" Margaret was busy cleaning up the very last of the dishes.

"I'll be just fine, Margaret. Don't worry about me. If it gets too cold here some nights, I'll stay the night with Mum. Or drive over to Windsor and look up Dan. Don't think I will need to, though – I've got shelter, even if it's not heated. I'm planning on putting in a vent for the coal stove as soon as I'm able. I should have heat in here before January. I'll take care of myself."

"Well then, we should be off. Jackie! Come climb in the truck."

Margaret headed to the passenger door while Robert put the last of the luggage in the truck bed. With Jackie between them, they set off for Hamilton, Ontario.

"Will ye come in, then?" A smiling Jeannie Wilson Brant stood at her front door. "Glad tae have ye, Margaret. I miss my friends from th' auld country." She held the door open wide.

Robert busied himself with bringing in the luggage, setting it just inside the door.

"Can I bring these suitcases somewhere?"

"Aye. Up th' stairs an' tae th' left. Jack will be stayin' with Will...across th' way from Margaret. Come wi' me tae the kitchen Margaret! We can catch up, and ye can help me wi' supper. Frank, stay th' night. It's nae guid drivin' back in th' dark. Ye can leave first thing in th' mornin'."

"You make a good point, Jeannie. Thank you for the offer. Is Bob around?"

"Nae, no yet. He'll be home from work shortly."

Robert headed out the back door, looking for Jack. He saw him up a tree with Will. Smiling, he headed over.

"I swear, son, you are part squirrel. Will...how you be?"

"Fine, Mr. Sharp."

"You don't mind sharing your room with Jackie, here?"

"Not at all. Like having a brother."

"Aye, that's good. Now, you boys come smartly when called for supper."

The two families built a campfire as dusk wrapped itself around the city.

"Come sit by me, Jackie." Robert sat cross-legged by the fire and hoisted his son on his lap. He leaned around so he could speak into Jack's ear.

"I'm going to miss you, lad. Now, you be a good boy for your mum, right? And be polite and helpful to Mrs. Brant. And don't be a bother to Will, okay?"

"Aye, Da. I will. But I don't want to stay here. I want to come home with you."

"We've talked about this. You can't be jumping schools. You and your mum will stay here until school's out in the spring. I'll come visit, I promise. And when school's out, you'll be coming home to a finished house."

Robert wrapped his arms around Jack and leaned into him.

"I'll come visit, Jack. You're my boy. It'll be spring before you know it."

The two watched the tendrils of flame flutter around the logs and the small pinpricks of embers rise above the fire.

"I'll be leaving at daybreak, Jack. We need to say our goodbyes tonight. I'll be back in a couple of weeks to see how things are going."

Jackie snuffled.

"Now, men don't cry!" Robert's voice was stern. "You must be a man. I'll have none of that from you."

Jack wiped his nose with the back of his hand. He snuffled again.

"Now, that's it." Robert lifted Jack off his lap. "Go to your mum. I'll not have a whimpering child. You're not a wee bairn anymore, Jackie. Stop acting like one."

Jackie ran over to Margaret, crying. She wrapped her arms around him but echoed Robert's message.

"You can't be crying now, Jackie. Nothing to cry about. We all do things we have to, even if we don't like to. Life is hard, and you'll not be doing well unless you toughen up."

The fire was soon down to glowing embers. Robert stood.

"I'll be off at daybreak. No need for anyone to see me off. I'll be back in a couple of weeks." He went over to Bob Brant and handed him twenty dollars. "This should keep for two weeks. Thank you for taking in my family. Good night to you."

He went over and gave Margaret a kiss on the head. "I'll see you in a couple of weeks, Margaret." He tousled Jack's hair. "Be a good lad, now."

He was gone long before anyone else awoke the next morning.

*　*　*

Robert had never awakened alone. He lay in bed for a few minutes, considering that fact. Everything was so quiet. There was no aroma of breakfast wafting through the window – no sleepy-eyed child getting roused to feed the chickens.

He rolled out of bed and looked around at the shell of a house. His work was cut out for him. He headed to the outhouse. Then he started a fire and put the coffeepot close to the flames. Looking west, he noticed clouds rolling in. While the coffee brewed, he brought several two-by-fours into the house and made sure the tarp was secured around the rest. It looked like rain – today would be studwork.

Robert became lost in his work, stopping only to bring up a can of chicken and a can of green beans. The rain had indeed come, extinguishing the fire. He ate the chicken and beans cold.

He fell into a predictable routine: two days a week, on dry days, he looked for day jobs. Every other weekend, he traveled to Hamilton. And when not working and not traveling, he worked from sunrise to sunset on the house.

By May, the house was ready…all except digging out the basement. That was left for the summer of 1934, when Jim Hooks and little Jackie dug out the dirt. A coal-fired furnace, complete with a coal bin, was installed before winter. It had taken the better of two years, but Robert had built a snug and sturdy little two-bedroom brick bungalow.

* * *

"Margaret, I've been having a hard time getting day work lately. There are so many men and so few jobs." Robert was discouraged. "Do you suppose we could move Jackie up to the attic and take in a boarder? That would help keep the house running."

"There's no heat up there, Bob."

"If we keep the ladder down, heat will rise. It won't be warm like down here, but it won't be freezing, either. We could use the money."

Margaret sighed. "I'd rather try to get my job at Banner back. Can I try that first?"

Robert put his head in his hands for a moment before looking back up at his wife.

"Margaret, I am so sorry. It's these tough times. It just seems it will never end."

"We're in this together, Bob. You've built us our own home – not many are that fortunate. Jackie's twelve now – he doesn't need me like he used to. I don't mind working. Let me see if I can get my job back."

"You're a fine wife, Margaret. I will make it up to you."

"I know you will, Bob."

The next day, both Margaret and Robert boarded the streetcar that ran down Warren Avenue and headed to Detroit – Robert didn't want to use what little money he had on gasoline. He got off to stand with the other men looking for day work, and Margaret headed to Banner Laundry.

It was a warm spring day, and more men than usual were looking for work. A couple of trucks pulled up and hired a few men... Robert and two other men were queried by the burly man in the third truck that pulled up.

"I'm looking for a few men to move demolition debris into trucks. Heavy work. You men interested? Twenty dollars each for a day's work. One day only."

Robert was the first to answer. "Yes! I'd love the work." The other two men were just as accepting. The three climbed into the back of the stake truck and took off.

"Hi. My name is Robert." He reached over to shake the other two men's hands.

"Bill," said the first, and the second followed with, "Harold."

"Glad to make your acquaintance. Good thing we got picked up today! I can use the work."

"You're not only sayin' it." Bill grinned. "Yer a fellow Scot, I see."

Robert grinned. "Aye, that I am. You've been here long?"

"Aye, since 1920. You?"

"Nineteen twenty-nine."

"Och – nae a guid time tae come, aye?"

"Could have been better." Robert turned to Harold. "And you?"

"I was born here. My folks came up from Tennessee for work right before I was born. I was working at Ford before I got laid off. Most of us were laid off. Been tough since then."

"For the lot of us. I worked at Studebaker, but only for a few months before getting laid off. It's been touch and go since then." Robert was careful not to mention how he had made money before Prohibition was repealed, and he didn't mention he had saved enough to build and own his own home.

The truck came to an abrupt stop in front of the old federal courthouse, half of which had been knocked down. Several trucks were waiting to be filled with debris. The three men got to work, and by sunset, the pile was gone. Dusty and exhausted, the three men collected their pay and wearily climbed into the bed of the truck to be taken back to their corner. By the time Robert had walked back home, it was already dark.

"I've some stew for you, Robert. Clean up – I'll set it out for you." Margaret busied herself with getting supper out.

"Where's Jackie?" asked Robert as he washed his hands.

"He's out back, securing the coop. Could ye change into other clothes before you sit? You're a bit of a dusty mess." Robert sighed and slipped out of his dirty clothes, leaving them on the floor as he went into the bedroom for cleaner garments. By the time he was back, Margaret had the clothes in the laundry basket and was pouring herself a cup of tea as she sat across from Robert.

She sipped while he ate. "Banner's no hiring right now, Bob." She stirred her tea absentmindedly. "I'm sorry. I left my name as interested. The manager remembers me and says, when there's an opening, he'll call right away."

Robert was busily eating his stew and bread. He was silent until he finished wiping the bottom of the bowl with the last piece of bread. "Well, you tried. I'll put an ad for a boarder tomorrow. Shouldn't be hard to find someone. What do you think, ten dollars a month?"

"I have no sense for that, Bob. Whatever you think is best."

"Well, maybe seven fifty. Ten might be a bit dear. Yes. Seven fifty."

Just then, Jack came in the back door.

"Jackie, come sit."Robert patted the chair seat next to him. "Son, you know times are tight."

"Yes."

"Your mum and I are putting an ad in the paper for a boarder. You'll have to move to the attic."

Jack hung his head. "It's cold and dark up there."

"I'll put in lights for you. We'll get you extra covers. I'm sorry, Jack. Work is hard to find, and your mum went to get her old job back. Not hiring. As soon as things turn around, we'll make it right. I promise. We don't have a boarder yet… No worries right now."

Robert paused.

"Tell you what… Let's you and me start a baseball team. I'll coach. Can you get your friends together for that?"

Jack suddenly wasn't so glum.

"I'll ask tomorrow! That will be fun!"

"Run along, then. Almost time for bed."

"Margaret, is there a spot of tea left?"

Margaret got up and emptied the teapot into Robert's cup. He took it to the living room and turned on the radio. Margaret followed, sitting next to the lamp and picking up a sock she was darning.

"Margaret, I was thinking to buy a gosling. By Thanksgiving, he should be nice and plump. What do you think?"

"That would be lovely."

A quiet settled over the home as Robert sat back and listened to Maxwell House's Showboat on the radio while Margaret darned.

* * *

"Hello. I'm here to answer your ad?"

Margaret opened the door and stood back as the young man entered.

"William Walker," said the man, extending his hand.

"Won't you come in, Mr. Walker? Let me go fetch my husband." Margaret led him to the living room and then left to call Robert in from the back.

Robert came striding in, extending his hand.

"Robert Sharp. Margaret says you are inquiring about the room?"

"William Walker," said the man, shaking Robert's. "Yes. I am interested in your room."

"You have a job, Mr. Walker?"

"I do. I work at the shoe store in Dearborn."

"How long have you been there?"

"Two years. My employment is steady – my uncle owns it."

"And how old are you?"

"I'm twenty-four, sir."

"Well, let me show you the room." Robert led the young man to the small second bedroom. "The room comes with breakfast and dinner. Seven fifty a month."

Walker looked around. "It's very tidy. I would like to take it, Mr. Sharp."

"Rules are no smoking or drinking. No partying. No women. We have a son, so we expect quiet after nine. If you will not be at dinner, you are to tell my wife that morning. Bundle up your sheets and clothes Friday night for washing. Rent is due bi-weekly – three seventy-five payable in advance."

"I'll take it!" Walker pulled out four dollars from his pocket. "I don't have change – can you put the twenty-five cents to the next payment?"

Robert took the money. "Certainly. When will you be moving in?"

"Will next Saturday work?"

"Fine." The two men shook hands. "Until Saturday, then."

"Nice to meet you, Mrs. Sharp." Walker took his leave.

By the time Jack came in for supper, all of his meager belongings had been moved up to the attic. Margaret put a bright, new calico quilt she had made on the bed, over a heavy, close-knit wool blanket. Robert had built shelves for Jack and run power for lights. It was significantly larger than Jack's old bedroom, and both Robert and Margaret tried to make it appealing to their son.

"I'll no be coming up here to clean, Jack. This is yours now. You're near a man, and this is your private space. You're to keep it tidy now."

"Yes, mum." Jack looked around, rather liking the independence he felt. His BB gun, bat, and glove were neatly placed on a shelf, with space for more things should he get them. "This will do."

"Have you spoken to your friends about the baseball team?"

"Yes – they are excited."

"How many said yes?"

"About a dozen. All the lads on this street and the next."

"Tell them to meet at the diamond Saturday at noon. We'll start practice, and I'll start looking for teams to play. You lads need to come up with a team name."

Jack grinned. "That shouldn'a be too hard. I'm partial to the Flyers."

"You'll have to get agreement. Let others suggest names, too."

* * *

Saturday came quickly, and a good dozen lads turned out with their bats and gloves, ready to play baseball.

"Okay. My name is Coach Sharp. How many of you have played baseball? Real baseball, with all of the rules about outs and strikes and the like."

Most of the hands went up.

"Okay, then! We'll need to have position tryouts. Can you name the positions?"

The boys rapidly called out positions.

"Catcher!"

"Pitcher!"

"Outfield!"

"Shortstop!"

"Excellent! We will have pitcher tryouts first." Robert had built a tripod using some old plywood and had drawn a prominent box in the middle. He placed it behind home plate.

"Okay. Lads, line up behind the pitcher's mound." He brought out three baseballs. "You each get three tries a turn. The area inside of that box" – he turned and pointed to the plywood tripod – "is the target. Try to hit inside the box. After you've made your three throws, run and pick up the baseballs, give them to the lad behind you, and go to the back of the line." I will keep track."

Robert took his clipboard and walked down near the tripod.

"First up! What's your name, lad?"

"Peter, coach."

"All right, Peter. Show me what you've got."

Peter missed all three times. He ran to pick up the baseballs.

"Just warming up, then, are you? You'll have another chance. No worries. Go give the balls to next in line, then, Peter."

"Next up! Your name?"

"Johnny."

"When you're ready, laddie."

Johnny did markedly better. He was grinning as he came to fetch the baseballs. "You've pitched before, have you?"

"Yes, coach."

"Good job. Now give the balls to the next lad and go to the back of the line."

"Next! Ah, Jackie. Give it a go, son."

Jackie's first ball was outside the square, the next was fairly dead center, and the third hit one of the lines squarely.

"One in, two out."

"But Da, the last one was spot on the square!"

"Can't let the other lads think you've got an advantage. I call it out."

Jackie scowled as he picked up the balls to take them back to the line. "No fair," he mumbled as he left.

"I'll have none of that, Jack." Robert's voice was quite stern.

Practice continued for an hour, and then Robert called the boys over.

"Have you decided on a team name?"

Johnny piped up. "I think we've settled on the Edgewood Eagles."

"Do you all agree?" Robert waited as the boys nodded. "The Edgewood Eagles it is, then. See you next Saturday. Plan on two hours. We'll assign positions at the end of next week's practice."

Robert placed his hand on Jack's shoulder as they were walking home.

"Well, did you enjoy yourself, son?"

Jack was silent for a bit. "Naw, not much, really. Not fun to be picked on by the coach." He pulled his shoulder away from his dad's hand as they continued home.

CHAPTER THIRTEEN

"I've gotten a full-time job. In fact, we all have." Robert elatedly threw his cap onto the coat rack and turned around, smiling.

"What?" Margaret looked up, startled.

"Jackie! Come on down, son," Robert called up the stairs.

The family assembled in the parlor.

"You know the movie house in Dearborn? The one on Michigan? The three of us are going to run it. Six days a week. Margaret, you can keep it clean and sell concessions. Jack, you can be the usher. The job comes with the uniform. And I will run the mechanicals. It also comes with free housing – an apartment over the bank next door."

"But we've a home, Robert. Here."

"I'm going to talk to Walker. We can rent it to him. The whole house. Extra money for us. If he doesn't want to rent it, we can find another."

"Did you already agree?"

"I did! We can earn twenty dollars a week, the three of us. Plus free housing and another twenty a month for this house... That's at least one hundred dollars a month for us!" Robert was giddy with glee.

"You agreed? Did you see the apartment?"

"No, I didn't. We can go tomorrow, though. I asked if we could take a look tomorrow."

Margaret hung her head in resignation and turned to head into the kitchen. "You're the man of the house, Robert. If that's what you've decided…"

As she crossed the threshold into the kitchen, she turned. "An apartment? No garden. No chickens. Food will cost a pretty penny more." She retreated into the quiet of the kitchen.

"Jackie, you can have five dollars a week."

"Six days a week? What about after school? What about sports? I want to try out for the wrestling team. I can't do that if I'm working six days a week."

"Earning a wage is more important that wrestling, Jack. You'll understand that someday. You'll be working with us, just like I worked with my da and brothers when I was your age."

Jack glumly turned and headed back up to his attic room.

Robert headed into the kitchen. He walked up behind Margaret and wrapped his hands around her waist.

"Full-time work, Margaret. After all these years of struggling with day jobs. It's my job to support my family, and here is our chance. I would have preferred just me, but let's not look a gift horse in the mouth, shall we? Full-time work. For all of us."

"No garden. No yard. No space."

"Tell you what, Margaret. We will save our money. I will buy you a better home. As soon as we have enough money. This apartment won't be forever. Jack is in high school now. He won't be home with us much longer. It will be just you and me. You will have the home of your dreams in a few years. I promise you that."

"We'll see." Margaret just kept cooking.

* * *

The apartment was actually larger than the bungalow. It took up the entire second floor above the bank and was bright and sunny, with large windows in every room. It had a large kitchen with a breakfast table in the middle, two bedrooms, a parlor, and a formal dining room. The bathroom had a large clawfoot tub right in the middle. The kitchen had a new refrigerator and an electric stove and oven. There was no coal furnace to tend to – heat was provided by the bank below. Margaret walked around, examining all of the rooms and the floor plan.

"'Tis a nice apartment, Robert. I'll give you that. It's big and modern. But how can I hang clothes to dry?"

Robert looked out the back window. There was a strip of grass between the building and the parking lot.

"I'll get a clothesline there, in the grass. Come look. Will that do?"

Margaret looked out the window.

"That will have to do, I guess. It is a nice apartment."

Robert smiled. "I thought you might like it. Let's walk over to the movie theater and take a look around."

As he opened the door, he casually said, "I think we should apply for citizenship. Would you like to become an American, Margaret?"

"Well, we'll not be going back home. Might as well make it official. This is our home now."

* * *

Jack burst into the house after school.

"Mum! Is Dad around?"

"Well, aren't you in a proper dither? What's so important? Da is at the movie house, loading the new film for tonight."

Jack put his books on the table and smiled broadly at his mom. "Mum, I've been invited to attend the Edison Institute!"

Margaret stared blankly.

"Mum, it's a college here in Dearborn. Henry Ford's school. I'll get to learn all about engineering and mechanics! It's invitation only. This is a big honor! I can't wait to tell Da!"

"Henry Ford's school? Isn't that for rich folks?"

"Mum, my grades in physics got me the invitation. The counselor said that it's part work and part study. I can be an engineer at

Ford!"

"That's fine, son. You'll have to speak to your da about it when he gets home."

Still beaming, Jack went to his room to do his homework before changing into his usher uniform. He wasn't finished when dinner was called.

"Robert, Jack has something he wants to talk to you about," said Margaret as she passed the stew around.

"And what would that be?" Robert replied while cutting into a fresh loaf of bread.

"Da, I've been invited to attend the Edison Institute!"

Robert put down his fork.

"Isn't that Henry Ford's school?"

"It is. I've been invited to the college. Not many get invited. Very few. It's a work and study program in engineering. I will learn all about automobiles and be offered an engineer's job at Ford when I'm done. Mr. Ford takes great interest in the students. We even get to eat Friday supper with him!"

There was a heavy silence at the table.

"Jack, it's not your place. We couldn't even afford the dinner suits you would need. I'm sorry, but it's out of the question. Those aren't our folk. You'd be out of place."

"But Da...."

"I'm sorry, Jack. We need you at the movie house Friday nights."

Jack sat in disbelief. He hung his head and then pushed himself away from the table.

"Not hungry. Think I'll do a little more homework before going to work." He abruptly got up and went to his room.

"Robert, are you sure? It seems like a wonderful opportunity. Our son – a Ford engineer! Wouldn't that be grand?"

"Margaret, Jack is not schooled in high-society ways. He would be a bumpkin with those folks. We couldn't even dress him properly. It would not go well. Trust me. It's for the best."

Dinner was finished in silence. After forty-five minutes, Robert called down the hall, "Time to go to work, Jack. Step lively. You mum and I are leaving straight away."

With that, Robert and Margaret left, followed shortly by a dejected and glum Jack.

* * *

The sun shone brightly on that perfectly glorious day in June 1940.

"John Paton Sharp, with honors."

Jack stood and crossed the stage to get his diploma. He shook the Dearborn High School principal's hand, took his diploma, and walked down the opposite stairs. After the graduating class recessed, he joined his parents in the crowd.

"Good job, son. I'm proud of you." Margaret patted Jack on the shoulder, beaming. "Such a braw laddie you've become!"

Robert reached out to shake Jack's hand. "You're a man now, son. Congratulations."

"I've made you your favorite, Jackie. Pineapple upside-down cake. Let's go have a lovely dinner. I've braised a lamb shank."

Jack removed his cap and gown and left it on the return table, and the three walked back to their apartment, climbed the stairs, and sat down for a very special dinner.

"Da, I want to go to college. I'm good at it. I can do well and get a steady job. I want to be an engineer."

"And where would you go?"

"Wayne. I can take the trolley right down Warren. They have a good physics department. I can get into engineering with a physics degree."

"And how will you pay for that?"

"I can get a line job at Ford during the summer. I can earn enough in one summer to pay for an entire year. I've already checked it out. Ford hires a lot of summer help."

"And will you pay room and board?"

Margaret angrily interrupted.

"Enough, Robert! We will not charge our son room and board! I will not have it, do you hear? I will have none of it!"

Robert looked at Margaret with great surprise.

"Ye kept him from the Edison Institute, and now ye would keep him from Wayne fer money? Nae, I willn'a have it. He wants to better himself, and you are gang tae let him. And that's the end of it!" Margaret was furious. She threw down her napkin and glared at her husband. It was an outburst Robert had never seen from Margaret before.

"Well then, all right. Earn the money for tuition, and you can go. See if you can get a shift and still usher."

* * *

"Not another war." Robert read the headlines with dismay. He shook his head and looked at Margaret. "Not another one. I'll not be enlisting this time. I learned my lesson. And Jackie, don't you be thinking of running down to enlist. You need to tend to your studies."

"As long as I can, Da. I promise. But they're already drafting men."

"You and I both have to go register for the draft, but hopefully, that's as far as it gets. School is going well? Are they drafting men in school?"

"Not yet. And yes. I'm doing well, and I like it a lot. At least, I like the science classes. Not so much history or English. We have to take those classes to graduate. The only thing good about history is this really cute girl who sits in front of me."

"Now, don't be tending to the lassies instead of your studies."

"What if I can do both?" Jack grinned as he said that. "Her name is Elizabeth – Betty – and she's a wee little thing. And a sassy one at that."

"Just tend to your studies, Jack."

"A laddie's got to have some fun. I'm going to ask her out to a movie."

Robert's face softened into a slight smile as his mind wandered back to the dance hall, the Grand March, and the fresh-faced lass with startlingly blue eyes and long dark ringlets on his arm.

* * *

"Da, some of my classmates have been drafted into the army. I don't think I can avoid it, so I'd at least like to enlist in the Air Corps. Better than the regular army, don't you think?"

"You need to finish this semester, Jack. Then you can enlist if you like. I agree – it's better than the army. I would think anything is better than the army. Wait until May, when the school year is over."

Robert was speaking as he was going through the mail. "What's this?" He looked at the return address… It was a government letter. He turned the envelope over, tore open the flap, and pulled the letter out. His face turned stony.

"Margaret. MARGARET!"

"What's wrong, Dad?" Now Jack was concerned. Margaret came running from the back room.

"I've been drafted! Labor drafted. Not a citizen two years, and I've been drafted? At forty-one years old? I have to report to the enlistment office in ten days."

Robert looked at Jack. "If I have to go somewhere, you must promise me that you'll take care of your mother. Promise!"

"Of course I will, Dad. Of course!"

Robert appeared as instructed ten days later.

"Robert Sharp?" The enlisting officer looked so young.

"Aye."

"You are not native born?"

"No. Born in Scotland."

"And are you a citizen of the United States?"

"I am. Since 1938."

"You are…forty-one, correct?"

"Aye."

"Have you ever served in the armed forces?"

"Aye. I was in the Forty-Second Blackwatch in the Great War."

"What was your rank?"

"Lance corporal."

"And did you see action?"

"Aye. I was on the Western Front in France."

The enlisting officer was quiet for a moment, and then he stood.

"May I shake your hand, sir. That was rough duty."

Robert was taken aback, but he extended his hand.

The officer sat back down and returned to the papers in front of him.

"You will not see active duty again. Tell me, what are your skills?"

"I'm good with my hands. I can turn wood and iron."

"What is your current occupation?"

"I run and maintain the mechanicals in a movie house."

"How much schooling do you have?"

"Just primary, back in Scotland."

"Have you ever built anything?"

"Built my house, sir – just me, my brother-in-law, and my son. Just the three of us."

"Did you install all of the mechanicals and electricals?"

"Aye, I did that by myself."

"And the house passed inspection?"

"First time, aye." Robert was proud of that fact.

The officer busied himself with writing for several minutes.

"Mr. Sharp, the country needs you and your skills. I am going to recommend that you be sent to construction or engineering school so you can help build plants for the war effort."

Robert tried not to look too excited.

"You should hear from us in a few weeks."

"Thank you, sir." Robert extended his hand. "Thank you very much. I'll work hard for my country."

* * *

"Well, Margaret, I'll be heading off for some schooling." Robert tossed his hat onto a coat hook as he entered the house.

"I thought you were drafted?"

"I was – am. But they told me I wouldn't see action. They said they needed me to help build plants for the war effort. They will be sending me to construction school – or engineering school. One or the other. I should hear from them in a few weeks."

Margaret was visibly relieved.

"That's a fine position, Robert! I am very pleased for you. For the both of us."

Robert walked over to give Margaret a hug. She was receptive at first, but then she stiffened up. "I should get back to the kitchen."

A week later, a similar letter came for Jack. After reading it, he glanced at the clock.

"Dad, I'm going down to try and enlist in the Air Corps."

"Right now?"

"Aye. Right now. Tell Mum I should be back by supper, but don't wait for me."

Robert and Margaret were just finishing up supper when Jack came in. There was no mistaking his irritation.

"Well, damn it all. I should have enlisted weeks ago. They aren't taking anyone into the Air Corps anymore." He grabbed a plate and went over to the stove to serve himself dinner.

"Watch your tongue, Jack. I'll not be having any profanity under this roof. Does that mean you'll be off to the army?" Margaret tried to keep the worry out of her voice.

"Yes, but in the Signal Corps. Not what I wanted, but the

officer suggested it when he heard I was a college physics major. He said it would be a good fit. I need to report for basic training next week."

"Where?"

"Illinois. It's the closest to here. I'm to take the train to Chicago, and then they will bus me to the training camp."

There was a silence at the table.

"Do what they say, son. No questions. I learned that the hard way in the Great War."

Jack looked up from his plate.

"You never talk about the war, Dad."

"Nothing I want to remember or dwell upon. It was terrible, and that's all I will say about it. Pray that you don't end up in the trenches."

Jack finished his dinner, put his plate in the sink, and went to the coat rack.

"Well, I guess I need to go tell Betty that I'll be leaving soon." He put on his cap and walked out the door.

* * *

"Margaret, come to my graduation. It's not a big ceremony, but I'd like you to be there. I passed with distinction. They are making me a construction foreman."

"You've always been a clever man, Robert. Will we stay here?"

"Aye. There are plants going up all over the place. I'll be home every night, that's for sure. Dozens of plants are going up. For planes and tanks and jeeps. And then there are the supporting plants: foundries and transmission plants and engine plants...several dozen here in the Detroit area. Pontiac, Grand Blanc, Flint, and Toledo too... I'd have to stay there during the week if I end up in Flint or Toledo, but there are so many here that I'm not worried."

"That's a relief, Robert." Margaret held up a book of stamps. "I went and got our ration stamps today. Mostly for sugar, but there's one for a pair of shoes and one for some coffee."

"We'll be saving money for sure, Margaret. Jack being gone and things starting to be rationed – and me earning $300 a month! I'll buy you a nice house, Margaret. A nice house with a big garden – on a quiet street. Already built. I promise. It shouldn't take more than a year or two."

Margaret gave him a slight smile. "That will be lovely, Robert. We need a house of our own again. Oh – we got another letter from Jack. He's in Florida teaching officers all about some top-secret something or other. He can't say. He did say that he's had several officers – he calls them "full bird colonels" – offer to take him into their units. He says his commanding officer won't let him go. Says he's too valuable where he is. He says he can come back home on a short leave next month. Says he misses Betty."

"Better than mucking in the trenches, that's for sure. Good for him. Hope he can stay stateside. Care to take a stroll, Margaret? We haven't done that in such a long time. Now it's just the two of us again. A stroll?"

Margaret shrugged. "It's a lovely evening, Robert. Let me grab a sweater."

Robert was happily surprised. He grabbed his hat, and the two took off for a stroll down the sidewalk.

* * *

"I've been promoted, Margaret. To general supervisor. It means another fifty dollars a month for us. And so…I've been looking at houses. I found one for sale. On Barton Street. It's a quiet street – only four blocks long. Near Middlebelt and Cherry Hill. Want to go look at it with me?"

Margaret smiled. "I would love to, Robert! It's time to have some land around us again. This has been a lovely apartment, but I would like somewhere without all the street noise."

"All right, then! I'll bring the car around. Meet me downstairs, in front of the bank."

219

Robert pulled up to a tidy bungalow with white siding and black shutters. It was set back from the street, which was lined with recently planted oak trees.

"Here it is, Margaret. Two bedrooms, a half-acre lot. See how quiet the street is?"

It was true: only four blocks long, the street was only used by the people who lived on it.

"Oh, this street is lovely! So quiet!" Margaret was beaming. "I hope the house is nice inside."

"It looks very well kept, Margaret. And if there's something that needs to be done inside, I can do it for you to make it right. Shall I call the realtor and set up an appointment to see it?"

"Oh, yes! I think I might like living here."

"I will call in the morning, then." Robert was thrilled at seeing Margaret happy again.

"Margaret – see? There's room for a flower garden in front. You can grow roses… I know you love your flowers. And there's room in back for a nice vegetable garden. I will call first thing tomorrow morning."

Margaret was chatty all the way back to the apartment. "We got another letter from Jack. They are sending him to Officer Candidate School. He's doing very well, it seems. He's going to be in Alabama – I think that's what he said. He also said he thinks he'll be sent to study for the medical corps. Wouldn't that be grand? Medical? He always has been such a clever boy. He says that Betty has transferred to Michigan State College, in East Lansing. He's coming back to visit her. I think they are serious. I wrote him and told him he should bring her around so we can meet her. Her father is an attorney, he says. A girl in college… What is this world coming to? What will she do with all that education once she marries? I will never understand that. I wonder if she has airs."

"Jack's a grown man now, Margaret. He can choose whomever he wants. There's no good to come from disapproving of someone he chooses. We should remember that."

"I suppose you're right, Robert. Whoever marries Jack will be our only daughter. We've precious little family left here – just Lill, her husband, and their two children."

Conversation drifted off as Robert pulled up to the apartment. "I'll be up after I park the car."

* * *

"I like it here, Robert. I like it a lot!" Margaret was beaming in her new home on Barton Street.

"I see you've planted a lovely flower garden, Margaret. It really sets off the front yard. I've a wee present for you. Stay here a minute."

Robert went out to his car and brought out a large box.

"This is for you."

Margaret lifted the lid, and out popped a little black head.

"It's a puppy! A Scottie?" She reached in and brought out a wiggling, wagging, and licking little girl.

"Oh, isn't she a bonnie one! Thank you! Has she a name?"

"No, that's for you to choose."

Margaret peered at the puppy's face.

"Bonnie. She'll be my little Bonnie." She laughed as the puppy licked her chin.

"Are you hungry, Bonnie? Do you need to wee? Come to the backyard, and then I'll fix you supper." She smiled broadly as she walked around to the back.

Margaret was still smiling when she brought little Bonnie back in, cradling her in the crook of her arm.

"I love my little Bonnie, Robert. Thank you."

Robert squirmed slightly. "I got her to keep you company, Margaret, because the government is sending me to work building a plant in Cleveland. I'll be second in command! But I'll only be able to come home every other weekend."

Margaret's smile quickly disappeared. "You have to go off?"

"I do, Margaret. Orders. At least I won't be terribly far. It's not like I'm off to the trenches again. I am truly sorry, Mag, but I have no choice. It's wartime."

He stepped over to her and lifted her head gently by her chin. "You know I hate to leave you. I truly do. I'll come back every chance I get. I promise. And I will call you every night. It will be hard to be away from you."

A solitary tear ran down Margaret's left cheek. She wiped it away with the back of her hand.

"I will miss you so, Robert." She looked around. "All this work for me to do. And no car. 'Twill be a heavy load."

"I'll have Jim Hooks look in on you if need be to fix anything that breaks or if something is just too much for you to handle alone. And I'll be back every other weekend. Hopefully, the big things that need done can wait. You know I would never ask for this."

"I know." Margaret was silent as she stroked Bonnie's head. She sighed. "I waited for you once for war. I'll do it again," she said with quiet resignation.

"That's my girl." Robert kissed Margaret on the forehead. "We'll get through this."

Robert left the following Sunday, his car packed with two weeks' worth of clothes. He stopped for gas, using the special, nearly unlimited gas stamps he had been given with the position. He got into Cleveland after supper, and he pulled into the motel where his room had been prepaid. After unpacking, he called Margaret.

"I made it, Margaret. I start tomorrow. Are you all right?"

"I'm fine, Robert. Lovely day here. I worked in the garden. Wee Bonnie fancies digging."

Robert chuckled. "She's still a pup, Margaret. She'll grow out of it."

"Oh, I don't mind. She's so cute I can hardly be angry with her."

"Well, I think I'll turn in. It was a long drive, and I need to be at the plant at six in the morning. You can leave messages for me at the front desk if need be. I left the name and number on the side table by my chair. I'm in room one oh six."

"All righty, then. Talk to you tomorrow. Good night, Robert."

"Night, Margaret." Robert hung up the phone, got undressed, flopped onto the bed, and immediately fell asleep.

Robert was fifteen minutes early at the plant. He pulled in through the construction gate and parked his car by others he found. As he was getting out, a burly man in a construction helmet walked up to him.

"May I help you?"

"Robert Sharp," said Robert as he extended his hand. "I'm your new construction superintendent."

The man, somewhat flustered, extended his hand. "Mr. Peterson said you'd be here today. I'm James Thomas, lead construction engineer. Glad to meet you. Please come this way."

James walked Robert to the steel girders and beams that would become the main assembly line for tank production. He picked up a construction helmet from a table near the entrance and gave it to Robert. "You must wear this at all times."

Robert smiled. "Of course. Not my first plant, you know. Safety glasses?"

"I'll get you some." James walked Robert past the drawing tables and over to a short, balding, paunchy man with a sour expression on his face. "Mr. Peterson? Mr. Sharp is here."

Peterson squinted through his safety glasses.

"Sharp? Glad you made it. Early, I see. There might be hope. You know anything about building plants?"

Robert was only slightly taken aback. "I do, Mr. Peterson. This will be my third plant. I believe you will find me quite competent."

"Don't know why they sent you. I told them I could handle this myself. But no – they think I need help. Six weeks behind schedule. Told them I could handle it."

"What's been the hold-up?"

"It's these damn plans. Project schedule is too demanding. Men can't easily make heads or tails from these drawings. They've had to rebuild the west end twice."

"Can I take a look?"

"Be my guest." Peterson grabbed a thick set of architectural drawings from one of the tables and shoved it at Robert. He let out an exasperated sigh as he turned unceremoniously and left to go talk to a cluster of men arguing on the far side of the area.

James shook his head. "He's a hard man to like, Peterson."

Robert unrolled the plans on the table. "Thomas, tell me – where is the problem?"

"There's nothing wrong with these plans. I'll swear to it. It's Peterson mostly. He loses his temper and calls men off plan to do this or do that. The man couldn't follow a project plan if it were drawn on the floor with chalk. Thinks he knows better than these plans. That's why things have needed to be rebuilt."

"Well then, tell you what. Can you walk me through where we are? I can run interference between the crews and Peterson and let you men do what you know best."

"I would like nothing better. I'm starting to think having you here is a brilliant idea."

Thomas pointed to an area near the rebuilt west end. "See this? This needed to be built first – before this part of the west end." He circled an adjacent area. "Peterson would have none of it. But look here…" He pointed to a support. "Peterson wanted to rush around this, so he told us to put it off. Now we have to go underneath all Peterson told us to build, and it has become a nightmare."

Robert studied the area pointed out by Thomas. "Do you have a fix?"

"Sure I do. We need to remove this superstructure" – he pointed again – "and reinforce this support. Then we need to put the superstructure back in place. We won't have a solid structure doing it backwards."

Robert took a few minutes to absorb what Thomas had told him. He finally slapped the table. "Do it. How much time will it take?"

"If we correct it now, the superstructure will be behind schedule by a couple of days. If we keep trying to work around it, we will be behind a good week."

"Two days. Change the project schedule to reflect that and send me the revision. When can I get it?"

"I'll have it to you by tomorrow."

"Great. Tomorrow it is. Can I get it by two?"

"I'll make sure of it."

* * *

Peterson was waiting for Robert in the parking lot Thursday morning.

"What the hell are you doing, overriding my direction?"

"Are you speaking of the support reinforcement?"

"Damn right I am! Listen, Sharp. I never wanted you here. If I could, I'd fire you on the spot. But the Army Corps of Engineers assigned you here, and there's nothing I can do about that. If this wasn't the war, you'd be out on your ass."

"The superstructure will not be sound if we try to reinforce it after it's up, Peterson."

Peterson's face reddened as he screamed. "Don't you dare undercut me, Sharp. Never! Do you understand?"

Robert stopped, and a calm came over him as he assessed the rage building in Peterson.

"Yes, sir." He turned and walked into the building, leaving Peterson sputtering. Robert sought out Thomas straight away.

"Hey, Thomas. Did your fix work?"

"Yes, Mr. Sharp. It worked fine."

"Still on revised schedule?"

"Yes, sir."

"Thanks, Thomas. Good work, by the way. I'd stay clear of Peterson for a while if I were you. He's positively apoplectic."

Thomas grinned. "He gets that way sometimes."

* * *

Robert was just coming into the house from one of his twice-monthly weekends home when the phone rang.

"Da? It's Jack."

"How are you, son? Still in Alabama?"

"Yes. Listen, I can't stay on the phone long. Betty and I are getting married next weekend. I know it's short notice, but I've heard I'll be shipping out soon."

"How much leave have you got?"

There was a pause, and then Jack lowered his voice and whispered into the phone, "I couldn't get leave, Dad. I'm going AWOL for the weekend. We're getting married Saturday in the Grosse Pointe Memorial Church. We'll spend Saturday night up at the St. Clair Inn, and then I have to rush back."

Robert didn't say a word.

"I've made captain, Dad. I'm an officer. I've been transferred to the infantry. We are shipping out to the Philippines in a few weeks. I've got to act fast."

'Let me get your mother."

Robert walked out through the kitchen, squinting against a bright, blinding, low sun as he called out the back door, "Jack's on the phone."

Margaret picked up Bonnie and scampered in.

"Jack! How ya be?"

Bonnie barked.

"Your da got me a wee puppy!"

"That's nice, Mum. Listen, I can't stay on the phone long. Betty and I are getting married next weekend. In Grosse Pointe. Sorry for the short notice – can't wait to see you. Oops – got to go. Love you, Mum." With that, the phone went dead.

Margaret hung up the phone, bewildered.

"Just like that?"

"He's been transferred to the army, Margaret. He's shipping out soon. Going to the Philippines."

"And where's that?"

It's in Asia. Far away. Near Japan."

All the joy went out of Margaret's face.

"He's made captain, Margaret. He's an officer. That is far better than being a foot soldier."

Margaret looked up. "Well, there's nothing to be done about it now, is there? A wedding next week. I'll have to see if I have a decent frock. If not, I'll wear the best I've got. It will have to do. Come on, Bonnie. Let's go take a look-see."

Margaret carried Bonnie to the bedroom with her. She rifled through her dresses, pulling out a light blue belted dress. She carried it out into the front room.

"Robert, what do you think of this one?" She held the hanger up with her left hand, pulling the dress in around her waist. "Will this do?"

"You will look lovely in it, Margaret. The color suits your eyes."

"We should host the bridal party Friday night, don't you think? I wonder who is standing up. Would you mind if I called Betty and asked?"

"Not at all." Robert shuffled through some papers sitting next to the radio. "Here. Here's the number at her parents'." He handed a slip of paper over. "I'm going to work outside a bit before it gets too dark."

Margaret was off the phone when Robert walked back in.

"Well, the maid of honor is a woman named Ginnie Smith, and Betty thinks that Jack has asked his cousin Jack Hooks. There'll be eight for supper here Friday night. Best we can do is roast chicken. I think I have enough sugar to make a little cake. Do we have anything for a toast?"

"Aye. I have a bottle of single malt. That should be good."

"I'll need to go get more flour for rolls. I hope it's clear tomorrow… I would hate to walk back from the bus stop in the rain."

She took the dress back to hang it in the closet, her mind busy with all of the things needing to be done for the dinner.

* * *

Betty and her parents were slightly early for dinner: Jack was not yet back from picking up the maid of honor or the best man. Robert opened the door wearing the only suit he had. He was sporting his one and only bow tie. His dress shirt, though, was brilliantly white and perfectly pressed; Margaret had seen to that. Betty entered first, smiling diffidently at Robert as she stepped to the side to allow her parents room to enter.

Andrew entered next, followed by Maria. The two were diminutive in stature and dressed in obviously expensive clothes. As Robert closed the door behind them, he noticed they had driven up in a new car. He turned and extended his hand.

"Robert Sharp. Glad to meet you. May I take your hat?"

"Thank you. Andrew. And my wife, Maria." Andrew handed over a hat made of the finest felted mohair, smiling broadly. "You've a fine son, Mr. Sharp."

Margaret came out from the kitchen after hastily removing her apron.

"Margaret, these are Betty's parents, Andrew and Maria."

Margaret dipped ever so slightly in a curtsey. "Pleased to meet you."

Robert directed the guests into the front room. "Come have a cocktail. Margaret will have supper ready soon." With that, Margaret headed back into the kitchen and donned her apron once again.

* * *

"Mum, you were awfully quiet tonight. Something wrong? Did you not like Betty's parents?"

Margaret turned away uncomfortably. "Nae, they are lovely people. But…" She put her hand over her mouth. "Did you see them smile? Lovely teeth, Jack. I have rotten teeth. I didn't want to let on. I'm not on their level, that's for sure."

She paused.

"I'd rather them think I am a quiet sort than some neer-do-well."

Robert had been listening. He walked up to her and gently grabbed her shoulders.

"Now, don't you go thinking that, Margaret. You are still a beautiful woman. However, you do have a point. For the both of us. Let me look into dentures for both you and me. It's been a long, long time since either of us felt comfortable smiling broadly. I don't want you to think less of yourself. And I certainly want you to feel comfortable around people. Let me see how much they cost. We've quite a bit put away, being that it's been fairly impossible to spend much." He kissed her on the forehead.

Still uncomfortable, Margaret lowered her head. "Now I need to see to the kitchen. I hope they don't end up thinking less of us."

"They don't, Mum. I'm sure of it," Jack said. "Dinner was delicious, as always. You did a fine job. Big day tomorrow. Think I'll turn in."

CHAPTER FOURTEEN

Jack slung his rucksack over his shoulder and walked the several blocks to his parents' house on Barton Street. His uniform hung on him limply – his malaria and amoebic dysentery from serving in the Pacific theater had made him a mere shadow of his pre-war self. He heavily climbed the few stairs to the front door and knocked instead of walking in – his parents were not expecting him.

Margaret came to the door, wiping her hands on her apron. "Jack, is that you? Are you not well? You are so thin! Come in!! Come in and let me get you something to eat." She took his rucksack from him and shooed him to the table. "Now, you just sit right down."

Jack sighed as he sat. "Sorry I didn't let you know I was on the way. I've spent the greater part of the week getting from California to Wisconsin, where I was discharged. That took some time, too, getting the papers all arranged." He let out another sigh. "It's good to be home."

"Does Betty know you're back?"

'No. I came here straight away." He interrupted his mother. "Now, don't get me anything heavy or rich – my stomach's not in great shape for that. Maybe only oatmeal for now."

Margaret brought oatmeal, toast, and a glass of milk. "Now, you eat this slowly, then. I'll go make up your bed fresh. It's so good to have you back." She smiled broadly.

"Mum! Your smile! You look great!"

At that, Margaret smiled even more broadly. "Aye, dentures. So much easier to eat now, and both your da and I look better, that's for sure. Now, let me see to your room."

Jack finished his meal, put the dishes in the sink, and headed to his room. Margaret was just finishing putting clean linens on the bed.

"Mum, I'd love to take a nap. I'm awfully tired."

Margaret turned down the covers, fluffed the pillows, and pulled the drapes shut.

"You sleep as long as you like, Jack. You need to get your strength back. Is there anything else you need? I put clean towels on the dresser. Leave your dirty clothes by the door, and I'll get them when you wake up. Do you want me to call Betty?"

"No – let me do that. After I rest. Thanks, Mum."

Two hours later, Margaret heard Jack moaning. She ran into the room to find him with a raging fever. She ran out and returned with a wet washcloth and put it on his forehead.

"I'm calling the doctor."

"Malaria, Mum. Tell him it's a malaria flare-up. Can you walk me to the tub? Fill it with lukewarm water."

"Now, you stay right here for a minute, Jack. Don't be foolish and try to walk on your own."

Margaret ran to turn on the tub spigot and then headed to the phone. Several minutes later, she got Jack up and into the bathtub.

By the time the doctor arrived, Jack's temperature had dropped, and he was back in bed.

"Evening, soldier." The doctor was unnervingly cheerful. "Malaria. You served in the Pacific, obviously. I've seen several of these cases recently." The doctor took Jack's vitals. "Not too bad. I've brought you some quinine. Take two pills three times a day. Get to the VA hospital as soon as you're able, though. Do you know where it is?"

"No, I don't."

"Southfield and Outer Drive. Quite close, actually. Lucky for you. I will send over your record – they should do a complete work-up on you. They're doing that for all sick Pacific theater soldiers."

Jack sat up to take the quinine and then laid his head back down. "I will. Thank you, doctor. Think I'll sleep a little more."

Margaret had been standing at the foot of Jack's bed.

"Mrs. Sharp, you can give him aspirin if his fever goes back up. He needs to rest."

Margaret pulled the covers up to Jack's chest and left with the doctor, closing the bedroom door behind her.

"Thank you, doctor. Will he be better soon?"

"You can expect flare-ups for a while, Mrs. Sharp. And there might be other issues – we've seen it often with these soldiers. Dysentery is also common. The VA can take care of both issues. Make sure he goes in when this spell passes."

"I will. Thanks again." Margaret showed the doctor out.

* * *

Jack slept through the night and most of the next day. When his fever abated, he washed up and headed to the kitchen, where Margaret was peeling potatoes.

"Think I'll call Betty and tell her I'm home."

Margaret simply nodded in acknowledgment, keeping to her work. Before Jack could dial, however, Robert walked in the front door.

"Aye, Jack! Your mum told me you'd come home. Said you'd taken quite a fever." Robert stood back and assessed his son. "You're a rail of a man, son. Didn't they feed you?"

"Living on C rations will do that to a man, Da. That and being sick. I never want to see a jungle again."

Robert stood silent.

Jack said softly and slowly, "Now I know why you never spoke of the Great War, Da."

Robert nodded sorrowfully. "Men should never have to witness what I saw, Jack. I imagine you feel the same, from the looks of you."

He then snapped to, regaining his usual countenance. "You'll be getting your service pay shortly, Jack. You should look for a house for you and your wife. Want me to scout around for you?"

"We can go together, Da. Once I feel strong enough to be out and about, not worrying about a relapse. I'm going to make an appointment at the VA hospital as soon as I tell Betty I'm back. The doctors should be able to tell me when these bouts of malaria will end. And maybe what to do with my bad stomach."

"Give Betty a call, then. And make your appointment. When you're done, we need to talk."

Jack joined Robert in the front room a half hour later.

"Everything fine?"

Jack smiled. "I thought Betty would snake right through the phone line. And I have an appointment at the hospital tomorrow morning! I didn't think I'd get in that fast." He sat down.

"Son, I've been discharged from the labor draft. I'm selling this place, and your mother and I are moving to California."

Jack was stunned. "I'm surprised Mum is leaving."

Robert paused uncomfortably.

"I haven't told her yet. But I'm opening a bar there. Scotty's Bar. I've found a place in Orange County – that's near Los Angeles. I don't want to leave until you and Betty are settled in a house. So, once you are well enough, I'd like to help you find a place and move in. Have you a plan for work?"

"I'm going back to school, Da. The government will pay for all of it. The GI Bill."

"Do you know what you'll study?"

"Something in the medical field. Not quite sure yet."

"And what will you do to put food on the table?"

"I've a good four years of officer's pay that I could not spend. I figure that will get me through school."

Robert sat quietly for several moments before standing up.

"Don't mention this to your mother. I think dinner should be ready. Let me know when the doctor clears you for house hunting."

Jack sat alone for several minutes, only rising when Margaret called that dinner was on the table.

* * *

Several weeks later, an excited Jack and Betty brought Robert to a newly constructed bungalow on Ludlow Street in Oak Park. All the houses were brand new: all the same, in neat little rows, with no trees and no grass.

"Da, come in and tell me what you think."

The three walked in, and Jack and Betty waited in the front room while Robert looked around, inspecting the main floor, basement, and attic.

"Seems fine. The whole subdivision is new?"

"Yes. Built for returning servicemen and their families. That's what we were told."

"And you have no problem affording it?"

"No, I don't think so."

"And you like it, Betty?"

"Oh, yes! It will be fun having my own house! I just wish we could afford carpet. Hardwood floors are so cold."

"Well then, Jack, I think you've found your house."

Betty beamed at her husband and, with an excited little squeal, went into the kitchen to look at it once more.

Robert pulled Jack towards the front door, still open and allowing the late afternoon sun to stream across the freshly finished pinewood floor.

"Jack, I will get carpet for the front room for you. But you have to make me a promise."

"What's that, Da?"

"If I ever ask – ever – you must promise you'll take care of your mother."

Jack, obviously surprised, furrowed his brow as he looked at his father.

"What? That's a strange request, Da. Are you ill?"

"No, son... It's just that you never know what's going to happen. Will you do that for her? For me?"

"Of course, Da. She's my mum."

Robert extended his hand, and Jack shook it.

"We are men of our word, Jack. What color carpet?"

* * *

Robert pulled into the driveway on Barton as the sun was low in the western sky. It filtered through the elm tree, still a sapling, that stood leafless in the front yard. Winter was on its way, and the brisk wind foreshadowed the cold, gray days to come. Robert bent into the wind and hurried into the house. He hung his coat, took off his hat, and went into the kitchen. Margaret was straining cooked potatoes over the sink.

"Are you getting tired of winter, Margaret?" He leaned over the sink. "You know I love mashed potatoes." He kissed her on the cheek.

Margaret, surprised at the kiss, smiled. "Makes no nevermind if I'm tired of winter or not, Robert. Winter comes, and that is that."

"It's not winter everywhere, Margaret. It's never winter in Southern California."

Margaret put the pan down on the counter. "Southern California? Are ye daft, man?"

Robert stepped back and quickly changed the subject. "What are we having with those potatoes?"

"And there you go, changing the subject. Stew beef and carrots. Supper will be ready shortly... You might want to wash up."

The two at dinner in silence. Robert paused with a forkful of beef halfway to his mouth. "Margaret, I have been looking at places in Orange County, California. I found a little bar we can run. The weather's always warm – and you know, the doctor told me years ago I need to stay out of cold weather."

Margaret paused and then put her fork and knife down. "You've made up your mind, haven't you? We're moving to California. When?" She looked dejected. "What about Jack and Betty? What about grandchildren? I won't be around for the bairns." She pushed her chair back strongly, stood, and took her dishes into the kitchen.

Robert didn't follow her; instead, he quietly finished his supper. Then he went into the front room and turned on the radio. Margaret cleared his dishes, and after washing them and putting the kitchen in order, she walked into the front room.

"So, tell me what you've done."

Robert turned down the radio. "I've put a deposit down on a little bar. You're right. I've already made up my mind. You'll like it, Margaret. It's lovely. You can tend your garden year round."

"Robert, there's no garden that can take the place of family. You took me away from my family coming here, and now you're taking me away from my family again." She started to cry, and then she turned and hurried into her bedroom.

Robert shook his head as he turned off the radio and stood. He looked down the hall at the closed bedroom door and sighed. Then he grabbed his coat and hat and walked out the front door. The stars twinkled in the cloudless early darkness. Robert took a deep breath as he shoved his hands deep into his coat pockets. He looked back at the front door, turned, and went for a walk.

He returned a half hour later, walking slowly up the couple of entry steps and turning the door handle. The front room was dark. He briefly turned on a lamp to hang up his coat and hat and then went to bed.

* * *

Margaret was silent and dejected as she slowly, carefully packed up the china and knick-knacks in newspaper. She wiped a tear away with the back of her hand as she wrapped the lovely teacups and saucers Robert had bought her. There wasn't that much to pack, so it didn't take long.

"Margaret, please don't be so sad. You will like California! It's never cold, and it's rarely too hot. The sun shines most every day. We will have a good life there. We can run the bar together – you can chat with the patrons. It will be easy to make friends, running a bar. We can even serve a bit of food – you're such a good cook, I'm sure it will become a favorite for a lot of people. Besides, there's so much pent-up demand – and money. It's been a long, dreary war. People are ready to have fun and spend the money they were forced to save."

Margaret remained silent.

"It will be a fine road trip across the country. We can stop at all of the national parks. We can visit the Grand Canyon! Look – here's a picture of it." Robert opened up a copy of *National Geographic* and showed Margaret a picture.

"Margaret, there are amazing wonders in this country. It will be something to remember forever. A vacation! You and I have never had a vacation. Ever. Don't you think it's time?"

Margaret finally spoke. "I'm a homebody, Robert. You should know that by now. I have never had a yen to travel about. Give me my garden and my kitchen, and I'm quite content."

"Wait till you see what I bought!" Robert ducked out to his car, returning with a medium-sized box. He placed the box on the table, reached in, and pulled out a khaki-gray contraption unlike anything Margaret had ever seen.

"It's a movie camera, Margaret. Watch." Robert recorded Margaret as she watched him.

"And what are you doing now, Robert?"

Robert smiled. "I'm recording you, Margaret. And when this is developed, you'll be able to see yourself in a movie."

"In a movie? Like at the movie theater?"

Robert laughed. "Yes, dear. And I want to record our cross-country trip. Now, won't that be grand?"

Margaret couldn't help but be intrigued. She had only seen

herself as a reflection in a mirror. Seeing herself projected on the wall would be fascinating.

"That's quite something, Robert. Quite something."

"We will have a marvelous time, Margaret. I promise. You and me, without a care in the world. On vacation. Taking moving pictures. What an adventure!"

"Well then, Robert… Here. Take these boxes and pack up your books." Margaret smiled slightly. The sight of that made Robert's spirits soar.

* * *

It was a bright, hopeful, mild November morning when Robert and Margaret climbed into their newish Ford coupe and headed west. The sun streamed into the small rear window as they headed down Michigan Avenue. They hoped to make Chicago by dinnertime.

* * *

Three weeks later, Robert and Margaret pulled into a tidy, small ranch house in Orange County, next to a cozy neighborhood bar.

"Finally! This is our house?"

"Aye, Margaret." Robert turned his head and looked at his wife. "We had fun, didn't we?"

"I'll admit, it was a marvelous trip. I never saw anything like it! That Grand Canyon…simply amazing. Not very fond of the desert, though. I'm glad we finally made it. I didn't realize we'd be so close to mountains."

"And the ocean's not very far away. Let's go get a bite to eat."

"Let me take wee Bonnie out for a little walk first."

After, Margaret kissed her beloved pup and put her back in the car. "We won't be long. I'll bring you a treat."

A kindly-looking elderly gentleman came up as Robert and Margaret entered the bar, and he shook Robert's hand, smiling. "I take it you're Mr. Sharp?"

"I am! And this is my wife, Margaret. I'm glad to finally meet you in person."

"Pleased to meet you, ma'am. I'm sure you will do well here. I'm getting a bit too old for this."

"Can we get a bite to eat?"

"Certainly!! Have a seat at the bar. I'll get some menus. We don't have a lot of variety, but it's good food."

He quickly returned with two menus, mostly filled with different types of beer and cocktails. Chicken soup, chili, and three different types of sandwiches were listed at the bottom. Cookies and ice cream. That was it.

Margaret smiled. "I can do better than this," she said quietly. Robert grinned back. "I know you can."

* * *

Robert and Margaret spent the next three weeks scrubbing and painting. Scotty's Bar opened up with mild fanfare from the town mayor and the local paper. The place was spit-shine clean and polished, and it quickly drew a crowd beyond the established clientele. Wee Bonnie was as popular as Margaret's hearty menu additions: stew, cock-a-leekie soup, and marvelous pies. It was arduous work, but Robert and Margaret fell into a busy but pleasant routine.

CHAPTER FIFTEEN

Nine months later, Robert answered a very early phone call.

"Mr. Sharp? This is Gerald MacNamara."

"Yes. I'm sorry, but we are not open at the moment."

"Gerald MacNamara from Bates and Collins Construction. I'm calling from Cleveland. Sorry it's so early – you are three hours behind us."

"How can I help you, Mr. MacNamara?"

"You were assigned to the Cleveland plant by the Corps of Engineers, right?"

"Yes, I was. I wasn't there that long, though. The war ended well before the plant was up and running."

"We know. Construction stopped dead in its tracks when the war ended, and the unfinished building has been sitting there since. Ford bought it and intends to turn it into an engine plant. We got the contract and were wondering if you would come back and finish the job for us. The construction engineer speaks very highly of you."

"Thomas?"

"Yes."

"Have you hired any others from the war project?"

"We're talking to several of them."

"Cal Peterson?"

"Yes, we've spoken to him."

Robert took a sharp breath. "If Peterson is on the job, I'm sorry, but I will have to turn down your offer."

MacNamara chuckled slightly. "That seems to be a common theme. So, what would it take, Sharp?"

Robert paused. "You put me in charge of the job and pay me adequately for that, and I will consider the offer."

"How much would you be looking for?"

Robert thought for a moment. "Six thousand a year. Plus moving expenses."

"Hmmm. Let me see what I can do. I'll be getting back to you."

Robert hung up the phone and smiled to himself. He shouted, "Shoot for the moon!!" to a very empty room as he wiped the bar down. He started happily humming.

The phone rang four days later, again very early.

"Mr. Sharp? This is MacNamara, from Bates and Collins. Have a minute?"

"Good morning, Mr. MacNamara! Yes, I have time to speak."

"I discussed your requirements with management, and we are offering the following: full control of the project, travel expenses back to Cleveland, and house hunting assistance. As regards salary, we couldn't go the full six thousand. We are offering fifty-five hundred, but we will provide pension and health benefits plus three weeks paid vacation. And if you can get the plant up on schedule, there will be a bonus in it for you."

"That's a very tempting offer, Mr. MacNamara. I will need to find a buyer for the bar I own here. Is your timing critical?"

"I'm afraid it is, Sharp. We would need you here at the start of next month... That's only two weeks away. Are you sole owner of your bar?"

"I am."

Robert thought a minute.

"Tell you what. I can find a competent bar manager faster than I can find a solid buyer, although that shouldn't take too long. We've become quite popular. If I can find a good manager and a good agent to sell Scotty's, I'll fly back next week, if you need me to, and have my wife follow when she's ready. Can you ask your management if they would stand behind the transition and loan me money, if I need it, while my place sells? Not that I think I'll need it – I just don't want to be in a position of owning a going concern in California when I will be so far away. My money's tied up in the place, and I won't be able to float a new mortgage until Scotty's sells. And given the timing, we will need professional packers. I would never leave all of that work to my wife alone."

"If it were just up to me, I would say we have a deal. Let me float this upstairs, and I'll get back to you."

"Good talking with you, Mr. MacNamara."

"You, too, Sharp. Have a good day."

Robert locked up and walked back home.

"Margaret! Margaret, where are you?"

A voice came drifting in through the open window. "I'm back here, hanging laundry."

Robert walked out back to the clothesline.

"Margaret, are you happy here?"

Margaret stopped, dropping the remaining bar cloths back into the basket.

"And why would you be asking me that, Robert?"

"Come on inside for a minute, Margaret. I think we've a good chance to move back closer to Jack, Betty, and the baby. Not back to Detroit, mind you, but to somewhere within driving distance."

Margaret pulled the bag of clothespins off of the line, dropped them into the basket over the damp bar cloths, picked up the basket, and went to the kitchen table. She dropped the basket to the side and sat down.

"Now, what are you talking about? You've gone and bought this place! What – are we just going to leave it?"

"Listen. I got a call from a big construction company. They

want me back in Cleveland to finish the plant I was working on when the war ended. Ford bought it and is turning it into an engine plant. It's behind schedule, and they've asked me to come back and finish it. I'd be top boss man. For twice what we're making here, plus medical insurance, a pension plan, and three weeks paid vacation."

Margaret stared at him in disbelief.

"All that?"

"All that."

"But what will we do with this place?"

"Sell it, Margaret. But I'd hire a manager to run it until it sells. The company will send packers to pack up everything and move it. I might have to fly to Cleveland to work and then come back to drive you back...unless you think we should sell the car here and fly you back. That might be easier."

"Fly me on an airplane?"

Robert laughed. "Yes, Margaret, fly you on an airplane."

"I've never been on an airplane."

"I haven't, either, but there's always a first time, right?"

"How far is Cleveland from Detroit?"

"A day's drive. Eight hours, I'd say. But with that kind of money, we could fly to Detroit to visit."

Margaret sighed. "I miss the new bairn, that's for sure. I've never even seen him. A wee one, Betty said. Premature. Only two pounds, twelve ounces. He didn't come home from the hospital for months, she said. I'd love to hold him."

"Well, if this works out, you'll be able to."

"When will you know?"

"In a few days. If I have to leave before you, will you be all right here for a while?"

"I was all right when you left for the war. I was all right when you were only home every other weekend while you were working in Cleveland during the war. I'll be all right here – as long as you have a manager to take your place."

Robert stood and planted a kiss on Margaret's forehead.

"Margaret Sharp, I think our day has come. Now, I'd best get back to tending the bar."

* * *

"Margaret, does this house suit you?"

Robert and Margaret were standing in the front room of a newly built, tidy, wood-sided ranch in Brook Park, not too far from the plant.

"Oh, Robert – it's lovely!" Margaret had never even entered a professionally built new home, and she was enthralled with the amenities.

Robert smiled widely. "Margaret, I told you…one day, I would make everything up to you."

"I never thought I would have a home like this." Margaret was positively beaming. "This is wonderful, Robert. Simply wonderful." She walked through the kitchen to look out over the fenced back yard.

"Perfect." She sighed contentedly.

"I thought you'd like it. Now, if you don't mind, I need to get back to the plant. Let me take you back to the hotel. I'll see how fast we can move in."

Margaret was silent all the way back, but as she exited, she turned and quietly said, "Thank you, Robert."

Robert leaned over and grinned at her as he put the car in gear.

"I told you, Margaret. It would all be worth it. See you tonight… We'll have a celebration dinner. I'll make reservations for seven at the best place in town. Wear your prettiest frock."

* * *

Margaret smiled shyly at the waiter as he took their drink orders.

"I really don't drink…" she started to say.

Robert interrupted her. "What about a spot of sherry? I know it's for after dinner, but you like it." He turned to the waiter. "Will there be a problem bringing the lady a spot of sherry before dinner?"

The waiter smiled politely. "Not at all, sir. And for you?"

"I'll have a scotch, straight. Single malt. What do you have?"

"I'd recommend the MacAllan 18, sir."

"That will be fine."

As they waited for their drinks, Robert perused the menu.

"Mag, would you like a steak for dinner?"

"You know, I have never had one, Robert. Is it good?"

Robert smiled broadly. "You just wait."

After drinks were served and dinner ordered. Robert reached into his pocket as they were waiting.

"It's June 6th, Margaret. Happy anniversary." He pulled out a ring case.

Margaret smiled. "You always do remember." She reached for the ring case, opened it, and gasped. Inside was a matched white gold wedding and engagement ring set sporting a full-carat diamond.

"My Lord, Robert! What's this?"

"Margaret, I have always felt a bit ashamed by your modest ring. It doesn't fit over here, and I want you to wear a ring the other wives will accept as equal to theirs. White gold – that's what they are wearing here in the States. Do you like it?"

Margaret's eyes teared up. "Never in all my born days… This is amazing." She removed her small garnet and gold daisy band, placed it in the box, and put on the two rings. Then she held out her hand, fingers up, to admire it.

"Never in all my born days. I don't know what to say." She reached into her pocketbook, pulled out a fine linen handkerchief, and dabbed the corners of her eyes.

"Margaret, I have put you through a lot. I know that. And you've always stood by me, even when you were sad and alone and probably miserable. I sent you to Canada, and you canned all the chickens to feed me while you were away. I took you from your family in Scotland… I took you from your family in Detroit. I left you for weeks at a time while I traveled for work. You took work at the laundry when times were tough, taking the bus. You never complained. You are a treasure, and I wanted you to know that."

At this, Margaret couldn't control the tears. She stood abruptly and went to the ladies' room, and she didn't return until she could muster dry eyes.

"Robert, I'll admit it hasn't been easy. It hasn't been easy for either of us. You are a good husband, and because of that, I try to be a good wife. I will be by your side, Robert, come what may."

"And I pledge to none other than you, Margaret, no matter what. Not now, not ever. That I promise you."

* * *

It was the dead of winter when Betty arrived, alone, bringing along a two-month-old baby girl to Cleveland.

"Margaret, can you please look after Cameron while I look at institutions for her?"

Margaret stared at a beautiful, wide-eyed, and alert little baby with a malformed right leg and arm, speechless. It was as if Martha, her long-dead first born, had come back from the dead.

"Institutions? Why?"

Betty flung open the blanket that wrapped around Cameron. "Look at her!" she snapped. "She's handicapped! How am I supposed to take care of a handicapped child?"

Margaret picked up the baby and held her protectively. "I will have her for as long as she needs me to." She cooed at the baby, who smiled back. "I'll take her forever if you want."

"No. I need to find a place for her."

"You do what you need to do. Take however much time as you need. The bairn and I will be fine. Did you bring diapers? Formula? Should I go out to get things?"

"I brought diapers and formula for a week."

Margaret looked with disgust at Betty but said nothing.

"I'll have Robert drive me into town this weekend. When are you going back?"

"Tonight. I'll take a taxi back to the airport... I need to tend to my son Jeff. He's staying overnight with a friend, and I need to pick him up tomorrow."

Betty was obviously uncomfortable around this imperfect child with the face of an angel.

"You go, then, Betty. I need to tend to the bairn and make a place for her to sleep." Margaret matched Betty's discomfort with as much unwelcoming demeanor as she could manage. "Have a safe trip back."

Margaret left Betty standing in the front room as she took the bairn with her back to the bedrooms.

"You're my little Martha, back again! Born nearly the same day...you look so much like her! No harm will come to you, little one. I will see to that," she said in a quiet sing-song, rocking the baby gently. "No harm, wee one. You are safe with me." The baby nestled down into Margaret's arms and nodded off.

Margaret took the baby to her armchair and held her for hours while she slept. It wasn't until she noticed it was 4pm that she realized she needed to start dinner and change into a clean dress. She placed the baby in the middle of her bed, surrounded by pillows, and went into the kitchen to start dinner. She had just managed to put on a clean dress and pearls, arrange her hair, fix her makeup, and return to the kitchen for a clean apron when Robert walked in.

"Jack called me at work. Where's Betty?"

"She's left. The baby's in the bedroom asleep."

"Jack was against bringing Cameron here. Betty didn't stay long – anything wrong?"

"I didn't want her to stay. What mother gives up her beautiful baby?" Margaret looked intently into Robert's eyes. "Robert, it's Martha, back again. Wait until you see her."

"We said we'd never speak her name again. Never!!" Robert's tone was surprisingly sharp. He didn't notice the hurt look that washed over Margaret's face. Curious, though, he silently went back into the bedroom to look at the sleeping child. Returning, he simply said, "The resemblance is amazing. She really is a beautiful child. I couldn't tell from the swaddling, but she looks normal."

It's only her right arm and leg. They turn in – they are bowed. And the foot and hand aren't right. I'll tend to her forever if need be. An institution! What is that woman thinking?"

"Now, Margaret, there's no good to come from causing a rift with the wife of your only son. And she's the mother; what she says goes. You don't want to be cut off from your grandchildren."

Margaret paused. "Well, if it takes years for her to decide, it won't bother me any. I'll be in no rush to ask her to come fetch the wee bairn."

The baby started to rustle. Margaret put a bottle into a pot, turned on the stove to heat the surrounding water, and left to tend to the waking child.

Dinner was slightly late that night as Margaret fed, changed, and rocked the baby back to sleep.

"Sorry dinner is a bit late, Robert."

"Don't apologize, Margaret. It's been a long time since you tended to a baby." He cut a piece of roast, piled a few mashed potatoes onto it, and stuck it into his mouth.

"We've been invited to a dinner next Friday night at my boss's house. Can you find a babysitter?"

"I'll ask the girl two houses down. I'm sure she'll sit. Friday night…is the dress after five?"

"I believe so."

"What about my black sheath, with pearls? Will that do?"

"You will look lovely in that, Margaret."

* * *

Margaret and Robert arrived at the Scavos' house at five after seven. A smiling Ed Scavo opened the door and stood back to let them in. "Welcome! Please come in! You are the first to arrive… let me take your coats."

"Are we early? You did say seven, didn't you?"

Ed laughed. "Nobody's ever right on time in this town. Don't worry." He took their coats and hung them in the front hall closet. "Please introduce me to your lovely wife."

"Ed, this is my bride, Margaret. Margaret, this is my boss, Mr. Scavo."

"Pleased to meet you, Mr. Scavo." Margaret held out her hand.

"Now, what are you drinking?"

"A highball for me, Ed. Margaret doesn't really drink… Might you have a soft drink for her?"

"Of course! Seven Up?"

"That would be nice, thank you," Margaret said quietly, trying to disguise her insecurity.

"Have a seat in the living room." Ed turned and called down the hall. "Madge, our first guests are here." He turned, waving his arm into the living room. "I'll be right back."

Madge started down the hall to greet Robert and Margaret, but the doorbell rang again. She smiled at the Sharps as she headed for the door.

Ed returned with a couple of glasses.

"How are you finding Cleveland, Mrs. Sharp?"

"It's not as nice as California," replied Margaret. Robert glanced sharply at her. "Our house is wonderful, though," she added quickly. "I'm sure we will be happy here."

Within the next half hour, the remaining four couples arrived, and the group split into men and women.

"Those Browns are hot this year! Undefeated! Five bucks say they'll win the championship."

"I certainly wouldn't bet against them." The men nodded in agreement.

"Hey, Ed. You and Madge going back down to Florida anytime soon?"

"Wouldn't miss it, Pete. Going again in March. Robert, have you ever been deep sea fishing?"

Robert was just taking a sip of his drink. Hastily swallowing, he replied, "No, Ed. I haven't. Something I've always wanted to do, though. I have always loved to fish."

"After things get settled and the plant's up and running, maybe you and Margaret would like to come down and join us for a week or so. I have a great fishing rig down there."

"You should really consider going, Robert. Peg and I went last year, and we had a wonderful time." Pete mashed his spent cigarette into an oversized ashtray.

Robert grinned. "Let's get the plant up and running first, shall we? Then we'll see."

"Do you think we will make plan?"

Robert looked Ed straight in the eye. "I will make plan, Ed. You can count on it."

As Robert took another sip, he saw Margaret standing in the doorway. "Excuse me a minute," he said as he put down his glass.

"Margaret...something wrong?"

"Can we leave, Robert?"

He looked at her questioningly as he led her to the front hallway, away from the crowd.

"Are you not well?"

Margaret wore the saddest expression. "I simply don't fit here, Robert. I am so uncomfortable. I have nothing in common with these women. I don't shop where they shop, and they talk at length of the latest fashions. I don't even know the latest fashions. They talked about their antics in high school... I left school at twelve to work as a house servant. They play bridge together –I was asked to join, but I know nothing of the game. They go out to lunch on Wednesdays, but I've got the bairn to tend to. Besides, I don't have a car, and I don't drive." There was an audible catch in her voice. "I just don't fit." Her voice was merely a whisper.

Robert cupped Margaret's chin in his hand.

"I am sorry you are so uncomfortable, Margaret. I'll say you've taken a headache. We can leave."

"Thank you. I'm so sorry."

Robert made his apologies, grabbed their coats, and took Margaret out to the car. The car was silent until they were halfway home.

"Margaret, it's important that we socialize with the people I work with. Very important… It's how things are done. So, first thing on the agenda: I will teach you how to drive. If you go to lunch with the ladies, you'll need to also learn how to play bridge."

Margaret remained silent.

"And where do these women shop? We will go there and get a knowledgeable saleslady to help you with fashionable clothes. You are a beautiful woman, and you still have your figure. You will light up the room in no time."

Margaret hung her head. "You know I'm a bit shy, Robert. This is very important to you?"

"Yes, Margaret, it is. In fact, I would say it's an absolute necessity."

She sighed. "If you say so, Robert. I will do my best."

He smiled and reached over to squeeze her hand. "That's my Margaret."

There was another long silence.

"Oh – and Margaret…this is a little thing. Remember when my boss asked you how you were finding Cleveland? You said that it's not as nice as California. That is very true, but could you please try and be a little less candid? People expect niceties with small talk. You can make people uncomfortable if you are too direct."

Margaret sighed. "You know I'm very honest, Robert. It's not as nice as California – you know that."

"Well, you're right, but please try to say something positive. You can even change the subject... Say something like, 'This opportunity was too good to pass up,' or, 'I love the park two blocks away.' Anything positive, especially at a social gathering."

A tear streaked down Margaret's face. "I told you I don't fit."

"I'll help you, Margaret. This is our life now... I'll help you adjust."

After a few minutes, Robert spoke again. "Jack called – he's coming to get Cameron. Betty has decided that Cameron can stay home. You'll have plenty of time now to get to know the wives."

* * *

Robert walked into Ed Scavo's office nine months later.

"You asked to see me?"

"Scotty, you did well! We even got a bonus for finishing ahead of schedule. Grab your coat... There's someone I would like you to meet." Ed reached for an umbrella and his coat, and he slung it over his arm as he walked through the door.

Robert fetched his coat and fedora and followed Ed to his car. They drove to a local restaurant, where the valet took the keys. Robert took note but said nothing; he had never used a valet service.

"Mr. Scavo! Good to see you. Your table is ready." The host walked Ed and Robert to a table in the far corner, away from the kitchen, restrooms, and entrance. A rather dapper man in a fine suit and Brylcreemed, perfect brown hair was already seated and buttering bread. He stood as he saw Ed and Robert approach.

"Ed! Good to see you. It's been a while."

"Good to see you, too, Mr. Waters! Yes, it's been a while...but we had to get the plant up on time, you know?"

Ed turned to Robert. "Scotty, I'd like to introduce you to Mr. Waters. He owns Detroit Fabricating and Engineering Company."

"Nice to meet you, sir." Robert reached over and shook Mr. Waters's hand, and then the three sat down.

Ed raised his finger, and the waiter came over promptly.

"Can we get a round for the three of us? It'll be Manhattan for me and, if I remember correctly, a martini for Mr. Waters. Scotty?"

"I'll take a highball, please."

The waiter came back quickly with the drinks and took lunch orders, which appeared just as promptly.

"The food is always excellent here, Ed," Mr. Waters said halfway through his salade niçoise. "I asked to meet you because I am interested in expanding my operations beyond fabricating and engineering. I've had a long-standing contract with Ford, and they have spoken very highly of the two of you and your management and project expertise. I am looking to hire executives to run my new enterprise, and it is my hope that I can convince you to move back to Detroit and run my new company."

Robert was glad he was between mouthfuls when he heard that – he thought he might choke if he had food in his mouth.

"This is such an honor, Mr. Waters. What will this business be doing?"

"Looking at the heavy commercial construction players, we see a nice opening in moving, rigging, and erecting heavy machinery. At the moment, there is little competition in this space, and it fits neatly with engineering and fabricating. I think it's a natural next step in my company's expansion, as a sister ship, so to speak. I've already discussed this with Ed… I've offered him the position of president. Not to be repeated, but he has accepted."

"And what role do you see me playing?"

"How does vice president sound? You would be in charge of all operations."

This time, Robert nearly choked on his sandwich. Almost. He quickly composed himself.

"How close is this to reality?"

We've already been incorporated, although we haven't filed with the state, and obviously, operations have not yet started. When we get the executive team in place, we'll be ready to bid on projects and start hiring."

"Ed, in addition to running things, I'll be expecting you to garner new contracts."

Ed smiled. "I don't think that's going to be much of an issue, Scotty. Mr. Waters is very well connected at Ford."

Scotty set down the rest of his sandwich and wiped his mouth with his napkin. "I'm in, gentlemen. As long as the terms are acceptable."

"I will make sure they are, Scotty. Well then, it's settled. A toast?"

The three men raised their half-empty glasses as Robert asked, "Do you have a corporate name?"

"Detroit Machinery Movers."

"Here's to Detroit Machinery Movers! To Detroit Machinery Movers and extreme success!"

Glasses clinking, the men toasted their next business adventure.

* * *

Robert was very excited that evening.

"Margaret!" He put his hands on her shoulders, beaming. "I have great, great news!!!"

Margaret was very apprehensive. "And what might that be?"

"How would you like to move back to Detroit?"

Margaret gasped. "Detroit? Really!! Oh, Robert, that would be so wonderful!!!" Now she was beaming, too.

"I've been offered an executive position at a new company – vice president. In charge of all operations for Detroit Machinery

Movers."

"A new company? Brand new?"

"Yes, but it has the backing of a very established firm in a related field. They also offered a position to Ed Scavo, so we will both be going."

"I'll be close to Jack and Betty! This is…" Tears ran down her face, and she wiped them off with the backs of her hands.

"Oh, Robert… I always hoped we would go back, but I never really expected it would happen." Her voice trailed off, and she gave Robert a big hug.

"So, in a week or two…shall we go house hunting?"

Margaret just smiled broadly and gave him a wink. She was going back to Detroit – full circle to where her American dream began.

CHAPTER SIXTEEN

"Come with me, Margaret. I think I have found a place." He shepherded Margaret to the big, new deluxe Buick he had purchased – one with four chrome airflow holes, and not just three. Together they drove downriver and across the bridge to Grosse Ile. He drove the length of it, crossed over to Meso Island, drove over the low, pink-painted bridge at the southern end, and was again on Hickory Island. He pulled into a driveway four houses in and turned off the engine.

"On the water?" Margaret was astounded.

"On the water," Robert said, smiling. They pulled in front of a brown wood and brick ranch. The entire front of the house was a two-car garage. To the left was a tall stone wall with an arched opening between it and the neighboring property. To the right was a two-story, wood-sided home.

"This house is for sale? I don't see a sign."

"That's because Mr. Waters found out about it before it was advertised. He asked the real estate agent to hold off for us. Come on – the owners are waiting for us."

Just then, an elderly couple came from the south side of the house, down the sidewalk, and around front.

"Mr. Sharp! Good to see you again! Mrs. Sharp? Pleased to meet you. I'm Joe, and this is my wife, Liz." Joe extended his hand in a warm handshake.

The foursome entered a sun-filled entrance-cum-sitting room, and from there, they turned left and walked down a short hall to the front room. There, on the east wall, was the biggest window Margaret had ever seen, looking over the bay and across the water to what appeared to be a military installation. She could see men moving rapidly around an airplane, far enough away that they looked like toy soldiers in their uniforms.

"What's that?" she asked, unable to contain her curiosity.

"That's the naval air station. It's always a flurry of activity."

Margaret walked over to the window and stared out for several minutes. She then turned to examine the fireplace and the dining area to the left. She walked over to it and then walked through it to the kitchen.

"Let me show you the rest," said Liz. She took Margaret into the hall, turning left towards the two bedrooms and the bathroom.

"That door at the end goes into the garage," she said. "The house also has a full basement. It is not finished, but there is a lot of space down there. There is plumbing for a washing machine."

Margaret nodded as she headed back to the front room, where Robert was discussing house mechanicals with Joe.

"It's lovely, Robert," she said as she headed back to gaze out the picture window.

"Well then, the deal is sealed," said Robert, grinning. "Joe, I'll have a purchase agreement here first thing in the morning."

Joe smiled. "Mr. Waters will be quite pleased."

"How so?"

"He holds the mortgage on this house…and the house next door. Liz and I are retiring, and Mr. Waters wants the funds for other purposes."

"The wood-sided house?"

"Yes. Normally, he rents it out, but at the moment, it's vacant."

Robert made a mental note of that as he turned to his wife.

"See you tomorrow, Joe. Come on, Margaret. Time to go! We've a dinner with Jack and the family. Don't want to be late!"

Robert purchased both houses.

* * *

Detroit Machinery Movers hit the ground running. Within the first week it had six contracts. Robert walked into a meeting Ed had called, only to see several people he had never met.

He was a bit flustered and spoke a bit out of turn. "Ed, we don't have the manpower yet! How are we going to meet these deadlines?"

"Slow down, Scotty, and meet your new team. JL is our new treasurer and a listed executive. Dorothy is our new corporate secretary and is also a listed executive. And this..." Ed extended his arm, palm up, and pointed to a rather burly man in an expensive but slightly rumpled suit. "This is Jimmy O'Reilly, the president of the Riggers Union."

Robert shook hands all around before Ed motioned for everyone to sit down.

"So, yes, we have six contracts. We brought in Jimmy to help us find qualified help."

"Qualified? All of our members are supremely qualified." There was an uncomfortable silence, finally broken by Jimmy. "Just joking, folks. Just joking. I can have a dozen men here tomorrow if you need them. Do you need more?"

Robert spoke first. "We could use twenty, Jimmy."

"Twenty and done," said Jimmy. "Union rates, of course. And make this a clean union shop – that's all I ask."

"Of course," interjected Ed. "Wouldn't have it any other way."

"When do you need them?"

"It'll take six to do this first job," said Robert, pointing to a stack of project papers. "Six men, two days – that should do it."

"Done! Am I done here? I have other business to attend to," said Jimmy, standing.

"Thanks for coming, Jimmy. We look forward to a long, mutually profitable relationship." Ed stood and reached across the table to shake Jimmy's hand."

"Likewise," said Jimmy, and then he grabbed his fedora and left.

Ed sat back down. "And now on to corporate business. Mr. Waters has built the specialized machinery we need and has agreed to loan us the money to buy it from his fabricating company at five percent, five years. JL, will you handle the transaction?"

"Yes, sir." JL made a note in the leather-bound, monogrammed binder in front of him.

"Dorothy, have you completed all the required registrations for the corporation?"

"Almost, Mr. Scavo. I have not received the stamped, approved corporate papers back from the state yet."

"Let us know when you get them. We can start work as long as it begins after the stamped incorporated date, correct?"

"I sent them in last week, so we can start immediately."

"Robert, you've got the green light. Anything else you need?"

"Not that I can think of."

"Good. Let's get to work, team."

Robert stopped by Hudson's department store before he headed to evaluate his next job site. He went to the stationery department and ordered a monogrammed leather binder.

* * *

It was another long day. Robert returned to the office to finish some paperwork before heading home. He saw Ed still in the office.

"Ed – still here?"

"Like you, Scotty. Our cup runneth over."

Robert entered Ed's office and sat in the leather chair across from him.

"I'm really curious, Ed. How in the world have we gotten so much business so fast?"

"It's Waters, Scotty. His connections run deep. Let's not

question the golden goose, though. Listen, Madge and I are having a party next weekend. You and Margaret are invited."

"Sounds good, Ed. When and where?"

"Our house, Saturday night, seven o'clock." Ed hesitated. "Margaret seemed out of sorts last time… Is she all right?"

"Ed, Margaret is having a bit of a struggle adapting, that's all. I pulled her to California, then to Cleveland, and now back here. It's all happened so quickly, and she needs some time to put down roots. That's all."

"Good to know. See you tomorrow, Scotty."

"Night, Ed." Robert stood and went to his office to tie up a few loose ends before he headed home.

He got up at daybreak and headed into the office the next morning. He hadn't been there five minutes before Dorothy walked in with a hot cup of coffee and a message for him.

"Here's your coffee, Mr. Sharp. And the local union steward is here. He'd like a word with you."

"Thank you, Dorothy." Robert took a sip as he sat down. "Send him in."

Buddy Witkowski was what you would expect a Rigger union steward to be: muscular with a bit of pudge, large as a football player, with a rugged face that belied too many beers after work.

"Hello, Buddy. What can I do for you?"

"Mr. Sharp, you've scheduled eight men for the Ford Foundry job."

"That's right. Is there an issue?"

"I've gotten word that O'Reill would like you to add two more men."

"Explain to me why the job needs them."

Buddy closed the door and took a seat.

"That's how it works, Mr. Sharp." His voice was low. "Do you think all of this work awarded to DMM was dumb luck? O'Reilly and

Waters have an agreement. It's in everybody's better interest to do what we are told."

Robert was taken aback but kept a poker face. "I'm not top dog, here, Buddy. Let me fly it by Scavo. That okay by you?"

"Then it's as good as done." Buddy got up out of the chair and headed to the door. He stopped with his hand on the knob and turned halfway around.

"It's how things are done here, Mr. Sharp. You'll get used to it."

Robert waited five minutes to make sure Buddy had left the offices and headed to Ed's office. He poked his head in.

"Got a minute?"

"Sure, come on in." Robert entered and closed the door behind him.

"Buddy says we are to add a couple of extra men to the Ford Foundry job."

"That's right."

"We don't need them, Ed."

Ed put down his pen and looked at Robert intently.

"Yes, we do, Scotty."

"So, you want me to add them?"

"Yes."

"Can you tell me why?"

"You'll figure that out soon enough, Scotty. Don't bite the hand that feeds you."

"But the expense won't come in under bid."

"That's been handled."

Robert's eyebrows furrowed. "If you say so, Ed. You're the boss." He turned and left. The next day, he did exactly as he was instructed.

As Robert drove home, he turned over in his mind all the possible reasons he had been told to pad the manpower on that job.

Obviously, the union wanted it – that made sense from a union perspective. But what incentive could a company have to increase expenses against a set-bid job? By the time he pulled into his driveway, he vowed he would figure it out.

* * *

"Margaret, we've been asked to the Scavo's for dinner."

Margaret sighed. "Again?"

"Come on and sit on the sofa with me, Margaret."

Robert took Margaret's hand and brought her over.

"It's very important to us that I succeed – do you agree? Do you like living here? Do you like having your own car? Being able to buy whatever groceries you want, with nary a care? To go to Hudson's and buy new clothes? Do you like those things?"

"Of course I do, Robert. But I am uncomfortable with those people. With the smoking and the drinking and the talk of country clubs and bridge games. I much prefer spending an afternoon with Jeannie Wilson. She understands me. Every time someone brings me a soft drink at one of your business parties, I feel people are snickering at me behind my back."

Robert held Margaret's face in his hands. "I can't go alone, Margaret. I can't get ahead, either, without a wife. It's how things are done. Please – for us, do your best."

"I do try, Robert. It's just so difficult for me. It always will be."

"Put on your best face, will you? And could you wear that lovely dark blue dress with the full skirt and patent belt? You look so pretty in it."

Margaret gave a slight nod and went to get dressed for the evening.

Most of the other guests had already arrived when Robert and Margaret got to the Scavos' – JL and his wife, the Waters, the Witkowskis, and Jimmy O'Reilly and his wife. Ed handed Robert a highball as Margaret went to the bar and poured herself a Seven Up.

Then she headed for the front room, where the wives were gathered.

"Hello, Margaret… How are you this evening?" Madge Scavo was a very gracious hostess.

Margaret smiled wanly at her. "Fine, thank you, Madge." She stumbled for something to say. "I wish it would rain, don't you? This dry spell is not good for the garden."

Just then, the doorbell rang, and Madge excused herself to get it. Ed reached the door just before she did, however, and opened it to Dorothy Steinhauser, without escort.

"Hello, Dorothy! Glad you could join us! Come on in. Madge, this is Dorothy Steinhauser, our corporate secretary. She keeps all of us organized and on track – we'd be lost without her administrative skills."

Madge smiled warmly and extended her hand. "Come on in, Dorothy, and welcome."

"What are you drinking, Dorothy?" Ed smiled broadly.

"Scotch on the rocks, please."

"You've got it!" Ed went to fetch Dorothy's drink. When he returned with it, he said, "Dorothy, can you come with me? Madge, excuse me while I kidnap Dorothy for a bit – we have some business to discuss."

"Certainly, Ed. Dorothy, the ladies are chatting in the front room, when you are finished."

Margaret had been watching with interest.

"Who is that, Madge? I've never seen her before… Is her husband ill? She came alone?"

"She works for the company, Margaret. I didn't see a ring on her finger. I would guess she isn't married."

"Where did she go?"

"Ed asked her to join the men for some business discussion."

"A woman? With them? Never in all my born days…" Margaret shook her head. "Never in all my born days."

Dorothy never did join the women in the front room.

* * *

"Mr. Sharp, have you a moment?"

"Yes, Dorothy. Please come on in. What's on your mind?"

Dorothy sat down across the desk, looking somewhat diffident.

"I have a sister, Esther. She is an executive assistant at Ford Headquarters. I was telling her about my job here, and she thought she could arrange a meeting between you, Mr. Scavo, and her boss, Mr. McNab."

Dorothy's words caught Robert quite by surprise. "Vice President McNab?"

"Yes, sir." Dorothy gave him a weak smile. "I thought you might be interested."

"I most certainly am. Let me brief Ed. We can take McNab to lunch. Can you ask your sister what's his favorite restaurant?"

"Certainly." Dorothy's smile became more confident. "I'll find out and let you know." She stood up to leave.

As she reached the doorway, Robert said, "Thank you, Dorothy. That shows initiative."

Dorothy merely nodded and left.

Robert got up and headed to Ed's office.

"Ed? busy?"

"No. Come on in."

"Did Dorothy tell you about her sister? Executive assistant for Rick McNab."

"You've got to be kidding! No...she didn't mention it to me."

"She's going to have her sister set up a lunch with him. This could be big, Ed."

Ed grinned. "That news made my day. Whenever it's set, let me know. I'll clear my calendar for it. And while we're on the subject of lunches, can you join McNamara and me tomorrow at Lelli's at noon?"

"Sure. Anything I need to prepare?"

"No. I think he wants to talk about an outside opportunity for us."

"Great! I'll put it on my calendar. Anything else?"

"Not at the moment."

On the way back to his office, Robert stopped by Dorothy's desk. "Dorothy, please put lunch at Lelli's tomorrow, noon, on my calendar. Reservation in Ed's name. And remind me to leave on time."

"Absolutely, Mr. Sharp."

"Thank you."

Robert was in great spirits when he got home that evening. As always, Margaret had the table set and a full dinner waiting to be served, and she was in a clean frock with sensible heels, makeup, and pearls.

"You look lovely this evening, Margaret. That dress suits you. What have you made for us tonight?"

"Lamb chops, neeps and tatties, chopped salad, and a lemon pie."

"Sounds delicious! I'll meet you in the dining room after I wash up." He gave her a peck on the cheek and went to the washroom.

"You must have had a good day, Robert," she said as she set his dinner plate before him. "You are in quite a good mood."

"It was a good day, Margaret. A very good day. Things seem to be really taking off. I have lunch tomorrow with Ed and the head of the Riggers union, and the secretary is arranging a meeting with us and a vice president at Ford."

"That's very impressive, Robert. I'm happy for you. It does me good to see you in such high spirits."

"If this unfolds like I think it might, it won't be long before you'll have your very own car. Not many families have two cars. Can you imagine? Who would have thought we would be in this position? Can you imagine us talking about owning two cars when we were taking our walks in Cowdenbeath?"

Margaret shook her head. "We wouldn't have ever been able to imagine this life, Robert. That's a fact. It was difficult coming here for me, but you were right. This is beyond my wildest dreams. When I write home and tell Bessie about our life, she can't believe it. She and Oliver, still in a row house, with no phone or car, to this day. And here we are… It's truly astounding."

Margaret paused, and her voice was quiet. "Thank you, Robert. You were right. Right about everything."

She then changed the subject. "Would you mind if I babysat two days a week for a while? The neighbor down the street asked me."

"That would be fine, Margaret. Just fine – as long as it's during the day and not at night."

"It is. Mrs. Reynolds is taking a class Tuesdays and Thursdays. Then, on Thursdays, she is meeting some women friends for lunch."

"That's fine, then."

"Good. I'll tell her tomorrow. I'll be glad to do it. I miss the wee bairns."

Conversation lulled as dinner was finished.

"Wonderful as always, Margaret. Think I'll go and read some… It's been a long day, so I'll say goodnight now in case I fall asleep."

Margaret silently picked up the dishes and took them to the sink as Robert went to his bedroom. It was on the left, off the hallway. Except for holding a wardrobe and a bed, it could have been mistaken for a man's study. It had dark wainscotting under dark painted walls, a dark leather club chair, and a full bookshelf of manly books: books about the two wars, books about famous sea battles, car books, photography books, and history books. Robert was filling in where formal education had left off, educating himself and learning about hobbies he wanted to pursue.

Margaret sighed as she did the dishes. Then she fed the dog, let her outside, and tidied up the dining room. Once done, she went into the front room for a while to stare out over the water, and then she turned on the television to watch the end of the news. She turned it off when the sun set and silently went into her bedroom, down the hall, on the right. Her room was soft and feminine, painted pale green with a matching pale-green satin quilted coverlet on the bed. A small ceramic figurine stood on her nightstand: it was a little Bible with the Lord's Prayer written on it. A mirrored and filigreed plate lay on the dresser, and on it rested a matching filigreed jewelry box.

She took off her sterling silver charm bracelet and put it in the box – she had taken to collecting charms of places and things important to her. Her bracelet had a little poodle, a charm for each of the now-three grandchildren, a little tea kettle, and a little chapel that you could look in and see a good representation of the inside of a church. There was room for quite a few more charms, but at the moment, there was not much more to Margaret's life that could be commemorated with charms.

CHAPTER SEVENTEEN

Four men dodging the pelting rain ducked into Lelli's. The coat check girl came out of her station to take the wet coats and hats, passing out tokens as she gingerly held the drenched coats away from her clothing.

"Nice to see you again, Mr. Waters. Mr. O'Reilly – always good to see you. Gentlemen." She nodded to Ed and Robert and then went back to the coatroom.

The maître d' smiled broadly as he led the men to their table, secluded in a quiet corner.

"Shall I bring the usual, Mr. Waters? Mr. O'Reilly?"

The two men nodded. "Yes, and thanks, Norman," said Waters.

"And for your two guests?"

"I'll have a Rusty Nail," said Ed. "Scotch on the rocks," said Robert.

"Single malt or blend, sir?"

"Single malt, please."

Waters waited until Norman left before starting the conversation.

"I'm quite pleased with how you've grown the company over the past three years, Ed. You've exceeded my expectations."

"Thank you, sir. Couldn't have done it without Scotty, here. He really knows how to get a job done."

Waters smiled. "You and Madge still travel to Florida frequently?"

"Yes, we do. Every chance we get. We bought a small place in Islamorada. Great fishing! And Madge loves the beach. She's picked up painting seascapes."

"Jimmy and I have a proposition for you, then. We would like to incorporate Detroit Machinery Movers in Florida, but only for a corporate presence. We were thinking that under that umbrella, we could expand into real estate – and even commercial fishing if you like. Jimmy and I see a great future in Florida and want to get in on the ground floor. We would need you to be the principals, though… I will not bore you with the intricate reasons why. You two would be our face to the public and our agents."

Robert had remained silent until now. "It sounds amazing, but I don't see how we can run businesses both in Michigan and Florida."

"Oh – don't worry about that. You will continue as you always have, except for the three or four trips to Florida a year that you would make. We will staff the Florida office and manage the day-to-day operations – as I said, it would mainly be in real estate anyway, and that's not what Detroit Machinery Movers is all about. And of course, we would fund the operation so you can concentrate on the things that have made you successful to date."

"Ed?" Robert turned to his boss. "I think this is mainly your call."

Ed said, "Intriguing, Mr. Waters. Of course, I'll have to get the approval of JL and Dorothy, but I doubt that will be an issue."

"Make it formal, Ed. Write it up in your next board meeting as an approved resolution. Have Dorothy file the papers. We have three of the five principals here at this table, so I believe it's a done deal."

Robert turned to Jimmy. "Mr. O'Reilly, I'm curious of your interest in this."

O'Reilly cleared his throat, giving him time to construct an adequate answer.

"The Riggers can't really have a real estate arm, Sharp. Or a

270

fishing company, for that matter. And I can't set up a company and be on its board, especially with companies that use our union labor. I can't do it on my own because I have to focus on running the union. I think that it's a wise business move, though, and I think Florida real estate will soar. I will be a silent and anonymous investor.

"Keep your nose to the grindstone and do what you've been doing, Sharp. From time to time, we'll suggest moves we want you to make in Florida. Get that paperwork done and bank on a trip to Florida in the near future. Corporate expense, of course."

O'Reilly took a rather large sip of water. "Oh – and Scavo, did you put in a bid to place that new Marshall Fredericks statue? The Spirit of Detroit?"

"Submitted it two days ago, Mr. O'Reilly. We were early. Bids aren't closing for another month."

O'Reilly winked. "Get ready for it – a little birdie told me it's yours."

Waters placed an envelope on the table, next to Robert's plate. "This is the first of hopefully many incentives for you, Scotty. Don't open it here."

He then raised his finger, and Norman promptly came over. "Bring rib-eyes and baked potatoes all around, Norman. Medium rare, sour cream, bacon, and cheddar on the side."

Waters raised his glass. "Here's to sunshine and palm trees, gentlemen."

Scotty silently put the envelope in the inside pocket of his suit jacket. Later that night, when he got home, he took the envelope to his room and opened it. There were several thousand dollars stuffed inside.

* * *

"Scotty, please see to the details of setting up shop in Florida."

"Yes, sir."

Robert headed to Dorothy's office.

"Dorothy…a minute?"

Dorothy looked up and smiled. "You know I'll always make time for you."

Robert didn't let his minor discomfort with that level of familiarity show.

"We need to incorporate in Florida, per the board resolution yesterday. Have you made any progress in finding out what that will entail?"

"Yes, sir. We need to file as a foreign corporation, but beyond that, it's simply submitting a form and a check to the state of Florida. I've already asked them to send me the form. It will need to be signed by all five of us."

"That's it?"

"Yes. We don't even need to establish a local office to incorporate – we can use this address. It seems very simple and straightforward."

"Very well. Let's get the paperwork finished right away – let me know when the document comes in. You really are very efficient, Dorothy. Well done."

As Robert turned and left, Dorothy's gaze followed him until he was out of sight. She smiled to herself, her hands under her chin, admiring his forceful stride, trim, muscular build, and broad shoulders. She closed her eyes and imagined his chiseled face, his pure-white, wavy hair – striking for a man in his fifties; his deep-set, cobalt blue eyes. Her obsession was broken when the phone on her desk suddenly rang. Composing herself, she answered it.

The call was short, and Dorothy returned to completing the incorporation paperwork. She filled in the principals' names role by role. When she got to corporate secretary, she stopped and stared down the empty hall. *Who will know?* she thought. *No one looks at these documents.* She wrote in the space "Dorothy Sharp." She quickly sealed the filing in an envelope, stamped it, and put it with the outgoing mail.

* * *

Robert was late for dinner that night.

"I'm sorry that the meat is dried out, Robert. I didn't expect you so late." Margaret took off her apron after she placed the full plates on the table.

"I called, Margaret, but you didn't pick up the phone."

"I was next door, helping Mrs. Wyzbinski with her children. I'm sorry."

"No matter."

Robert started eating his roast beef, string beans, and mashed potatoes.

"Let's have a spot of sherry after dinner, Margaret."

"Are we celebrating?"

"Not exactly. Let it wait until after supper."

Supper done, dishes cleared, and sherry poured, Margaret sat back down.

"The company is incorporating in Florida, Margaret."

Margaret paused, her glass in mid-air. Raising it to her lips, she took a sip and set it down before speaking.

"Does that mean we are moving…again?"

"No…at least, not in the foreseeable future. I've been told I'll be doing what I have been doing here in Detroit. However, I will need to fly down a few times a year."

"Robert, I can't take care of things like I used to, and this house and property are larger than anything we've ever had. When you leave, can you get your man Gilbert to come around and help me with things when you are gone?"

"Well, I was thinking that you might want to come with me to Florida."

Margaret clasped her hands in her lap and looked down.

"Robert, you know I'm a homebody. You'll be at work all day long, and I'll be left in a hotel room. I'll know no one. I won't know the area. What will you have me do while you are at work?"

"I won't be going alone – Ed and Madge will most likely be going, too. You and Madge can shop, go to the beach, have lunch by the water… you might like it!"

"I'll think about it, but at the moment, I think it would be awkward. Madge and I are nothing alike. Spending all of that time together might highlight just how different we are. Now, if it was a vacation, that would be different. I think I'd really like spending time – just the two of us – in Florida."

"Well, nothing's set in stone at the moment. Let's see how this plays out, shall we?" Robert raised his glass and finished his sherry.

Margaret still had half a glass left. She took another sip before talking.

"The grandchildren are coming next week for their summer vacation. Jack and Betty are bringing them down Sunday. Shall I buy steaks for the grill? And ice cream for dessert?"

"That will be fine. And don't forget the charcoal. How long will they be staying?"

"Several weeks."

Robert smiled. "I've been thinking about what I would do next time they are here. I've got a great idea to keep them entertained."

"Margaret stood to clear the table. "You have always been good with the bairns, Robert. I'm sure they will be delighted." She picked up the plates and silverware and took them to the kitchen sink.

When she returned for the glasses, Robert said, "I'm having some men come and pour a seawall, but I'll have them hold off for a month."

"A seawall?"

"Yes – and I'll be building a covered boat well with a heavy-duty winch to pull the cabin cruiser out of the water for the winter."

"A cabin cruiser? We don't have a cabin cruiser."

Robert grinned widely. "Not yet, Mag. But we will – as soon as it's built. I bought one. We can cruise up to Georgian Bay. It will sleep all seven of us. I'm going to christen it the *Sharp Seven*." Robert winked. "Clever, huh?"

"Aren't such things dear, Robert? I know you are doing well, but do we have enough money for a cabin cruiser?"

"Work has been going very well, Margaret. Don't think about it another minute. We are in fine shape." He raised his glass. "A spot more?"

* * *

Robert got up with the sun – he always did. He took a half-dozen scraps of paper – he made sure they looked rough – and wrote something on each one. Then he took a small cloth sack, put a couple of shiny quarters in it, and pulled the drawstrings tight. He ran downstairs to his workroom, grabbed a handful of tacks and a hammer, and went into the backyard.

The sun was barely up over the horizon, but the sailors across the bay were already busy on base. He nailed the first note to the tree closest to the house. Then he placed the notes here and there in the yard and ended up tucking the drawstring bag into a corner of the grill. Content with his work, he put the hammer away and left for work.

Margaret was busy getting the grandchildren up, cleaned, and fed their daily porridge and tea with milk.

"You can't go out yet – it's too early. Don't want to disturb the neighbors."

"If we can't go out, why did you get us up so early?" Cameron always was the one who asked all the questions.

"Up with the sun, to bed when it sets. That's the proper way." Margaret was busy picking up the breakfast dishes and putting them in the sink. "Now, go watch cartoons while I tidy up. Go along, now." She shooed the children into the front room.

An hour later, she allowed the kids outside. As they headed down the sidewalk, towards the water, Jeff stopped. "What's that on the tree?"

He went over to the note nailed to the tree. Cameron was not far behind.

"It's a note!!"

Jeff pulled it off and read it aloud.

"Aye, matey. I've been watching you. Follow this trail for a treasure – or face the plank! Dead-Eye Dick, the Dirty One."

Jeff's eyes were round and large with wonder. "It's a pirate note, Cameron! A real pirate note!"

Cameron grabbed at the paper. "Let me see!"

Jeff held the slip of paper high over his head. "No – there's an arrow under his name. It points that way." Jeff extended his right arm. "Let's go over there and see if we can find the treasure!"

The two happily spent most of the morning looking for notes and clues. They finally discovered the treasure hidden in the grill, right before Margaret called them in for lunch. They burst into the kitchen, chattering about their morning adventure.

"Look, Gram! Look! There was a pirate here during the night, and he left us clues and treasure. His name is Dead-Eye Dick, the Dirty One! Look!!" Jeff held out the small drawstring bag. "Quarters!" He then held out his other hand, clutching the collection of notes.

"Now, share with your sister, Jeff. Put that down and go wash your hands and faces, and see to it you do it smartly. Then come and eat."

Margaret put egg salad sandwiches on the table, plated with apple slices, and glasses of cold milk. She picked up the crumpled notes, read a few of them, and smiled to herself. Yes, Robert was very good with the bairns.

Margaret had put the children down for an afternoon nap and was taking her afternoon tea when there was a gentle tap on the side door.

"Mrs. Sharp?" A thin, middle-aged Black man stood to the side of the door, holding his cap in his clasped hands.

"Hello, Gilbert! Thanks for coming. I was wondering if you could help me better arrange the garage before you mow the lawn."

"I would be happy to, Mrs. Sharp." Gilbert's voice was as gentle as his tap on the door.

Margaret wiped her hands on her apron. "Follow me, then." She went out the door and into the garage, speaking to Gilbert as they walked.

"Mr. Sharp is leaving on a business trip next week, Gilbert. Can you come maybe every other day and make sure everything is taken care of? I have my hands full with my grandchildren, and this property requires a lot of tending."

"Mr. Sharp told me, Mrs. Sharp. I'd be glad to come. Just make me a list of things you want me to do."

Margaret pointed out what she wanted done in the garage.

"I'll be in the house, Gilbert. The children should be getting up soon. Just come in if you have any questions of me."

"Yes, ma'am."

* * *

"Dorothy, did you make the hotel and rental car reservations for next week?"

"Of course. We have rooms at the Penn-Sheraton for two nights. I've also secured a Lincoln Continental for the duration."

"Traveling in style, I'd say."

"Mr. Waters insisted on it, Mr. Sharp. I can't say I disagree." Dorothy smiled. "Are you sure Mrs. Sharp will not be coming?"

"No – she's tending to the grandchildren for two more weeks. Waters's, Ed's, and JL's wives are all coming?"

"And Mrs. O'Reilly."

"Well, I am quite sorry my wife won't be joining us. I guess you and I will have to pair up to make it even. Have you come up with activities for the wives while we are working?"

"I have, and I think they will be pleased."

"Good. Thank you, Dorothy."

Robert headed towards his office.

Dorothy's eyes once again followed Robert down the hall. *Pair up.* A thrill ran through her frame as she considered those words. Her mind drifted into a pleasant daydream of Robert and her walking along the river at sunset. She smiled at the thought, tapped her pencil on the desk absentmindedly, and reluctantly got back to work.

* * *

The Riggers were holding their national convention in Pittsburgh – Ed, Waters, JL, Robert, and Dorothy were enjoying a leisurely breakfast as the O'Reillys opened up the convention.

Dorothy had planned a shopping excursion for the women, and as she was directing them to the small bus, Ed called after her, "You go, too, Dorothy."

"I'd rather stay, Mr. Scavo... It's my job."

"No, no – go and enjoy yourself with the gals. I'm counting on you to make sure they don't buy all of Pittsburgh. We'll see you at dinner."

A frown of disappointment washed over Dorothy's face, but she boarded the bus.

"We've reserved a conference room, gentlemen. Follow me." Waters stood and headed out to the lobby and down a short hall, opening up a door to a well-lit room with an oval table surrounded by a half-dozen leather chairs. A coffee station had been set up in the corner, and pads of paper and pencils were in front of every chair.

"Take a seat." Waters claimed the head chair, furthest from the coffee, and headed to pour himself a cup. Returning, he sat down and waited briefly until the rest of the men were settled.

"Jimmy invited us here because there may be business coming out of the convention that will potentially involve us, especially in Florida. It's a great opportunity for us to strengthen our relationship with the union."

Halfway into the meeting, Jimmy O'Reilly stuck his head in the room. "Sorry to interrupt – I've only got a sec. Russ, can I see you for a moment?"

Waters excused himself and left the room. Several minutes later, he returned.

"Robert, next week, you and I are flying down to Florida. We'll discuss the details later. Now, where were we?"

* * *

Robert and Waters stood in the midst of acres of palmetto trees and scrub.

"O'Reilly would really like this property."

"You think so, Mr. Waters?"

"Robert, please. We've known each other long enough for you to call me Russ. Yes, I think this would do nicely. I think you should buy it."

Robert concealed his shock with a cough. "Sorry – it's the humidity. Buy this? How many acres did you say…eighty?"

"Yes, it's a nice piece of property."

"I'm not in a position to buy this, Mr.…Russ."

"We will get you the money, Scotty. All you'll have to do is sell it to the riggers when they ask. They told me they were planning on building a retirement home. This would do nicely. Can you do that for us?"

"Simply buy this and hold on to it? That's it?"

"That's it."

Robert considered the proposal.

"I imagine that would be easy enough." Robert paused. "I was wondering if you could do me a favor."

"What would that be?"

"My son is a dentist – I think I told you that. He's been in solo practice in Royal Oak. However, they've taken his office to build the expressway. I was wondering if he could work for the riggers in their medical center."

"Sure, I'll ask them and let you know."

"Then I think we have a deal, Russ."

Waters grinned and slapped Robert's shoulder. "That's the spirit! I'll have the paperwork drawn up. Go down to Southeast Bank – the main branch, downtown Miami – and open up a checking account. The money will be there once you call me with the account number. Use that for the transaction."

Waters reached into his suit jacket and brought out another envelope.

"Here's a bonus, Scotty. Or an incentive; it doesn't matter. We'll take care of you if you take care of us."

Robert took the envelope, and the two headed back to the rental car and left.

"Scotty, Ed's going to start a fishing business down here."

"A fishing business?"

"Yes. Do you like deep sea fishing?"

"I've never been, but I do like to fish."

"There may be things Ed asks you to handle. Would you be up for that?"

"My first priority is Detroit Machinery Movers, Russ. At least, that's how I see it. Are things changing?"

"Not at all. Ed won't ask for much of your time, and it won't have anything to do with running the business down here. Just know that if he asks, it's fine by me."

"Yes, sir."

The two men sat in silence for the rest of the short car ride back to the hotel as Robert mused about how fishing and property holdings fit with Detroit Machinery Movers.

The two entered the hotel lobby, and Russ checked for mail at the front desk. He turned to Robert after picking up a few pieces of mail. "Meet me in the bar? Half an hour?"

"Sure, Russ. See you then."

Robert took the half-hour opportunity to call Margaret.

"Hello Margaret. How are things? Everything okay?"

"Yes. Gilbert's been a great help, and the children are leaving this weekend. When will you be back?"

"In a few days. Wish you were here, Mag."

"Maybe I can come with you on one of your trips. I'm not fond of being here all alone."

"That's the spirit! You and I will have a great time down here. I'll be home soon. I miss you."

"I miss you, too, Robert."

* * *

Robert was back in the office bright and early Monday.

"Dorothy, please book a flight for you and me for Thursday. We need to go to Pittsburgh to meet with Jimmy Reilly and Russ Waters. Make a note to bring your notary seal. We'll fly back on Friday."

"I'll clear your calendar and make the arrangements, Mr. Sharp. Is there anything else?"

"Just a quick trip in and out to finalize some business arrangements and get the paperwork in order. And since I've been traveling so much, can you please arrange to have my household bills sent here? Gas, electric, water, phone... I think that should do it."

"I'll do it right away, Mr. Sharp."

As Dorothy started to leave, Robert spoke again.

"Do you suppose you could pay those bills for me when they come in? I'll give you a bank of personal checks."

"I'd be happy to, Robert. Anything else?"

"No – that should do it." Robert got back to the papers on his desk. It seemed that in no time at all, the day had passed.

Dinner was on the table when Robert arrived home, as always. The house was immaculate, as always. Margaret was in a clean dress, with pumps, pearls, and makeup, as always…and dinner was delicious, again as always.

"You're quiet this evening, Robert."

"Margaret, you're a fine wife. A fine housewife. I know you're much more comfortable in that role, but you and I are supposed to socialize for my career to advance. I can't help but feel we could do better if you and I socialized with the proper connections. We've been asked to dinner Thursday night in Pittsburgh with the Waters and O'Reillys. Fly back on Friday. Will you come?"

"Here we go again." Margaret was uncharacteristically angry. "You knew who I was when we married. I haven't changed. I have followed you across land and sea, moved several times, kept the home fire lit for you while you pursued your career. That I did willingly. We've been around and around on this, Robert. I hate pretending to be friends with those people! It's fake. I don't smoke, and I don't drink, and I don't play bridge. I'm sorry, but I don't want to have this conversation again. You want to be chummy with them – fine. I don't. I don't care what you tell them. You spend eight to ten hours with them, five days a week. That should be enough. Please don't keep trying to drag me into it."

The force of her rant took Robert by surprise.

"Well, fine. I won't ask you again. But don't complain when I'm not home as much. I'll go by myself to Pittsburgh."

"Fine."

CHAPTER EIGHTEEN

Ed Scavo called an emergency leadership meeting on a bright but cold Monday morning in March.

"I'm sure you're all aware of how well we have done over the last decade. I'm sure this has not been lost on you. I want to thank each of you for your contributions to our success. However, Mr. Waters and I have decided to dissolve Detroit Machinery Movers."

There was a stunned silence in the room.

"Effective when?" JL appeared quite concerned.

"Unfortunately, it is effective immediately. I am announcing my immediate retirement – my wife and I are moving to Florida to run the charter fishing business. Mr. Waters has resigned from the firm, also effective immediately."

"Anything else to add?" Robert's tone was brusque as he broke the awkward silence.

"Yes, actually. You all will be receiving rather handsome severance packages. Checks for a portion of your severance will be handed out by the end of the day… The balance will be paid once the company assets are sold."

The awkward silence returned as the men absorbed the abrupt and massive change to their lives. After a minute or two, Robert stood up and headed to the door.

"Fine. Are we done here? I have work to do."

"Scotty, wait."

"No, Ed. It's clear we are done here. We've had a good run, haven't we? You've announced your next step... now, if you don't mind, I have to work on mine." Robert turned and walked out, not bothering to shut the door behind him.

Robert walked out onto the shop floor and found Buddy, the union steward, looking over some blueprints.

"Buddy – have a minute?"

"Sure, Mr. Sharp. What's up?"

"Can you come to my office? Right now? It's rather important."

Buddy took off his gloves and hard hat and followed Robert. Once in his office, Robert closed the door."

"Buddy, looks like this place is shutting down, sooner than later."

Buddy was caught off guard. "What do you mean, shut down?"

"Everyone's getting laid off – today. Doors are being shuttered for good, effective immediately. I was wondering, though – would you come over with me if I started a new business?"

Buddy stared at Robert and then narrowed his gaze. "Does this have anything to do with O'Reilly?"

"What do you mean, Buddy?"

Buddy lowered his voice to a conspiratorial near-whisper. "Word is, O'Reilly's going to jail. The Riggers and everybody close to them are under a microscope."

Suddenly all of the pieces fit.

"So, Buddy – would you come over to my company? A new start?"

"Personally, I would immediately say yes. You're a straight shooter. But you know how these things go... I have to run it up the flagpole."

"I understand. Can you let me know, though, as soon as you hear?"

"Definitely."

Buddy paused.

"Between you and me, I would follow you in a heartbeat, Sharp."

"Thanks, Buddy. You're a good man. Just let me know."

Robert's next stop was at Dorothy's desk.

"It's 11:45, Dorothy. Want to catch a bite?"

She reached into her bottom drawer and pulled out her purse. "Shall I call ahead? For how many?"

"Yes, please. Lelli's maybe. See if you can get us in right away. Table for two."

Dorothy's faced flushed, which she tried to hide by pulling out a notepad and writing down the reservation request.

"I'll be in my office. Come get me when everything's arranged."

* * *

Forty-five minutes later, Robert and Dorothy were sitting at a table along the wall, waiting for their drinks.

"Dorothy, the company is folding."

Dorothy gasped slightly and attempted to recover by taking a sip of water.

"I spoke to Witkowski, and if the Riggers allows it, he said he would come over to work with me. My question to you is, would you come, too?"

Dorothy almost choked on her water.

"Come over where, Robert?"

"I'm thinking I can start my own company, and frankly, I don't think I can do that without you. I don't even know how to start a company. If we can get adequate financing, we can buy DMM's assets and hit the ground running, at least from an equipment standpoint. Will you come and work with me? Form a company with me?"

Dorothy reached over and placed her hand on Robert's. "I would follow you anywhere, Robert. You should know that."

He withdrew his hand from under hers.

"Dorothy, please. This is a business arrangement. It's not personal."

Just then, their drinks came. Robert took a big swig of his single malt before continuing.

"It hasn't escaped me that you have an interest in me that exceeds a normal working relationship."

Dorothy looked down at her hands, flushed and silent.

"You must know that I am a married man. I love my wife, even though she has made my career a bit more difficult because of her personality and reluctance to play the corporate wife. That being said, she is my wife, and I made a pledge to her. If nothing else, I am a man of my word. I will never divorce her. I took her away from her family in Scotland, moved her across the ocean and all over this great country, and she's put up with more than her share of hardship. She has been steadfast throughout. She rarely complains, and she is a good wife. She will remain my wife forever."

There was a long silence at the table, and then Dorothy quietly said, "Robert, I will follow you to the ends of the earth. You are taken; I understand that. I will settle for being able to see you every day. Your terms, no questions. I will only say this once, and then I will drop it. You are the man of my dreams. I admit I adore you. If a working relationship is all I can get, then I will take only that and be glad for it. I can't imagine my life without you."

Robert's discomfort was saved by the arrival of lunch.

"So, what do you think of the name Detroit Rigging and Erecting?"

"That's a fine name."

"Start arranging the paperwork. I'll speak to JL to see whether he might join us. Also, please set up a meeting with Mr. Waters – tell him I'm interested in exploring the purchase of the company's assets. Let's also try to get a meeting with union officials – we're going to want a labor agreement."

Dorothy pulled out a steno pad from her roomy purse and switched to shorthand to keep up with the flow of requests.

"Anything else?"

"See whether we can take over the existing offices. If not, start looking around. Did Ed talk to you about the executive severance package?"

"I haven't spoken to him all day, Robert."

"You should make it a point to talk to him this afternoon. I'll pay you your current salary from my severance, but not until you pay yourself from your severance until it runs out. Fair?"

Robert took a bite of his club sandwich, put it down, and took a sip of water.

"I don't want us to miss a beat. I'll speak to all of our current customers and see whether we can step in – hopefully, we can make it seamless and carry forward the existing book of business. I hope Buddy gets back to me soon."

The two ate the rest of their lunch in silence.

"Coffee?" asked the waiter as he cleared the table.

"No, not for me," answered Robert as he looked at the check and laid a fifty on top of it. "Keep the change."

"We've got to get back, Dorothy. I have a lot to do."

When they returned and were heading to their respective offices, Robert stopped in the hall.

"Oh – and please get a flight to Miami for my wife and me – make it for the week after next."

* * *

"Margaret, I've made arrangements for us to spend a week in Florida. It'll be nice to leave this long winter and get some warm sunshine. We're leaving a week from Sunday."

Margaret turned from setting the table and smiled. "Oh, that sounds grand, Robert! Thank you!"

"Bring that big straw hat of yours – I've made reservations in Marathon, and we're going deep sea fishing."

"Did you rent a boat for the whole week, too?"

Robert grinned. "No, Mag – I bought one."

"You bought a boat. "

Robert winked.

"We'll be going down a lot, then, will we?"

"Only in the cold months here. Lovely here in the summer."

"You'll keep the boat in Marathon? It would be difficult to bring it back."

"I've already made arrangements for mooring and storage."

"Of course you have." Margaret served herself a second helping of vegetables. "It sounds rather nice, Robert. I think we can have a lovely time."

Margaret paused.

"We'll be back in time for Easter, right? Jack and Betty have invited us to church and dinner."

Robert hesitated a minute before answering, having forgotten entirely about Easter.

"Easter's the tenth? Sure – we'll be back in time."

"Maybe we can take the two older children with us during spring break one of these times. I think they would enjoy it."

"We'll see, Margaret. We'll see." Robert pushed himself away from the table. "Dinner was delicious, Mag. I'll be down in my workshop."

Margaret silently cleared the table, did the dishes, picked up her knitting, and worked in silence before heading to bed.

* * *

A week later, Robert was standing in Russ Waters's office.

"As I said in our brief phone call, I would like to buy the assets of Detroit Machinery Movers. I can put down fifty percent and was wondering if you would also agree to finance the balance over a five- or ten-year period."

"You would pledge the equipment?"

"Yes. You know that I can run this business, Russ. You've watched me for years."

"Would you agree to a callable note?"

"Callable under what circumstances?"

"Missed payments for certain. I have to work out other potential circumstances – probably related to the sale of the equipment... I don't know. Certain business or economic conditions... I'll get with my attorney and see if we can draw up something that you and I can come to terms with."

"Thanks, Russ. I'm eager to get this underway, so let me know right away."

"Will do, Scotty."

Robert's hand was on the doorknob as Russ called out after him.

"Good luck to you, Scotty."

"Thanks."

Robert left and met Dorothy at Lelli's, their ad hoc office ever since DMM had shuttered.

"Dorothy, I'm not sure I trust Waters with this financing deal. He wants to make the note callable. I think I need to shelter all the other assets I can. Something just doesn't feel right."

"What are you thinking?"

"Well, I was wondering about moving all after-tax profit to you – to us but in your name. That way, if things go south, we have sheltered all of what we have made."

"That's putting a lot of trust in me, Robert."

"Would you betray me?"

"Never. You know that."

Robert paused and looked directly into Dorothy's blue eyes. "There are only two people I trust totally, and you are one of them."

Dorothy bit her lip and fumbled with her sandwich. She took a small bite, put it down, and grabbed her glass of water.

"I think I've found an office, to start. It doesn't have a yard big enough for all of the equipment, but it's available immediately, and I think it can get us started. It's on Springwells, down near the Rouge River."

"Have you walked it?"

"Not yet – I've got an appointment tomorrow to see it."

"If you think it's good, secure it."

Robert pulled out his checkbook and quickly filled it out for several thousands of dollars.

"Here. Put this in a new account in your name. If there was one thing I learned from O'Reilly and Waters, it is this. Keep it safe for our business future, Dorothy."

"What's this?"

"The part of my severance I don't need at the moment. You and I have kind of been in business for quite a while...and now it's cemented."

"The sooner the better for an office, Dorothy. If you think it's good, bring me the lease papers so I can sign them. I'm heading home."

* * *

It was one of those cold, wet April days – low, dirty gray clouds spitting out rain driven by gusty winds. It was early to be home – much earlier than normal. Margaret was sitting in the living room, watching her favorite soap opera, "General Hospital." It was her three o'clock ritual. Robert's entrance startled her: she hadn't yet prettied herself up for his usual suppertime arrival.

"You're home early, Robert!" She instinctively patted her hair and smoothed the front of her dress. "I tried calling your office earlier to ask if you wouldn't mind if I drove up to Jack and Betty's tomorrow with a pot of soup. Must be something wrong with the service, though – the call would not go through."

"We've been having issues with the service, Margaret. Don't worry about it – we're getting new phone numbers soon. It will be in a different exchange."

"I haven't yet started supper. I'm sorry." Margaret got up, switched off the television, and headed to the kitchen. "I was planning on pork chops with baked apples. I can start them now, and dinner will be ready in forty-five minutes."

"Don't rush. I'm not hungry yet. I'm going to change and go work on the boat a bit before supper. Boating season will be here before we know it."

* * *

One month later, Detroit Rigging and Erecting was settled into its new offices and had completed the purchase of heavy machinery, brought up a union shop, and just signed its first job. Robert stuck his head out of his office door. "Dorothy! Buddy! Come in, will you?"

Robert was pulling out a bottle of scotch as the small team entered.

"Celebration time! We just signed our first job! Margins are razor thin, but we got it. I didn't realize how easy we had it before, with all the work falling into our laps. Buddy, you're on to run it. Not a city job – it's commercial. We're bringing in all the machinery for a new tool shop. Not huge, but it's a start."

He poured shots for the three of them and handed them over. Then he raised his high in the air. "To us!"

* * *

"The numbers don't look very good, Dorothy." Robert had been poring over the books. "We've our heads above water, but not by much. We can't gain enough momentum to land big jobs."

"Growth takes some time, Robert. Don't despair. No one could be working harder than you are, and no one runs a tighter ship. As long as we're making headway."

"Not so sure I have time to wait like I used to. I'm nearly sixty-five. I'm short on time."

"We'll be fine, Robert. You've got me, and I'm seventeen years younger than you. We can keep this company going."

Robert sighed. "You truly are indispensable. Had you been a man, you'd have been running your own business decades ago. I've said it before: I don't know what I would do around here without you."

He handed Dorothy a check. "Not much to move over to you this quarter, Dorothy. This is it, I'm afraid."

"Better than nothing, Robert. I'll deposit this right away."

"Well, we best be getting back to work." He closed the book, stuck it in his right-hand drawer, pushed back his chair, and stood. "I need to go find Buddy."

He walked back into the shop and stopped the first laborer he saw. "Have you seen Buddy?"

"He got called out on union business, Mr. Sharp. He's at a meeting at the union hall. He said he'd be back in an hour or two."

"Send him to my office when he returns, will you?"

"Sure enough, Mr. Sharp."

Robert returned to his office and spent the rest of the day making cold calls...his least favorite chore. As he left for the day, he realized Buddy hadn't shown up. Thinking he'd catch up first thing in the morning, Robert left for home.

Margaret was chatting as she served dinner to Robert.

"Jeff's graduating high school next month, Robert. I was talking to Jack... Do you suppose we could go in together and get him a used car?"

"That's a bit much, Margaret. Can we maybe simply give him a hundred dollars?"

"If you say so, Robert. I'll let Jack know that he's on his own with a car. Can't say I don't agree with you. Can you imagine getting anything so extravagant when you left primary?"

"Heavens, no. Times have really changed, haven't they? What's

Jeff going to do?"

"He's going away to Michigan State."

"Ah...extending his youth, I see. He's not working his way through?"

"Not that I've heard."

Robert shook his head. "And to think that at his age, I was coming home from the war. Times certainly have changed."

"I don't think it's all bad, Robert."

"Not all bad, but certainly not what makes a man, in many ways."

The rest of dinner was eaten in silence.

*　*　*

The parking lot was uncharacteristically empty when Robert arrived the next morning. He checked his watch – he didn't think he was that early. He wasn't. He walked in, turned on the lights, and started walking around the shop. No one was there. He headed back into the office and called the union hall.

"This is Robert Sharp from Detroit Rigging and Erecting. I'm concerned that there's no one here. You haven't called a strike and not let me know, have you?"

"Let me put you through to the vice president, Mr. Sharp. One moment."

The switchboard operator connected Robert right away.

"Harry? This is Bob Sharp, Detroit Rigging and Erecting. What's going on?"

There was a long silence.

"I'm sorry, Mr. Sharp. We got word yesterday from the top. O'Reilly's been removed from all involvement with the Riggers. New leadership has instructed us to immediately sever all ties with anyone with connections to O'Reilly. You can sue us if you want, but in the meantime, I can assure you that we will not honor our contract with you."

"I can't survive waiting for a court ruling, Harry. I don't have the funds to ride it out. Anything you can do? You know I've been square with you."

"Sorry, Scotty. I have no wiggle room."

"Thanks for being straight with me, Harry."

There was a pause on the line.

"For what it's worth, Scotty, good luck. This is a raw deal."

"Thanks, Harry." Robert hung up the phone.

Dorothy arrived ten minutes later and went straight to the break room to make a pot of coffee. Once it was perking, she headed to Robert's office.

"What's going on? Did the Riggers call a strike or something?"

Robert sighed as he put his head in his hands. "We're done, Dorothy. The Riggers have shut us down."

"What do you mean, shut us down? Why? How can they do that? We have a labor contract."

"We do, and we would probably win in court. But we don't have enough to ride it out. It would take months. We're done."

"Let me bring you a cup of coffee." Dorothy left and quickly returned with a steaming mug. Placing it in front of him, she sat down. "What about Waters?"

"I'll give him the machinery back or sell it and give him the proceeds. I'll show him the books – can't get blood from a turnip. He's smart enough to take what he can get and run. He's our only creditor and won't get anything more by suing us. If there's one thing he is, he's a smart businessman."

Dorothy took a sip of coffee. "So, that's it, is it?" She paused. "What's next, Robert?"

"I have no idea, actually."

"Well, what would be a dream of yours?"

Robert turned his chair to gaze out the rather dirty window, onto the street and beyond, to the other industrial buildings and parking lots that filled the area. He strummed his fingers on the chair arm as he pondered.

"Something with boats and water, I suppose. I love boats, fishing, and water. Maybe a marina. With a shop where I could fix engines and things. I think I would like that. No more unions or depending on other people to make a living."

"You certain you don't want to simply retire?"

"That's not in my character, Dorothy. Whatever would I do with all my time? And besides, just between you and me, spending all day, every day, with my wife is not terribly appealing. We have grown so far apart."

"Well then, let's both look to see whether there's a marina we could buy. We have quite a stash of money we've been squirreling away. That was brilliant of you to think of that, by the way."

Robert finished his coffee, set his jaw, and handed the mug back to Dorothy. "Well, it's useless twiddling our thumbs here all day. Turn off the coffee pot; we can handle wiggling out of the lease and formally dissolving this business later. I think you and I should drive down towards Toledo and check out marinas between here and there. And if that doesn't work, we can go east of Toledo for a bit or go up towards Harsen's Island. Let's close up shop."

Robert and Dorothy headed downriver, stopping along the way at every marina and speaking with the owners or managers. They didn't get past Wyandotte before it was time to turn around. The next day, they picked up where they had left off, and they did the same thing day after day. After a week, they had visited every marina between Detroit and Monroe, and after that, they headed further south, towards Toledo. As they pulled off of I-75 in LaSalle, heading toward the Toledo Beach marina, they passed a small, rather tired marina situated on a canal amidst a marsh. It appeared shuttered, so they headed on to the much larger Toledo Beach Marina.

"Hi! I was wondering if the owner was around."

"Sure – let me get him." Soon an athletic-looking man in his late fifties appeared. He strode energetically over to Robert and Dorothy and extended his hand.

"Tim Gladieux – how can I help you?"

"Robert Sharp. I'm looking to learn about marina ownership and possibly investing and running a small one. You've got quite an operation here." Robert looked around with obvious appreciation.

"Thank you! We are proud of it."

"I couldn't help but notice that small, rundown marina as we came here. What do you know about it?"

"Well, the owner passed away, and none of his children were interested in running it. It's tied up at the moment in the estate, I think, but it will be sold when the dust settles. It needs a lot of work, as you might imagine."

"It never would be much competition for your operation, that's for sure. Do you know who's handling the estate?"

"Some attorney in Monroe. I sure you can get his name from the probate office."

The man paused.

"Not a very good place for a marina if you ask me. Two miles away from the lake, and the canal keeps needing to be dredged. No idea what possessed the owner to put a marina so far away from the water's edge. Takes all kinds."

"Thanks for your time, sir. We'll not keep you any longer. You've been very helpful."

Robert and Dorothy headed to the car. "That's it, Dorothy. I can feel it. Let's head into Monroe and see what we can find out.

CHAPTER NINETEEN

"Margaret, we're moving. I've bought a marina – and the house next door. It's a lovely, two-story brick house. Solid as a rock and much larger than this one. I think you'll love it."

Margaret looked at Robert in total shock. "Just like that? Where is it?"

"Down past Monroe. It's maybe forty-five minutes south of here. You'll get used to it… It feels as if it's out in the country."

"And what of your job?"

"Retired from that. I am sixty-five. It was time to do something I think I will love."

Margaret looked around at the house she had become so comfortable in with sad resignation.

"I'm going to miss it here."

"Come with me now, Margaret. I'll drive you down there and show you around."

Robert was brimming with happy anticipation, and it had been so long that Margaret had seen that. She grabbed her purse and headed towards the garage.

Forty-five minutes later, the two of them were standing next to the two old gas pumps that stood in the middle of the crumbling asphalt lot in front of a smallish, sorry-looking building with dirty picture windows revealing empty display cases and shelves. To the left was, as promised, a two-story, solid-brick, classically colonial home: center door, double-hung windows on each side.

"Come on, Mag. Let's go in the house."

"Margaret couldn't help but stare at the storefront.

"It's a gas station, Robert. A gas station. And look at the reeds behind! That's not open water – that's a swamp."

"That's an overgrown canal, Margaret. I will clean it out. There are boat slips behind the building. You'll see. I can clean it all up. But come into the house."

Robert headed around to the back of the house and unlocked the back door. He headed into the landing that served both the basement and the kitchen to the left. Margaret reluctantly followed him. She silently walked around the kitchen, opening the stove and refrigerator doors, and then headed into the dining room and then the living room. She wandered upstairs to the three bedrooms and bath. Then she came back down and headed into the basement. Robert didn't follow her.

She finally came back into the kitchen, where Robert was waiting.

It's a lovely home, Robert. I'll give you that."

She walked out the front door and gazed at the surroundings.

"We have no neighbors."

"We do, but they are a mile or so down the road. Nice and quiet here, right?"

"I'll have no neighbors. And where is shopping?" She looked over at the commercial building.

"And that! Robert, are ye daft? That's nothing but a rundown mess!"

"I will bring it back, Margaret. I can't wait to start. I am calling it Rainbow Marina. It's my dream – my gold at the end of the rainbow."

Margaret sighed. "If it makes you happy, Robert. If it makes you happy."

She went back and sat in the car, pulling out the linen handkerchief she always carried to dry the tears she could not stop.

Robert slipped behind the steering wheel. "I'll make sure you know where everything is, Margaret. And I will be right next door if you ever need anything. Right next door, working."

The houses on Hickory Island sold right away, and in a whirlwind of activity, Robert and Margaret moved to LaSalle, Michigan.

It only took a few days to get the house in order, and once the kitchen was organized, Margaret fixed a nice lunch for Robert that she planned on taking next door – for the first time. She hadn't mentioned she was going to do that, and her little surprise pleased her greatly. She packed it up carefully in a picnic basket, went out the back door, and headed over to the building with a little smile on her face. When she walked into the open back bay, she heard voices up front, so she headed that way. There she saw Robert and Dorothy leaning over the glass display case, deep in conversation about the drawing lying there.

Margaret was in shock.

"Robert?"

Robert looked up, obviously surprised.

"Oh – Margaret. I didn't expect you."

She offered up the picnic basket. "I brought you lunch." She stared at Dorothy.

"You remember Dorothy, don't you? I've hired her to help me here."

Margaret stammered. "I only made lunch for one."

Robert took the basket. "Thank you, Margaret. That was very thoughtful of you. Very unexpected."

"Well, I've got to get back. I have many things still needing tending. Dinner is at six." She stared at Dorothy again, turned, and hastily left. She managed a dignified walk back to the house, but once inside, she ran up the stairs and flung herself on her bed, sobbing. Robert did not follow her into the house, but kept on working, sharing his sandwich and grapes with Dorothy.

Dinner that night was eaten in stony silence. Margaret picked up the empty plates and threw them into the sink, chipping the bottom plate. She stormed back into the dining room.

"And just how long has this been going on?"

"What do you mean, going on? We work together."

"How very chummy. Funny that you never mentioned her. You're hiding something."

"My business affairs have always stayed outside of our house, ever since you refused to be my corporate wife. You made it difficult and uncomfortable for me for years, but I never forced you into that role. Dorothy is an astute businesswoman, and I appreciate her talents. I rely on her to keep things straight and accounted for. You can't do that: she can."

Robert's tone was very cold and matter of fact.

"I want her fired."

"That will never happen."

"So I'm supposed to sit here quietly as my husband flaunts his lover in full view, right next door?"

"I never said she was my mistress."

"I don't think you have to. Everyone will just assume. And I am here, right next door – forced to look at the two of you carrying on right under my nose?"

Robert stood forcefully, knocking his chair over as he did.

"I need Dorothy to help run the business, and that's that. If you don't like living here, I suggest you call Jack and Betty and move in with them. That's my final word." He stormed out the back door and headed over to the shop.

Margaret threw down the dishtowel in dismay and ran back upstairs, sobbing.

* * *

Breakfast was on the table by six in the morning, and next to it was the picnic basket, loaded with lunch – for one. Margaret said nothing as she made sure she was busy in the kitchen while Robert ate. Mid-morning, she fixed her hair, put on makeup, heels, and a good dress, and drove herself down the road a mile or so. She noticed a woman hanging laundry, so she pulled in, stopped, and got out of her blue Ford sedan.

"Hello. I'm sorry to bother you. My name is Margaret Sharp, and my husband and I just moved into the brick house by the old marina. I'm obviously new to the neighborhood and would like to invite some ladies over for tea to get to know you."

"Clara Stevens. Welcome! Would you come in for some coffee? I hear an accent!"

"Yes – I'm Scottish. I would love a cup of coffee! Thank you."

Clara set the kitchen table for two and brought out cream and sugar. "Coffee is still a bit warm – do you mind reheated?"

"That would be just fine."

Clara sat down. "I'm glad someone finally bought that old place. I see it's being fixed up, and I'm so very glad to see the gas pumps are open again. Really convenient. So, tell me a bit about yourself!"

Margaret retold her story, leaving out her deceased son and daughter: how she and Robert had left Scotland, spent several years in Canada, moved to California after the war, then to Cleveland, and then back to Michigan. She also mentioned proudly that her son was a dentist, that she had three lovely grandchildren, and that she loved her garden and was keen to keep her home "just so."

"I do have a favor to ask. Since I know only you, could you ask a handful of women friends to come to tea for me? Next Tuesday, say ten in the morning?"

"I certainly will! I'm sure that they will be very welcoming."

Margaret finished her coffee. "Well, I can't thank you enough. I am sure I've interrupted you, and you have to get back to your chores. Very nice meeting you, Clara. I really look forward to next week."

Margaret went home smiling. She suddenly realized just how long it had been since she had offered to host a ladies' tea party.

Excited, she checked her pantry to see what she already had and started a grocery list.

* * *

"Robert, we have over two dozen empty boat slips. That's a good half of what we can accommodate."

"Well, now that we are fully open for business, I think we should put ads in the local papers and see if we can't get referrals from local boat dealers and outfitters. We can berth boats much more cheaply than Toledo Beach – that's what got the boats we have. Hopefully, our customers will help spread the word."

Robert and Dorothy were chatting in the front over morning coffee, where they could watch for gas pump traffic. A sedan pulled up, and Robert quickly put down his coffee and went out to pump gas and clean the car windows. The driver rolled down his window to pay.

"That'll be three dollars and a quarter. Are you a boater?"

"I am! I have a little fishing boat."

"Well, we're fully open out back – refurbished docks. We also have a full-service engine repair shop. I think we can beat most prices around. Why don't you come by this weekend and take a look around?"

"I just might. If your docks have been refurbished like the building, I just might be very interested."

"Great! Have a good day, sir."

Robert went back in and put the money in the till.

"That gent might return this weekend to look at berthing his boat here."

"I think we might want to stock candy and snacks up front."

"That's not a bad idea, Dorothy. Can you handle that?"

"Of course. And what about a small retail space with things boaters might need: hats, sunglasses, marine paint for touch-ups…"

"We don't have a ton of space, but yes, we have some. I'll start putting together a list – you can, too. We can compare notes."

Robert looked out to see Margaret leaving. "Wonder where my

wife is going so early." He looked at the calendar. "Oh – probably to the grocery store. She usually goes on Tuesdays." He turned back to his coffee as another car pulled up and Dorothy headed out to the pumps.

*　*　*

Just before ten o'clock, two cars pulled up to the house, and a half-dozen women exited and walked up the front door. Margaret greeted them and ushered them in. She had set a lovely table and brought out her best china and tea set. Scones and Devonshire cream were sitting on a delicate, hand-crocheted tablecloth next to shortbread and jam, coffee, and tea.

"Margaret, let me introduce you to a few of the local ladies." Clara smiled as she introduced them, one by one. "This is Mary – she lives three doors down from me. And this is Susan, and this is Joan. Susan and Joan are sisters. This is Betty – her husband runs the hardware store in LaSalle, and finally, this is Donna. Donna teaches piano."

"So nice to meet you all," said Margaret. "Please come in and make yourselves comfortable."

An hour of coffee, tea, treats, and small talk later, the women were gathering their purses to leave.

"This was lovely, Margaret. We should do this again!"

There were approving murmurs.

"Yes! I'll host the next one. Week after next?"

"Joan, that would be lovely!"

"And I'll do the one after that!"

"Do you sisters always compete?" Clara laughed.

Margaret stood by the opened door. "Thank you all for coming!"

She leaned her back against the front door after they left and smiled to herself. These women were housewives, like her. They chatted about children and grandchildren, recipes and gardens...subjects familiar and comfortable. Margaret hummed a little tune as she carried the dishes into the kitchen.

Dinner was on the table at six, as usual. Margaret was still basking in the warmth of her ladies' tea, and an occasional smile flitted across her face as she remembered conversations.

"You're in a good mood this evening, Margaret," Robert commented as he buttered a roll.

"I had some ladies over for tea this morning. We had a lovely time."

"That's nice."

It didn't even bother Margaret that Robert wasn't more interested.

* * *

Several months later, Margaret was late getting supper on the table.

"Sorry – dinner's not quite ready. I need fifteen more minutes. I was busy working on this afghan for the ladies' flower club benefit, and I lost track of time."

She pulled out the small pot roast and set it aside to make gravy and mash the potatoes.

"I'm glad you've made some friends, Margaret – just don't let it get in the way of your duties." Robert's tone was unusually sharp.

"Don't be so sharp with me, Robert. This is the first time dinner has ever been late. After over forty years, that's not such a bad track record."

Margaret's retort surprised Robert, and he said no more on the subject.

"I'll be hiring two or three lads to help with the winterizing. Short term – only about three weeks. Do you suppose you could arrange lunch for them every day? Nothing special, sandwiches and apples. I would really appreciate it."

"When will they start?"

"Next week."

"Let me know how many sandwiches to make, then."

"Thank you, Margaret. I'm sorry I was sharp. Lots of pressure at the moment. I'm a bit worried about making it through the winter with only gasoline sales."

Margaret plopped a large spoonful of mashed potatoes on Robert's plate, put down the saucepan, and sat across from him.

"I'm sure you'll figure it out. You always do." She said no more, focusing on her roast beef and green beans.

When finished, Robert pushed his chair away from the table. "I'm going back to the shop to wrap up some things. Dinner was good – thank you."

He left Margaret to clean up the kitchen, watch a couple of game shows, and head to bed.

* * *

Charlie Stevens entered the shop after filling up with gas.

Robert rushed up, a big smile on his face as he stretched out his arm. "Good to see you, Charlie! Looking to winterize and store your boat for the season?"

Charlie did not take Robert's hand. "Um, no, Robert. I've come to move my boat from Rainbow."

Robert's smile vanished. "Did something happen? Something I did? How can I make it right?"

Charlie hesitated. "It's not that, Scotty. It's my wife, Clara. She insists."

"But why? Has she ever been in here?"

Charlie squirmed, put his hand on Robert's arm, and steered him outside.

"My wife won't have me doing business with you anymore, Scotty. It's because of her." He cocked his head towards the door. "She won't have me doing business with a man cheating on his wife in plain view."

Robert was stunned. His eyes widened, and his jaw dropped. "What? Where did that vicious rumor come from?"

"Come, now, Scotty. Everyone is saying it. Truthfully, it couldn't look any clearer. You've been seen going back over after dinner, lights on till late, alone with her. Clear as day, looking at the lights in your house, that your wife has gone to bed. This is a small community. A small, conservative community."

Robert was silent as he absorbed the words.

"I'm sorry, Scotty. I'm pulling my boat out. Can you get it up on the trailer for me by the weekend? Thanks, and send me anything I might still owe."

Charlie climbed into his car and left.

Robert turned and smacked the gas pump in anger. He paced for a few moments and then headed over to the house, storming in the back door.

"MARGARET!!" he roared more loudly than he had ever done before.

Margaret came up from the basement, wiping her hands on her apron.

"What's wrong, Robert? I've never heard you so upset."

"You and your lady friends! What have you been saying to them? That Dorothy and I are having an affair? Is this your doing?"

"Well, aren't you? Everyone thinks so," Margaret said matter-of-factly.

Robert could barely contain himself, and he smacked the wall and kicked the stove.

"Come, now, Robert – you're going to damage the oven, and then how will I make your supper?"

Robert whirled around and grabbed Margaret by the shoulders.

"You may never visit with them again! You may not leave this house except to go shopping and visit with Jack and the family. Do you understand? NEVER!!!"

Margaret was silent.

"You are forbidding me to leave this house."

306

"Yes, I am. You are ruining my business! People are leaving! Do you know what that means? If I lose business, we lose everything – this house included. So, if you want a roof over your head, you will heed me. Forbidden to leave this house. Period."

Margaret quietly turned and headed back down to the basement to work on the laundry, leaving Robert to his untamed anger.

Dinner was on the table that night, as usual.

"Robert, I want you to buy me a round-trip ticket to Miami in January. I want to go stay with Cameron for three or four weeks. She has invited me."

Robert looked up, trying to read Margaret's face.

"Things are a bit tight now, Margaret."

"That is none of my affair, and it hasn't been for our entire marriage. It's winter, and I have honored your wishes of not seeing my friends. I will not stay prisoner in this home with no diversions. Either you figure out a way to buy me a ticket, or I shall go visiting."

Robert clenched his jaw. "Fine."

"Thank you. I'm sure you'll manage to keep the house up, do your laundry, shop, and make your meals. If you get a little overwhelmed, I'm sure you can ask Dorothy to help."

Margaret picked up her place setting and carried it into the kitchen.

* * *

Spring came late that year, and the marina opened a bit later than usual. Robert was busy in the shop when Dorothy came in with an opened letter.

"Robert, they are closing the South Otter Creek exit off of I-75 for six months."

"That's our exit! How in the world are we supposed to manage over the summer if people can't get to us?"

"They are routing them from Erie and La Plaisance."

Robert sat and held his head in his hands.

"The entire summer? There goes our gasoline income. We won't be getting any of the traffic headed from the expressway to Toledo Beach."

He sighed heavily.

"I don't know if we can make it, Dorothy. We're tight as it is, and I'm approaching seventy. I'm not sure I have any fight left in me."

Dorothy peered at him over her glasses.

"I think we need to ride out the exit closure, Robert. Then I think it might be time to sell. Have to wait, though. The closure will depress the selling price."

She sat across from Robert. "You gave me the money from Detroit Rigging and Erecting. I've invested it. Esther is about to retire from Ford, and she'll have a nice pension. Esther and I were thinking of building a house in the Keys and having Archie move in. Since it will actually be some of your money used, we would like you to move in, too. You can help take care of our father if he needs it. I think it's time."

"I need to think about it, Dorothy. It is tempting, but I need some time." Robert sounded resigned. He looked around his very clean and tidy shop.

"This was my dream, you know? My pot at the end of the rainbow." He walked over to the tool bench and ran his hand over the smooth surface.

"My timing has always been bad. I've always overcome it, but this one…I think I've run out of time. Run out of grit and time. I think, this time, I'm defeated."

Dorothy walked over to put her hand on his shoulder, but Robert turned away.

* * *

Three weeks later, Robert invited Jack for lunch at his old haunt, Lelli's.

"We've not chatted for a long time, son. How's it going? I hear you divorced Betty? And I hear that Jeff and Tracy are struggling, but Cameron is doing fine?"

"Cameron had graduated college – she's the smart one. Got a really good job. Tracy has gotten herself kicked out of every high school she's attended. Betty finally sent her down to live with Cameron. And Jeff – well, Jeff's just a bum. Let his hair grow long, dropped out of college with only a year to go… He's a goddamned hippie. No idea how he's supporting himself. Not me, that's for sure."

"And how are you doing?"

"I'm back at dentistry, but I picked up orthodontia. The physics of it interests me. I'm having fun with a great bunch of guys… We have a social calendar going out an entire year. We got together and bought a ski house in Charlevoix, and we're all going to Munich for Oktoberfest. A couple of us got together and bought a seventy-foot cruiser – we're taking it to the islands after Munich."

Jack took a few bites of his club sandwich.

"How's Mum?"

"That's what I want to talk to you about. I'm pushing seventy, and it's time for me to retire. I am probably going to move to the Keys, and I want to ask you to make good on a promise you made me a long time ago."

"And what was that?"

"I want you to take care of your mother. We have been distant for a very long time, and we will both be happier apart."

"Are you divorcing her?"

"No – I would never do that. I made a vow, and I am a man of my word. I just can't live with her anymore. I will be moving in with Dorothy, her sister Esther, and their father, Archie. So I am asking you to fulfill your promise to me."

Jack put down his sandwich and stared intently at his father. After a rather long and painful silence, he finally said, "I am also a man of my word. I will take her, Dad. I will make sure she's cared for."

"Thank you, Jack."

"When will all of this take place?"

"By the end of the year, I hope. The expressway exit to the marina is closed for construction all summer long. Once it's back open, I'll be putting the marina up for sale."

"Have you told Mum?"

"No, I haven't. We probably should do that together, don't you think?"

"Yes, but not right now. I need to figure out where she's going to live... I think a condo might be perfect for her. Give her some privacy, away from the crowd I'm hanging with. Let me look around first – I'd like to be able to take her to see it right after we tell her. Might give her a better sense of security."

That's a good idea. We have quite a bit of time."

Jack paused after finishing his sandwich.

"I hope you'll be happy, Dad."

"Me, too, Jack. Me, too."

* * *

"Mom, this house is getting too much for you. I've found you a condo near me. Let me show it to you."

Robert stood silently as Jack tried to put the best spin he could on the uncomfortable situation.

"By you? Robert, isn't that too far from the marina?" Margaret looked at Robert, her expression changing as she started to understand what was happening.

"You are selling the marina. I wondered, with the exit being closed for as long as it was. I noticed people weren't pulling up like they used to."

"Margaret, I think it's best you go with Jack now."

"And what about you?"

There was a long silence.

"I'm leaving, Margaret. I'm moving to Florida with Dorothy,

her sister Esther, and their father, Archie."

There was another long silence.

"It's for the best, Margaret. You know it. You belong here. You and I have been distant for a very long time. I know I've made you unhappy… It's time for you to try and find some happiness. I can't give it to you."

Margaret's lip trembled, and she wiped her nose with the back of her hand. She bit her lip, holding back the tears. Then she straightened up and composed herself.

"Going to live with that hussy? And you've said all along you weren't having an affair. Well, now the truth comes out. You just go along, now. It will be nice to be able to go out and see friends again. I'm sick and tired of being a prisoner in this house because of you. You just go along with your life, Robert. You just go along."

"Margaret, you've been a good wife. You really have. If it means anything to you at all, you are, and will forever be, my wife. I'll not divorce you… I'll not remarry. You were the love of my life. I will honor you with that."

"Funny way of showing that, Robert."

Margaret turned to Jack. "A condo? Well, let's get on with it." She walked out the door.

* * *

Robert looked at the purchase agreement and shook his head.

"Well, looks as if I've lost pretty much everything, Dorothy. I'm going to sign everything I have over to you, but it's not nearly enough to put a roof over our heads."

"You've given me enough over the years, Robert. Because of you, we've been able to build this house. I will forever be grateful."

The house was on concrete piers, as were all new houses in the Keys.

"Archie, Esther and I will live upstairs. This…" Dorothy swung her arm around the lower level in back of the garage. "This will be yours. You still have your boat... You can moor it right outside."

The lower level was dark, with no windows because of hurricane building codes. Upstairs, however, was bright and sunny, with floor-to-ceiling windows.

"This will be perfectly fine, Dorothy. Thank you." Robert looked around and then headed outside. There was a dock along the edge of the canal, which was sheltered by a short strip of land. Because of it, waves didn't hit the shore by the house. However, also because of it, the current through that small canal was strong. He looked up at the palm trees swaying in the breeze and took in the salt air. It was perfection.

He went back inside and climbed the stairs.

"Dorothy, I'll give you my Social Security checks for my upkeep if that's all right with you."

"My my, Robert... That won't be necessary."

"But I insist!"

"If you must..."

Their conversation was interrupted by Esther, who had just returned from the grocery store.

"Here – let me help you with those." Robert went over, took the bags from Esther, and put them in the kitchen. "Don't worry about the rest – I'll fetch them." He stood to the side as Archie slowly climbed the stairs.

"Getting your exercise, Archie? Take your time." Robert smiled as Archie passed him and then ran down the stairs to bring up the rest of the groceries.

CHAPTER TWENTY

Maggie sat in the living room of the assisted living facility Jack had put her in, quietly holding hands with Harold. The facility was a refitted residential home, with only a half-dozen or so inhabitants. As much as she did not like the idea at first, she had to admit she was happier here than alone in her condo. She thought of the conversation that had placed her in the Silver Bell Road facility.

"Mum, you can't live alone anymore. Look, you have nothing in the refrigerator! What happened to everything I put in there last week?"

"I thought it had gone bad, so I threw it all out."

"Mum, it was all fresh! You need someone to look after you more than I can do, with you living in this condo by yourself. I'm going to move you to where you can have people around."

Harold was kind – Harold thought she was beautiful. It was pleasant being cared for… At eighty-four, Margaret had a boyfriend.

She was sitting, waiting for a visit from her granddaughter.

"Hey Grandma! How are you today?"

Cameron walked in, swaybacked from the child she was carrying.

Margaret smiled. "My! Aren't you huge!" She laughed.

"That's wasn't very nice, Grandma." Cameron bent down and gave Margaret a kiss on the cheek. "How are you?"

Margaret scowled a bit. "Nae so good, Cameron. I've not been feeling very well. Your dad is taking me to the doctor tomorrow. I've got pains in my stomach."

Cameron reached into her bag. "I brought you some chocolate, Grandma. Sanders. Your favorite!"

Margaret took the box and placed it on the end table, unopened.

"Don't you want to grab a piece or two?"

"No, not now, Cameron. I'm not hungry. It's my stomach."

"That's not like you, Grandma." Cameron looked worried. 'I'm glad you're going to the doctor tomorrow."

"It's all right, Cameron. I'm just tired. Tired of this. I've had a good life… It might be time to go."

"No, Grandma! No! You love the bairns… You'll love this little boy. Please hang on for him. For me…"

"There's something not right with me, Cameron. I can feel it. It's fine, though. Don't worry. This is not much of a life anymore."

Through all of this, Harold said not a word. He didn't even look as if he knew Margaret had a visitor. He simply sat there, holding her hand, staring down at the well-worn carpet.

"Grandma, hold on. Please. I'm going to give you a great birthday present… I promise. Please hold on."

Margaret smiled at Cameron. "Really, child. I think it's getting time for me to move on. I don't mind. I don't mind at all. I feel it's getting to be time."

Cameron leaned over and gave Margaret a hug. "Please hang on, Grandma. Until your birthday. Please," she whispered. "Just hang on."

As winter lingered, Maggie stopped eating. She wouldn't even taste ice cream. On a blustery February night, Cameron got a phone call. "We've put in a feeding tube." Several hours later, a second call came in. "Your grandmother has passed."

Even though it was two in the morning, Cameron called her father.

"Pops, grandma has died. The facility called."

The line stayed silent.

"Pops – are you still there?"

"Yes, I am. You just caught me off guard. I'll manage everything – you take care of yourself and that baby you're carrying. Good night, Cam."

"Night, Pops." Cameron hung up the phone and fell back asleep.

The next morning Jack called his father."

"Dad, I have some sad news. Mum passed away last night."

Jack patiently waited for his father to absorb the news. Robert finally spoke.

"Was she in pain?"

"Not that we've heard, dad. She's been failing for a while and not eating. I think she wanted to go."

"You'll handle the details? She should remain in Michigan. Will you have a service?"

"I don't think so, Dad. I don't think there are many left who knew her – just us. Cameron is not supposed to risk the winter weather, since she's nearing her due date. I think I'll just inter her... we can get together to remember her later, when the weather is better. Maybe after Cam's baby is born."

"Well, I'm sorry she's gone but grateful she didn't suffer. Thanks, son, for letting me know. Even though I left, she was my one and only."

"Talk to you later, Dad. Good bye."

* * *

Robert sat on the edge of his bed for quite a while. His mind drifted back to the dance hall, where he first laid eyes on that stunning young woman with long dark ringlets. He remembered coming back from the war, taking those long walks in Cowdenbeath. His dear, stalwart Margaret – moving away from her family across the ocean, and then criss-crossing the United States with only a whisper of complaint. He laid back down and put his hands behind his head, remembering how she made do during the Depression with strong resolve. She really was as perfect a housewife as could be had: always neat, changing into a fresh frock for the delicious dinners she made. A perfect mother... a perfect grandmother.

I put her through so much. I should have let her be the perfect housewife. That's what she did best.

Robert rolled out of bed and went to his desk. He pulled out a pen and paper and wrote one last letter to his wife.

Dearest Margaret:

I am sorry. I am sorry for so many things. I am sorry I tried to force you to become who you weren't. I am sorry I put my career so far ahead of us. I am sorry for causing you so much pain. It's all my fault, not yours. I am sorry I couldn't stand by you as you stood by me. Please forgive me. I have always loved you. I have never loved another. I will remain true to you, even in your death.

I have so many regrets. Please forgive me. I would give anything to do it differently.

Love, Robert

For the first time in his life Robert allowed tears to run down his face. He took the letter with him as he went out to his dock. The breeze was warm and stiff. Whitecaps were breaking against the seawall, and the current in the water off the dock was swift. Robert ripped the letter into small pieces and sent them sailing in the breeze until they hit that strong current and were swept out to sea.

* * *

Cameron went into labor on a warm and sunny late April day. And although her due date was May 5, on April 28 she delivered a healthy little baby boy – on what would have been Margaret's eighty-sixth birthday.

* * *

"Dorothy, I'd like to go visit my family. Cameron's had a baby boy. I'd like to go see him."

Dorothy clenched her jaw.

"It's such a long way back to Michigan, Robert. Are you sure?"

"They are my family, Dorothy. You and Esther and I can go – we'll have the neighbors look in on Archie."

"If that's what you want, Robert." Dorothy faked a wan smile.

"We can also stop and see your nephew, Peter. It will be a great trip." Robert, unaware of the undercurrent, kept chatting. "I've decided to work on hybridizing hibiscus. The garden club here is marvelous, don't you think? I like the work they are doing. They are trying to raise money. Think I could donate some of the stained-glass nightlights I've been making? Think I'll make one for baby Chris. From pictures, he's a strapping lad."

"I think the garden club would love your work, Robert. That's a great idea."

Dorothy got up and headed into the kitchen. "Think I'll make some potato salad."

Robert went down to his quarters, where he had set up a little workshop. He started working. Then he stopped to write letters to both Jack and Cameron, telling them of the upcoming visit.

His writing was interrupted by Dorothy coming down the stairs.

"Robert, you are a widower now. You and I have been together for so long... I don't want to sound forward, but don't you think it's time we married?"

Robert froze and then put down his pen. He turned in his chair to face Dorothy, but he didn't stand.

"Dorothy, I...I can't. I'm sorry. I simply can't."

"Why, Robert? After all these years? Don't you agree we get along very well?"

Robert looked at her directly. "No, Dorothy. I can't. I made a vow to forsake all others, and I did not fully live up to that promise. I have a family in Michigan I have been ignoring. If I couldn't fully honor my vow when my wife was alive, I certainly can honor it now. I told her I would never remarry. At least I can keep that promise. No, I will not marry you. Please don't ask again. If you want me to leave, I will understand. I can always go back to Michigan."

Dorothy hung her head, and a tear dropped from her cheek and onto the wood floor.

"No, Robert. Don't leave. I said years ago, if this is all I can get of you, it will be enough. I just thought after all of these years…"

"I'm sorry, Dorothy. I really am. I simply can't. I've done wrong, and I need to try and make it right. As best I can. You and Esther are like family, but you are not family. You are not of my blood, and I have been steadfast in my position. I am sorry that I have let you down – but then, I think I've let a lot of people down in my day."

Dorothy didn't say another word and slowly trudged up the stairs.

Robert returned to his letters.

* * *

"He's a braw lad, that's for sure. You're going to have your hands full, I can tell you that. It's genetic. It was me; it was your dad… He's going to be a handful."

Robert fondly gazed down at little Christopher, who kept crawling over to the bookcase to pull down the books.

"I was a sassy lad, I was. Thought I knew everything. It took many long nights marching in full regalia for me to realize I wasn't going to win." He laughed. "You've certainly got your hands full."

Cameron picked up her son and took him into the kitchen, where Esther and Dorothy were waiting.

Robert looked around the open floorplan of Cameron's California contemporary house.

"You know, I don't like it. It's too open."

"Robert!" Dorothy chastised him.

He turned to her. "Well, where do you think I'll end up if something happens to you?"

Dorothy's mouth flew open in surprise, and Cameron laughed.

"Gramps, you're always welcome, but I'm not so sure it would be a picnic with this wild child pulling at your trousers."

Dorothy hastily interrupted. "Let's go to lunch, shall we? Your favorite place, Robert – Bill Knapp's."

Cameron looked at Christopher. "I think we'll be better off going to Pasquale's. Better all around with the young'un. Let me go change him – we'll be right back."

While Chris was on the changing table, Cameron whispered to him, "You know that Batman that's in the counter at the restaurant? The one you wanted? If you are perfect for lunch – absolutely perfect – I will buy it for you. Deal?"

Christopher grinned in excited anticipation.

"Perfect – okay?"

Chris nodded.

*   *   *

Not long after Robert, Dorothy, and Esther returned to the Keys, Robert got a letter from the duke of Argyll, addressed to Frank Sharp. Surprised, he opened it right away.

"Greetings! On behalf of the Forty-Second Blackwatch, I am extending an invitation for you to visit me at my castle. Our records indicate you are the oldest living survivor of your unit, and we would love to honor you for your service. Please reply at your earliest convenience."

Robert ran up the stairs.

"Dorothy! Esther! What say we all go to Scotland!"

The two women hurried into the living room, and Robert handed over the letter.

"Do you think we could arrange it?"

Dorothy smiled as she handed the letter to Esther. "Sounds wonderful!"

Robert was nearly dancing in excitement. "I will write back right away! We will have a marvelous time!" He went back downstairs to answer the duke. Then he stopped.

I lied about my age. What if I'm not really the oldest one? But how can I refuse this? Tell the duke I lied? If the records say I'm the oldest, who will ever know? I'll just say I am older."

He accepted the invitation.

* * *

"Jack and Cameron and the two boys are coming to visit, Dorothy. Can you have lunch ready?"

Dorothy clenched her teeth again, but she replied through a fake smile, "Of course. How lovely."

When Robert's family arrived, he took the two young boys to the dock and gave them each a fishing pole.

"Here – let me bait this for you. This is how you fish." Robert reveled in instructing his two great-grandchildren in one of his personal loves – fishing.

"That's my dad...always great with the children." Jack was looking at his father with a grin on his face.

"He does have a way, doesn't he? I'll always remember Dead Eye Dick, the Dirty One." Cameron laughed. "We were totally enchanted."

The conversation continued through lunch. Lunch was hot: meatloaf sandwiches and cooked carrots. Pieces of cake were already served and sitting above the dinner plates – an incentive to belong to the Clean Plate Club. Robert looked at the table and then at his great-grandsons.

"Trade you my carrots for your cake." Everybody laughed but Esther, who tut-tutted and chided Robert for setting a bad example. The two young boys were wrapped up in Robert's enchanting spell.

* * *

Archie passed in 1991, two months short of his hundredth birthday. In those final months, Robert would lift Archie in and out of bed.

"Thank you so much for helping us with our dad, Robert." Esther was rather melancholy as she went through her father's belongings, sorting things to give to charity.

"I said I would, Esther. I like to keep my word if I can." Robert was boxing the items to give away.

"I want to make it longer than Archie did. I want to make it past a hundred."

"The way you look and move, I wouldn't doubt it, Robert. You've been a great help to us."

The two silently went about their business.

"When are we taking Archie back to Michigan?"

"The memorial service is in two weeks. Most of his friends are long gone – we're just planning a small internment in the family plot in Roseland Park. Next to our mother. Dorothy and I will also be there."

"Are you sorry you never married?"

Esther paused.

"I probably would have done my life differently if I could. I think I missed a lot, not having a family. I've been feeling pretty isolated. We've got our nephew and his family, but that's about it. And aunts and uncles come in second to parents and children – as we get older, that's becoming more and more apparent. Yes, I probably would have done it differently. But here we are. No use crying over spilt milk, as my mother used to say."

Robert pondered those words.

"I probably would have done things differently, too. I think I would have liked to have more children. I had two others, you know. They both died as babies. Three children, three grandchildren, and now three great-grandchildren. I do miss them."

321

He folded a pair of trousers and placed them in a box.

"I think I also regret not teaching my grandchildren about Scotland. I used to think it was so terrible, but it wasn't, really. There was a sense of pulling together there that I didn't appreciate at the time. Very strong family values, which, again, I did not fully appreciate. Amazing how a person sees things so differently as they become old."

"Like they say…if we knew then what we know now…" Esther's voice trailed off.

"You're not only saying it, Esther." Robert paused again.

"I want to see my family when we're up in Michigan."

"Well, that will irritate Dorothy."

Robert looked up. "I didn't know you were aware of that."

"Oh, Robert…how could I miss it? Every time you mention your family, she gets this sourpuss expression on her face. Pretty hard to miss."

"She has always wanted more than I was willing to give. I wish in retrospect that she would have found someone to marry."

"She's always wanted you, Robert."

"So, here we all are. Nobody's really happy. Many regrets, all around."

"I wonder how many people are truly happy with their decisions when all is said and done."

"I think only a lucky few are blessed."

Robert finished up and went down to his workroom. He had purchased a few Scottish standards, and he busily mounted and framed them. He packed a couple in his luggage to take to Michigan.

* * *

"Dorothy, we need to stop by Cameron's."

"Can't we just meet them at a restaurant?"

"No. I told her we'd be there. We don't need to stay very long, but I've something to give her."

Dorothy's sour face reappeared, but she said nothing. They

drove up to Bloomfield Hills after Archie's ceremony.

"Hi, Grandpa! Good to see you!"

Cameron gave him a big hug as Dorothy stood uncomfortably by. Esther remained in the car left running on the driveway.

"Can you stay for supper? The boys should be back from their dad's in an hour or so."

Dorothy's reply was rapid and terse, "No – we're on a rather tight schedule."

"Well, come in, then. Can I get you anything?"

Cameron shepherded in Robert and Dorothy, heading to the kitchen. "A glass of water, maybe? A cup of coffee?"

"No, thank you. I needed to stop by to give you this." Robert pulled out a framed Scottish standard from the bag he was carrying.

"Here. This is for you. Now, you're gang tae hang it whair ye can see it an' never ferget yer a Scot!"

Cameron looked at Robert with surprise – after all the years of downplaying where he was born, Robert's sudden outspoken pride in his heritage surprised her.

"I will, Grandpa. I will."

"And tell those lads about Scotland now. We're a strong and proud breed. There's lots to be proud of."

"I promise, Grandpa. I wish you could stay."

Robert looked over at Dorothy, who was finding it impossible to hide her irritation.

"We've got to go, Cameron. We have to get back."

"Good to see you, Grandpa. Love you." Cameron gave her beloved grandfather a hug.

"You take care, Cameron."

"I will, Grandpa. You, too."

With that, Robert and Dorothy took their leave.

* * *

Robert achieved his goal of outliving Archie and living to the great age of 100 on the 15th of July, 1999.

"Well, I beat Archie." Robert laughed. He was sitting before a large birthday cake, surrounded by most of the local garden club. The local newspaper had sent a reporter and a photographer, and a very lengthy article about Robert had been published. Robert blew out the candles to the tune of a bagpiper that had been brought in for the occasion.

"I'm surprised that Jack and Cameron didn't come."

"Probably too busy, Robert." Dorothy didn't look at him as she replied.

"You did invite them, didn't you?"

Dorothy must not have heard, because she quickly walked away for some errand.

* * *

Four months later, Robert stumbled while coming up the stairs. Esther came running.

"Are you all right, Robert?"

He was having a difficult time getting up.

"There's something wrong, Esther. I just don't feel right. It feels hard to breathe."

"Dorothy, come quickly!" Esther called over her shoulder as she hurried down to Robert.

Dorothy scurried to the top of the stairs. "Oh, my! What happened?"

"Come down and help me get Robert back to his bed." The two women grabbed Robert's arms and, with great difficulty, got him back to his bed.

"Now call the doctor, Dorothy." Esther checked Robert's arms and legs for cuts and bruises, and maybe worse. "Ask him whether we should take Robert to the hospital."

Dorothy was back in five minutes.

"Doctor says, at his age, take him to emergency."

"Can you get Archie's walker? I think we need it for Robert."

"No – I can walk."

Robert sat up and then tried to stand. He sat back down on the bed.

"Can you wheel me in my chair instead?" He pointed to the wheeled office chair he had by his desk.

"That's a good idea."

Esther rolled the chair over to the side of the bed for Robert to get in. She rolled him to the car and opened the passenger car door. Dorothy climbed behind the wheel, and Esther climbed in the back.

* * *

"It's his heart." the doctor said with no emotion. "It's remarkable he's lived this long. He survived the trenches on the Western Front? Amazing he made it to a hundred. That was one interesting story."

"What can be done, doctor?"

"Not much, unfortunately. His heart is functioning at thirty percent. We'll put him on oxygen, but beyond that, there's not much else we can do."

"Have you told him?"

"Yes, but he already knew. He's sharp for his advanced age and told me to give it to him straight."

"Thank you, doctor. Just take him home?"

"Yes – take him home and keep him comfortable."

Esther climbed the stairs after she and Dorothy settled Robert in to his bed.

"I'll take his meals down, Dorothy – your knees can't take it. You cook, and I'll deliver. You should probably let Jack know."

"Yes, I probably should." Dorothy said no more.

* * *

Robert passed in his sleep two months later.

"I'll take care of everything, Esther. You did all of the delivery up and down. Let me handle the details."

Dorothy called the medical examiner to report the death.

"Parent's names?"

"I don't know."

"Next of kin?"

"None."

"Your relationship?"

"Intimate friend."

"Place of birth?"

"Firth of Forth, Scotland."

She then went down to the funeral home – alone.

"I'd like to make arrangements to have remains prepared for travel to Michigan."

"You are his wife?"

She hesitated.

"No. But he has no next of kin. Just me."

"I'm sorry for your loss, ma'am."

"Thank you."

"Where will the remains be sent?"

"Roseland Park Cemetery in Berkley, Michigan. To be interred in the Steinhauser family plot. There will be a memorial service there, too."

"We'll take care of it for you, Ms...."

"Steinhauser. Dorothy Steinhauser."

* * *

Two months later, Cameron received a call from Esther.

"Are you going to come get your grandfather's belongings?"

Cameron was stunned.

"His belongings? What? Did he pass?"

"Yes, he passed – and neither you nor your father even came to the service."

"Esther – nobody told us."

"What?"

"Nobody told us."

"Dorothy said she called."

"Absolutely not. You think I would have missed that? I'm going to hang up now. I'm calling my father.

Cameron hung up and promptly called Jack.

"Pops, did Dorothy call you to tell you Grandpa died?"

There was dead silence on the line.

"No."

Cameron was furious. "Let me handle this, Pops."

She hung up and started making calls. The first was to the closest funeral home to Marathon.

"Hello – this is Cameron Sharp. Did you happen to make the arrangements for Robert Sharp?"

"Yes, we did. And may I ask your relationship?"

"I am his granddaughter."

The line seemed to go dead.

"Hello? Are you still there?"

"Yes, I am. I handled those arrangements. I remember him well. We were told there were no next of kin."

"That was an abject lie. My father and sister are still alive, as well as three great-grandchildren."

"I am so, so sorry!!! I didn't know…"

"I am sure it's not your fault, but you were lied to. Where are his remains?"

"Give me a minute – somewhere in Michigan… Let me see." A rustle of fumbled papers was audible over the receiver.

"Ah – here it is. Roseland Park, Berkley, Michigan."

"Thank you."

"I am so, so very sorry…. We didn't know…"

"I understand. It's not your fault. Thank you – you've been very helpful."

"Good luck to you."

"Thank you."

Cameron had breakfast with her father the next morning.

"Well, I know where Grandpa is. Roseland Park. In the Steinhauser family plot."

Jack said nothing.

"You want to go make it right? Want to move him to Kirk in the Hills?"

Jack took a forkful of scrambled eggs, crunched on a piece of bacon, and took a sip of coffee.

"Yes, I do."

"Well then – let's make it happen."

After breakfast, Cameron gathered three birth certificates: hers, Jack's, and Robert's.

"How do you have all three?" Jack was curious.

"Genealogy's a great thing, Pops. Let's go to Roseland Park."

Cameron and Jack drove down Woodward and pulled into the Roseland Park Cemetery. They stopped at the office and asked where the Steinhauser plot was. Given the directions, they drove to it.

This was not your normal, simple grassy area with headstones. No, these were vaults – five of them, raised, in a row: two for Archie and his wife, a partially engraved space for Esther, one for Dorothy...and there was Robert Sharp, entombed right next to where Dorothy would eventually be.

"That bitch."

"Come on, Pops. Let's go back to the office."

Cameron and Jack walked into the office.

"We need to speak to the manager."

"Is there anything I can help you with?"

"No – we need to speak to the manager."

A serious-looking, black-suited, and somber man showed up shortly. Cameron took out the three birth certificates, opened them, and laid them on the table in front of the manager.

"Hello, Mr…?"

"Mr. Tubman. And you are…?"

"I'm Cameron Sharp, and this is my father, Jack Sharp. John Sharp, actually. Jack is a nickname."

"What can I do for you?"

"We need to move our grandfather from the Steinhauser vault to Kirk in the Hills."

"I can't do that."

"Oh, most certainly you can."

"I need the Steinhauser's permission."

"No, you don't." Cameron bubbled with anger. "You were lied to. You were told that there was no next of kin. We are next of kin, and in front of you is proof positive. You were deceived – that is not your fault. But now that you have been informed that you were the victim of deception, you have an obligation to make it right."

Mr. Tubman looked at the paperwork before him.

"This is most unusual. I'm not sure what to do. I can tell you that you have to get a funeral home to make the arrangements. I can't do that. I really should get the Steinhauser's approval."

"I should really just sue you – how's that? Or maybe I should simply call a reporter – this would make a great story, don't you think?"

Tubman's face went pale. "Can you get a funeral home to call me? I'll see what I can do."

"Very good, Mr. Tubman. Until next time, then. Thank you for your assistance." Cameron gathered up the birth certificates, and she and Jack left.

"Wow. Do you always go at it that hard?"

"Pops, there are times when it's necessary. I cannot let this stand. Let's go."

They headed back up Woodward, into Birmingham. There, at the corner of Woodward and Maple, stood Hamilton Funeral Home, a large, red brick building on the southeast corner. A sign across the front read: "We are going out of business."

Cameron and Jack got out of the car and pulled at the front door – it opened. They looked at one another and walked in. They were quickly greeted by a slender, kindly-looking, silver-haired man.

"May I help you?"

"We have a bit of an unusual request. Can we go sit down somewhere and explain our situation?"

"Come with me. By the way, my name is Jean DeMarais."

"I'm Cameron Sharp, and this is my father, Dr. Sharp." DeMarais ushered Cameron and Jack into a wood-paneled office lightly littered with World War II memorabilia.

"You a veteran?" Jack looked around at the pictures and plaques.

"Yes. Pacific theater. Air Force."

"I was in the Pacific, too. The Philippines. Army."

The two warmly shook hands.

"What can I help you with?"

Cameron looked at Jack and relayed the story.

Jean listened quietly, looked at the birth certificates, and sat back with his fingers touching and his elbows on the arms of his chair.

"That's quite the story. What happened to you is unconscionable. I owe it to a fellow vet to make this right. This will be the last thing I do at Hamilton – I can't imagine a better way to end it all."

Mr. DeMarais stood, followed by Jack and Cameron.

"I will be in contact with you."

"Thank you so much!"

A month later, Cameron got a phone call.

"Ms. Sharp? This is Jean DeMarais. I just wanted you to know that I have gotten your grandfather moved to Kirk in the Hills."

"Wow! I can't thank you enough, Mr. DeMarias."

"Roseland Park was not very cooperative. They had the body

moved, but they told me they absolutely could not remove your grandfather's name from the vault."

"That cannot stand, Mr. DeMarais."

Jean chuckled.

"It has been handled, Ms. Sharp. The name is gone."

"How did you arrange that?"

"From one veteran to another...my gift."

"You are awesome, Mr. DeMarais. We cannot thank you enough."

"Well, thank you for the most fitting capstone to my working career. God bless you, Ms. Sharp."

"God bless, Mr. DeMarais."

Cameron hung up the phone, smiling. She promptly called Jack.

"Pops, can you come over tomorrow morning? I've something I want to show you."

Jack showed up the next morning.

"Come eat first – I made you porridge. Just the way you like it." She placed a steaming bowl of porridge, sweetened with maple syrup and swimming in cream, next to a hot cup of coffee.

"My favorite!" Jack dug in.

"Come with me, Pops. I've something to show you." Cameron motioned for Jack to follow her into the garage.

"Climb in."

Cameron drove to Kirk in the Hills and parked.

"Follow me, Pops."

As she headed up the stairs to the columbarium, the sun sparkled across the Island Lake water, which was separated from the niches by a manicured swath of emerald-green lawn. The Kirk itself, a magnificent stone structure fashioned after Melrose Abbey, towered over it all, its massive bell tower keeping silent watch along with the statuary and Celtic cross.

There, tucked into a black marble niche, next to two unmarked niches, was inscribed:

Robert F. T. Sharp

1899 – 1999

Jack looked around at the serene setting, quietly contemplating.

"Those two empty niches are ours, Pops. Now we need to move your mom here."

Cameron leaned down and softly touched the name.

"Pops, we brought him home."

THE MAN FROM BURNT ISLAND

ABOUT THE AUTHOR

Wendy Sura Thomson is a five-star author with several previously published works: *Summon the Tiger* (2016), *The Third Order* (2018), *Postcards from the Future* (2019) and *Ted and Ned* (2019). She holds two degrees in business; an undergraduate degree from University of Miami (Coral Gables) and a graduate degree from Florida State University.

She finds herself incredibly busy for someone who ostensibly retired several years ago, still freelancing in the financial arena for a few clients, as well as writing, painting, and gardening. She lives in Bloomfield Hills, Michigan, with her four Setters; Riley, BeBe, Shiloh and Rowan. Visit her at www.quittandquinn.com, follow her on Twitter @1amwendy, on Facebook at Wendy Thomson, and on Instagram at wsurathomson.

Made in the USA
Monee, IL
28 October 2021